"The pony ride

Vicki turned to see Dan standing beside her. Everything inside her lurched when she saw he was in full uniform, gun on his hip. A tan deputy's uniform was different from the Austin PD's blue, but not different enough. It reminded her sharply that this man lived a life she wanted no part of ever again.

He'd been watching her little girl on the pony and smiling, but he looked at her when she didn't answer immediately.

"Yes," she said, finding her voice. "She's loving it. I can't thank you enough for all of this, including all the tickets. You didn't have to do that."

"No, I didn't. I wanted to. Some dreams just need to come true. Are you taking pictures? Because you'll never again see your four-year-old taking her first pony ride."

She nodded, feeling like she needed to catch her breath.

WYOMING
★ COUNTRY LEGACY ★

A SHERIFF'S HONOR

New York Times Bestselling Authors

Rachel Lee

Allison Leigh

Previously published as *The Lawman Lassoes a Family*
and *Sarah and the Sheriff*

Recycling programs
for this product may
not exist in your area.

ISBN-13: 978-1-335-50008-3

Wyoming Country Legacy:
A Sheriff's Honor
Copyright © 2020 by Harlequin Books S.A.

The Lawman Lassoes a Family
First published in 2015. This edition published in 2020.
Copyright © 2015 by Susan Civil-Brown

Sarah and the Sheriff
First published in 2007. This edition published in 2020.
Copyright © 2007 by Allison Lee Johnson

This edition published by arrangement with Harlequin Books S.A.

For questions and comments about the quality of this book, please contact us at CustomerService@Harlequin.com.

Harlequin Enterprises ULC
22 Adelaide St. West, 40th Floor
Toronto, Ontario M5H 4E3, Canada
www.Harlequin.com

Printed in U.S.A.

CONTENTS

Rachel Lee was hooked on writing by the age of twelve and practiced her craft as she moved from place to place all over the United States. This *New York Times* bestselling author now resides in Florida and has the joy of writing full-time.

Books by Rachel Lee

Harlequin Special Edition

Conard County: The Next Generation

A Soldier in Conard County
A Conard County Courtship
A Conard County Homecoming
His Pregnant Courthouse Bride
An Unlikely Daddy
A Cowboy for Christmas

Harlequin Intrigue

Conard County: The Next Generation

Cornered in Conard County

Harlequin Romantic Suspense

Conard County: The Next Generation

Undercover in Conard County
Conard County Marine
A Conard County Spy
A Secret in Conard County

Visit the Author Profile page at Harlequin.com for more titles.

THE LAWMAN
LASSOES A FAMILY

Rachel Lee

To all the stepparents
who open their hearts.

Chapter 1

On a warm summer afternoon, Conard County Sheriff's Deputy Dan Casey steered his truck around a rental truck half parked in Lena Winston's front yard, and then into his own driveway. Lena had been a friend for years, an older woman whose company he enjoyed. On Lena's porch he saw a little blonde girl, maybe four, sitting on the swing and rocking gently. She had her thumb in her mouth, a teddy bear in her arm and a sad look on her face.

Lena's niece, Vicki Templeton, must be moving in with her daughter. He looked at that van, not a very big one, but still wondered where they were going to put everything.

He was glad, though, that he'd had to leave his patrol unit at the garage for some work today. Climbing out of his car, he hurried inside to change into civvies before going to offer his help. Fewer reminders of cops might be welcome right now.

He knew from Lena that Vicki was a cop's widow, that she'd lost her husband a little over a year ago. Lena had stewed about it off and on for all this time, worried about her niece and grandniece, thinking it might be best for them to get away from reminders and come live with her.

Apparently, it had happened. As he wondered why Lena hadn't mentioned it would be so soon, he pulled on jeans and a black T-shirt blazoned with a wolf, and made his way next door. The little girl was still sitting on the swing. Female voices came from inside.

"Hi," he said from the yard, on the other side of the railing. "You must be Krystal. I'm Dan Casey. Are your mom and Aunt Lena inside?"

She took her thumb from her mouth and regarded him from eyes the color of the sky overhead. "I'm not supposed to suck my thumb."

"I didn't notice anything."

A shy smile curved her mouth, just a little. She pointed to his shirt. "That's not a dog."

"You're right, it's a wolf. A wolf from Yellowstone Park. Maybe you can see them one day."

Just then a young woman poked her head out the door. Blue eyes and black hair struck Dan immediately, as did a pretty face that looked tired almost beyond words.

"Krystal? Are you talking to someone?"

Krystal pointed and Dan moved closer to the steps. "Just me. Dan Casey. I live next door. Lena said you were moving in and I came to see if I can help. You must be Vicki."

The woman hesitated, then stepped out fully, brushing her hands on her jeans. "It's amazing how much dust seems to have moved with me." She wore a blue checked shirt with rolled-up sleeves, and tails knotted around her tiny waste. Her black hair had started to come loose from a ponytail set high on her head.

Dan stepped forward, reached up across the three steps to offer his hand. "It's a pleasure to meet you. Lena's been looking forward to this." Then he smiled. "Two fairly strong arms here, ready to pitch in. You can't turn me down."

She should have laughed, but all he saw was the flutter of a smile. "I think…"

Whatever she thought was lost as Lena came through the door behind her. Lena was in her midfifties, a little rounded by her years, with dark brown hair that was showing a lot of gray. Her eyes were a kindly brown. She, too, wore jeans and a man's tan work shirt.

"Dan! You arrived just in time. We got all the small stuff out, but now we've got Krystal's bed and some other big pieces. The three of us ought to be able to do it."

"I can call for more help if we need it," Dan assured her. "But where are you putting everything?"

Lena put her hands on her hips, a wry expression on her face. "That is a problem we'll deal with later."

Vicki looked at her aunt. "I could get rid of some of these things."

Lena shook her head firmly. "Nothing that's a comfort to Krystal or you is going anywhere. If we need room, I can easily get rid of some of my junk. God knows, most of it is far older than I am. Besides, you'll both sleep better in your own beds, and I like that sofa you brought. Never had a recliner before."

Dan paused. "You two moved a sofa?"

Lena laughed, a deep, throaty sound. "Not yet. I was waiting for you to get home."

He joined her laughter, but noticed that while Vicki smiled, she didn't laugh with them. Still grieving, he supposed, and now a huge move on top of everything. He felt genuine sympathy for her, and for the little girl, who looked utterly lost at the moment.

He wished he could gather them both in a hug, but knew the urge was ridiculous. He was a stranger to them, and he sure couldn't do anything to ease the pain of losing a husband and father.

He decided the best thing to do was focus on the moving.

"Let me see what's left in the truck," he said. "Then I'll know if I need to call for some help. And, Lena? Maybe you could show me where you want the big pieces?"

Dan called some friends, and soon there was a swirl of men moving from the truck into the house and back again. Vicki sort of got pushed to one side as Lena supervised the unloading. Occasionally her aunt questioned her about where she wanted something, but mostly Vicki just sat with Krystal curled against her side, and watched the activity.

Had she really brought so much with her? Apparently so. She felt a twinge of guilt for dumping so much on her aunt, but she'd spent a great deal of time beforehand selling things and giving them away.

Yet she had to bring things that were important to Krystal, or that would become important to her later. Her father's awards. All the photographs. Her toys. Krystal had been allowed to help with the decisions, and made it clear what was to come with them.

Nor was Vicki entirely blameless. There were some items she just couldn't let go of, either. Memories of Hal had attached themselves everywhere, and parting with some of them had been downright painful.

Maybe she should have put stuff in a storage room, but she had discovered she wasn't ready to make that big a break yet herself. Struggling to move forward with her life had meant moving to a new place, away from the constant attentions of Hal's colleagues and their spouses, who had gone out of their way to make sure she always had someone available, that she was left out of nothing they did. Even Krystal had been included in their caring, as various people from the department took her on outings, or just made themselves available.

At some point it had hit her: she could continue to live as Hal's widow, surrounded by his well-meaning friends, which made it impossible for her to move on. Or she could take her aunt's repeated offers and just do it.

Vicki hoped she hadn't made the biggest mistake of her life.

She worried about Krystal, who seemed to be adjusting to her father's absence, but didn't appear to understand he would never come home. Vicki worried that this move might stress the girl even more. Now she had lost every single thing that was familiar except for what they had brought with them.

Maybe Vicki's decision had been selfish.

"Mommy?"

"Yes, honey?"

"I sucked my thumb. The man saw me."

Vicki felt her eyes prickle with tears she couldn't allow herself to shed. Gathering her daughter onto her lap, she hugged her tight. "That's okay, honey. When you're ready to stop doing it, you will."

Krystal had stopped sucking her thumb by eighteen months of age. The habit had returned within days of her father's death. Vicki wasn't going to give her a hard time about comforting herself.

"But I'm a big girl," Krys said. "Big girls don't suck their thumbs."

"Who told you that?"

"Jenny."

Jenny had been a friend at preschool. "Well, that's not always true, Krys. Some grown-ups still do it."

Krystal stirred and looked up. "So I'm still a big girl?"

"You're a wonderful big girl."

"Aunt Lena's house smells funny."

"She uses sachets. We'll get used to it."

Krystal sighed, closed her eyes and melted into Vicki. A precious moment.

Vicki's gaze strayed to the men who were unloading her life, and saw they were about finished. She knew Dan Casey was a deputy, because Lena had mentioned him occasionally over the years. A good neighbor, Lena had judged him.

He was certainly being a good neighbor now. Vicki watched him and three other men carry the recliner sofa across the ramp and into the house. A good-looking man, maybe getting near forty, although she couldn't be sure. He definitely looked older than Hal, and Hal had been thirty-three, just a year older than Vicki.

Cops, she thought. Hal's friends had helped her load, and now Dan and his friends were helping unload. No escape, but at least these cops hadn't been her husband's friends.

Suddenly she realized he was looking at her. Dark hair, gray eyes, very fit. He stepped over.

"Well," he said, "Lena's house is packed. We'll be back to move some stuff to her basement or garage once she makes up her mind what she wants to do with it. But listen, I'm going out to get dinner for everyone. Is there anything Krystal doesn't like to eat?"

"She's not picky." Not anymore. She'd outgrown that stage a while back.

"Then what about you? What would you like her to eat?"

Krystal stirred. "I want a hamburger." As clear as a bell.

Dan looked at Vicki, who nodded. Then he squatted and smiled at Krystal. "A hamburger just for you. What do you want on it?"

"Ketchup. I hate pickles."

"You got it. Vicki?"

"Whatever you all want is fine by me. Thank you."

He nodded and straightened. The ramp was being shoved back into the truck, the rear doors closed and locked. Then they parked the truck on the street behind her little car, still sitting on the towing trailer.

It was done, Vicki thought. She'd broken with her past. She just hoped she hadn't broken her daughter in the process.

Before Dan returned with food, the other men headed home, explaining they had families, but promising to come back when needed. Vicki could feel the blue wall enclosing her in its comforting grip already. What had she thought she was escaping? But she knew: familiar faces that inevitably reminded her of her loss. At least these were all new faces, with no connection to Hal.

She was still sitting on the porch with Krystal in her lap when Dan returned carrying big brown bags.

"Dinner bell," he said cheerfully. "And one big hamburger for Miss Krystal here."

The words galvanized Krystal for the first time in hours. She squirmed off Vicki's lamp, left her teddy bear behind and excitedly followed Dan into the house.

Vicki followed more reluctantly. Tired as she was from the long drive and unloading, not to mention getting ready for this big move, she hadn't felt hungry for a while. She ate only because she had to, not because she wanted to. It was like the period right after the shock of Hal's death.

Maybe this move had been a bad idea for a whole lot of reasons.

Lena had a big house, as local houses went, but right now it was full of boxes and excess furniture. The dining room was still clear, though, and they ate there at a table that showed the effects of the years, with scratches, faded stains and a few deep dings.

Lena brought out plates and flatware, but Krystal wanted to eat from the foam box. Her burger was huge, so Vicki cut it in half for her, and tried not to look at the mound of french fries. Of course, Krys went first for the fries, a rare treat.

Two of the containers held huge salads, so Vicki put some in a bowl next to Krys. "Eat your salad, too, honey."

"I will."

Lena spoke. "Sit down and eat, Vicki. You're exhausted. I can look after Krys's needs, can't I, hon?"

Krys nodded. Whatever else might be going on inside her, her appetite hadn't diminished.

Vicki took a seat at last, with Krystal between her and Lena, and Dan across the way.

"You must be tired," he said to her. He still hadn't

opened the box in front of him. "I can just take my meal and run."

Considering how he had helped, and that he'd run out to get this meal for them, letting him leave would be churlish, no matter how fatigued she was feeling.

"No, please," she said. "You've been so kind to us today. I'm tired, but not that tired." She tried for a smile and apparently managed it, because he returned it with one of his own.

"Mommy worked hard," Krystal announced, at last reaching for her burger. "I had to stay with friends lotsa times."

"Yes you did, honey. But you helped me choose, didn't you?"

Krys nodded, then disappeared behind the huge burger. She wouldn't be able to get her mouth around it, a mess would ensue and Vicki didn't care. She was just glad to see Krys enjoying herself.

Vicki looked at Lena. "We took over your house. I'm sorry."

"And I'm not," her aunt said. "This is a big house for one woman." She looked at Dan. "I don't know if I ever told you, but this is the family house, from the earliest days of Conard City. It's been passed down for nearly a hundred years, and here I am, rambling around in a house that was meant for a big family. There's plenty of room for two more. We just need to do some sorting and arranging. I might not have it all settled by tomorrow, though."

"Probably not," Dan agreed, holding half a sandwich in his hand. "Just let me know when you want help and how much you need. But take your time." He glanced toward the front room with a humorous twinkle in his eyes. "That's a lot of boxes, never mind furniture."

"I probably overdid it," Vicki said. "Maybe I just gave up. Sorting, selling things, giving them away…" She looked down. "I guess I just couldn't do it anymore."

Lena reached out and patted her hand. "You did just fine. I wasn't kidding, Vicki. I didn't want either of you to give up a single thing that you want. It's not necessary. As for some of the old stuff around here, I'll be glad to have a reason to see the last of it." She laughed and reached for her bowl of salad. "You know, more than once I've had a fantasy about bringing in a decorator to do the whole place over. Beyond my means, I know, but I'm not going to mind the changes." Then she leaned over and looked at Krystal. "And you, my dear Krys, have a whole room for a playroom. Or you will once we move a few things out."

"Goodie," said Krystal, her mouth full of hamburger. Vicki let it go.

"Should I groan now?" Dan asked. Lena laughed.

Vicki kept her eyes down, even as she tried to smile. It was impossible not to look at Dan and see the spark of male interest in his gaze. She wasn't ready for that, didn't know if she would ever be, but she was absolutely determined never again to care for a cop. One trip through that hell had been enough for a lifetime.

Right now she had only one concern, helping Krys through another major upheaval. Vicki hoped it would be the last one, but she wasn't going to throw anything else into the pot for the girl. Now her daughter had not only lost her father, but she'd lost everything familiar except what they could carry with them. All her friends, her preschool, the places they'd frequented. Ripped away from her.

Vicki barely heard the rest of the conversation as she

once again debated with herself the wisdom of her decision. She knew she needed to move on, both for her own sake and her daughter's. She had to build them a life of some sort away from the haunting memories. She had to set an example of strength, find some joy in life again.

So yes, she'd had good reasons for this move. But gazing at Krystal, who was beginning to look as if dinner had made her sleepy, she wondered whose interests had driven her more.

"Honey? Are you getting sleepy?"

Krys lifted her head, trying to look alert, but failing. "I guess. Read me a story?"

"You bet."

"Just take her up," Lena said. "I'll clean up. We can reheat her burger for her lunch tomorrow."

Upstairs, Vicki found the box with Krys's sheets and pillows, and soon the bed looked familiar again, with brightly colored balloons on the linens and comforter. Krys climbed in after allowing her mother to wash her face and hands at the bathroom sink, then waited expectantly for her story.

She wasn't going to last long, Vicki thought as she dug out one of her daughter's favorite Dr. Seuss stories. The Boston rocker had made it up here, so she pulled it over to the bed and held Krys's hand while she read the silly, hypnotic words.

Krys's eyes started to close, but Vicki kept reading so that the happy rhymes would follow her into sleep. Soon, though, the girl seemed fast asleep, her breathing deep and regular. Vicki eased her hand away and stood, placing the book on the chair.

The floor creaked a little as she crossed tiptoe to the door, and Krys's voice stopped her.

"Mommy? Don't go away like Daddy did."

The words froze Vicki like an electric shock. Anguish she had believed was lessening seized her in a painful grip, twisting her heart until she wanted to cry out from it. She squeezed her eyes shut briefly, then turned, knowing she had to answer her daughter.

But Krys had already fallen back asleep. A little murmur escaped her and she rolled on her side, hugging her pillow.

Vicki crept out. At the top of the stairs she sagged until she sat on a riser, and let hot, silent tears fall.

"Your grandniece is cute as a button," Dan said as he helped clear the table. Lena put on some coffee and invited him to stay.

"She certainly is," Lena agreed. "Now stay for a few minutes, Dan. I know how you love your coffee, and it's the least I can do after all your help."

"Any neighbor would have helped," he said dismissively. "Glad to do it."

"Stay anyway. What are you going to do? Head home and sprawl in front of the TV with some soccer game?"

Dan laughed. "You have me pegged."

Lena arched a brow at him. "Yeah. As a man who works hard and wants to relax when he gets home. Instead you moved half a house."

He shook his head. "Don't make too much of it, Lena. I had an easy day and the workout felt good. As for sprawling in front of the TV, I do less of that than you think."

She laughed. "Maybe so. I don't exactly keep an eye on you."

"Thank goodness. My reputation probably wouldn't survive it."

They carried their coffee into the front room. "That's

a really nice couch," he remarked. He'd like one himself, a dual recliner such as that. But he didn't sit on it. He wasn't a dullard, and he was willing to bet one end or the other had been Vicki's husband's seat. Dan didn't want her to see him on it when she came back down.

He picked his way to Lena's old sofa and took his usual place on it. She often invited him over for dinner or dessert, especially when he did some little thing for her around the place that she couldn't do herself. And Lena could do quite a lot herself, so it wasn't as if she imposed.

Boxes, shoved to the side, made the room feel tiny, which it never had before.

"How much are you planning to get rid of?" he asked. This house had been the same the whole time he'd known Lena, and even in its current jumbled state he could see the place he knew. He wondered if she was going to find it more difficult than she was letting on.

Lena waved a hand. "As much as I need to. Probably won't be as much as it looks like right now. Everything I have are hand-me-downs. I never got a chance to do this place the way I wanted, except for some curtains and small things. I feel like the caretaker of a museum sometimes. The Winston Family Museum. There are a number of things I'm attached to, but most of it is just here. No history, no old memories, no meaning."

"I don't know whether to say that's good or that's sad."

"Both," she said wryly. "Vicki gets it next. It might as well be more to her liking."

Dan leaned forward, holding his mug between both hands as he rested his elbows on his knees. "Hey, you've got a lot of good years left. Don't be talking like that."

"Like what? I'm almost fifty-five, young by the reckoning of most. I might have another thirty years. Then again, I could slip on ice this next winter and be done. You never know, Dan."

"No." This conversation was taking a maudlin turn, and he wondered if it had to do with Vicki. Not that she had started it, but maybe what had happened to her niece had caused Lena to start thinking about these things. He sought another avenue.

"So Vicki is your sister's daughter? I know you told me, but I've never had the instincts of a genealogist."

Lena barked a laugh. "That's right. She took off out of here when she was eighteen, and never came back. I used to go visit her, the way I went to visit Vicki."

He began to remember stories from over the years. Shortly after Vicki had graduated from college, Lena's sister had died. Vicki's father had apparently vanished from the scene before she was born. "Lou, wasn't it? Your sister? Skydiving accident?"

Lena smiled faintly. "Live it while you have it, that's my motto. I just chose a less risky way of life. Lou, on the other hand, had a whole bucket list of wild things she wanted to do once Vicki was old enough."

Dan hesitated, but for some reason he wanted a clear picture of the situation. Maybe it was just the cop in him. "And no family on Vicki's husband's side?"

"Hal grew up in foster care. Near as I could tell, he felt closer to the Police Athletic League than any of his foster families, and there were a lot of them."

"So that leaves you."

"It sure does. And since I was never blessed with a family of my own, I'm considering myself blessed right now."

Dan grinned. "I don't get why you weren't snapped up."

Lena arched a brow. "Oh, there were snappers. I just kept throwing them back in the river."

He unleashed a belly laugh. "I love you, Lena."

She rolled her eyes. "Just not like that. I get it." Then she joined his laughter.

Upstairs, Vicki heard the laughter and decided that she needed to go down. After all, she'd made this move, wrenching her daughter away from the only home she'd ever known, so they could start fresh. That meant she had to rejoin the world again.

She stopped in the bathroom, wiped away the tears and applied cold water to her eyes. After a couple minutes, she realized that she couldn't erase the puffiness. They were going to know she had been weeping.

Oh, well. She'd do it again countless times. Grief was nothing to be ashamed of, and if it made Dan uneasy...well, he didn't have to stay. She took a brush to her hair, smoothing it back into a neat ponytail, then stiffened herself to face the world.

She entered the living room and found Lena sitting on a rocker and Dan sitting on the old couch. Habit led her to take her usual end of the recliner sofa, where she curled her legs under her.

"Want some coffee?" Vicki asked. "Just made a pot."

"I'll get it. Thanks, Lena."

Her aunt stood. "Stay right there. I'm not the one who spent weeks moving. Be right back."

Which left her alone with Dan. He sat with his legs splayed, the mug cradled in both hands, his elbows resting on his thighs.

"How long did you drive today?" he asked. "Austin's quite a piece."

"We broke it up. There's just so long you can keep a

four-year-old cooped up in a vehicle. We left Laramie this morning."

"Not too bad, then."

"No." Which kind of ended the conversation. She wanted to sigh as she realized that she'd lost the basic skill of making small talk. Over the past year, her friends and Hal's had taken up all the slack on that front, leaving her to join in when she felt like it. She hadn't filled any gaps or silences.

"Your daughter is cute," Dan said after a pause. "Adorable. Is she really attached to that teddy bear?"

"Off and on. Not like when she was a baby and she needed a particular blanket or stuffed animal. During the trip, the bear was handy." At least Vicki had managed more than a single word.

God, she felt so out of place and out of sync. All the weeks of preparation, the long drive, and now she had arrived, and felt as if she'd been cast adrift.

"You ever been here before?" he asked. "I don't remember seeing you, but I only moved in next door three years ago."

Lena returned with a mug for Vicki, and the coffeepot to pour fresh for everyone. "Never visited me," she remarked. "No, I had to fly to Austin to see her." She placed the pot on an old table and returned to her rocker.

Vicki wondered if she should apologize. Her head was swimming, trying to order things, make sense of everything, and she had no idea what she should say.

"Not that I wanted it any other way," Lena said, her eyes twinkling. "I got to travel the world. Well, Texas, anyway. I even got to meet the oversize Texas ego."

Helplessly, Vicki felt a small laugh escape her. "It's a state of mind, you know."

"I noticed," Lena said tartly. "Now, I'm not saying

they don't have a lot to be proud of, but if you ask me, it was really something back there for a while when Texans who'd moved away sent for bags of Texas dirt to put under delivery tables so their babies could be born on Texas soil. And the state issued honorary birth certificates."

Dan appeared astonished. "For real?"

"Unless I misread the story." Lena looked at Vicki. "Are they still doing that?"

"I have no idea, honestly. I thought it was just a brief fad when it occurred, and I'm positive the state isn't in the business of giving honorary birth certificates."

Lena chuckled. "Well, of course it would turn out to be a Texas-sized story."

"It's a good one, though." Dan smiled. "It probably even grew legs for a while."

"It grew legs for me," Lena said. "Now I'm wondering how many times I told that story. I may have a lot of apologizing to do."

"Don't bother," said Dan. "It's a good yarn, and apparently at least a few people must have sent for Texas dirt."

"That much was true," Vicki said. "A few people. Maybe occasionally someone still does it, but only for their own amusement. It doesn't make a real difference as far as I know."

Silence fell for a few minutes. Vicki felt uneasy. Surely she ought to have something else to contribute?

Then Dan spoke again. "I think you'll like living here. It's a pretty good town, as small towns go. People are friendly. We can't keep up with a place like Austin for excitement and entertainment, but we have other advantages."

He rose, putting aside his mug. "I'm going to go now,

Lena. Vicki looks exhausted, and we all have a lot to do tomorrow." He paused in front of Vicki. "I'm glad I finally got to meet you."

Then he was gone, leaving the two women sitting in silence.

"Did Krys go to sleep okay?" Lena eventually asked.

"Out like a light."

"Then I suggest you do the same, my girl. You're starting to look pale. Need help making up your bed?"

"Only if I can't find the sheets."

Lena laughed. "I got spares if you need them. Let's go and settle you."

Vicki wondered if she'd ever feel settled again, then made up her mind that she would. Compared to the past year, this was a small challenge. Feeling better, she followed her aunt upstairs.

Chapter 2

Lena was the bookkeeper for Freitag's Mercantile. She often joked that there was little as boring in the world as a bookkeeper, unless it was a CPA. Vicki, who found her aunt anything but dull, always smiled or laughed, but she didn't believe it. Besides, boring jobs sounded awfully good these days. For her part, until Hal's death, she'd taught kindergarten, but there wasn't a job available here yet.

Which was fine, she told herself as she fed Krys her breakfast, after Lena departed for a half day. Vicki wanted to spend as much time as possible with Krys, until the girl was truly settled here. In the meantime, Vicki had plenty in savings from insurance and death benefits, plus the money she and Hal had been saving toward a house. She could get by for years if necessary.

She had to deal with the present. Sitting at the table with Krys, who looked a lot perkier today, she said,

"How about we set up your bedroom and playroom this morning?"

Krys tilted her head, her blue eyes bright. "Okay. I can tell you where to put everything?"

"Most of it, anyway. We'll have to see how things fit."

"Aunt Lena has lots of stuff."

Vicki nodded guiltily. Lena had assured her there was ample room, and in terms of space, there was. The problem was that this house had accumulated so much over the years that the space was pretty full. With her additions, it was packed.

"We may not be able to get everything just right," she told her daughter. "We'll have to see where there's room."

Krys nodded and emptied her bowl by drinking the last of the milk from it. Vicki reached over with her napkin to wipe away a milky mustache and a few dribbles.

"Are there kids here?" her daughter asked as they headed upstairs.

"Plenty, I'm sure. Once we get some unpacking done, we'll go look for some."

"'Kay. I liked that man. He's coming back, right?"

"Yes, to help with moving." Dan Casey, another cop. Didn't it just figure? And even in her dulled state, Vicki had noticed how attractive he was. Well, that was best buried immediately. No more cops ever, and moving on didn't mean she was ready to dive into some relationship, anyway.

Time. She needed more time. Whoever had decided that a year was enough time for mourning evidently had never really mourned.

She pushed aside her mood and focused on enjoying Krys's excitement. For the little girl, opening boxes and rediscovering treasures that had been steadily packed away over the past few weeks seemed to be almost like Christmas morning. Every rediscovered belonging, no matter how old or familiar, was greeted as if it were brand-new.

The child's excitement was contagious, and Vicki joined in wholeheartedly. The bedroom was relatively easy. Lena had gotten rid of everything except a decent chest of drawers, and with Krys's bed and the Boston rocker, all they needed to do was unpack clothes and books, and some of the stuffed animals Krys wanted in the room with her.

The playroom turned into a bigger challenge. It already contained a narrow bed, a chest and a bureau. Vicki moved the bed over against the wall, thinking that she could probably cover it with pillows and a spread, and turn it into a daybed. Krys slowed down a little, having to decide where each and every toy should go.

Vicki didn't rush her. They weren't going anywhere soon, and the child might as well enjoy whatever control she could over a life that had changed so drastically.

It amazed Vicki anew the number of toys Krys had, even though she herself had packed them. She and Hal had tried never to overindulge their daughter, but during the past year that had gone out the window. So often one of Hal's colleagues would stop by bearing a gift. It was well-meant, but now Krys had way too many toys.

But she had refused to part with a single one, and Vicki hadn't had the heart to disagree with her. Krys had lost too much, the move was a huge change, and if she needed every one of those toys for comfort, then they came along.

By noon, when Lena returned, they were only halfway through the unpacking, and Vicki suspected that

Krys was dawdling a little. Getting tired or getting overwhelmed? She couldn't really tell, and the child didn't have the self-awareness yet to define why she was slowing down.

"Lunchtime," Lena called up from the foot of the stairs.

Krys seemed glad of the break and hurried down. Vicki took a little longer, freshening a bit in the bathroom and wishing she had a window into her daughter's head. Even teaching kindergarten, she sometimes found youngsters this age to be inscrutable mysteries. You could tell when something was wrong, but you couldn't always find out what the problem was.

Krys wanted her leftover hamburger, and seemed to enjoy it even after a trip through the microwave. Lena and Vicki ate ham on rye.

"Dan called this morning. He got a half day, too, and should be over soon. I guess I need to figure out what I want moved where."

"Lena…"

Her aunt shook her head. "No. Don't say it. I made most of the decisions already, once you agreed to come. Vicki, believe me, I wouldn't have kept pestering you to come here if I thought it was going to be inconvenient."

"But—"

"Hush. We're both going to do some adapting. It's not a major crisis."

Vicki wasn't entirely certain about that, but decided to let it go unless a crisis blew up on its own.

When Dan arrived, Vicki and Krystal were pretty much relegated to the front porch swing. Lena wanted to label items that needed to be moved according to where she wanted them, and Dan accompanied her, taking notes to determine how much help he'd need.

"I could hire some people," Vicki said at one point.

Dan merely gave her a wry look. "Don't offend me."

How was she supposed to take that? All she knew was that a big handsome man was moving in on her life. Her attraction to him made her feel a bit uneasy, and she quickly squashed it. Krystal yawned and curled up on the swing with her head in her mother's lap. That effectively put Vicki out of the action.

It was a perfect day, however. A gentle breeze blew, and the temperature was somewhere in the midseventies. For a Texan it felt like spring, but this was summer in Wyoming. With her hand resting on Krystal's shoulder, Vicki pushed the swing gently and decided to accept her exile from all the doings inside.

It was Lena's house, and it would be handled Lena's way.

It was nearly four when Dan emerged and went around the corner to the garage. He returned a few minutes later with two folding lawn chairs and set them on the porch. Lena appeared a little while later with a pitcher of lemonade and glasses full of ice on a tray. Krystal barely stirred. Evidently she was worn-out, whether from all the activity earlier, from the trip or from the changes, Vicki couldn't guess. She let her daughter sleep on.

"Okay," said Lena. "That's half the battle done."

"Which half?" asked Vicki.

"Everything's labeled that I want gone. Some for basement storage, but a lot for the garage." She grinned. "I'm going to have a big garage sale. Gawd, I've wanted to do that for so long."

Dan laughed quietly. "You should have told me."

"I dither sometimes. Like I said, this place feels like

the Winston Family Museum. Anyway, Vicki, I want you to go through. If you see any furniture I've labeled that you like, then let me know. I want the house to please you, too."

Vicki opened her mouth, then snapped it closed.

Dan flashed her an attractive grin. "Don't argue with Lena. There's no winning."

"I'm beginning to realize that."

He glanced out toward the street. "We need to turn in that rental truck and get your car off the tow trolley."

"There's supposed to be someplace here in town," Vicki said.

"On the west side. I can show you."

At that moment, Krystal sat up. The instant she saw Dan, her face lit up.

Vicki felt her heart sink. This could turn out to be bad. Another cop. Damn, why couldn't she escape cops?

"Go deal with it," Lena said. "Krystal can help me with a few things after she finishes her lemonade."

Krystal beamed.

While Vicki went inside the rental place to turn in the vehicle, Dan unhooked her car and rolled it off the trolley. It took him only a minute to reconnect her lights properly, then he leaned against the side of the truck to wait for her.

He had the distinct impression he was pushing himself into territory where he wasn't wanted. Why, he didn't know. It was something in Vicki's demeanor. Not that it really mattered. He wasn't going to stop helping Lena, and even if Vicki didn't want him around, he felt a duty to Krystal. That girl's daddy had been a cop, and he felt obligated to at least keep an eye on her and step up where he could.

If Vicki would allow him to.

He folded his arms and crossed his legs at the ankles, letting the afternoon sun bathe him with warmth. He knew a little about grieving. He'd lost his wife to cancer five years ago, and he still sometimes missed her so much he wondered if he could stand it. That might be what he was sensing in Vicki.

It had been only a little more than a year for her. A year was an infinity in terms of pain, but short in terms of recovering. The woman was probably a walking raw nerve ending.

He still wondered at her decision to come here. Oh, he'd been listening to Lena suggest it for months now, and knew it was what his neighbor had hoped for, but what about Vicki? She had left behind her support network, her friends, her home. And so had Krystal. Why? He'd never felt the least desire to leave Conard City after Callie's death. Yeah, he'd eventually bought a house, but that hadn't deprived him of anything. He and Callie had been living in one of the apartments near the college, and they'd always planned to buy their own place. He'd felt as if he was fulfilling the dream for both of them.

But it was entirely different for Vicki. And for Krystal. He kept coming back to that little girl and wondering if this were best for *her*. Of course, Vicki was her mother and must have had her reasons, must have determined this complete severing would benefit her in the long run.

Maybe it would. Krystal had been three when her daddy died. She probably hardly remembered him. She wouldn't remember all that much about being four, either. Dan sure couldn't. But she *would* remember this move.

At least he didn't have a kid to worry about, so those

were shoes that didn't fit him even temporarily. He and Callie had wanted kids, though. When they found out why they couldn't, it had been too late for Callie.

Hell. He uncrossed his ankles, straightened and scuffed his foot at the dirt. He didn't want to run down this road again, but Vicki's situation was reminding him. Funny how he thought he'd moved on, until something reared up to remind him he hadn't moved as far as he thought he had.

The smart thing to do might just be to stay away, unless Lena needed him. Keep his hard-won equilibrium in place. But then he thought of Krystal, a cop's little girl, and Vicki, a cop's widow, and he knew it wasn't in him to stay away.

A decent human being would help however he could. But for a cop it went beyond that. The family took care of its own, and Vicki and her daughter were family.

Simplistic, maybe, but every cop counted on that kind of support for his or her family when something bad happened.

He looked up at the sound of footsteps, and saw Vicki approaching from the office. Today she wore jeans again, but this time with a T-shirt emblazoned with the Alamo. Texan through and through, he thought, smiling faintly.

The smile she gave him looked brittle. "All done."

He gestured to the car. "All ready."

"Thanks."

He hesitated a beat, then said, "I can walk back, if you like."

Her expression turned quizzical. "Why should you do that?"

"You might be feeling a little overwhelmed."

Her blue eyes widened a shade, then she shook her

head. "Hop in, cowboy. I'm going to feel overwhelmed for a while."

So he climbed into her little Toyota while she started the engine. It was a tight fit, but he didn't want to push the seat back. Adjusting the car for himself struck him as an intrusion.

"Give yourself some leg room," she said as she turned the car and drove toward the street.

She was observant. Reaching for the lever, he pushed the seat back. He sought a way into conversation that wouldn't come out wrong. "Is this a big adventure for Krystal?"

"So far she seems to be reacting that way. This morning was like Christmas as she was unpacking her toys. And I need to find her some friends soon."

"There's a park just a couple blocks from the house. Swings, monkey bars, slides, sandbox. That might be a good starting point."

"Thanks. I'll take her there."

Okay, then. As a cop he had become fairly good at hearing what wasn't said. She hadn't asked him to show her the park. She didn't want him to. Vicki Templeton was setting boundaries wherever she could.

Fine by him. There was a difference between being there if she needed anything, and pushing himself on her. He could do the former, and it might be better in the long run. He had some rawness himself since Callie and hadn't even dated since her death. Eventually, he supposed he would again, but he'd know when the time was right. For now, however, he couldn't imagine anyone in Callie's place.

Deciding that Vicki might be wise, he settled back, intending to focus solely on helping Lena clear her house.

And on Krystal. Vicki might think it was a big adventure for the child, but he'd seen her sitting on a porch swing, sucking her thumb and looking like an abandoned, weary waif.

He would do everything he could for that child. Starting with finding her a friend.

"Where's Dan?" Lena asked, when Vicki stepped inside.

"He said he had something to do, and would see you tomorrow." From upstairs, she could hear Krys singing at the top of her lungs. Vicki looked up. "She sounds happy."

"For now. I left her to finish her playroom. There wasn't much left to do, and she's pretty certain about where she wants everything."

"She sure is." Vicki dropped her purse on the hall table. "I told her to put her toys where she wanted in there. I hope it was okay."

"Perfectly okay." Lena slipped her arm around Vicki's shoulders. "Now let's you and me have a quiet cup of coffee and relax for a minute. You've earned a chance to take a deep breath."

Vicki hesitated only briefly. Keeping busy had become a kind of refuge for her, a way to keep grief and despair at bay. Coming here had been a way to escape the constant reminders of loss. Somehow it just hadn't been getting easier.

Lena took them into her kitchen, which like many older ones didn't have a lot of cabinetry or counter space, but instead had a big round table for most kitchen chores. Despite its lack of the conveniences Vicki expected, it was a large room and probably worked well. One long bank of counters and cabinets provided enough room for a microwave and a food processor, and little else. A sink with a short counter filled a second wall. That left a stove and refrigerator side by side on the third wall, and the table, which sat beneath the wide windows.

The coffee had already brewed and Lena set out two mugs for them. Vicki slid into an old oak chair at the table, saying, "We must seem like an invasion force to you."

Lena laughed. "Actually, no. Why do you think I kept asking you to come here? This is a big old house, too big for one person, and it's going to be yours someday, anyway. You might as well make any changes you want. Better than being caretaker of the family museum."

Vicki laughed helplessly. "You've said that before. Do you really feel that way?"

"Sometimes, yes." Lena sat near her. "When your grandparents were alive, that was one thing. The three of us got along pretty well, and the place was...well, what it was. But it's been a while since they passed. This place echoes with just me, and I keep getting an itch to change it somehow. It always seemed like a ridiculous expense just for me. But now there's you and Krystal, and I think changing this house around is going to be good for me. For all of us."

"I hope so."

Lena regarded her thoughtfully. "Does something about Dan bother you?"

Vicki started. "No. Why?"

"I know he's a cop and you were trying to get away from being smothered by them, but he's not like that."

"No?" She waited, tensing.

"No. He's a widower, you know."

Vicki felt her heart jump uncomfortably. "He is?"

"Yup. Lost his wife to ovarian cancer a bit over five years ago. I knew her, too. Small town. Anyway, he's become a good friend of mine, and I'd hate for you to feel uncomfortable with him."

Vicki nodded and realized that she had indeed felt a resistance toward him. Not because of him; he hadn't done one thing to make her feel that way. But because she feared...what, exactly? He might be a cop, but he wasn't a reminder. She shifted uncomfortably. "I'm sorry, Lena."

"No need. You and I have been talking frequently since Hal died. I think I have some understanding of the problems you've been dealing with. It might give you some comfort to know Dan's been through a lot of it, too. Anyway, he's a good friend. He could be your friend, as well, but he doesn't have to be. I just want you to know that he is *my* friend."

Now Vicki felt just awful. She must have done something to cause her aunt to speak this way. "I don't want to make him feel unwelcome."

"I'm sure you don't. And you've been dealing with a lot. I only brought it up because...well, he was supposed to come here for dinner tonight. I expected him to return with you. Did something happen?"

"Not a thing. He was very helpful, and he told me about the park where I could take Krys."

"Well, then, I'm going to call that young man and find out what's going on."

If she hadn't felt so bad, Vicki might have laughed. Dan was young enough, but Vicki wasn't so old that she should be thinking of him as "that young man."

Lena went to the wall phone and called Dan. "I hear you're skipping out on dinner. You never pass on my fried chicken."

Vicki gestured that she was going to the bathroom, then slipped out. It seemed she couldn't escape Dan, but then she wondered why she should even want to. He'd been pleasant and helpful, and he had no ties with her past, other than Lena. What was going on inside her?

She wondered if she would ever get herself sorted out.

"Mommy?"

She looked up and saw Krystal at the head of the stairs. "Yes, sweetie?"

"I finished. Come see."

Vicki climbed the stairs to join her daughter in her new playroom. "I heard you singing when I came home. It sounded like you were having fun."

"Aunt Lena said I could do it myself. I'm a big girl now."

That was the second time in two days. When she reached the top of the stairs, Vicki stroked her daughter's blond head and wondered if she had somehow put pressure on the child, making her feel she needed to grow up faster. Even with all her experience with children, Vicki didn't know. They all seemed to want to grow up fast. But sometimes they had reasons that were darker than their years should justify.

The organization in the room existed only in her daughter's eyes, but Vicki praised it sincerely. This was one place Krystal could express herself and control her environment, and not for the world would Vicki take that away from her.

Then she saw a photograph on the shelf and felt gut-punched. It was a family photo of her, Hal and Krys, taken on Krys's third birthday. Balloons decorated the background, and all three of them were beaming.

Vicki hesitated, then said, "I thought you liked that picture by your bed."

Krys shook her head. "I can't see him when I sleep."

"Oh. I didn't think of that." The giant fist, so familiar over the past year, once again reached out and grabbed Vicki's heart, squeezing it until she almost couldn't breathe. Her knees weakened and she sat on the edge of the bed, which had almost disappeared beneath stuffed animals.

Krystal climbed up beside her. "See?"

Indeed, she could see. Krystal had found the place in the room where Hal's photo could see her everywhere. His dark, smiling eyes seemed to be looking at them right now.

"Daddy likes it here," she announced. "Tell me about my party again?"

Despite feeling as if her chest were being crushed, Vicki told the familiar story of Krystal's third birthday party. It had become a ritual, and if she skipped even one word, Krys reminded her.

Hugging her daughter, she forced life into her voice, when she felt as if she had no life left.

Dinner with Dan had been a pleasant time. They ate at the big dining room table again with the overhead chandelier adding some cheer. He and Lena spoke about doings around the county, and Dan included Krystal as often as possible, asking her about her new playroom, but in no way pushing any boundaries.

By the time Vicki took her daughter upstairs for a bath and bed, she felt more comfortable with the whole idea of Dan being around frequently. Unlike some of Hal's friends, he wasn't trying to play the father role for the girl. He just treated her as if she were another friend at the table.

Later, when she went back downstairs, he was still here, chatting with Lena in the living room. Vicki wished she could enjoy the kind of comfortable friendship they seemed to, and knew she was the only one holding back.

It was always possible she might not like him as much as Lena did, but she'd never know unless she joined the two of them.

Lena had made it clear that they were friends, and that wasn't going to change. Vicki still wasn't sure what she had done that had made Dan originally decide not to come for dinner, but she resolved to be friendlier.

If she could figure out how. She seemed to have become somewhat socially inept after the past year. But of course, she'd stopped meeting new people and had become enclosed by the blue wall of Hank's friends. If she sat for hours without speaking, they didn't worry about it. They just included her, then let her be.

Despite the passage of time, she'd seemed to want to be left alone more rather than less. It was part of what had driven her to accept Lena's invitation—the feeling that Hal's friends, despite their best intentions, were holding her in some kind of stasis. That with them she would always be Hal's widow.

Well, if she was to have any life at all other than being his widow and Krystal's mom, now was the time to start. And friendship was a good place to begin.

She went to the kitchen to pour herself coffee before joining them. Once again, she found Dan and her aunt on Lena's old couch. Vicki wondered if her recliner sofa was radioactive or something.

"Hey there," Lena said. "Is the tyke out for the night?"

"Totally. She worked hard on her playroom today." Vicki smiled. "And she loves it. Thanks, Lena. I can't quite tell how she organized it, but everything is where she wants it."

"I could get rid of that bed."

Vicki sat on the edge of the sofa. "I don't think you need to. It seems to have become the home for a bazillion stuffed animals."

"We should find some things to put on the walls," Lena remarked. "That old wallpaper just looks old, and the room hasn't been used in so long that if it ever had any charm, it was in another era."

Dan chuckled, and Vicki felt a smile lift her lips. "Krys seems happy with it."

"Krys put a lot of life into it," Lena agreed. "But I'm sure I could give her something cheerier to look at above little-girl height." She brightened. "Let's do that. Posters, whatever. Bright colors. I bet she'd love to help pick them."

Vicki had no doubt of that. "Just not too much," she said cautiously.

Lena eyed her inquisitively. "Why?"

Vicki hesitated, acutely aware that Dan would hear, and might take it wrong. "Well, our friends..." Yes, call them friends, not Hal's colleagues, not cops. "Every time they came to see us, they brought something for Krystal. That's why she has so many stuffed animals and toys. More than any child needs. Hal and I didn't want to spoil her, but..." Vicki shrugged, not knowing how to finish the thought.

"Well, thank goodness," Dan said.

Startled, she looked at him and found him almost grinning. "What?"

"Krystal was admiring the wolf on my T-shirt yesterday. You don't know how close I came to getting her a stuffed wolf. I guess that would have been the wrong thing to do."

Lena laughed. Vicki felt her cheeks warm. "It wouldn't have been wrong," she said swiftly. "I'm sure she would have loved it. It's just that she's spent most of past year living in a flood of gifts. That needs to slow down."

Dan winked. "Got it. I'll get the wolf next week."

In spite of everything, Vicki laughed. All of a sudden her heart felt a smidgeon lighter. "That'll work," she said.

Dan rose to get more coffee. Lena suggested he just bring the pot into the living room.

"So what's on the agenda for tomorrow?" Lena asked Vicki.

"Your house, your agenda."

Lena cocked an eyebrow at her. "You don't get off so easy. It's your house now, too. You still haven't gone through to tell me if I've labeled any furniture for removal that you might want to keep. And we need to get at your unpacking."

Vicki was glad Dan wasn't in the room at that moment, because what burst out of her sounded anything but adult. "Lena, this is so *hard*."

Her aunt instantly came to sit beside her and hug her. "I know, my sweet girl. I know. Don't let me pressure you."

"It's not that," Vicki admitted. "It's that I seem to have made all the decisions I can make. I don't know if I can make any more. And I'm not even sure I made the right ones. What if this is all wrong for Krystal?"

Dan froze in the foyer as he heard what Vicki said. The worn oriental rug beneath his feet had silenced his steps, and he was certain neither of the women knew he was there. Should he go back into the kitchen? But the anguish in Vicki's voice riveted him to the spot.

He understood the torment of losing your spouse, and he was intimately acquainted with the decisions that eventually had to be made. Few of them were easy; all of them were painful. You could either turn your life into a living gravestone, or you could chose to move ahead.

But moving ahead meant making painful choices. The day he had realized that he needed to take his wife's clothing to the Red Cross had sent him over an emotional cliff edge. Lena talked about living in her family's museum. Well, he'd done that, too. He'd lived in a museum of his life with Callie. He supposed Vicki had done the same thing.

But his choices hadn't been as broad or sweeping as the ones Vicki had just made. She hadn't just closed up her own museum, but she'd left the only place familiar to her, everyone she knew, and she'd taken her daughter on the journey with her.

Hearing her fear that she might not have done right by Krystal pierced him. How she must have agonized over making the correct decisions.

He heard Lena speak again, quietly. "I'm sorry, my dear. I'm truly sorry. I keep wanting to be cheerful, and keep moving us along, and I forget how hard this must be. I've never had to do anything like it. It was different when your grandparents died. They were old, they were sick, it was time. And I didn't have to do anything except stay right here and let time do its work. You've chosen a much harder path."

"What if it's the wrong one?" Vicki asked, her voice strained.

"I can't guarantee it's not. Only time will tell. But I listened to you enough to know all the thought you put into deciding to move here. And I know that never at any point did you forget about your daughter."

Silence. Dan closed his eyes for a moment, absorbing Vicki's fears and pain. He didn't know what he could do about any of it, but he was determined to try. Then he heard Lena speak again.

"All right," she said, "no more decisions for you unless you feel like making them. There's really no rush, you know. I shouldn't have pressured you. Take a break. We'll sort out everything when you're ready."

Dan suddenly realized he'd been gone too long. After stepping backward on the rug to the kitchen door, he headed for the living room again, making his footsteps heavier this time.

When he entered the room, Lena was still sitting beside Vicki.

"Coffee, anyone?" he asked casually.

Chapter 3

Two days later, Vicki was beginning to feel that she had her feet under her again. She spent a couple hours unpacking her own belongings and arranging her bedroom, with Krystal's guidance, then suggested they take a walk to the park.

Krys, dressed like her mother in jeans and a T-shirt, liked the idea, but ran to her room to grab a teddy bear first.

Vicki wondered what to make of that. Krystal had never before seemed inclined to carry a stuffed animal with her. Maybe the girl was still feeling insecure. Vicki hid her concern behind a big smile, stopped to grab her purse and keys, then opened the front door.

A young woman stood there, hand raised to knock, and beside her was a girl of about Krys's age. The woman wore a summery halter dress, and the little girl was dressed in shorts and a sleeveless top with a pink bear on it. They looked almost like peas from the same pod with their shoulder-length auburn hair and hazel eyes.

"Hi," said Vicki. "Can I help you?"

The other woman smiled. "Well, we'd heard a new little girl had just moved in down the block. I'm Janine Dalrymple, and this is my daughter, Peggy. She's been badgering me to come meet you, but I figured you might need a day or two to settle in a bit."

Vicki immediately offered her hand. "Nice to meet you. I'm Vicki Templeton and this is my daughter, Krys." She glanced down at her, wondering how she would react. Vicki didn't have long to wait.

"Hi," Krys said to Peggy. "Mommy's taking me to the park. Do you know where it is?"

"The park is great," Peggy answered. "Slides 'n' swings and everything."

Before either woman could say another word, the girls were off together.

Janine regarded Vicki wryly. "I think we'd better keep up. How are you at the fifty-yard dash?"

Vicki laughed, quickly locked the door behind her and hurried along. She noticed the teddy bear had been left behind on the floor.

God, she hoped that was a good sign.

The next couple hours slid quickly by as the girls played and Janine filled Vicki in on enough local gossip that she wondered if she needed to keep a crib sheet.

"Oh, you'll hear it all again," Janine assured her. "And again. Eventually, you'll even remember the names. Little enough else to talk about around here except each other. Although... I wouldn't want you to worry…most talk is kind and general. We have to live together, and hard feelings could last a long time."

She looked toward the swings. "I see a couple of girls who are getting tired. Or at least Peggy is. Let's do this again."

"Absolutely."

Krystal practically skipped the whole way home, and after they left Janine and Peggy at their house, en route, she turned into a chatterbox, words tumbling over one another. It was the most animated Vicki had seen her daughter in ages.

Maybe, she thought, drawing in a deep breath of summer air as they walked beneath leafy trees, she hadn't been wrong to move. Maybe the shadows that had been haunting her had haunted Krys, as well.

Lena, who kept so-called banker's hours at her job, was already there, humming as she emptied some grocery bags. She looked up as Krys and Vicki joined her. "Don't you two look a sight for sore eyes. Good day?"

Krys didn't give her mother a chance to answer. She started babbling on about the park and Peggy, telling her great-aunt every delightful little moment, before running to the bathroom.

"Don't have to worry about conversation around that one." Lena grinned as she and Vicki finished putting groceries away.

"Not today, anyway."

"What did you think of Janine? At least I suppose it was Janine, seeing as how I just heard all about a little girl named Peggy."

Vicki laughed. "It was Janine. She spent the whole time trying to clue me in on the town, and I'm not sure I remember a quarter of it."

"Most of it was probably old and outdated, anyway. We'll have new stuff to talk about next week."

Vicki laughed again. "So what can I do to help with dinner?"

"Not a dang thing. After all these years of cooking for one, and collaring Dan or the gals to come be extra mouths, I'm actually looking forward to making a meal big enough for four."

"Four?"

"I invited Dan over."

For some reason, this time Vicki didn't feel at all uncomfortable with the prospect. "Good. He's been scarce."

"All but invisible, if you ask me."

Vicki leaned back against the table, trying to stay out of Lena's way as she buzzed around. "You see him a lot?"

Lena glanced at her. "We're friends."

"I would have thought he'd have a more active social life."

"Than me? Thank you very much."

"I didn't mean it that way." Vicki felt her cheeks heat. The last thing she wanted to do was offend her aunt.

Lena turned from the groceries and eyed her. "I know you didn't. Like I said, we're friends. Just like I am with a bunch of gals. But if you're curious about him, ask him. The man's an open book."

Was she curious about him? Was that what had caused Vicki to speak in a way that had implied there might be something wrong with the man? Why should she care, anyway?

She couldn't answer those questions, but their existence scared her.

She didn't want to get involved. She didn't want another man in her life, most certainly not a cop. She shouldn't be curious about Dan at all...except that she was.

Oh, boy.

Dan had been trying to give Vicki the space she seemed to want, and life had cooperated. Last night there'd been a baseball game that he'd wound up umpiring, because their regular man had broken his foot. Tonight some of the deputies had suggested meeting at Mahoney's to watch a ball game on the big screen TV, and he'd considered it, but didn't really feel like it.

Lena's invitation had come as a relief, in a way. He could bow out of going to Mahoney's, and have a good excuse to see how Vicki was doing. Vicki and Krystal. He told himself he was more concerned about the little girl whose life had been upended, but he knew he was equally concerned about her mother. Been there, done that. He knew grief intimately, and he was worried about the woman.

When Callie had died, he'd stayed put for a few years, relying on his friends for distraction, and keeping as busy as he could. Occasionally, he had even allowed himself to wallow, not that his buddies would leave him alone for long.

Sometimes he'd resented their intrusions, but in retrospect he knew they'd helped him every single time they'd badgered him to come do something with them. Vicki had chosen to kick that all to the curb. He knew everybody was different, but he still worried. Other than Lena, she didn't know a soul here.

He guessed that left him, for now, anyway. Except she had sort of made it clear that she didn't want him getting too involved. Maybe she was right. All that stuff about her being a cop's widow, deserving of support and whatever else she might need, was true. It was even good. Cops took care of each other and maybe she hadn't had time to discover it. But if someone else had been walking in her shoes, she and her late husband would have been among the people trying to help as they could.

But over the past couple days, Dan had become wary, and not just because she'd intimated she didn't want him to become too close to her and her daughter. He'd become wary of himself.

His first reaction on seeing her had been quickly swamped in the awareness of who she was, and concern for her, her daughter and Lena. But the mental image of when he'd first seen her come out the door had become engraved on his brain, and he couldn't dislodge it.

Vicki was sexy. Her tiny waist had been accentuated by the way she had knotted that shirt at her waist. Her hips flared perfectly, and when she bent over to lift something, he couldn't help noticing her rounded bottom. Eye candy.

The woman turned him on.

Not good. He didn't want another woman. Some part of him felt as if he'd be betraying Callie, even though it had been years, and that wasn't a feeling he could reason with. Then there was Vicki's clearly wounded state. And a little girl who might well resent any man who hung around her mother too much.

So while his response to her was all natural male, Dan couldn't afford to let it grow, not even a bit. All it could do was make a hash of everything, maybe even damage his friendship with Lena. He suspected *that* woman would react like a she-bear with cubs if she thought anyone might hurt her niece.

"Ah, hell," he said aloud as he showered after a long

day of riding dusty roads and answering calls, most of which had turned out to be minor. He'd even had to pull a truck out of a ditch with his winch, all the while wondering if the driver, a ranch hand, had been drunk when it happened, but had had time to sober up and get rid of the evidence before Dan arrived. The guy had claimed to be waiting for a tow truck that hadn't yet shown.

It was possible, but not likely, so Dan had questioned him closely, hoping he put the fear of the law into him sufficiently that he wouldn't pop the top on a few beers again and then get behind the wheel. Or possibly enjoy the brewskis while he was driving.

It was easy out there on lonely county roads to sometimes get the idea you were all alone in the world. It was one of the reasons Dan liked patrolling, but it sometimes led people to do stupid things.

He glanced at the clock and realized it was time to get over to Lena's. The burst of activity rearranging the house had died down, or at least any part that might involve him. Lena had been all in a rush to get rid of furniture, enough of a rush that she'd labeled it all, but nothing on that front had happened since.

Of course, the other night he'd overheard Vicki saying she couldn't make any more decisions. He kind of understood that feeling, too. The way he had dithered about buying his own house…hell, it was a wonder the real estate agent hadn't thrown him out on his butt.

Now to go pretend he didn't feel attracted to Vicki, when in fact she was the first woman he'd felt attracted to since Callie… Didn't that beat all?

It also made him uneasy. Was he responding to Vicki especially, or was he just waking after a long period of quiescence? He didn't know. Dangerous ground, either way.

* * *

Krystal wanted to answer the door. Lena immediately said, "Let her. The worst thing that ever showed up on my doorstep was a guy selling life insurance."

So Vicki stayed in the kitchen with the delicious aromas of Lena's homemade mac and cheese—made with white cheddar and sausage instead of hot dogs—and tossed the salad.

She heard Krystal practically shriek, "Dan!" Then her daughter was off and running, relating everything she could about Peggy and the park. A short time later, Vicki heard footsteps approach and Dan's voice saying, "Howdy."

She turned and nearly gasped when she realized he'd picked Krystal up and was carrying her on his hip. "I want a horsey ride," Krys said. One of Hal's friends had taught her that, crawling around the floor on hands and knees while Krys straddled his back. Vicki's chest tightened a bit.

"Maybe we can get you a real horsey ride soon." Gently, Dan put the child down. "How are you ladies tonight?"

Their answers were drowned out by Krystal. "A real horsey? A big one?"

Dan squatted. "Maybe not so big for the first time, Krys. A deputy friend of mine, name of Sarah? Her husband has a horse ranch. He's got some ponies that might be great for your first ride. But only if it's okay with your mom."

That diverted Krystal straight over to Vicki, who, despite feeling a twinge of fear about what might happen to the girl if she fell from a horse, couldn't help laughing at her daughter's excitement. "We'll see," she said repeatedly. "We'll see. But don't bug me about it, kiddo."

Krys turned to Dan. "Bugging is bad."

"Yes, it is," he agreed, straightening. He looked at Vicki. "Did I put my foot in it?"

She shook her head with a smile. The offer had been intended kindly, and she wanted Krys to have every possible good experience. Vicki could endure the inevitable pestering.

"Go wash up for dinner," she told Krys. But her eyes seemed to have locked with Dan's, and she felt a warm tingle inside, accompanied by a slight speeding of her heart.

She turned swiftly back to the salad, resisting her response to the man. She'd cataloged his attractiveness at the very beginning, but it had been only that: noticing it but not responding to it. Now that she'd caught up some on her rest, her body seemed to be taking a different attitude.

She didn't want it. She absolutely did not want it. She wasn't ready for another man, any man, and least of all one who risked his life on a regular basis. One trip through that hell had been quite enough.

"Do I smell your famous mac and cheese?" Dan asked, returning everything to normal, especially for Vicki.

"That you do," Lena answered from the sink, where she was washing the cheese grater. "It's almost ready. Why don't you set the table?"

They gathered around the big round table in the kitchen instead of using the dining room. Krys was ravenous, and at first said very little. A couple times Vicki told her to slow down so she didn't get a tummy ache. Krys slowed down, but not for long. Her only comment was "I like white mac and cheese better than orange."

"A hit." Dan smiled. He was doing a pretty good job

of eating his portion. "So, are you planning to go to the county fair this year?"

Lena shook her head slowly. "Hadn't thought about it. Krys should go, though. She'd probably like the rides. And, Vicki, I think you'd love the crafts. Some of the women around here make amazing quilts, and the knitting…well, if I could ever knit even stitches, I might go over to Cory's place and join one of her classes." Lena explained that there was a sewing and knitting shop just down the street from the diner. "You might like that, too."

"I might," Vicki agreed pleasantly, but her mind was back on the county fair. Had Lena just attempted some matchmaking, saying Krys and Vicki should go to the fair? The suggestion was hanging there as if she'd wanted Dan to say he'd take them.

But he didn't, and Vicki relaxed again.

"I'm not sure if I'll be working the fair or not," Dan said, after a bit more discussion from Lena. "The schedule is still up in the air, but since most of the deputies with kids want to take them, the rest of us will probably plug the holes."

Which, thought Vicki, was a good explanation for not offering to show them around, even if Lena had been trying to encourage it. Astonishment filled her as she realized she felt mildly disappointed. *Steady, girl.* No point in bargaining for trouble. "How long does it last?"

"It's a whole lot of setup for three days," Lena answered. "Friday afternoon through Sunday evening. The rodeo's on Saturday. And of course, one of those traveling carnivals always shows up."

"Why so short?"

"Most folks around here are awfully busy on their ranches," her aunt replied. "But summer is the time for fairs. What can I tell you? Imagine holding one when the weather turns cold."

"It's just a small fair," Dan explained. "We pretty much get overshadowed by the state fair, which offers a whole lot more for people who can get the time to go. Here it's...a community social, basically."

"Good description," Lena said approvingly. "Anyway, in one afternoon you can see everything you want to see, and fit in the rodeo, too. Now, I like our rodeo. It's mostly local cowboys who compete, not pros who are on the circuit, although we occasionally get one or two."

"That *would* be interesting. I've been to the one in Austin, but the rodeo is professional, and so is the entertainment."

Dan laughed. "You might hear a few local country musicians here."

"Don't forget the old guys with their fiddles," said Lena. "Always gets my foot tapping." She eyed Vicki. "A good place to meet people."

"Speaking of meeting people," Dan said, "I presume the Peggy that Krys was telling me about was Janine Dalrymple's little girl?"

"Yes, it was," Vicki replied. "They both came over this afternoon, and before I could even invite them in, the two girls were running down the street toward the park. We dashed to keep up. I like Janine."

"I thought you might," Dan said. "Salt of the earth."

"Did you ask her to come?" Vicki didn't know if she liked that. She preferred to think that Janine had come because she wanted to.

"Of course not," Dan said. "I passed her on the street and she asked about the rental truck, so I told her you were here."

So he wasn't trying to micromanage her life even in small ways. Vicki had been through enough of that. Something that had been coiled inside her let go, and she was able to enjoy the rest of the meal.

After they made short work of dishes, Krystal wanted to play a game. She asked Dan and he agreed. Soon they were all playing a very childish board game with Krys, whose brow knit with concentration. One of these days the girl would realize the whole game depended on luck, but right now she gave it the attention of a major tactician.

Finally, Lena claimed an aunt's prerogative. "Let me get Krys ready for bed and read her a story."

Krys jumped up. "Can I pick the story?"

"Of course you can." Lena looked at Vicki. "I don't know about you, but I could use some coffee."

"I'll make it."

"And I could use a walk," Dan said. "Been sitting too much today." He glanced at Vicki. "I can wait until you make the coffee if you want to take a turn around the block with me."

Summer evenings were long in Wyoming, and Vicki wondered when she had last taken a walk around a block. Part of her felt a little nervous, and part of her thought she was entirely too hypersensitive. A friend was going for a walk. It would have been rude of him not to ask her.

She wondered at herself. How had she gotten to the point of overreacting to friendly overtures? Why should she have been even a tiny bit disturbed if Dan had suggested to Janine that she bring her daughter over? It would have been a neighborly gesture.

For the first time Vicki considered the possibility that

losing Hal had twisted her in some way. Suspicious of friendliness? Good heavens.

"I'd like that," she answered, then started making the coffee. "If you don't mind waiting."

"What, two minutes?" His tone evinced amusement. "Oh, man, I'm just panting to walk around the block. Vicki, I can't wait. Hurry! Hurry up!"

She had to laugh, and was still grinning when she finished preparing the coffee. "You're learning from Krys."

"That girl is a real experience. I never would have guessed a four-year-old could put an auctioneer to shame."

"She can spill those words out when she's excited."

Out on the street, with twilight beginning to settle, he said, "Vicki?"

"Yes?"

"If I was wrong to mention the horses, tell me. I don't suppose Krys is the type to forget."

"No, she's not." Vicki wished she'd brought a sweater. She'd left Austin at the height of summer, but the days were cooler here and the nights chilled fast.

"Well, I'm sorry if I caused you a headache."

"You didn't." She glanced sideways at him, and decided he had a great profile. He walked easily, like a man in great shape. "I never knew a girl who didn't want to ride a horse. If you hadn't mentioned it, someone else would have, and I really don't have an objection. I have to admit that I prefer the idea of a pony, though."

"Heck, no," he said humorously. "We'll put her on a stallion sixteen hands tall."

Another laugh escaped Vicki. "So your friend has ponies?"

"Yeah. Sarah Ironheart works with me. Her husband, Gideon, runs a stable, trains horses and gives trail rides. A decade or so ago he decided to get himself some American Shetlands. Kids often ride them."

"Sounds great to me. I think she'd like a horse closer to her size, at least to begin with. Then again," Vicki said wryly, "she might decide they terrify her. You never know with a child."

"I suppose you don't." He waved and called out a greeting to an older couple who were sitting in wooden rockers on their front porch.

"It's different here," she remarked suddenly.

"I suppose so. In what way do you mean?"

"Well, I was just noticing, this is a front porch town. Newer construction has banished the front porch to a backyard deck or patio."

He paused before answering. "You're right. I never really thought about it before."

"I never did, either. But it probably has a big impact on community dynamics. I wonder what started it."

He shook his head. They turned a corner and strolled on slowly. "I have no idea. TV? Lena tells me that when she was little sometimes neighbors would gather to watch TV together. These days, everyone has one at home."

"Well, I'm no social psychologist. It's just nice to walk down a street like this and see people out on their porches."

"The whole town isn't like this, though. After the Second World War some subdivisions were built. No front porches."

"Maybe it was a cost thing. I guess I should research it when I have some time."

He seemed comfortable with silence when it fell between them, so she didn't struggle to fill the void. She wondered if it had always been hard for her to chit-chat, or if this was a recent development. Honestly, she couldn't remember.

"Has Lena said any more about the furniture?" he asked.

"Not a peep." Vicki sighed. "That's my fault. I guess I need to get to it. I'm sorry."

"No need for you to be sorry. It's just that I need a heads-up to get some guys over to help. I may be strong, but that old furniture is heavy. Solid wood. Some of it I could trot around for her, but there are a few pieces where I'm going to be smart and say no way. They might as well be constructed of lead."

Vicki laughed quietly. "I've noticed. I tried to nudge an armoire around in my bedroom. No dice."

"I can help with it if you want. Just let me know."

She hesitated to speak. He was Lena's friend, after all, not yet hers. But still, she wanted to say something. "She kept telling me there was plenty of room, but I feel like we're crowding her out. And now she's saying she wanted to make the place over, anyway."

"She did. She mentioned it to me a few times before there was any possibility of you moving here. I've found that Lena can be as blunt as she needs to. If she had a problem with any of this, she'd say so."

Vicki looked at him, feeling an undeniable quiver of sexual attraction run through her. Was she trying to awaken as a woman again? Not good. "Thank you. So maybe I don't need to walk on eggshells?"

"Around Lena? No way." He flashed a smile. "She'd hate it if you did. That's one of the things I like about her. I can always count on her to tell me if I'm being a jerk."

A laugh bubbled out of Vicki. "You know, that's good to hear."

"I think she figured out a long time ago that leaving people to wonder what you were thinking created an awful lot of empty space for making trouble."

Vicki stopped walking. He halted beside her and faced her. "What?" he asked.

"I think that's a great observation. I'm going to keep that in mind." She smiled as they continued their walk, her heart feeling a little lighter.

From the outset she'd worried about Lena. It was good to hear from someone else that her aunt didn't pull her punches. Now maybe Vicki could let go of that concern and just worry about the day-to-day matters.

As they rounded the last corner and were walking back to the house, she looked at Dan. "Are you as blunt as Lena?"

"Yes, when it matters. Your husband was a cop, so you should know. We learn to have difficult conversations."

His easy, comfortable reference to Hal reassured her in some odd way, as if setting her free to just be open about it all.

She hadn't wanted to even mention him, because she felt as if talking about him could depress everyone around her. Some of that had come in the other direction, too, as people tried to avoid reminding her of her losses.

That left a big void in her conversation, and in her heart. Hal had been her husband, a major part of her life, and grief was part of her life now. Avoiding it didn't change a thing.

"Thanks," she said as they reached the porch.

"For what?"

She looked up at him. "For mentioning Hal. I feel like I can't even talk about him. It makes people uneasy."

"I know what you mean. After Callie died there was a burst of remembrances from our friends, and then it was as if she was erased."

Vicki warmed to him. "Exactly. That's it exactly. Well, you go ahead and talk about Callie anytime you want, if I can do the same about Hal."

"Deal," Dan said.

At the door he stopped. "I need to get home. I've got to be in at five in the morning. Will you thank Lena for me again? It was a great dinner."

"I'll tell her."

Vicki waited, watching him cross the yard to his own front door. He was a good man, she decided. She could see why Lena liked him so much.

Inside she found her aunt curled up on her own sofa with a coffee and a book. "Nice walk?" she asked.

"Lovely. It's gorgeous out there this evening. Dan asked me to thank you again for a wonderful dinner. Was Krys okay?"

"Krys was a doll, and fell asleep long before Bartholomew Cubbins ditched his tenth hat."

Vicki giggled. "I wonder if she'll ever hear the end of that story."

"Someday she can read it to herself. I understand that children like repetition, but for those of us reading, not so much."

Vicki sat facing her aunt. "I'll look over the furniture tomorrow. But I want you to do it with me."

Lena waved a hand. "I already made my decisions. The only question is whether you disagree with any of them. And you still have some unpacking to do."

Vicki bit her lip. "Most of what's left is mementos

of Hal. I'm not sure I want to unpack them, but I'm keeping them for Krystal. Can I put them in your attic or basement?"

"Not the basement. It gets damp sometimes. Set them aside and we'll get them into the attic."

A short while later, Vicki headed upstairs to shower and settle in for the night. The change to Mountain time might be part of it, or it could be due to all the hard work and stress over the past month, but she was going to bed earlier.

As she soaped herself in the shower, however, she experienced a strange moment when she felt lifted out of herself. Instead of her own hands running over her, her mind turned them into Dan's hands. Silky and smooth, gliding effortlessly over her every curve. Her breath started coming faster, and heat pooled between her thighs, a deliciously heavy and nearly forgotten sensation.

Then she snapped her eyes open. "No way," she said, her voice echoing in the shower. For the love of heaven, the man was a cop. If nothing else about him mattered, his being a police officer was a wall between them that she didn't even want to think about climbing.

She'd had enough of that. More than enough.

Angry with herself, she turned down the temperature of the water until it felt slightly cold.

If she ever, *ever* again had a love relationship, it wasn't going to be with a man who, every time he walked out the door, left her wondering if he'd come back alive. It had been hard enough when part of her believed that couldn't happen to Hal.

But then it had. And it hadn't even happened when he was on duty. No, he'd made a simple run to the convenience store because they were out of milk. A robbery. A man with a gun, and valiant Hal stepping into it like the cop he was. The robber was in jail, but Hal was in the ground.

No, she wasn't ever going to risk that again. And she wasn't going to risk putting her daughter through it. No way.

Stepping out of the shower, Vicki scrubbed her body with a towel until it felt as if she'd removed an entire layer of skin. She glanced in the mirror and saw a woman filled with furious determination.

Her hair, as it began to dry, started to curl wildly. Ruthlessly, she brushed it straight and caught it in a ponytail. Hal had liked those curls. She had no desire to flaunt them ever again.

Chapter 4

A week later, on Saturday, Dan showed up with four other guys to help move the furniture Lena had decided to get rid of. Vicki and Krys were banished to the park, while Lena remained to supervise.

Krys wanted to know why Aunt Lena was moving out.

"She's not moving out, sweetie. She's making room."

"For us? She's nice."

"I like her. I guess you do, too?"

"Yeah." Krystal grinned up at Vicki. "I like it here."

"Really?" Her heart skipped a few beats as an extraordinary sense of relief flooded her. She'd feared her decision to move primarily because of Krystal, but apparently everything was going to be all right.

"Yup," said Krystal, who had recently picked up the affirmative from Peggy. "I like Peggy and her mommy, too. And Dan."

"Of course." Dan especially, since he'd been remarkably patient with the girl, playing board games and Old Maid with her when he had the time. Often he did not, because, Vicki had learned, he coached a recreational soccer team for girls, and played on a baseball team that consisted primarily of local deputies. They often faced off against another local team.

Just last evening, he had taken Krys outside with a soccer ball and started teaching her how to kick it. Vicki had been surprised at how reluctant Krys was to kick the ball.

"That's not unusual," Dan told her. "This is the first hump we have to get over with almost all the kids. Later we worry about the other stuff." He turned. "No, not with the toes, Krys. Remember."

The girl's scowl of concentration had remained with Vicki. It had been adorable.

Now at the park, awaiting the arrival of Janine and Peggy, Krys asked, "When can I ride a horsey?"

Vicki looked at her.

"I'm a bug?" Krys asked.

Vicki pressed her lips together so she wouldn't laugh. "Uh, no, you're not a bug. But I can't answer that question, so you shouldn't bug me about it."

"Who can tell me?" Krys demanded.

"We can't do it until Dan can make the arrangements."

Krys's brow furrowed. "Like what?"

"Like, he's got to have the time off, and then he has to talk to his friend who has the horses, and his friend has to have the time to give you a ride."

"Sheesh. I'll never ride a horsey."

"Of course you will. Dan will see to it." Of that she had not the least doubt, after the past week or so. The man's middle name should be Reliable.

Janine and Peggy couldn't stay for long because Janine had to go clean her ill mother's house and make dinner for her. Vicki almost offered to keep Peggy for the rest of the day, then realized she couldn't. Until Lena's house was sorted out, they had to stay out of the way.

Some other children arrived to play, but they were all much older and didn't show any interest in Krys, understandably enough, so soon the child was left to her own devices. And soon she was growing bored.

"Let's go for a walk downtown," Vicki suggested, not knowing what else to do. If they went back to the house, she might enjoy watching sweating men grunting as they moved furniture, but Krys would continue to be bored and would probably manage to get underfoot. Vicki also suspected Krys's presence would put a damper on the males' most enjoyable pastime: cussing inventively while they worked.

She almost laughed at her own train of thought. By the time they walked the few blocks, Krys was beginning to drag her feet. Glancing at her watch, Vicki realized it was nearly lunchtime. Instead of wandering through stores, she took her daughter to the diner, hoping food would perk her up.

Vicki checked her cell phone for messages, but had none, which meant they weren't through with clearing the house. When she thought about the big pieces of furniture Lena wanted moved, she wondered if the job would even be done today.

The diner wasn't too busy yet, so they were able to get a small booth near the front window. Krys had no doubt about what she wanted: a hamburger. It arrived with the usual mountain of fries. Vicki didn't feel very hungry, so she ordered a chef's salad. It looked big enough to feed a crowd.

"Why's that lady so grumpy?" Krys asked, after Maude slammed their plates down.

"She's not grumpy," said a familiar voice. "She's Maude."

"Dan!" Krystal shrieked and wormed her way out of the booth to reach up for a hug. Dan obliged her, then set her on her bench and slid in beside her.

"Hi," he said to Vicki. "Tyke's getting tired?"

"A little. I think food will rev her up. Is the job done?"

"Not quite. We're taking a lunch break. I told Lena I'd bring back something for her. She wanted to feed us, but that's just a little bit difficult right now." He was smiling and relaxed, and he looked down at Krys. "Are you getting tired of not being able to go home?"

"Which home?" Krys asked.

Dan looked nonplussed. Vicki felt her heart stutter. "This is our home now," she said quietly.

"I know." Krys picked up another fry and bit into it. In her small hand it looked gigantic.

Vicki looked at Dan and saw understanding in his gaze. She guessed her concern had been written all over her face.

"What about my horsey ride?" Krystal asked.

"Honey…" Vicki instinctively wanted to hush her. It was important to learn not to press people for gifts. But Dan forestalled her.

"Next weekend," he said. "Gideon's going to bring his ponies to the fair, and he promised me you could ride as long as you want."

Krystal brightened as if a lightbulb had turned on inside her. "Next week? How many days?" She looked at her hands. "Seven. Seven days. That's a long time." But she didn't stop smiling.

"Thank you," Vicki said to Dan.

He smiled. "Plenty of other stuff planned, too. Listen, if you want to bring Krystal home, I think you can now. We moved everything from upstairs down, so she can use her playroom, bedroom and bathroom, and there won't be anything dangerous on the stairs."

Vicki blinked. "My, you have been busy."

"Many hands and all that." He started to ease out of the booth. "I think that's my carryout. Want me to get Maude to wrap yours up? I've got the car and I can drive you home."

Vicki looked at her daughter, who, despite that burst of excitement over the idea of the horse ride, was now fiddling with her food more than eating it. Vicki began to wonder if this was just fatigue or something else. "Thanks. I think we'd both like that."

"I don't have a booster seat for her. I should probably ticket myself."

A laugh escaped Vicki. "I didn't think of that. I'm so used to having one in my car. Okay, I'll walk her home. Krys, are you done eating?"

She nodded. "Doesn't taste good."

Vicki immediately went on high alert. She reached across the table and tried a fry. "They're fine. Okay, sweetie, we're going to put your lunch in a box and get you home."

"You think she's getting sick?" Dan asked.

"I don't know. Maybe."

"Let me take care of your lunches. You head on home with her right now. Or I could go get your car, or the booster seat from it."

It seemed as if every minute Vicki spent with this

man, she warmed to him more. Alarm bells clanged, but they were muffled by her concern for Krystal. Besides, liking a man was a long way from being involved.

"God, am I stupid," he said suddenly.

Startled, she gaped at him. "What?"

"Stay here. Give me five. Maude," he called out, "I'll be right back for those lunches. Could you pack these up, please? And just add them to my tab."

He dashed out the door. Maude clomped over to the table with two boxes for the meals. "You want me to fill them?"

"I can do that, thank you." Then Vicki saw the woman's face soften, just a teeny bit.

"The little one don't look so good. I'll get you a bag."

Vicki just finished moving the food into the foam containers when she saw Dan return out front, carrying a booster seat. Where had that come from?

It took him only a minute to install it in the back of his SUV, and then he came back into the diner. "All set," he said cheerfully.

He stopped at the register to pay the bill, and Vicki clearly heard Maude say, "On the house. You just take care of that little girl."

It seemed there was a heart of gold hidden beneath that rough, irritable exterior.

"Where did the seat come from?" Vicki asked as she adjusted the straps for Krys.

"The sheriff's office has about a dozen of them. I don't know how I could have spaced it."

"Why so many?"

"Community effort to ensure no kid rides unprotected just because their parents can't afford a seat. When they're no longer needed, they come back to us, we get 'em cleaned and checked out, and if they're still usable, they get used again."

"What a great idea!"

"I bet your husband's department did the same thing. We're not exactly unique that way. I went to a conference once and a cop from Georgia explained it to me like this. He said once you see what can happen to a kid who isn't properly secured, you never want to see it again. Thank God, I've never seen it."

Vicki looked at him. "Hal did once. He had to take time off and he spent three days cussing nonstop."

Dan touched her shoulder. "Did he get some professional help?"

"Of course not," she said with a bitterness that surprised her. "Cops don't want that on their records."

Dan didn't say another word. He loaded the bags into the back, then held the passenger door open for her.

Whatever he thought about professional help and cops who didn't get it, he never said.

That had been the other downside to being a cop's wife, Vicki thought as she rocked beside Krystal's bed. The girl hadn't argued about taking a nap, a sure sign that she wasn't feeling well. Sounds from downstairs were muted, as if the men helping to move Lena's furniture were trying to be quiet.

Which gave Vicki perhaps too much time to think. Being a cop's wife had been difficult in more than one way. Vicki sometimes wondered how so many women handled it. By not thinking about it? By staying busy? Staying busy had been her choice, a way to avoid worrying every time he went out the door. Maybe if they'd been married longer she might have become inured to it. At least until the violence struck too close to home.

She'd seen the other wives after Hal died, had noticed how they'd clung a little closer to their men. Every so often, the awful possibilities just couldn't be ignored.

But there'd been the other stuff, too. Hal had tried not to bring it home, but even in the five years of their dating and marriage, she'd begun to see changes in him. While he wouldn't talk about the ugly matters, she was sure there were plenty of them, judging by his occasional angry outbursts, and by the nights she awoke to find him out of bed and pacing.

Surprisingly, it had been a newspaper reporter who had told her, "We all get some PTSD. Cops, firemen, EMTs, reporters. You can't avoid it, because every so often you're going to deal with something so terrible you can't close your eyes without seeing it."

Since Hal wouldn't talk to her about things that disturbed him, probably because he was trying to protect her, she finally had learned to just let him be. After a few days, he wouldn't be so angry or irritable, and he wouldn't spend hours outside by himself shooting hoops at a nearby park. Somehow he always found his way back, and it wasn't as if it happened constantly.

But at some level she'd been aware of what he might be dealing with, and considered herself lucky that she never had to go to the scene of an accident or shooting. She was touched, too, by the way he sheltered her.

Hal was a good man, she thought, as she watched her daughter sleep. Like so many cops, he'd joined the force to help and protect people. Of course, Vicki had met the other kind, the thrill seekers, the tough guys, but Hal hadn't invited them into his personal circle.

Reaching out, she touched Krys's forehead and thought it felt just a tiny bit warm. Vicki was sure she'd packed a thermometer, but couldn't remember unpacking it. Well, it would be easy enough to get another, she supposed, if Krys started to feel too hot.

Lena poked her head in, asking in a whisper, "How's she doing?"

"Out like a light. Maybe a bit warm. I'm not sure because she's sleeping." Like her father, Krystal seemed to radiate heat when she slept.

"Need a thermometer? Want to go to the doctor?"

This was ridiculous, Vicki thought, the two of them whispering across the large room. She eased out of the rocker and tiptoed over to the door so she could step into the hallway. She was surprised to see Dan near the top of the stairs.

"How is she?" he asked.

All thoughts about the dangers of caring about a cop flew from her head as his concern touched her. She was making too much of nothing. Dan was just a nice man, and he truly seemed to like Krystal. Her daughter needed that. "I think she's okay. If she's sick, it's not bad."

"I can call my doctor to see her, if you get worried at any point," Lena offered. "Or there's the minor emergency clinic the hospital started a couple of years ago."

"I don't think we've reached that level."

"We're almost done downstairs," Dan said. "And by the way, I noticed you never ate lunch. Want me to bring your salad up?"

Vicki felt wrapped in caring. She'd been wrapped in it before and had struggled to break free, but somehow this felt different. "Thanks, both of you. I'm not hungry right now."

Lena patted her arm. "Of course not. When we're done below, we'll let you know. Maybe we can bring Krys downstairs if you want to keep an eye on her."

It was different here, Vicki thought, as she returned to the bedroom and sat again in the rocker. At home— her former home—she had been able to keep an eye on Krystal from the next room. No stairs between, no big gaping spaces as at Lena's house. Taking Krys downstairs and setting her up on the couch might be a good idea.

Assuming she didn't feel better when she woke.

Maybe it was just all the accumulated stress of the move and the changes. Maybe she was just tuckered out. Vicki could sure identify with that. Nothing was familiar any longer. The old routines were all broken. It was a bit tiring and stressful even for her. How much more so for Krystal?

Sitting and rocking, forced into a quiet moment by life, Vicki thought over the past year, even the painful times, and once again sorted her priorities.

She knew she needed to move on. She didn't need Hal to tell her; it's what he would have wanted. The question was, how much did she want it?

Evidently, enough to move here, away from everything and everyone that reminded her of Hal. Except for her daughter, of course. Looking at Krys would forever remind her that Hal had lived, loved and laughed with her. That he'd been the center of her existence for a long time.

Some things couldn't be left behind. No way.

Nor should they be.

Krys woke a couple hours later. She was hungry and thirsty, and a little cranky. Vicki pressed her palm to her daughter's forehead, didn't think she felt feverish, and after a trip to the bathroom, they headed downstairs.

The house suddenly looked empty.

"What happened, Mommy?" Krys asked when they were halfway down the steps.

"I guess Aunt Lena got rid of everything she didn't want."

"This is a big house!"

Indeed it was. It had pretty much absorbed two extra people and their belongings, while appearing only slightly crowded once the majority of boxes had disappeared. Now it looked almost empty.

Lena was in the kitchen cooking dinner, and turned at once to ask Krys how she was.

"Hungry," she answered promptly.

"I think I can do something about that," Lena replied.

"I can just get her lunch out."

Lena shook her head. "I can do better than a hamburger." She looked at Krys. "Watermelon?"

Krys clapped her hands together. "I love watermelon!"

"I thought you might." Still smiling, Lena looked at Vicki. "Dinner won't be for a while. I'm roasting a fat old chicken. Dan will be back. He said he'd move the boxes you want stored up in the attic."

"Wow. He's already done a lot today."

Lena nodded. "I know. But these guys...you'd think they just wanted to get all this done, the sooner the better." She winked, making Vicki laugh, and went to the refrigerator to pull out a watermelon that had already been sliced into wedges.

Krystal tucked into the watermelon, not caring that she smeared her face and got covered with juice. Vicki watched her, smiling faintly, wondering at what point in life people started to shed the exuberance of childhood. What did it matter if her daughter got covered with watermelon juice? It could all be washed up.

So of course, watching all this, she ate her own slices

carefully. She could have laughed at her own absurdity. "What can I do to help?" she asked Lena.

"Just keep me company. I'm in a cooking mood. Days will come when I'll holler for you to take over the chore for me, but right now it doesn't feel like one."

"I should thank everyone who came to help with all of this."

"I already did. But one of these days, if you want, we can have them and their families over for a barbecue out back."

Vicki almost agreed, but the words stalled in her throat. It would be just like it had been before, only the faces and names would change.

She spoke to Krys instead. "Are you feeling better?"

Her daughter nodded, her mouth full of watermelon.

So maybe it had been fatigue brought on by all the stimulation. Krys's entire world had changed, and now everything was new. But Vicki had already thought of that. She guessed the question she really wanted to ask, and didn't know if her daughter could even begin to answer, was whether she was homesick.

Vicki herself was past homesickness. Her entire heart centered around Krystal now, and she didn't even miss the home she had shared with Hal. She didn't miss any of it—not the town, lovely though it was, not the shady streets and lanes in some of the older areas, not the beauty of the Hill Country to the west, nor even her friends.

It was as if she had sliced something off at some point. Or she could just be fooling herself.

Later that evening, Lena took Krystal up to bed again. It had become a new routine, every other night Lena tucking Krys in and reading to her.

Tonight, as they headed upstairs, Lena looked back at Vicki, and at Dan, who had once again joined them for dinner. "Why don't you two take a walk or something? Get out of here for a while. Sometimes a woman needs to be something besides a mother."

Startled, Vicki looked at Dan, who just shrugged, as if he didn't get it, either. But there was a warm light in his eyes, and his gaze seemed to pass over her appreciatively. She was startled again by the strong tug of attraction she felt toward him, but this time didn't evade it. She trusted him now not to get out of line, and it did her ego some good to know the attraction wasn't one-sided. She also liked him far better in jeans and a fleece shirt than in his uniform.

Outside on the street, this time with a royal-blue hoodie to ward of the evening chill, Vicki asked, "What did she mean by that?"

"You'll have to ask her," Dan answered. "I'm just following orders."

Vicki might have taken umbrage, except that he sounded so amused. She had to laugh. "Is that what we're doing?"

"So it appears. A woman tells me to get out of her house and take a hike, I go."

Vicki laughed even harder. "It almost sounded like that."

"Maybe Lena needs some quiet after today. We sure made enough of a ruckus."

"But you were helping us out."

"Doesn't mean the helpers don't wear out the helpee."

"True." A shadow seemed to pass through Vicki, saddening her somehow and leaving her feeling a little cold inside. "Dan?"

"Yeah?"

"Do you know why I moved here?"

"Are you asking me or do you want to tell me?"

She hesitated. "I don't want to offend you. And I wondered how much Lena told you. Heck, I'm not even sure how much I told Lena."

"All she told me was that she'd been asking you to come, and that you started to feel a need to move on. Beyond that, I'm in the dark."

"Okay."

They walked in silence. He didn't press her, and Vicki was grateful for that. But he also didn't give her the feeling that he didn't care. She could feel his attention as surely as if he wore a sign, but he wasn't going to push her. Hal would have pushed her. Hal had hated it when he'd sensed she was thinking about something but wasn't sharing it. For the first time she realized how much that had annoyed her.

"Sometimes," she said, "I just need to think things through on my own."

"Understandable." They had reached the park. "Do you want to warm a bench for a while, or keep walking?"

"The walking feels good." So they kept on. Twilight was beginning to fade into night, and a gentle breeze whispered in the trees.

"Hal always wanted to know what I thinking," she said. "And sometimes I just wasn't ready to talk about it. I wasn't sure what I was feeling, wasn't sure where it was going, it was just something working around in my head, you know? A lot of the time it was about some child in one of my classes, but sometimes it was about other things. Regardless, I get quiet when I'm working something through."

"And he didn't like that."

"Not at all."

"Well, it's not my place to offer an opinion on that."

"Oh, go ahead."

Dan laughed quietly. "I've found it's best to keep my thoughts to myself until I understand them."

She halted sharply and looked at him. Overhead, a streetlight winked on, making him look strange, yet still familiar. "Exactly!"

His smile widened. "A meeting of minds?"

"Oh, yeah. Hal wasn't like that. Well, not exactly. When something from work really troubled him, he could turn into a clam. I'd know it only from the way he acted, and if I got any details it was from the newspaper. He was trying to protect me, I guess. But he could clam up."

"And you never could?"

"He didn't like it."

"So feel free to be a clam with me. I can take it."

She bet he could. She wrapped her arms around herself. "So I'm going to tell you something, and I don't want you to think it's in any way about you, because it's not."

He paused before responding. "Maybe we should have taken one of those benches." His tone conveyed humor.

"Oh, cut it out," she said, a tremor of laughter in her voice. "It's not about you. It's about a cop thing."

"Well, I'm a cop."

"Not in the way I'm going to talk about."

"Have at it, then."

But still she hesitated. When she thought about the subject, it felt one way, but she suspected she was going to sound like an ungrateful witch when she said it out loud. Steeling herself, she took the leap.

"I left Austin because I was feeling smothered."

He waited, letting her find her own way through. They approached the downtown area, but he waved his hand and they turned along another residential street. A Conard City police car started rolling slowly by, then came to a halt beside them. "Hey, Dan," said a voice from inside.

"How's it going, Jake?" Dan asked, pausing to face the car.

"Boring. As usual. Even the kids are behaving tonight."

"Vicki Templeton, this is Jake Madison, our chief of police."

"Nice to meet you."

"I'd heard you moved to town," the chief said. "I'd have helped except I'm holding down two jobs."

"Jake ranches, too," Dan explained.

"That's a lot to do," Vicki remarked.

"Keeps me out of trouble. You two enjoy your walk. Vicki, I'll tell my wife, Nora, to give you a call sometime. Or you can stop in the library and meet her. She works there three days a week. See you around."

Then the vehicle continued down the street.

Vicki didn't move for a minute. "Was that a cop thing?" she asked finally.

"What? Suggesting you meet his wife?"

"Yeah."

"I don't know. I doubt it. Why?"

God, this was going to sound awful. Maybe she shouldn't even bring it up. But then Dan astonished her. Reaching out, he gripped her hand gently and tugged until she started walking with him again. The warmth of his touch triggered an instant heat deep within her, and for a few moments she wanted to pull herself out of her thoughts and take a different direction.

Avoid the whole thing.

"You wanna tell me about it?"

Then it struck her that she needed to test her reaction against someone like Dan. Someone who could understand and maybe explain, and maybe tell her whether it would be the same here, or if that friendly little conversation had been just that, a friendly little conversation.

"I felt smothered back home." She repeated the claim, this time more vehemently.

"By what?"

"By Hal's colleagues and their families. Oh, God, I sound awful. It's just that... I never had a weekend to myself. My teacher friends gave me more space, but Hal's friends...it was like they were afraid that if I had to deal with a weekend alone, I might do something drastic."

Dan tightened his hold on her hand. "That's how they made you feel?"

"Yes."

"Oh, man. Maybe they went a little overboard."

"More than a little. I understand the point of the blue wall, and I was grateful, especially at first. But then it was as if I had to keep dancing or I'd have one of the women on my doorstep, wondering if I was all right. Oh, this is so hard to explain. But eventually, I got to thinking that I'd never be able to move on if I didn't move away. I was surrounded by so much caring I felt like I couldn't breathe. And it sounds just awful to say it."

She waited for his reaction, and glanced at him repeatedly, trying to read some reaction on his face. But as she had noted before, Dan's face revealed very little unless he chose to let it. Right now it was a mask, not stony, just unrevealing.

"After Callie died," he said, "I got the same sort of treatment. I appreciated it. Sometimes I wonder what I would have done during those last few months of her life if I hadn't had that support. It was different for me because we knew Callie was dying. And maybe because I'm a guy and people felt they couldn't push too hard. I don't know. The thing that irritated me most was that afterward, nobody seemed to want to talk about her. But we mentioned that last time we took a walk. I needed to talk about her, Vicki."

"Of course you did. I needed to talk about Hal. I still do sometimes."

"So, I kind of get it. I felt silenced. You felt smothered. And all of it with the best intentions in the world."

She nodded. "Exactly. The best intentions. Which makes it hard to say to somebody 'I don't want to come to your barbecue this weekend because I really need some time alone.'"

"Yeah."

Dan turned at another corner, and Vicki realized they were wandering even farther from Lena's. Good, because she wasn't ready to head back. She needed this break, and oddly, Dan's presence was giving her something, letting her lance an old emotional sore.

"Maybe I'm being unfair," she said after a bit.

"I don't think fairness applies to how we feel."

"No, of course it doesn't. But they are all good people, Dan. It's just that I started to feel as if I was always going to be Hal's widow. The person everyone felt an obligation to look after, but...oh, I don't know. Of course I'm Hal's widow. But I'm other things, too, and those other things were vanishing under the weight of being Hal's widow. I can't explain it any better than that."

"Frozen in time," he remarked.

"Or frozen in a role." She had certainly begun to feel that she'd have no other future, the way things were going. And she was equally positive no one had meant to make her feel that way. "I guess I should have just told them, instead of running away. Stood up to it. At the very least I wouldn't have put Krystal through all this."

"Krystal's going to be fine. At her age, you're the major stability in her life. If she were older, it might be different."

Vicki thought about that and decided at least to some extent he was right. Even at Krys's preschool the kids had been changing constantly. She hadn't had one friend who'd remained for an entire year. Young families moving up tended to move a lot. Or look for a more convenient day care, or whatever. Among Hal's friends and Vicki's teacher friends, there had been no other girls Krystal's age. Odd, but there it was.

So maybe here in this town, where change came slowly, Krys could find that kind of stability, as well. Certainly she and Peggy had become best buds. Whether that would last, who knew, but the start had been made.

Then there was Vicki herself. This was an odd kind of place to come make a new life, but she loved Lena, and the chance to move in with her had proved impossible to resist. She'd applied for her state teaching license and was sure she could find a job eventually, at some level, as a teacher around here. In the meantime she had plenty to do getting herself and Krys settled into life here.

Then, of course, there was Dan, who was still holding her hand as if it were the most ordinary thing in the world. Once again she noticed the warmth of his palm clasped to hers, the strength of the fingers tangled with hers. Damn, something about him called to her, but it could never be, simply because he was a cop.

"I'm not making you feel smothered, am I?"

Startled, she looked at him. "No. How could you think that? You've been helpful, but you haven't been hovering."

He laughed quietly. "Good. When you first arrived I had two thoughts. You were Lena's niece and I'm crazy about Lena, so I wanted to make you feel at home. The second was...wait for it..."

"Duty," she answered. "Caring for the cop's widow and kid." She didn't know whether to laugh or cry. It was everywhere.

"Of course," he answered easily. "Nothing wrong with it. Even around here where the job is rarely dangerous, we all like knowing that we can depend on the others to keep an eye on our families. Nothing wrong with that. But I can see how it might go too far. And everyone's different, with different needs."

She sidestepped a little to avoid a place where the sidewalk was cracked and had heaved up. His hand seemed to steady her.

"Promise me something," he said.

"If I can."

"If I start to smother you, you'll tell me. I wouldn't want to do that."

"I'm not sure you could," she answered honestly. "But I promise."

He seemed to hesitate, very unlike him. "There was a third reason I wanted to help out," he said slowly.

"What was that?"

He surprised her. He stopped walking, and when she turned to face him, he took her gently by the shoulders. Before she understood what he was doing, he leaned in and kissed her lightly on the lips. Just a gentle kiss, the merest touching of their mouths, but she felt an electric shock run through her, felt something long quiescent spring to heated life.

Instantly, fear slammed her. *No. Not with him. Not with a cop.*

But he let go of her before she could react, and resumed their walk. "Reason number three. You're a wonderfully attractive woman. But don't worry about it. That was just an experiment."

An experiment? God, now she felt utterly confused. The warring emotions inside her were bad enough, but now she had to wonder how his experiment had turned out. Good? Bad? Indifferent?

Surprisingly, she hoped she hadn't left him cold.

"Dan?"

He paused again, touched her lips lightly with his fingertip. "You don't need to say anything. Like I said, you're an attractive woman. Nice kiss. But you're not ready, are you."

He could tell all that? What, had she been sending out smoke signals? She couldn't even remember if she'd reacted to his kiss in any way other than to experience an astonishing flood of sexual longing, something that had been buried for a long time now. Then she remembered she had stiffened. Embarrassment flooded her, but she couldn't say anything.

"So tell me more about Hal," Dan said.

All of a sudden, she didn't want to talk about Hal. She wanted to talk about herself, about all the difficulties, about her fears, about her unexpected new yearnings. Or maybe not talk, but certainly think it all through again.

Maybe that was part of her problem, though. Initially paralyzed by shock and grief, she had drifted like a leaf on the breeze. But as she'd come out of shock, she'd turned to activity, to busyness, to focusing on everything outside herself. Then she had become concerned that no matter how busy she got, nothing was changing. She was taking no step in any direction to start a new life. Not one.

For a while, concern about Krystal had been her excuse, but finally Vicki had realized that the way she was existing couldn't possibly be good for her daughter. Not one new or interesting thing had entered their lives. They had settled into a routine within the comforting walls provided by Hal's friends. That was when she had realized that she was beginning to feel constricted. Smothered.

She blamed Hal's friends, but the truth was she had let them build that cocoon around her. Invited it. She could have stopped them at any time, could have created her own space, sought out her own friends.

But no, it had been easy just to drift. The easiest way to deal. Until finally the only solution she could see was to uproot herself and her daughter?

"Vicki?"

They were getting closer to home now, and part of her wanted to run away, just run away and hide in a cave. But she'd been doing that for more than a year now, until some survival instinct had brought her here.

"Vicki, are you okay?"

Of course he was wondering. He'd kissed her, she'd become outwardly stiff despite the inner firestorm of response, then he'd asked her about Hal and she hadn't answered. Dan must be wondering if she was furious with him.

"I'm mad at myself."

"Whatever for?" he asked.

"Because I just realized... Hal's friends weren't smothering me. I let them. I wanted them to. I was hiding in them."

Dan walked a bit before responding. She had noticed how unwilling he seemed to be to comment on her. She wondered if that was because he figured she was entitled to her own thoughts and reactions, or if it was because he just didn't know what to say.

Funny, she'd never thought of herself as some kind of puzzle box.

"I don't see anything wrong with that," he said finally. They could see the front porch of Lena's house now. Lights glowed from within as the summer night slowly deepened. "Healing is a very individual process. I don't think it's wrong to lean on others for whatever we need at the time, not if they're willing."

"Maybe not, but I think I took it to an extreme. And then when I realized I needed to make some changes, I practically threw it all in their faces by leaving town."

"I would bet they didn't take it that way. They were probably glad to see you ready to move on."

"Relieved, probably."

"Dang, Vicki."

"What? I must have been a drag."

"Just tell me one thing. Have you heard from any of them since you left?"

She thought immediately of all the texts she had been receiving. "I get text messages. Several a day."

"If they really wanted to be shed of you, they wouldn't be doing that."

He was right. She shook her head at herself, and wondered what other parts of her had vanished with Hal. His death had changed her inalterably. Maybe it was time to take a measure of the ways.

"Darn it," she said.

"What?"

"Just everything. I've screwed it all up and now I have to figure out how to fix it."

"Fix what?" They stopped in front of Lena's house, alone on a quiet street, the porch only six paces away.

"I took a huge leap into the unknown out of a manufactured sense of desperation, and I took my daughter with me. I may have been reacting more than reasoning."

"I don't know," he answered.

She gave him points for honesty. No calm, soothing words or aphorisms.

He looked away for a few beats, then spoke slowly. "It was awful when Callie got sick. Maybe when she finally died I felt some relief. For her. For me. Selfish, maybe, or just realistic. Those last few months were so hard on her. Then it hit me that I'd never see her again. I don't have to tell you what that felt like. Purely selfish then."

"Really?"

"Unlike you, I'd watched my wife waste away and suffer tremendous pain. I can't help but think my grief was selfish, because she'd had enough, and wanting to keep her longer…well, that wasn't for her benefit, was it?"

"Dan…" Vicki reached out to touch his arm, feeling such an ache for him. It reached past all her defenses, spearing her.

"It's all right." He gave her a crooked smile. "Long time ago, and I've worked through it. Grief is really something, though. It's not enough that we miss someone so much we can barely stand it, but it gets all mixed up with other stuff, like guilt. Kinda like walking across a glacier, never knowing when you'll hit the next crevasse."

She nodded, agreeing with him. She let her hand fall from his arm.

"And as for that stages-of-grief thing… I don't know about you, but they come in no particular order, and some of them keep popping up again for another go-round. It does start to get easier, though, Vicki. I can promise you that much." He looked toward the house. "Say good-night to Lena for me. I'll check with her tomorrow."

Vicki watched him turn and walk across to his own front door. He waved once, then disappeared inside.

For the first time she saw Dan Casey as a man who could understand her.

Chapter 5

"When can we leave?" Krystal demanded, practically bouncing with impatience. "Soon?"

"Soon," Vicki answered. The day of the county fair had arrived. For the past week, she and Lena had spent a lot of time putting prices on the things Lena intended to sell out of her garage that day. Vicki had often thought the prices too low.

"I just want it gone," Lena had answered.

"You can always haggle. Start higher."

"Ah, the garage sale guru."

Vicki had laughed. "People expect to bargain. They're not going to pay your asking price, no matter how low."

Muttering something about interfering nieces, Lena had complied. She'd been running an ad in the local paper all week, and Vicki and Krystal had busied themselves putting up signs on light poles and passing out fliers. If anyone in town hadn't heard of the sale, it would be a miracle.

Vicki gathered a handful of fliers to take with her to the fair, and glanced at her daughter. "Ready?"

Krys looked about ready to pop. "Yeah," she said eagerly. "My pony ride. And cotton candy."

"There's other stuff, too," Vicki reminded her, but these two things had been Krys's major preoccupation all week.

They took the car, because Vicki fully expected that by the time Krys wanted to leave, she was going to be awfully tired. Vicki's cell phone rang just as she was pulling away from the curb. She stopped to answer it.

"Hi," said Dan's familiar voice. He was on duty for the first half of the day. "You guys coming?"

"We're on our way."

"Gideon's got the ponies here, at the north end of the field. Try to park close, because Krys gets as many rides as she wants."

Vicki laughed. "I'll try." After she disconnected, she twisted to look at Krys in her booster seat in the back. "That was Dan. The ponies are waiting for you."

Krys clapped her hands together and gave a little squeal of delight. "Oh, goody!"

All the traffic was moving in the direction of the fairgrounds, if you could call them that. It was a big vacant lot just to the west of town, on the north side of the train tracks. Bleachers had been hastily assembled, probably for the rodeo later, and plenty of folding tables had been set up beneath canopies. Just to the west of the booths a carnival had risen almost overnight, and the Ferris wheel was already spinning slowly. To the north side of that were some ramshackle lean-tos that Vicki assumed held prize livestock hoping for blue ribbons.

The fair wasn't huge, but it was big enough. An afternoon might be sufficient for an adult, but for Krystal it might be too much to do. A man in a reflective vest, holding an orange-coned flashlight, directed her toward a row of parked cars. She slipped into place and turned off the ignition. They'd arrived.

Overhead, a blindingly blue sky held only a few puffy clouds, what a pilot she had once known called "popcorn clouds." Rain later? Well, now was not the time to wonder.

She helped Krys out of her booster seat. "Now remember, don't let go of my hand and don't wander away from me."

"I won't." But Krys's eyes were already on the delights awaiting her, her head full of excited anticipation.

"Krys," Vicki said firmly.

The girl looked at her.

"Rules?"

"Hold your hand and don't go away from you."

Satisfied, Vicki locked the car and held out her hand. Krystal took it and skipped alongside her.

"What first?" Vicki asked as they approached the gate, even though she already knew the answer.

"Ponies!"

She laughed. As they reached the gate, she saw a face that had become familiar from somewhere. "Howdy," the man said. "You're Vicki Templeton?"

"Yes, I am, and this is my daughter, Krys. And you are?"

"Jake Madison, sometimes chief of police. We met when you were out walking with Dan. Right now I'm temporary ticket-seller extraordinaire. Make sure you come by the sheds to see my prize Angus." He winked. "She'll be heartbroken if you don't." Then he reached into his hip pocket and pulled out a white envelope. "Dan Casey left this for you. Come on in. Your entrance is already paid."

Once they passed the gate, Vicki looked in the envelope. "Oh, my!"

"What, Mommy?" Krys asked, tugging impatiently at her hand.

"Dan left us tickets for everything. All the rides, the rodeo…"

"Cool. Can we see the ponies now?"

Vicki looked around, trying to locate them. The north side, Dan had said.

Jake called out. She turned and he pointed. "Dan said ponies first."

Vicki had to laugh. An orchestrated day at the fair, and she didn't feel at all suffocated. She tucked the envelope full of tickets into her old fanny pack, which she wore around front so she could get to it, and the two of them set off.

The dry grass, already fairly well crushed even though it was still early, crunched beneath her feet. Tinny, cheerful music issued from loudspeakers on poles. The narrow paths between booths weren't overly full of people yet, but everyone nodded and smiled, and she returned the greetings. She found the booth to leave the flyers for Lena's garage sale, and the two women there oohed over Krys, who kept impatiently pulling Vicki toward the ponies.

Little kids bounced along like balloons that were barely tethered to the ground. Older kids wandered in small groups, most of them eating something, most of it food on a stick. Everything looked deep-fried one way or another. The only thing Vicki didn't see were the deep-fried turkey legs that were a staple at home.

At home. She caught herself. This was their home now.

They found the ponies without any trouble. A rope corral strung from metal posts contained four Shetlands, all saddled and ready, and tethered to the rope.

A strongly built man sat in a folding chair nearby, wearing jeans, cowboy boots, a plain Western shirt and a battered cowboy hat. He stood as they approached, and smiled. Very definitely Native American, he had his long black hair caught in a thong at the nape of his neck.

"Gideon Ironheart," he said, holding out his hand and shaking Vicki's. "The Templetons?"

"That's us." Vicki smiled. "I'm Vicki and—"

"I'm Krys," the little girl announced, bouncing on her toes. "These are real ponies?"

Gideon squatted to her eye level. "They sure are. Just about your size. What do you think?"

Krys studied them. "They're not too big."

"That's why I brought them. Smaller people can get afraid of the big horses. I know dogs that are bigger than my Shetlands."

Krys giggled. "You're teasing me."

"Not really." But he winked. "Wanna take a ride?"

Oh, yes, she did. Gideon helped her into one of the miniature saddles, adjusting the stirrups for her, showing her how she should press her feet into them. He kept up a patter the whole time, telling her the horse was called Belle, and her favorite thing in the whole world was a carrot.

Vicki realized her cheeks hurt from grinning so widely. She couldn't remember having felt this good in a long time, and she just loved watching Krys have so much fun.

"The pony ride's a success, huh?"

She turned her head to see Dan standing beside her. Everything inside her lurched when she saw he was in full uniform, gun on his hip. A tan deputy's uniform was different from the Austin PD's blue, but not different enough. It reminded her sharply that this man lived a life she wanted no part of ever again. But even as fear tugged her in one direction, attraction pulled her in a very different one. The man could have posed for a movie poster. Male to the last inch of him.

He'd been watching Krystal and smiling, but he looked at her when she didn't answer immediately.

"Yes," she said, finding her voice. "She's loving it. I can't thank you enough for all of this, including all the tickets. You didn't have to do that."

"No, I didn't. I wanted to. Some dreams just need to come true. Are you taking pictures? Because you'll never again see your four-year-old taking her first pony ride. I've got to keep circulating, but I'll be done early this afternoon. I hope I catch up to you."

He nodded and moved on, leaving Vicki with the feeling she needed to catch her breath. She pulled her cell phone out of her fanny pack and snapped some photos of Krys as Gideon led her on horseback around the small corral. Her daughter, who had appeared nervous at first, had now relaxed and was enjoying repeated turns around the small corral.

Other little kids were beginning to line up for rides, too, and soon two tall teenage boys appeared. One glance at them said they were related to Gideon. Soon other children were mounted and riding around, led by the boys.

And soon enough Krys's first pony ride came to an end.

By early afternoon, Krys seemed worn out by all the stimulation. There had been rides that had left her shrieking with delight, stops to play various games. She'd had her face painted, and taken another ride on the ponies, and now even Vicki was starting to forget everything they'd done. She finally found them some food that wasn't deep-fried, and a place at a picnic table under a canopy. Since the girl had been running at full tilt since she'd awakened that morning at six, Vicki was concerned that she needed a rest break. Krys was eager to eat her nachos and chili, and kept worrying that her face paint would disappear.

"If it does, we'll go get some more."

That settled her, and she dived into her meal with all the energy and concentration she'd expended on every one of her new experiences that day.

The breeze felt good to Vicki, as did the shade. Being from Austin, she was used to a more brutal sun, but that didn't mean she never wanted to escape it. Probably time to put on more sunscreen, too.

"Hi, ladies." Dan approached smiling, still in uniform. Despite her reaction to the fact, Vicki couldn't help noticing how well he filled it out. A powerful figure of a man.

Vicki managed to smile back despite wishing he could change into civvies. Inwardly, she scolded herself, though. This was the same man who was becoming a friend to her and her daughter, and no uniform could change that. But her reaction to it told her she had some serious thinking to do.

Maybe she had moved Dan into a different category without realizing it. Maybe she had successfully managed to forget what he did for a living. Nothing else could explain her earlier reaction to seeing him in uniform. It shouldn't have felt like such a shock.

He sat across from them with a paper plate full of

various foods on sticks, and a stack of paper napkins. "Been having fun?" he asked.

"Yup," Krys answered, her mouth still full of nachos.

Dan looked at Vicki and she nodded, smiling. "We've been running ourselves ragged. I think we tried a little bit of almost everything."

"I still want my cotton candy," Krys announced.

"After lunch," Vicki promised.

"There are rules even at the fair," Dan remarked. He was grinning at Krys.

"And another pony ride," she said stoutly.

"If Mr. Gideon has time. Lots of other kids want pony rides, too," Vicki said.

"What about the rodeo?" Dan asked.

She hesitated. She liked rodeos well enough, although she preferred small local ones to the big affairs some places held, where everyone was a pro. But while she'd expressed interest, she'd begun to question whether it would be a good experience for Krys at her age. Remembering the tickets in the envelope, she knew Dan had bought them admission, and it would seem rude, but...

As Dan noticed her silence, his grin faded and his gray eyes caught hers. "There could be lots of reasons for skipping the rodeo," he said, barely audible over the endless music playing from speakers, and the crowd noises.

"Like someone being so young."

"Hadn't thought about that." He glanced toward Krys. "Is someone counting on it?"

Vicki shook her head. Her daughter hadn't said a word about going to the rodeo, probably because she had no idea what one was. Vicki had been thinking about it in odd moments throughout the morning, and wondering if it might scare or upset Krys. All those bucking horses and bulls, riders being thrown to the ground… how would she interpret that? And what if something went wrong?

"I always thought," Dan said, "that a rodeo was like waiting for an accident."

Vicki blinked. "You don't like them?"

"Not my most favorite thing. The cowboys around here like a chance to show off, and some are pretty good. Still not my favorite thing. I spend a lot of time wincing for other people."

That brought a laugh from her. "Good description." At least she knew now that he wouldn't be offended if they didn't go.

"Peggy!" Krystal nearly screamed in her delight. Dan rose to his feet to greet Janine and her daughter, and soon they were all seated around the same table.

"George couldn't make it." Janine screwed up her nose. "And Peggy couldn't wait for tomorrow. Lena's still working her garage sale? She ought to be able to close that down soon."

"Unless it's going well. Are you taking Peggy to the rodeo?"

Janine shook her head. "Absolutely not. Those idiots are welcome to break their necks to prove their machismo, but I don't have to watch. What are you guys doing this afternoon?"

"At least one more pony ride and cotton candy. Beyond that… I think we've done everything that Krystal wanted to."

Krystal and Peggy chattered happily to each other about the things they'd done. Vicki thought Dan had to be feeling like a fifth wheel. He sat there eating, occasionally smiling. For the first time, it struck Vicki that it couldn't be easy for him to see families when he had none of his own. He seemed to like kids, but he didn't have any. A wave of sadness washed over her. Life could be cruel sometimes. Terribly cruel.

When he spoke, it was to bid them farewell. "I've got to clock out and get home. I'm going to see how Lena's doing. You all have a great time."

Then Krystal said something that froze Vicki's breath in her chest.

"Don't leave, Dan." She turned toward him and threw her arms around him. "Don't leave."

That night, Vicki sat on the front porch swing. Krys had fallen into an exhausted sleep, and the only altercation they'd had was over the face paint. Finally, her daughter had agreed to having her face washed. Little was left anyway but a smear, and while Krys demanded they go back tomorrow for more, Vicki hadn't caved. She probably would, though. Krys's words still rang loudly in her head. *Don't leave, Dan.*

Lena poked her head out. "Young or old, depending on how you look at things, I'm taking my weary butt to bed."

"It was a good garage sale." Lena had spoken about it at dinner.

"Better than I expected. People will probably be bringing trailers off and on for the next few weeks to pick up their purchases, but I've only got two unsold pieces. I'll probably donate them." Then Lena stepped out. "Are you okay, Vicki?"

"I'm fine. Chasing Krys today wore me out a bit. She was running on excitement. I was just trying to keep up."

Lena laughed. "Now you know why children are

born to young people. She sure talked about it at dinner. Good night."

"Sleep well."

"No question of that," Lena answered, then disappeared inside.

With one leg curled under her, Vicki used her toe to push the swing gently. It was a beautiful night, cooling down rapidly, but she was learning. She'd brought an afghan to wrap herself in.

Twice since moving here, Krys had expressed the fear that someone was going to leave her. Vicki had been hoping her daughter didn't have much memory of her father's death, that she could move on more easily because she wouldn't remember much except what Vicki told her.

But apparently, emotional connections ran deeper than memory, and this move might have reawakened a fear that Krys hadn't been able to express before.

Vicki heard a sound and looked next door, to see Dan step out onto his own porch. His house was smaller than Lena's, but it had been built when every house had a porch.

Evidently, he heard the swing creaking, because he turned toward her.

"Beautiful night," he said.

"It sure is."

"Do you want company or solitude?"

She bit her lip, then realized she didn't want to be alone, even if they didn't speak a word. "There's room on the swing."

He crossed the yards and sat beside her on the swing. It shifted a little beneath his weight, then he started pushing them gently, giving her a break. "Krys seemed to have a great time today."

"She sure did. She wants to go back tomorrow. She's mad that we had to wash off the face paint."

He laughed quietly. "As I recall, there wasn't much left."

"Nope."

"Are you taking her?"

"I haven't decided yet. She wants another pony ride, too. I'm in one of those mixed-up-mother states. The fair only comes once a year, she'll only be four once, but I don't want to spoil her."

He sighed. "I'm no help with that. Utter lack of experience. One thought, though, if you won't be offended."

Vicki tensed a little. "Fire away."

"You matter, too. If you don't want to go tomorrow, you shouldn't have to. Just sayin'."

It was true. "I just don't know. I look back over the past year, and I wonder if I overcompensated with her."

"To some extent you probably had to. I mean, you became the only parent. But honestly, she doesn't strike me as a little tyrant, so whatever you did couldn't have been that bad."

"Thank you."

The swing continued to rock; the breeze ruffled the hair at the nape of Vicki's neck, chilling her a bit. She pulled the afghan up until she was wrapped to her chin.

Dan was a comfortable companion. Not in any way did he make her feel it was necessary to chat. The night's quiet settled into her, disturbed only rarely by a passing car.

"I had a great time today, too," she said after a while. "Thanks so much for the treat."

"My pleasure." He paused, then drove straight to the heart of her worry with unerring precision. "She's afraid of losing someone else, isn't she?"

"Oh, God." Vicki twisted until she could make out his profile, shadowy though it was beneath the porch roof. "You noticed."

"Kinda hard not to. Has she been doing a lot of that?"

"One other time, when we first got here. She asked me not to go away."

He swore quietly.

"My sentiments exactly. I guess Hal's death had a bigger impact than she showed before. Of course, it had to. I mean, her daddy never came home anymore. But after a few weeks she stopped asking, and seemed to accept it. Now this. I don't know if she's been feeling this all along and just didn't know how to tell me, or if this is something new because of the move. If it's the move, I'm going to hate myself."

Dan shifted closer until he could put an arm around her shoulders. "It's gotta be rough. I mean, does she even begin to understand death?"

"I don't think so. It's not that I didn't try. It's not that I didn't tell her he wouldn't be coming back, with all the sugarcoated stories about going home to heaven. I didn't lie to her, for heaven's sake!"

"I didn't think you had. It's just that she's so young. People my age have trouble comprehending it."

"Sorry," Vicki said. Dan's arm felt good around her, a friendly kind of support, and she needed support right now. She was truly worried about her daughter.

And about herself. Despite all her promises, she was letting another lawman into her life. Any convenient amnesia she had been suffering the past couple weeks had been broken by his appearance at the fair. A gun and a badge, two things that now had only bad associations for her.

"You know, I thought I got used to Hal being a cop. I lived in an alternate universe."

"Meaning?"

"Oh, I convinced myself that while bad things happened, they weren't going to happen to him. After all, most cops get to retirement without ever drawing their guns. Most never get hurt at all in any serious way. It was only when he got home and the relief washed through me that I realized how tense I'd been. How edgy."

Dan tightened his arm briefly, just briefly, but didn't say anything. Letting her talk if she wanted to. He was good at that.

"If there's a level of denial deep enough, I never found it," she said slowly. "You *have* to believe that everything's going to be fine, but at some level you don't quite make it. Or at least I didn't."

"I pretty much went into denial for a while after we got Callie's diagnosis," Dan murmured. "Somehow we were going to cure her. I'm not sure I didn't make it harder on her. I didn't want to accept the truth. Sometimes that's a good thing, sometimes not."

"Yeah." Vicki hesitated, wondering how much closer she wanted to get to this man. Knowing more about him would probably make it worse, but she plunged in, anyway. He was her friend, after all, even if he could never be more than that. "It must have been just terrible, Dan."

"It was." A bald statement. "Took me a while to accept it. But eventually, I realized that even with all the anguish and pain at the end, I wouldn't have wanted to miss loving Callie."

"What are you saying?" Vicki felt a flicker of anger, as if he were scolding her in some way. She resented that. But his next words calmed her again.

"Only that I know how hard it is. We each have to find our own ways to cope. I found mine. You'll find yours. Maybe you have. And then there's Krystal. I can't imagine trying to do what you're doing. Just when life seems to freeze in a pain so consuming that all you want is to die, you have to live for someone else. Put on a good face. Be upbeat. At least I got to wallow for a while."

"Did wallowing help?"

"I don't know. I just did it. Hid in the apartment, neglected to take care of myself, damn near a cliché." He laughed quietly. "I look back at it now and wonder if I was doing what I thought I should be doing. Who knows? I just know that for a while I'd wake up, turn over, see the bed beside me empty, and I'd pound the pillow, hating the fact that I had to face another day. It was hard on the pillows."

Vicki couldn't help herself, because she felt her heart reach out to his pain, the same pain she had known. She leaned into him a bit and rested her head in the hollow of his shoulder. His arm around her tightened a little, like a hug. Nothing to alarm her.

"I pounded a few pillows, too," she told him. "Once—and I'm ashamed to admit this—while Krys was at day school, I stood in the kitchen and smashed every single dinner plate we'd gotten as wedding presents."

"Did it help?"

"Not a whole lot. I cussed myself out the whole time I cleaned up, worried that Krys might step on a pottery shard. When she came home that day, I was on my hands and knees using damp paper towels to be sure I got everything."

He squeezed her again. "Wow."

"Then I put on the bright face and we went out and bought new dishes. Very different ones. She was too young to even wonder about it. I did any number of stupid things at first. Well, they look stupid now. At the time I wasn't questioning myself very much. Maybe it was just expressing the inexpressible."

"Yeah. I hear you."

"And now this with Krys. Man, I hope it wasn't a stupid decision to move here."

"God, I hope not," he answered. Then, astonishing her, he caught her chin in his hand and tilted her face up. She looked at him in surprise, trying to read his shadowed face, wishing there was some light. But then he bent his head and kissed her.

This time it was no experimental touching of lips. This time his mouth was firm against hers, and when she didn't immediately resist, he ran his tongue across her lips, asking for entry.

She should have refused, but the fire he'd ignited with the first kissed leaped to renewed life, filling her with all the hungers and yearnings that life brought. She was alive. He was alive. Surely they were entitled to this little bit of pleasure?

His tongue dipped inside her mouth, teasing hers, learning her contours, finding ways to make shivers pass through her. Just a kiss, just a simple little kiss, but it seemed as momentous as a huge earthquake. She leaned into him, forgetting everything but the need he had awakened. She wanted him. If her arm hadn't been tangled in the afghan, she'd have wound it around his neck to pull him closer.

But then, with apparent reluctance, he withdrew. Vicki didn't want to open her eyes, didn't want reality to come crashing back. For just a minute, he had taught her that she could be free, alive and vibrant again.

He ran his fingertips lightly across her lips, then wrapped his other arm around her, holding her close as he pushed the swing to and fro.

"Now that," he said after a while, "was no experiment."

No, it hadn't been. The night seemed alive, suddenly, as if the darkness held promise. The whisper of the breeze in the trees felt like a song echoing the sensations he had evoked in her. Maybe he was the wrong guy, but it didn't matter. She'd just taken a step forward for the first time since Hal.

The front door opened slowly. Immediately, the two of them jerked apart.

"Mommy?" Krys sounded barely awake.

"I'm right here." She hoped her daughter didn't notice how breathless she sounded. "Do you need something?"

"You were gone." The answer that came was heart-wrenching. Bare feet padded on the wooden slats of the porch floor and soon the little girl in her night-gown stood in front of them. Before Vicki could move, Dan reached out and lifted Krystal, placing her between them. Vicki pulled the afghan free and wrapped it around her.

"You should be in bed, sweetie. I'm not going anywhere. Did you have a bad dream?"

"I dreamed a monster was chasing you."

Vicki stroked the girl's hair gently. "Well, you can see he didn't get me. Want me to put you back to bed?"

"No."

Vicki looked over Krys's head at Dan. He seemed to meet her gaze.

"That was a scary dream," he said. "We'll keep the monsters away, okay?"

Then, without a word, he wrapped mother and daughter in his arms and held them close. Krys snuggled right in, and the swing kept moving, rocking to and fro.

Reality was biting Vicki in the butt again. There was no longer any question in her mind that the move to Conard City had disturbed and awakened her daughter's deepest fears. Fears she had never expressed before. Maybe now she was old enough to speak them, but Vicki wondered just how much of a silent hell Krystal had been going through even as her mother had fought to make their days as normal as possible.

But what could she do now? Moving back to Austin would just create more problems. Krys was already attached to Dan, and Vicki felt uneasy about it. Dan was a neighbor. He might be around for a long time or he might choose to go away. He certainly wasn't bound to her daughter by anything except his friendship with Lena. And perhaps now by his friendship with Vicki.

Of all possible men for Krystal to attach herself to, she'd chosen the worst, a cop. A man who might go off to work one day and never return. God, what if Vicki had walked her daughter into another nightmare?

Krys had fallen asleep again, snuggled between the two of them.

Dan spoke, little more than a whisper. "Want me to carry her to bed?"

Vicki nearly refused, wanting him no more intimately involved with her or her daughter, but when she looked down, even in the poor light she could see that Krystal's hand had knotted itself into Dan's sweatshirt. Hanging on for dear life.

Whatever was going on here, she didn't want to make it worse. She looked at Dan and nodded.

He scooped the girl into his arms before he rose. He didn't try to take the blanket away, but kept her bundled in it.

"Lead the way," he murmured.

Krys made a small noise but didn't wake, merely curled more tightly into Dan.

Vicki's heart felt as if it were being torn in two. The child's trust in him overwhelmed her and worried her. Maybe it was time to take Krys to a psychologist. She clearly had anxieties Vicki couldn't begin to imagine how to soothe.

Dan eased Krys down onto her bed, leaving her snuggled in the afghan. She sighed and rolled onto her side, sticking her thumb into her mouth.

"I can let myself out," he whispered.

"I need to lock up."

"I have a key." Surprising her, he pulled her into a quick, tight hug. "I'm off tomorrow. I'll see you."

Then he slipped from the room with amazing quiet for a man so big. Vicki sagged onto the Boston rocker, determined to be there if Krys woke again.

But it left her an awful lot of time to sit in the dark, pondering her past mistakes and wondering if she was making a bunch of new ones.

Nothing about life seemed simple anymore. Everything had turned into a tangle of potential complications. But maybe it had always been that way. Maybe before, she'd just been too happy and secure to notice it.

Still rocking, concerned about leaving Krystal alone, Vicki slowly fell asleep, remembering the peace of a group hug on the front porch swing.

Chapter 6

Sleeping in a hard wooden rocking chair all night left Vicki aching almost as soon as she stirred. Every muscle, every joint protested.

Then she heard voices downstairs: Kystal, Lena and Dan. Krystal mostly. Vicki recognized that tone. Her daughter wanted something. Vicki had to get down there before someone gave in to her.

When she stood, she groaned. Twisting and bending, she tried to ease the kinks out. What she needed more than anything was fresh clothes and a shower, but she decided that would have to wait. First she had to find out what was up with Krys.

Good heavens, it was already past nine. The alarm clock beside Krys's bed scolded her. She must have been more tired than she realized. Whatever, she had to get downstairs now, even if she looked like a witch, with tangled hair and rumpled clothes. Some things couldn't wait, primarily a four-year-old who sounded like she was on a campaign.

Vicki reached the bottom of the stairs in time to hear Dan say, "That's up to your mother, Krys. She's in charge."

Thank goodness for that, Vicki thought, feeling a flicker of amusement. She paused long enough to gather her hair into a tighter ponytail and rub some of the sleep out of her eyes. Then she walked into the kitchen, to find Dan, Lena and Krys gathered around the big round table having breakfast.

"Good morning," the two adults said.

Krys chirped, "Hi, Mommy."

Vicki returned the greetings while she poured herself some coffee. Dan pulled out a chair for her. Today's breakfast seemed to be sweet rolls from a bakery, Krys's inevitable Cheerios and milk. Krys had a mustache from the milk, but no one seemed to care.

"I must look awful," Vicki remarked. "I need a shower and a change."

"We'll forgive you," Lena said. "You want something else to eat?"

"This is fine." Finally, she glanced at Dan and saw him smiling as he looked at Krys. Vicki sensed he was enjoying something.

But all of a sudden she remembered their kiss and hug last night on the porch swing, and both warmth and desire washed through her. The man had given her and her daughter comfort, but he'd also given her something else. She wasn't sure that was a good thing.

"I'm not s'posed to bug you," Krys said, a bit of milk dripping from her chin. "Dan said."

Vicki propped her own chin on her palm. "But you're going to be a little bug, anyway."

Krys grinned.

With her free hand, Vicki grabbed a napkin and wiped her daughter's mouth and chin. "Next time you do the wiping."

"'Kay."

"So were you bugging Aunt Lena and Dan?"

Another grin, but no answer. Vicki looked at Dan and Lena. "Well?"

"She wants to go to the fair again today," Lena said.

"Pony rides," Dan added. "Oh, and face paint."

"I see." Vicki looked at her daughter. "You had that much fun, kiddo?"

"Yup."

Vicki could almost see the desire to plead written all over the girl's face, but so far she was heeding Dan's stricture not to bug her mother. Interesting. The child must be ready to explode.

Vicki pretended to think about it, although in truth she was going to say yes. Krys had enjoyed it, the fair wouldn't happen again for a year, and it seemed churlish to deny her. "First," she said finally, "I need to take a shower and change. That rocking chair was *not* a comfortable bed."

Krys surprised her. Milky mouth and all, she jumped down from her chair, then wormed her way onto Vicki's lap. "You stayed," she said simply.

"Yes." Vicki barely got the simple word out as her throat tightened painfully and a weight seemed to settle in her chest. *So many kinds of sorrow*, she thought helplessly. Maybe the biggest one now evidenced in Krys's insecurity.

Bowing her head, she pressed her face into Krys's silky hair, inhaling her daughter's wonderful, familiar scent, hugging her tightly. "Do you wish we'd stayed in Austin?"

"No!"

The vehemence of the answer surprised Vicki. She looked down and Krystal looked up at her. "I like it here."

Well, of course, she thought, as Krystal slid off her lap and went back to eating her cereal. Dan and Peggy and Lena and the fair…it seemed her daughter was sprouting new connections rapidly. But still, she had climbed out of bed from a nightmare that something was chasing her mother.

Sipping her coffee, Vicki watched her daughter eat, once again amazed by the complexity of a young child. Finally, she ate a piece of roll to tide her over, and excused herself to go clean up.

The shower washed away the last stiffness from her body. For the first time in forever, she didn't try to brush the curls out of her dark hair. Let them come. It would probably look like a wild cloud, and she was overdue for a cut, but today she just decided to let it do its own thing.

Another step, she thought as she once again dressed in jeans, and a lightweight, blue polo shirt. At least her Austin casual clothes fit in here. Soon it would be time to think about getting some serious winter clothing, she supposed. While they had an occasional touch of winter in Austin, she was certain it was nothing like Wyoming.

Random thoughts flitted around in her head, a break from more serious occupations. She must need it.

Downstairs she found Krys, who had dressed herself in her favorite T-shirt and jeans, with pink running shoes, practically bouncing up and down in her excitement. Lena appeared ready to go with them, and she remarked, "Dan's going to meet us there."

Well, well, Vicki thought sourly. *One big happy family outing.* Shame filled her an instant later. She really had to do something about her resistance to friendship. All Hal's friends had ever tried to do was help in every way that they could think of, and if it had overwhelmed her, maybe she should have found a way to let them know that she needed space, rather than running away.

But run away she had. Now she was here, and trying to fall back into her old habitual thinking. She looked at Krys as she put her in her booster seat, and wondered if she needed a mental health check. She'd run, claiming she felt smothered, and had perhaps caused her daughter more problems. Moving hadn't sound like such a bad thing when she had justified it, including thoughts of Krys that had always ended with *Well, she's so young.*

"Yeah," Vicki muttered to herself. Maybe she had utterly misjudged how much more secure her daughter might have felt in familiar surroundings. She guessed now she had a whole load of new guilt to live with, because she couldn't take back her decision.

"Mommy?"

She finished buckling the harness and looked at Krys. "What, honey?"

"You sound grumpy."

Caught, Vicki almost colored. "I'm a little mad at myself," she admitted.

Krys touched her cheek with small, soft fingers. "Don't be mad, Mommy. This is fun."

Wisdom from a child, Vicki thought, as she climbed in behind the wheel. Lena was already in the passenger seat.

"Maybe you need to talk a bit later," Lena remarked casually. "Been getting that feeling. I'm available. So's Dan if you want a man's perspective. Although to my way of thinking, us gals do a better a job of the thinking part."

A small laugh escaped Vicki. "Maybe so."

As it was Sunday morning, the fair wasn't as crowded yet as yesterday. Most people were probably in church, Vicki thought, and knew another pang of guilt. That was something else she'd let slip since Hal. It might be good for Krys, the nursery school, the Bible school classes. Or then again…

"You went away again," Lena said as they walked toward the ponies. "What's going on?"

Vicki took the safe path. "Just wondering about church around here. I haven't taken Krys in a long time. Would you recommend one?"

"Good Shepherd," Lena answered promptly. "Good pastor, nice folks for the most part. Great children's programs from what I hear. But don't be rushing into it."

Vicki, whose arm was swinging as Krys hung on to her hand and skipped beside her, looked at her aunt. "Are you trying to say something?"

Lena snorted. "Not in front of the girl. You may not approve of my heretical notions."

That surprised a laugh from Vicki and she let the subject go.

Gideon Ironheart was there with his ponies and welcomed them warmly. Then he introduced them to a teenage girl. "Kiana, my daughter. Took me a while to get her away from her swords and sorcery games."

Kiana, who had long, inky hair and beautiful dark eyes, laughed and gave him a shove on his shoulder. "I'm only impossible part of the time, Dad."

Gideon's eyes crinkled as he looked at Vicki. "She takes after her mother."

"Like you're easy?" Kiana asked. She squatted down and held out her hand. "You must be Krystal? That's such a pretty name. My dad says you liked Belle a whole lot yesterday. Wanna feed her a carrot?"

Krys, her eyes huge, nodded. She took Kiana's hand and let herself be led over to the string of ponies.

"Break out that camera, Vicki," Lena said.

Vicki was already reaching for it. Any nervousness she might have been feeling vanished the instant the pony snatched the carrot from Krys's tiny hand and the girl laughed with sheer delight. Kiana then showed her how to pet the horse, and soon it was clear Krys felt she'd made a friend for life.

Kiana seemed endowed with amazing patience for someone her age. She walked the horse and Krys around the small corral countless times, all the while chatting with her about horses and how she could come up to the ranch anytime Kiana was home and Vicki could bring her. The teen talked about the dozens of horses her dad had, and all the work involved in caring for them. "They say," she told Krys, "that my dad is a horse whisperer."

"What's that?"

"He speaks in a way the horses understand."

"Oh, I wanna hear!"

"It's not something you hear," Kiana said. "I'll get Dad to show you someday."

"My daddy's dead."

Silence ensued. Vicki's heart plunged so fast she felt as if she were in free fall. A strong hand gripped her elbow and it was a moment before she realized Dan had joined them. "Easy," he murmured. "Take it easy."

Vicki didn't know what else she could do. If Krys had mentioned it, then she'd needed to say it. Everything now depended on a girl who couldn't be more than sixteen.

"I'm sorry," Kiana said. "You miss him?"

"I have his picture in my playroom."

"That's good," Kiana replied.

"He sees me," Krys said with absolute certainty. "Is Belle sleepy?"

"Not yet. Are you?"

"Nope." Another word she had learned from Peggy. "I like this lots!"

"Belle likes little girls like you, too. When I was smaller, she was my favorite. Now I have to ride bigger horses."

Finally, Kiana called a halt, explaining that she didn't want Krys to get saddle sore. Then she had to explain what that meant. "You won't be able to sit down for a few days."

The thought made Krystal giggle, and she accepted that her ride had come to an end. They moved on, with an invitation from Gideon and his daughter to come up to the ranch soon. That seemed to thrill Krys, who announced in no uncertain terms that she wanted to see bigger horses.

More people were arriving, and tempting smells were issuing from a lot of the food booths. Silence had fallen over the three adults, but Krystal skipped merrily along, hunting for the face painter. When they reached the booth, her face sagged. "She's gone!"

"Maybe she's just late," Dan said. "A lot of people come late on Sunday. Are you hungry? Because I sure am."

Vicki's stomach growled as if in answer, making everyone, including her daughter, laugh. "I guess I am," she said, laughing at herself and shrugging.

"Well," said Lena, "there are two good reasons to ignore a diet. This is one of them. Let's go stock up on all the fat we can find."

"What's the other one?" Krys asked.

"To break a diet? Holidays, like Christmas and Thanksgiving."

Krys slipped her hand into Lena's. "Can I pick?"

"Anything you want."

Dan, walking beside Vicki, said, "You weren't really thinking you could feed her fiber and low-fat, were you?"

Vicki had to laugh again. "I don't do that to her. Balance is my goal. No balance today, I guess."

Krys got the corn dog she'd wanted the previous day, and a deep-fried pastry that was loaded with powdered sugar. Vicki gave in and had a corn dog, too. Dan once again filled a plate with a variety of fried foods, and Lena chose a big order of fries. "Fried in lard," she said with satisfaction.

At long last, Vicki allowed herself to really look at Dan. She'd been avoiding it since he'd gripped her elbow, but as the four of them sat at a picnic table, there was no way to avoid it any longer. Out of uniform today, he looked amazing in a blue chambray shirt that stretched across his broad shoulders. A cowboy hat, clearly one that had seen a lot of use, was tipped back on his head. Behind the table, his narrow hips were concealed, but Vicki couldn't help remembering them, anyway. If ever a man had been built for jeans, it was Dan Casey.

Without realizing it, she slipped into a dreamy state of mind, into a place where she and Dan were alone, where everything else had ceased to exist. Absently, her eyes wandered his face, remembering how his lips had felt on hers, how his arms had felt around her. Her whole body craved a repetition, and finally she closed her eyes, letting the anticipation and hunger fill her. Why not? At the moment she was safe, and daydreaming wasn't a crime.

"...in Denver."

Abruptly, before her daydream could turn her into a torch, Vicki snapped back into the conversation. "Denver?" she repeated.

"You're falling asleep there, Vicki," Lena remarked. "Do we need to get you home?"

"Face painting," Vicki said automatically. "Not before that. You said something about Denver?"

"It's that time of year," Lena explained. "The girls and I go on our big shopping trip, take in a play or a concert. Which reminds me, we're playing bridge tonight. You want to join us?"

Vicki shook her head. "Thanks, but I'm not much into cards. When are you going?"

"Next weekend. Everybody—well, except me, of course—ditches their husbands and we have a hen party. Maybe when Krys is a little older you can join us." Lena laughed. "By then you'll be eager to see a city again."

Vicki managed a laugh, but she felt strangely disoriented. Lena was going away for a weekend. Why should that bother her? What was going on inside her?

Then her gaze leaped across the table. Dan was looking toward Lena, for which Vicki was grateful, because she feared what he might see on her face in that instant. Lena was going away. That meant her chaperone would be gone.

Only then did she realize how much she was relying on Lena to keep her safe from temptation.

Vicki looked down at her plate and decided that she really, *really* needed to get her head straight. Any more self-delusion might get her into serious trouble.

Daydreaming about a man in a dangerous profession, and then expecting her aunt's presence to protect her from her foolishness? Oh, boy. She'd been in a cocoon too long. She was a grown woman and needed to deal better than this.

Krys put an end to her soul-searching. "I want my face painted now."

Vicki looked at her half-eaten corn dog and knew she couldn't swallow another mouthful. "Let's go, then, kiddo. Aunt Lena and Dan can catch up when they're done."

Escape. Right then she needed it.

The following Friday night, Lena left for her bridge game about five thirty. "Call me if you need anything," she said as she prepared to go. "I'll try to be back before eleven."

"Take your time and have fun."

"We will. A bunch of husbands have probably already headed for Mahoney's Bar." She laughed as she walked out.

Vicki had been looking forward to an evening alone with Krys. While she enjoyed sharing the house with Lena, it had seriously cut into their mother-daughter alone time. Early morning over breakfast, weeknights when they'd spent hours playing games or just watching TV. Admittedly, there hadn't been a whole lot of that, thanks to Hal's friends, but there had been more of it when she was living alone with her daughter.

But almost as soon as Lena was gone, Vicki realized

how big and empty the house felt now, even with Krystal's energy practically filling the place.

"Should we go for a walk?" she asked. Bedtime seemed out of the question if the girl didn't slow down a bit.

"'Kay," Krys answered.

Hand in hand, they started down the sidewalk, bathed in the pleasant summer evening that lasted so much longer here. "Let's practice crossing streets," Vicki suggested.

Krys grinned up at her. Wired or not, the girl seemed happier since the fair. Vicki's heart settled a bit and she gave her daughter's hand a squeeze. It was going to be all right.

Dan, wearing a long-sleeved gray shirt, jeans and jogging shoes, was sitting on his own front porch, doing some heavy thinking, one foot propped against the porch rail.

He saw Krys and Vicki walk away down the tree-lined street. They made a cute pair, Vicki wearing a lavender T-shirt and jeans, and Krys skipping along beside her in the pink that appeared to be her favorite color. They hadn't glanced in his direction, and for some reason he'd failed to call out a friendly greeting.

Of course, he'd been trying to keep a low profile since the fair. He wasn't a dunce. As a cop he'd gotten really good at reading people, and he'd picked up on cues that Vicki wasn't entirely comfortable with the amount of time he spent around her and her daughter.

He understood. He was a cop, after all, and he hadn't missed Vicki's startled reaction when she'd seen him in full uniform last Saturday at the fair. Bad reminders.

And from what she'd said about being afraid every time her husband had gone out the door, Dan got it.

He idly wondered if telling her that a cop was three times more likely to be struck by lightning than killed on the job would help her relax, then decided little could probably do that in the wake of Hal's death. Availability bias. He'd studied it in one of his college classes. She was seeing the whole world now through a single incident. As for whether her fears all along had been as great as she'd said, or amplified by Hal's murder, there was no way to know.

He had known cops who thought they were in danger every time they went on duty. They expected it. Funny thing was, expecting it seemed to cause it. Yet some recent stats he'd read said about 90 percent of cops retired without ever having fired their guns except on the practice range. He'd likely be one of them.

He sighed, and knew he was having a pointless argument with himself, because he doubted any of that would persuade Vicki. He didn't see his job as at all dangerous. Domestics were the only time he got edgy. But how he felt about it couldn't change the way Vicki felt.

Feelings were immutable things. Burned deep, they guided actions more than thought. You sure as hell couldn't reason with a feeling, no matter how hard you might try.

Which was part of what was giving him a problem. His feelings for Vicki were going places he was sure she didn't want. He should never have kissed her. Doing so had started a wildfire in him that wouldn't listen to his brain. He wanted that woman. He liked that woman. As for her daughter...well, he was fast coming to love that little girl. It was far too easy to imagine a future that contained both of them.

His foolishness almost amused him. He wasn't usually a foolish man, although like everyone else, he had his moments.

So he'd been staying away to give Vicki the space she seemed to want, and to avoid enhancing Krystal's attachment to him. That, too, had caused concern to flicker over Vicki's face a time or two. The woman was under enough stress with just the move. She didn't need to be wondering if her daughter was growing too close to a man she didn't want to become a permanent fixture.

Dang! The spinning of his own thoughts was growing frustrating. It should be so simple. Dan wanted the woman, and if something grew between them, he'd gladly welcome her daughter, too. No problem there.

Except Vicki. He knew damn well she wanted him, too, but she was afraid of it. Kinda turned things into an emotional time bomb.

But Vicki was creeping into his dreams, popping up in his thoughts without warning, and every time he thought about her he hardened a bit. Well, that wasn't enough for the long term.

Staying away this week had been tough. It was not only putting a distance between him and Lena, but he found himself wondering every evening what Krys and Vicki were doing. Missing them.

So he was a damned fool. Fair enough. There ought to be some reasonable way to handle this that didn't involve avoiding the three of them entirely. Lena must be wondering what the devil was going on, and he prized her friendship.

At least he had a game to coach tomorrow. That would help. And two nights this week he'd had a game to play in. That helped, too. Maybe he needed to take up some additional sports. Bowling?

He could have laughed at himself. He liked bowling well enough, but not enough to commit to a team. Anyway, his schedule was often erratic. Hard enough to keep up with baseball and the soccer team he coached.

But he was aware of something else changing in him, too. He'd rather sit here on his front porch mooning over Vicki than go down to Mahoney's and join the others to watch a game and have a few beers. Oh, that was bad.

He waved absently as cars drove by, passed some idle words with his neighbors who were out strolling, but all that seemed to barely scrape his internal fascination with thinking about Vicki.

The street quieted down as twilight descended. Fewer cars, almost no people now. Everyone was headed home to spend the rest of the night with a book or the TV.

Which was what he ought to do, instead of trying to solve unsolvable problems.

Removing his foot from the porch railing, he stood, deciding to go inside and pick up that book he needed to finish. Some distraction would do him good.

"Dan!"

His hand had just reached for his door latch when he heard Krystal call out. He almost pretended not to hear her, but then he heard something else that made him pivot quickly.

It all happened so amazingly fast, but in that instant time seemed to slow to a crawl. The sound of a car coming way too fast. Vicki crying her daughter's name. Everything suddenly became acutely clear, from the deepening shadows, the car coming at a fast clip without headlights, the leafy trees motionless as if frozen.

The girl had slipped away from her mother and was

running out into the street, heedless of the car. Vicki hit a dead run. So did Dan.

With horror, he saw Vicki trip over a tree root and land on the ground. Saw Krystal still running his way. Gauged the distance and started an almost incoherent prayer in his head as he hit top speed and ran into the street to grab the girl.

He got to her in the nick of time, grabbing her, tumbling to the ground and rolling away just as the car roared past, so close that he could feel its heat.

Krystal started crying. Vicki came running, screaming her daughter's name. The cop in Dan took a mental snapshot of the vehicle and driver. All in an instant. Then people began to pour out of their houses onto their porches.

He sat up with Krystal in his arms, hugging her so tightly that he might have scared her more. "It's okay," he heard himself say. His heart thundered like a galloping horse. Fury at the driver filled him, but his main concern was the sobbing little girl.

Then Vicki scooped her from his arms. "Are you all right? Is she okay?"

Dan rolled to his feet. "I think she's okay." He was fairly certain he'd protected her well enough. He suspected the same couldn't be said about himself. "Out of the street. Now."

The words penetrated Vicki's fear for her daughter, and she scurried with her over to the sidewalk in front of Lena's house. Only then did she set the girl on her feet, studying her anxiously.

Dan called out to the neighbors. "Everyone's okay, folks." They began trickling back inside, probably wondering what had just happened.

Vicki knelt in front of Krystal. "Does anything hurt, sweetie?"

"No." Krystal's sobs were turning into hiccups. "I was scared."

"Oh, baby, so was I."

"Get her inside and check her out. I'll be right there." Dan pulled out his cell phone, amazed he hadn't crushed it when he'd rolled with Krystal, and called the dispatcher. "Jay, Junior Casson just came speeding southbound down Collier at about fifty in a twenty-five. Nearly hit a little girl crossing the street. I want him picked up now."

Inside, he found Vicki and Krys sitting together on the couch. Vicki had protective arms wrapped around her daughter. Krys's tears were drying, but Vicki's face was still almost white. He squatted in front of them, noting that Vicki had a few small abrasions on her chin.

"How are you?" he asked her. "Did you get hurt when you fell?"

"I'm fine. Dan, I can't thank you enough..."

He shook his head. "Don't. I'm just glad I reached her." Then he looked at the girl. "What about you, pumpkin?"

Krys, who had been sucking her thumb again, pulled it out of her mouth. She wormed out of her mother's hold and landed between Dan's thighs to give him a big hug.

"Not mad at me?" he asked her.

"No. You helped me."

He stood up with the girl in his arms, feeling the adrenaline seeping away. With its departure came the awareness that he was probably growing some good bruises on his hip and shoulder. Turning, he sat beside Vicki on the couch, so the child was with them both.

At once Vicki reached out and drew her daughter close again. Dan forgot about everything that had been troubling him earlier, and wound his arms around both of them. For a long time nobody said a word.

"That guy was driving like a maniac," Vicki said eventually.

"They're going to pick him up. One nice thing about being a cop here. I recognized the idiot behind the wheel."

"Good." Although Vicki didn't sound as if satisfaction was going to ease her terror anytime soon. "Dan, if you hadn't…if…"

"Shh," he said gently. "No point worrying what didn't happen. I'm just glad I was there. Of course, if I hadn't been, Krys probably wouldn't have run into the street." And she'd have been less eager to see him if he hadn't been staying away. Guilt struck him, hard on the heels of fear for the child.

"Don't blame yourself. My God, you saved my daughter." Vicki made a choked sound. "Would you believe we'd been practicing how to properly cross streets while we were out walking?"

The irony didn't escape him.

"I was bad," Krys said. "Look both ways first."

Dan didn't have a clue how to respond to that. Saying she hadn't done anything wrong would be untruthful. Blaming it all on the driver would only be partially correct. He looked across the top of the soft blonde head cradled between them and met Vicki's gaze. She still appeared pinched, but a little less pale.

"That's right," she said. "Look both ways. Sometimes cars come really fast."

"Sorry."

Vicki sighed shakily. "It's good to be sorry, but it's even better not to do it again. Okay?"

"'Kay."

Her hand still trembled as she lifted it to stroke Krys's hair. She looked at Dan again. "What about you? Are you okay? That was a hard fall."

"Just a few bruises. I've rolled before."

"God, I never saw anybody run as fast as you did."

"You were doing a pretty good job yourself."

"I tripped." Anguish laced the words, and he watched as she drew a few deep, steadying breaths.

Dan wondered if they needed to change the subject, get her and Krys's mind off what had just happened. He doubted it would be as easy to make Vicki move past it quickly, but he wanted to see Krys smiling again. What had almost happened was probably meaningless to her, and a lot of her terror likely had come from being grabbed that way. It had probably conveyed more to her than the whole rest of the situation.

"How about I read a story," he said. "Or maybe we can play a game?"

"Game," said Krys promptly. She gave up sucking her thumb and wiggled free of the confinement of two hugs.

"Go get one, honey," Vicki said. From the expression on her face, Dan got the distinct feeling that letting her daughter out of her sight, even to run upstairs, was difficult right now. It might be difficult for a long time to come.

Vicki turned back to him after watching Krys disappear around the corner. "Dan, I've got to thank you—"

He shook his head, about to tell her it wasn't necessary. As if he was going to stand by and watch any child get hit by a car? But just then his cell rang. He rolled his eyes at Vicki, who smiled wanly.

It was Dispatch, of course. "Good. All right, I'll be in shortly, Jay." He disconnected and rose. "I'm sorry. They caught the driver, but by the time they did he'd slowed down to a legal speed. His dad's screaming they need to let him go, and while we could hold him for seventy-two hours without a charge, we don't do that around here for anything less than real mayhem. I've got to go in and file my report. Knowing that family, Junior will skip the county before morning."

Dan saw her face become pinched again. "I understand," she said, her voice muffled. Just then Krys bounced into the room carrying a board game.

"I'm sorry, Krys," he said. "I've got to go to work for a little while. We'll play tomorrow, okay?"

Krys's smile faded, but she nodded. "Will you come back?"

"I promise. If you're asleep, maybe your mommy will let me come up and peek in on you."

"Of course," Vicki said swiftly.

That brought the smile back to Krys's face. "Okay," she said. "Mommy can play with me."

From the look on the child's face, Dan figured she was going to fight sleep with all her might until he got back. He guessed he'd better hurry.

Chapter 7

Dan filled out his incident report in record time, insisted that Junior's blood be tested for illicit substances, then raced back to Lena's house.

Sure enough, when he let himself in, Vicki was on the couch with Krys, and it was after ten. Way past the girl's bedtime. His heart squeezed with concern and caring for both of them. He was definitely in it up to his neck, and right now he didn't care.

"She wouldn't go to bed until you got back," Vicki said.

At the sound of her mother's voice, Krys stirred, opened her eyes and smiled. "Dan," she said with satisfaction.

He perched on the edge of the couch beside her. "Do you know the story of Cinderella? How her fairy godmother turned her pumpkin into a coach?"

"Yup," Krys said sleepily.

"And then if she didn't get home in time, it turned into a pumpkin again?"

Krys nodded.

"You're going to turn into a pumpkin if you don't get to bed soon."

A sleepy giggle emerged from Krys. "You called me a pumpkin before."

"And you're a very cute pumpkin. But you still need your sleep."

"Carry me?"

Dan quickly searched Vicki's face and she nodded. He scooped the girl up in his arms, suppressing a wince as he felt the bruise on his shoulder protest. Oh, it was going to be a good one. So was his hip, come to that.

Ignoring both, he carried his precious cargo upstairs, then said good-night and slipped out while Vicki got the girl into bed.

"Dan..." Vicki's voice trailed after him. "Stay a bit?"

"Sure."

Since he knew his way around Lena's house as well as he knew his own, he started a pot of coffee. It had almost finished brewing by the time Vicki appeared.

"That smells good," she remarked. She looked so weary it troubled him.

He was leaning back against the counter, waiting for the coffee, when she approached. "Turn around."

Surprised, he obeyed, then nearly jumped when she touched his shoulder, and he realized her fingertips met bare skin. Hunger surged in him.

"I didn't say anything before," she said. "I didn't want Krys to notice. But your shirt's torn. Dan, that's an awful bruise you're getting."

"I'll survive." He felt frozen in place, wanting her touch to continue. But her fingertips went away.

She said, "I guess it's too late for ice."

"Probably. It'll be okay, Vicki. If that's the worst to come out of tonight, I'm grateful. I'm also grateful we got Junior Casson."

Dan heard her move to the table, so he turned around again.

"Is he a problem?" she asked.

"Wild child, although he's getting a little too old for that. Every place has a family or two like the Cassons, always on the edge of trouble, always creating it if they can't find it. Mostly stupidity and orneriness. Anyway, he's going to be off the streets for a little while, longer if we find out he was under the influence."

She nodded, then gave a start. "Let me get your coffee. You sit down. If your shoulder looks like that, other parts must hurt, too."

He eyed the hardwood chairs, gauged his hip and said, "Living room?"

"Fine by me. And for goodness' sake, if you want to use the recliner, use it."

He paused in the doorway. "I didn't want to take Hal's seat."

She sighed. "I kinda guessed. But Hal hasn't been using it. Make yourself comfortable. Please. If that was going to be a problem, I wouldn't have brought the sofa with me. I expect other people to use it."

So Dan risked taking the end of the sofa away from where she always perched, and accepted a mug of hot coffee gratefully. When she sat, she curled one leg under her, leaned back against the overstuffed arm and faced him, holding her own mug in both hands.

"This is going to be some story to tell Lena," she remarked.

"Wouldn't surprise me if she went down to the jail in the morning to give Junior a piece of her mind."

Vicki laughed quietly. "I wouldn't mind doing that myself."

"He's sure as hell going to get one from me. I'd have done it tonight except I got the feeling Krys wouldn't go to bed until I got back."

"You called that right." Vicki sipped coffee, then astonished him with what she said next. "You've been avoiding us. Did I do something wrong?"

Crap, he thought. *Called out.* He gave her points for it, though. Apparently, she was a lot like her aunt. "I got the feeling you didn't want me so involved with you and Krys." He could be blunt, too.

She nodded slowly, looking pensive. "I told you about my fears. But that doesn't mean we can't be friends. Krys really likes you. So do I, for that matter." Vicki's eyes lifted, meeting his. "We can do friends, right?"

It might be a new kind of hell, given how badly he wanted her, but he wasn't a proud man. He'd take what he could get. This past week of trying to do what he believed Vicki wanted had been a kind of hell, anyway. "Sure," he said. No point in being blunt about *this*. It was tough enough and he didn't want to bring her fears back.

"Good." She hesitated, then astonished him anew. "And do me a favor?"

"If I can."

"Next time you decide to read my mind, tell me what you think I'm thinking. You were the one who mentioned that silence leaves a lot of empty space to imagine things."

He laughed. Somehow he just had to. "Okay," he agreed. "So what *was* going on?"

"I was worried about Krys. She's said a few things, done a few things, that make me think she's having separation anxiety. I suspect the move was harder on her than I expected. And while I'm not sure she remembers Hal much, if at all, she's been through a lot of loss in little more than a year. Anyway, she's attached to you, obviously, and I don't mind. Honestly."

"Are you sure about that? I heard what you said about cops."

She bit her lip. "Okay, I'm a little worried. But it's crossed my mind that I can't protect against everything, and she has needs to be met. You're apparently meeting one, and I'd have to be a witch to deprive her."

He paused before responding carefully, "My job isn't all that dangerous, Vicki. I've been a deputy for seventeen years. Do you know how many times I've had to pull my gun? None."

"Really?" She hesitated. "I think Hal did a couple of times."

"Big cities are different. And I'm not saying it never happens around here, but it's been two decades since we lost a deputy. We have our share of problems, I won't deny it. But I think it's more dangerous to be a crab fisherman."

"Maybe so. Anyway, I don't need to pass my fears to Krys. She's struggling to make new connections here, and she needs every one of them."

He'd already figured out Vicki was remarkable in a lot of ways, but it floored him to see her put aside a very natural fear of her own in favor of what she believed to be her daughter's best interest. "So I'm not smothering you?"

Her expression turned wry. "To do that, you'd need to try a whole lot harder, cowboy."

He grinned. "Fair enough. I'm coaching girl's soccer tomorrow. The six-to-eight group. You wanna bring Krys to watch? There'll be some younger kids there watching, too."

"That'd be good for her," Vicki agreed.

"And what about you? What would be good for you?"

The question seemed to startle her, but before she could answer, the front door opened and Lena swept in. Clad in her usual Western shirt and jeans, her only concession to playing bridge with her girlfriends had been a dab of makeup.

"We slaughtered them," she said cheerfully. Then she took in the scene on the couch, and evidently something got her attention. "What happened? Is everything all right?"

"It is now," Vicki said. "I'll let Dan tell you. A cop can do it without breaking down."

Lena sat on the other sofa almost as if her strings had been cut. "Krys?"

"She's fine," Vicki said swiftly. "Thanks to Dan."

So he sketched what had happened, almost as if he were filling out a report, but adding a few details, such as how Vicki had tripped, and why her chin was abraded.

"Well, I never," Lena said. For a minute or so she didn't say any more, then demanded, "Junior Casson? He's in the jail?"

"Yes," Dan answered.

"Shoulda let that young man run. Maybe he'd never come back." She shook her head. Then she took in Dan. "Are you all right, too?"

"Bruised but fine."

Lena rose. "I'm gonna get me some of that coffee—there's more, right?"

Vicki nodded.

"Good. I'm getting some, then you're going to take me through this again, Dan Casey. And this time not like an abbreviated police report."

He flashed a smile. "Yes, ma'am."

She was tutting as she walked out. "Junior Casson. I'm going to have some words for him."

The soccer game the next afternoon turned out to be a lot of fun for both Vicki and Krys. Krys soon met three children near her own age, and it provided a perfect entrée for Vicki to become acquainted with some of the other women. The young girls running wildly on the field, occasionally getting confused about where to go and what to do, provided an endless source of conversation and some amusement.

Mothers cheered loudly, but refrained from any critical remarks, which was a pleasant surprise for Vicki, who'd gone to some recreational league games with friends and discovered that some parents took the game as seriously as if it were the World Cup. The women surrounding her that afternoon remained a whole lot more laid-back, apparently thinking their children were here to have fun, not get college scholarships ten years down the road.

When it was over, Vicki was encouraged to come back next weekend, and even had an invitation to join a local church.

She had noted, however, that Dan seemed to be moving a bit stiffly and felt a pang for the discomfort he must be feeling. Her heart wanted to reach out to him even though it was nothing terribly obvious, but when they met up after the match, as the girls and their families scattered to cars or along the neighborhood side-walks, she asked him about it.

"Just bruising, but I guess I got some road rash on my shoulder. My skin is annoyed with me." He smiled. "I'll be fine. Now how about I take us all for ice cream?"

"Yay!" Krys squealed. Then she added, "Mommy, I wanna play soccer."

Vicki opened her mouth to say she wasn't old enough yet, but Dan spoke first. "There's a group of four-and five-year-olds. One of the elementary schoolteachers runs it as a kind of intro-to-skills group." He turned to Vicki. "And lest you worry, no heading of the ball allowed at that age." He chuckled. "Not that most of them are in any danger of getting their heads that close to a ball."

"Thanks. I'll check into it." She looked down at Krys. "We'll see what I can find out."

The ice cream parlor was just off the town's central square. Vicki was able to find parking nearby, and Dan almost as close. They met at the door and he ushered them in.

Retro would be a good word for the place's appearance. Vicki wondered if it just hadn't changed in fifty years or if it had been designed to look like something out of *Happy Days*. Most people were buying cones or cups and leaving with them, so the three of them found seats easily at the counter, which was where Krys wanted to sit, on a high stool. Vicki and Dan sat on either side of her, and Vicki helped her daughter read the menu. While the child did fairly well with simple children's books, the menu was full of a lot of words she had to sound out. Vicki was not surprised, however, when they got only partway through the listing and Krys made her decision.

"Chocolate with chocolate sprinkles."

"Cone or cup?"

Krys thought about it for a second. "Cone," she announced.

Dan ordered a double scoop of chocolate chip and Vicki a cup of frozen yogurt. She soon discovered why most people probably didn't stay here with their ice cream. Dan was greeted by everyone, while his ice cream began to melt down the cone into the napkin he'd wrapped around it. He introduced Vicki and Krys to all comers, which took a fair amount of time, as well.

He winked at Vicki over Krys's head. "Great place to have a meet-up."

"So it appears." Glancing down at Krys, Vicki saw fatigue beginning to appear. Her daughter had stayed up late last night, had gotten up early this morning filled with excitement about going to the soccer game, and had been running at full speed ever since. She was still enjoying her ice cream, licking round and round to make sure she caught all the drips, but she was slowing down.

Just then Dan's cell phone beeped. He shook his head a little and pulled it out, quickly scanning a text. "Gotta go. I'm sorry. Work. See you later?"

Vicki nodded, watching as he dropped a kiss on the top of Krys's head. "Later, pumpkin," he said, before hurrying out.

Vicki looked up from her ice cream at her mother. "He works a lot."

"Yes, he does." Apparently, around here hours weren't as regular for cops as they'd been in Austin. Smaller department, she decided. Sometimes they probably needed officers on call, more than she was used to. But really, she had little on which to base that. This might be unusual. Regardless, she somehow seemed to be getting in tune with his job and becoming more accepting of it.

"Mommy?"

"Yes, honey?"

"Wanna go home."

So, ice cream in hand, with plenty of napkins, they went out to the car and drove home. Krys kept up licking her ice cream until it was down inside the cone, but then she nodded off, just as they pulled into Lena's driveway.

Vicki climbed out and looked into the backseat. Krys was sound asleep, with the contents of the cone dribbling onto one of the napkins. Smiling, Vicki caressed her daughter's head gently, then grabbed the cone in a wad of napkins. She heard the front door and saw Lena come out.

"Need help?" her aunt asked.

"If you could grab the ice cream mess, I'll grab Krys."

Lena took the wad in both hands. "My, she's tuckered. Of course, she's been going like ninety."

Vicki laughed quietly, unbuckling her daughter, then lifting her out of the car. "That she has."

With her hip she shut the door, then used the auto-lock button on her keys and settled Krys more comfortably on her hip.

"You can just put her on the couch if you want," Lena said as they headed inside. "We can klatch in the kitchen."

"Sounds good to me. Dan had to run in to work. He said he'd be over later."

"'Bout time he started coming by again."

Krys stirred a little, her eyes fluttering open as Vicki laid her on the couch and spread an afghan over her.

"Mommy?"

"Sleep, little dove. I'll be in the kitchen."

Krys sighed, rolled over and stuck her thumb in her mouth. Evidently all the problems weren't gone yet.

Sitting at the kitchen table with Lena felt relaxing to Vicki. Her aunt was a good woman, always great to talk with about nearly anything. She might joke that bookkeepers were boring, but she was a widely read woman who could discuss almost anything if she chose.

Her sights were set a little lower at the moment, however. She eyed Vicki with concern. "Are you all right? I can see that Krystal is, but you were the one who got the biggest shock last night."

"It rattled me a lot," Vicki admitted. "Right now, I don't want Krys out of my sight."

"We can move into the other room if you want. I doubt the two of us talking will wake her. She's out like a light from what I saw."

"Yeah." Vicki stared down into her coffee cup. "You know, Lena, even with all that's happened, I don't think I've ever been as scared as I was last night. If not for Dan…" She could barely stand to think about it.

"A long time ago, I decided kids must all have guardian angels. How else do so many of them ever grow up?"

A weary laugh escaped Vicki. "She sure had one last night."

"And I'm mad at the jailers."

At that, Vicki lifted her head. "Why?"

"They wouldn't let me scold Junior Casson. Now I ask you, the man nearly kills my grandniece and one of my best friends, and if he doesn't want to see me I don't get to tell him off?"

Vicki's laugh came a little easier this time. "Dan may do it for you. He said he was going to give Junior a piece of his mind."

Lena ruminated a moment, then said, "He'll do a good job of it, too. I've heard him dress down some youths before. Junior will have no doubt that he's an idiot by the time Dan is done."

"Good."

Lena peered at her. "Did you sleep much last night?"

"Honestly? No. I kept seeing it over and over—Krys running into the street, me falling, Dan running faster than the wind. He barely made it, Lena. However casually he treats it, except for him…" The tears came then, running freely down her cheeks. A choked sob escaped her.

Lena jumped up and came to hug her tightly. "Let it out, girl. Let it out."

Vicki couldn't stop it. She'd remained calm for Krys's sake, but she couldn't do it another moment. Her daughter had come within a second of being run over by a car. The scene ran repeatedly in Vicki's head like a horror movie on infinite loop.

Lena patted her shoulder, made comforting sounds, but didn't do a thing to make Vicki feel she should stop crying. She'd lost her husband, and had just almost lost her daughter, and the pain surged in her, needing an outlet.

It took a long time, but finally she began to run out of tears. Her chest felt so tight she could hardly breathe, but finally she managed a ragged one. Lena straightened and passed her a fresh kitchen towel to wipe her face.

"Maybe you should take up kickboxing."

Startled, Vicki raised her head, holding a now damp towel. "What?"

"There must be enough rage in you to want to take on the universe sometimes. Pounding something might do you some good."

"I agree." The deep voice startled her even more and she swung her head around to see Dan standing in the doorway, arms folded, leaning against the jamb. "Sorry, I let myself in. If I should go, tell me."

She didn't want him to go, although she was sorry he'd seen her such a mess. But then she remembered he'd lost his wife. He was probably as familiar with her reaction as anyone could be.

"Stay," she said, her voice still hoarse from crying.

He came into the room, poured a coffee and joined the women at the table. "There was a spell after Callie died that I went to the gym nearly every day just to pound the punching bag until I couldn't punch it anymore."

"Did it help?"

He tilted his head. "I don't know that anything really helps. But it sure does wear you out. So the anger gets expended, and the grief moves back in, until the next time anger takes over." He shrugged his uninjured shoulder. "It eases, Vicki. That's all I can say."

Silence fell. When Vicki at last reached for her cup to moisten her throat, she found the coffee had grown cold. The instant she stirred as if to rise, Lena snatched the mug, emptied it in the sink and refilled it.

"Thank you."

Lena smiled sadly at her. "I can't do much else except keep the coffee coming."

Vicki reached out to squeeze her aunt's hand. "You've done a whole lot for Krys and me. A whole lot."

"Time will tell." She turned her attention to Dan. "So did you give Junior a piece of my mind for me?"

"Yeah, I did," he said. "And a piece of mine, as well. Sorry you couldn't do it yourself. I know you'd have felt better."

"I feel good enough that you did it."

"First he was angry, but I just kept at him, Lena. You know how stubborn I can get."

"Pretty stern, too," she agreed.

"By the time I was done I saw something I thought I'd never see on a Casson face—shame. Doubt it'll last, though."

"How long will he get?"

"I don't know. A lot depends on whether he was under the influence. As it is, reckless endangerment carries a decent sentence. Maybe assault with a deadly weapon. It's up to the county prosecutor now. We'll see."

"If the county attorney feels like most of us in this county, she'll throw the book at him," Lena said. "About time a Casson got sent away for a while."

A quiet laugh escaped Dan. "He's going to have trouble finding a sympathetic jury, that's for sure."

Vicki was only half attending to the conversation as she waited for her emotional storm to settle completely. All she had to do, all she ever had to do, was take one step at a time. Then the next. Since Hal's death, looking too far forward occasionally daunted her, and right now she wasn't the least interested how long Junior Casson spent in jail. It was enough that he'd been caught.

What mattered was that her daughter was all right. Vicki wasn't feeling especially vengeful, although she might later. Right now she was absorbing the fact that she had something to be truly grateful for. Krystal was fine, apparently less disturbed by last night than anyone else.

Vicki closed her eyes a moment, accepting a quiet sense of blessing, a blessing that existed because of Dan. She opened her eyes and looked at him, to find him regarding her with concern.

"Thank you," she said again. "And don't tell me I don't need to thank you. I do."

He nodded once, saying nothing, his gaze steady.

He was a remarkable man. Handsome, of course. She liked the way time and the sun had put fine lines around the corners of his eyes, lines that crinkled when he smiled. She liked the warmth she almost always saw in his gray eyes. She liked the way he treated Krys, and with the passage of time she had stopped worrying that he might overstep with her daughter. He never did, and the more he became involved, the more comfortable Vicki felt. He had good instincts, and she didn't mind it when he made a suggestion. Not now. She no longer feared him encroaching.

He was very different from Hal. She had loved Hal with her whole heart, but he'd been a different man, more excitable, more hyperkinetic. Everything about Dan created a calming atmosphere, which she appreciated.

Well, except for her attraction to him. Traitorously, it was rising in her again, the longing for another kiss, for more than a kiss. She looked quickly away for fear he might read her reaction.

How could she be feeling such things hard on the heels of her near breakdown? It seemed impossible and made her feel both guilt and shame. But as soon as she recognized it, she caught herself. It was simply a sign that she was still alive. And like it or not, she was very much alive.

Just pass it off as life trying to reassert itself. That was inevitable, and it was surely no crime.

The conversation between Lena and Dan flowed into slower, easier channels. Lena asked about soccer practice, then talked about her plans with her friends the coming weekend.

"I'm going to spend more than I should, eat more than I should, and laugh until my ribs hurt," she told them. "Say, Dan, aren't you about due for vacation again?"

"Yeah, but I'm waiting. I always go in August or September, and I decided this year to take a winter vacation."

Lena cocked a brow. "Heading for the sun?"

"I don't know. I haven't been skiing in a while, and I was thinking about that."

Lena snorted. "Talk about spending more than you can afford!"

Dan laughed. He glanced at Vicki, but didn't make any effort to get her to talk. Nor did she feel any desire to. It was enough to ride the flow of their conversation while matters inside her tried to settle. All the changes, especially Dan and last night, had altered her internal landscape. It might take a while for her to become comfortable inside her own skin again.

"I think I'm going to run to the store and pick up something easy for dinner," Lena announced. "I don't feel like cooking tonight."

"I could cook," Vicki offered immediately. "I've been feeling bad about you doing it all."

Lena eyed her. "I told you I'd let you know when I want you to cook. And don't think I haven't noticed the way you've been cleaning this place. I don't believe it's been this clean since it was built."

Vicki managed a smile. "It's the least I can do."

Lena looked at Dan. "She won't listen to me. She insists on helping out financially, too. I ask you, do I look like I'm poor?"

Dan spread his hands. "I'm not getting into this with you two. Anyway, now you can spend even more than you thought in Denver."

Lena barked a laugh. "Maybe I will."

"As for dinner, I could make chili," Dan said. "You like my chili."

Lena shook her head. "Vicki might not. She's from Texas, don't you know."

At last Vicki was able to let go enough to join in. "Hey!"

"Might be too hot for Krys, though," Lena said, standing. Evidently her mind was made up. "I want something different tonight, so just let me go take care of it. I won't be long."

That left Dan and Vicki sitting at the table by themselves. Vicki had nothing to say, afraid that she would only talk about last night again. Then Dan surprised her back into the present.

"Callie and I wanted children," he remarked.

She looked at him and saw that his face was shadowed. "You didn't get the time?"

"Oh, we had time, we thought. When it finally struck us something might be wrong, we went to the doctor to find out. That's when we learned she had ovarian cancer."

"Oh, Dan. Oh, my…" Words seemed so inadequate. Vicki reached out and he took her hand.

"It still kills me that we didn't know until it was too

late. Sometimes I still read all the articles about warnings and signs that need to be checked out, but if Callie ever had any of them, I didn't know it. One day she seemed perfectly healthy, with a whole future ahead of her, and the next day we were facing death. Those kinds of things haunt you. But you know that."

"Yes." But Vicki didn't dare say any more. She waited, giving him some space to talk. After all, they'd agreed they could talk about their late spouses, a subject that generally made others uncomfortable. But apart from that, she really hurt for him.

He averted his face for a few seconds, and she could almost see him absorbing the blow all over again. But then he turned to her again and squeezed her hand. "Krystal's a doll. You're lucky to have her, and I'm lucky I met her."

Vicki answered with a wryness that surprised her, given what she'd been feeling and what they'd been discussing. "She gets her energy from her father. He didn't like holding still. She's not easy to keep up with sometimes."

A smile washed away Dan's haunted expression. "A definite powerhouse."

"Until she runs empty." Vicki hesitated, thinking of the little girl in the next room. She ought to check on her, then told herself she was being overly protective. She'd been trying hard to avoid that, because she didn't want to deprive Krys of a normal childhood, or instill any unnecessary fears in her. The urge was strong today, however, exacerbated by last night.

But she had to consider Dan, too. She didn't want to pop out when he'd been sharing something important with her. It would be rude at the very least, and possibly cruel.

He sighed, rubbing his thumb lightly over the back of her hand. An instant shiver of pleasure passed through her, and a self-protective instinct almost made her snatch her hand back. But she liked his touch. What was so wrong about enjoying it? Besides, he already knew how she felt about a relationship with a cop, how it terrified her. He'd have to be an idiot to have misread that.

He pressed her hand gently, then let go. "How'd we get so maudlin?" he asked. "Oh, yeah. Junior Casson started the show last night. Scares. Reminders. But this time no loss."

Dan's gaze grew intent, earnest. "Just keep reminding yourself of that, Vicki. Krys is all right."

"No thanks to Junior," she said a bit sharply, but then admitted he was right. Maybe she needed to reexamine herself in light of last night's near miss. Apparently cops weren't the only people who could walk out a door and never return.

What a thought! She banished it, not wanting it to pop into her head every time she was away from Krys. "You know," she said suddenly, "it would be so easy to get neurotic."

Dan's eyes widened, then he laughed. "Yeah, it would. I'd really rather not."

"Me, either. I've got enough problems I don't want to pass on to my daughter. Additional ones are not welcome."

His expression softened. "I think you're doing pretty darn good, actually. She seems totally normal to me, in every way."

"Except for the separation anxiety. I hope that passes."

"Too soon to be sure, but she also seems resilient.

We must have scared the dickens out of her last night, but she seems fine today."

She certainly did, Vicki thought. Unlike her mother. But maybe that was a blessing of childhood. Last night had scared her, but today everything was happy and upbeat again. Vicki could take some lessons from her. "She seems to have an innate wisdom."

"Or maybe she's far more willing to live in the moment than adults. We're always thinking about tomorrow, or the past, and often overlooking the moment right in front of us."

"Too true," Vicki acknowledged. "Except when we get shocked out of our shoes. That kind of wakes us up." But maybe only briefly. How much time had she spent thinking about last night, instead of just being grateful she still had Krys? Except for a short time when she had felt the blessing, she'd been back-and-forthing about things that had happened and things that might never happen.

"Seems to be human nature after a certain age. God knows how much time I could have spent with Callie that got wasted because I was so busy with anger and grief in anticipation of losing her. Unfortunately, I don't think we can change the way we're built. Nor, I suspect, would the world do so well if nobody learned from the past or looked toward the future."

Vicki gave a quiet laugh. "True. But we could probably spend a little more time actually being here and now."

"Worth a try."

They heard the back door open. Vicki snatched her hand back instantly and Lena entered the kitchen carrying two cloth totes. "Get ready, folks. The butcher will never forget my visit. Big juicy T-bones, specially cut. Dan, you're in charge of grilling. Found some good sweet corn, too, so, Vicki, you can wrap the corn for the grill. You up to it?"

"I thought you didn't want to cook," Vicki said, smiling.

"Did I say *I* was cooking? I seem to be designating everyone else."

Krystal appeared in the doorway, rubbing her eyes. "Can I help, too?"

"See?" said Lena with satisfaction. "Pass me a mint julep. Y'all just got your orders."

Chapter 8

Watching Lena and her friends depart for Denver turned into a hoot. Six ladies had to load two cars with luggage, decide who was going to sit where and try to decide what hotel to stay in. Vicki suspected some of the lighthearted arguing was for the benefit of their audience, herself and Krys. Finally, Lena jammed her last bag into the back of Rebecca's Toyota.

"It's only three days," Vicki teased. "How are you going to bring anything home with you?"

Rebecca, a slender woman of Lena's age, laughed. "That's what laps and half the backseat are for. Although one year we rented one of those little trailers."

Vicki blinked. "For real? What in the world did you buy?"

"Too much," Lena said drily. "We're older now. We take it to the post office and ship it home."

All the women started laughing and were still laughing when at last they set out.

The Friday afternoon was bright and warm. Vicki took Krystal to the park for a playdate with Peggy, and spent the time talking with Janine Dalrymple and a few other women, one who pushed a stroller back and forth steadily as she watched her two-year-old son play. Her infant slept peacefully the whole time.

In fact, the whole scene was peaceful and nearly perfect. Vicki felt herself uncoiling, in part because she loved the sound of children having a good time.

When the other women learned she had taught kindergarten in Texas, they suddenly bubbled with ideas for her. "You should try to teach at the preschool at Good Shepherd," one said. "I think they need more help."

"Or start your own," said another. "Good Shepherd is too crowded."

"That would be too expensive," Janine said, before Vicki could point it out. "A building, a playground, licensing, hiring other people... That's why the only one we have is at a church."

"I was thinking something else," said the other woman, Daisy. "More like just a couple of hours a day, where kids could get a leg up on reading, the alphabet, numbers. The academic stuff. More personalized attention."

That actually appealed to Vicki. Even though she'd applied for a license here before she'd left Austin, she wasn't sure she was ready to get back into full-time teaching. Her decision to be available to Krys after Hal's death remained with her. It was too soon, especially considering Krys's separation anxiety, for Vicki to be gone all day. She understood plenty of other mothers weren't blessed with her choices, but since she was, she had chosen what she thought was best.

Which, as with so many things in parenting, might be a two-edged sword.

"I'll think about it," she said as Daisy continued to press her. Vicki returned her attention to Krys, who was now on a swing, talking to another girl as they passed each other in endless arcs. It was also possible that Vicki was making Krys more dependent on her. Crap. Were there no easy, clear answers?

After the park, they walked to town. Krys wanted a hamburger, and since it had been a while since the last junk meal, Vicki decided to give it to her. Besides, she didn't feel like cooking tonight. Her mind seemed preoccupied, though she wasn't exactly sure why.

Dan had been among the missing most of the week, although he had a reason for it. They were approaching championship season in baseball, which seemed a little ludicrous to her. Apparently, the Little League needed some extra umpires, so he was there every evening he could be, helping out. At least he'd dropped by on his way home, staying for a brief chat with her and Krys.

Vicki missed him, and was surprised that Krys hadn't been carrying on about it. She always greeted him with huge excitement, but didn't seem to have a problem with him being needed elsewhere. Once, Krys had said that she wanted to go to a baseball game, and Vicki had promised they'd go next week.

She was just entering the courthouse square, right before the turn to Maude's, when she saw Dan come out of the sheriff's office. Once again, for the first time since the fair, she saw him in full uniform. Her heart jolted and she would have frozen in place if Krys hadn't spied him and cried his name. *It's not the same*, Vicki told herself. Hal's uniform had been dark blue. This uniform was khaki. Different.

Oh, hell, it wasn't different at all. The badge, the belt with the gun, the white plastic restraints hanging like loose loops on his hip…no, it wasn't different.

Dan heard Krys call his name. He smiled and waved, and trotted toward them, making an exaggerated effort to look in every direction before crossing the street. In spite of herself, Vicki had to laugh.

"Two of my favorite ladies," he said warmly when he reached them. "How's my pumpkin?" he asked as he lifted Krys for a hug.

"Super," Krys answered, her new favorite word. "I'm getting a hamburger."

"Oh, that sounds yummy. No pickles, right?"

"Nope. Mommy always gets pickles." Krys made an exaggerated face.

"So she's a sourpuss?"

That sent Krys into a gale of laughter as Dan set her down. He smiled at Vicki. "How's Mom doing?"

"I'm just fine," she answered. "Are you off on an important mission?"

"Actually, I was about to go in search of food. We had a busy day, and I haven't eaten since breakfast. I was thinking about calling you and asking if you wanted me to bring dinner home with me, but you beat me. Mind some company?"

"Of course not."

Krys clung to both their hands as they walked, crossing one more street, then turning toward the City Diner.

"What was so busy?" Vicki asked.

"Youthful miscreants. Too much time on their hands this summer, school's about to start again, and I guess they figured this was their last chance to misbehave.

Heck, I don't know. The Little League championships have some people wound up, too, and a lot of folks have come to town for the weekend games."

"For real?" It amazed her.

"Hey, for some it's important. Important enough to overimbibe, to forget that the sun is supposed to pass the yardarm first...you get the idea. Speeders, vandals and inebriates, and some fisticuffs. You could almost swear something gets into the water from time to time."

She noted the way he tried to phrase it so Krys couldn't follow, and Vicki expected a raft of questions from her daughter. But Krys seemed to be more interested in getting to the diner.

"Summer's almost over," Dan said as they approached the restaurant. "The last hurrah. Until cabin fever sets in sometime this winter, anyway."

Coming from Texas, Vicki couldn't imagine summer being over already. "I'd still be thinking fall was a bit down the road in Austin."

"I imagine so," he said as he opened the door. "We'll probably see our first snow flurry here while you Texans are just starting autumn. Or not." He looked down at Krystal. "Ever been sledding?"

She shook her head.

"We will definitely have to take care of that."

She imagined sitting behind Dan on a sled, her legs and arms wrapped around him, and decided they would definitely have to try sledding. A small smile danced across her face.

The place was fairly crowded, but Dan managed to get them a table near the window. Or maybe Maude, the owner, did. She kind of pushed them toward it.

"She's sweet on you," Vicki couldn't resist murmuring to Dan, although she suspected she might be projecting her own feelings. Was she getting sweet on him? Instead of being terrified by the thought, she actually tucked it away and savored it.

"Hey, I'm a sweet guy." He winked humorously.

Their dinners were served, and Vicki talked about the school idea the women had suggested, because it seemed utterly safe. Dan listened, nodding, and Krystal appeared more involved with her giant hamburger.

"I agree setting up a preschool would be an awfully expensive venture," he said. "But a tutoring kind of program for an hour or two a day? I bet a lot of people would be interested. The church preschool *is* overloaded. They're trying to raise funds right now to expand, because they've reached their code limits."

"Well, it's just an idea, and that's all it's going to be, at least for a while."

He smiled. "Try taking some deep breaths and getting your feet under you first."

He was right about that. She felt far from settled yet, and while she was beginning to make some community ties herself, she still had to put Krystal first. The women at the park had been fun and encouraging, very welcoming, but Vicki was still waiting to feel as if she and her daughter had truly landed. Something a little like jet lag struck her every so often, a sense of unreality. She guessed her big move wasn't yet complete, at least emotionally.

Still, it was kind of nice to play around with the tutoring idea. Her days were full enough, with Krystal, and helping Lena take care of the house, and while Vicki hadn't thought about it much in the past year, she was beginning to feel some needs of her own, such as wanting to accomplish something. Teaching kindergarten had often given her the sense that she was doing something important that extended out beyond her immediate family. Apparently, that need hadn't entirely gone away. Little by little it was reawakening, and tutoring seemed like a gentle way to reintroduce Krys to the idea that her mom worked.

A good example for the child, a necessity for herself, and something that probably would wait until Krystal started school next year. Vicki's whole purpose in leaving her job last time had been to make sure Krystal got over the hump of losing her father, that she knew at least one of her parents was always there.

Maybe that wouldn't be so important a few months down the road, but so soon after their move, Vicki still worried. Krys seemed to be transplanting well and thriving, but there were still those moments that worried her.

When it came to true stability for Krys, Vicki figured she was it.

After their early supper, the two of them walked back to the house carrying a bag of leftovers. Dan returned to the sheriff's office, mentioning he'd probably be home soon.

"Come see us," Krys invited.

Dan looked at Vicki, who smiled and nodded. It no longer totally terrified her that she wanted to see this man often. Just as long as she kept things in safe limits, that was.

"You got it, pumpkin. I'll be there soon."

It struck Vicki as they were walking home that it might not be good for Dan to make such promises. She'd already seen that he could get called in on a moment's notice. What's more, a department with only about twenty-five deputies probably needed a lot of officers to step up if something happened, or if one got sick. Filling in the gaps was probably a large part of Dan's job.

And then there was the other problem: the possibility that he might not come home at all. She felt only marginally better since he'd told her that they hadn't lost a deputy in a couple decades. It could still happen.

But for the first time, she wondered if her fear might be irrational. Yes, being a cop could be dangerous, but when she looked back over her years with Hal, the only death had been his. And he hadn't even been on duty.

Her throat tightened and she swallowed hard. Hal going to the store to get milk. Sometimes she got so angry, wondering if he wouldn't have been killed if he hadn't tried to be the good cop. He hadn't even been on duty. Maybe interfering in the robbery had cost him his life. But on duty or off duty, he'd been a cop. He could have just as easily walked into that mess wearing his uniform.

She tried to tell herself it could have happened to anyone in the store that night, but she didn't quite believe it. Hal had put it all out there, trying to protect the store manager and other patrons. It was too late to second-guess his decisions, to wonder whether, if he hadn't challenged the perp, the guy might have walked out with his miserable twenty bucks. A man's life for twenty dollars. It still appalled her.

"Mommy?"

Yanked back into the present, Vicki glanced down. "Yes?"

"Will Dan really come?"

There it was again, tightening Vicki's throat once more. Maybe she should speak to Dan about saying things with much less certainty. "He said he would. But he has to work, too, so we can't be sure."

"I know."

There was something dark in the girl's tone, and it frightened Vicki. What demon was she dealing with now?

Vicki squatted on the sidewalk and Krys automatically turned to look at her. "Krys, are you worried Dan won't come?"

She tilted her head before answering. "No," she said finally. "He said he would."

"Then you're worried about him being late?" God, Vicki hoped that was all it was.

"Yup. Can we go home and play a game?"

"Of course." They resumed walking, but Vicki's heart felt like lead. Late? Oh, she didn't think that was it at all, especially since Dan hadn't promised a time. Maybe seeing him in uniform had stirred some reaction in Krys, one she wasn't even aware of.

Was Vicki making a mistake, allowing this friendship? But how could she stop it now? Her daughter wasn't the only one who'd become dependent on Dan.

Dan didn't keep Krystal waiting for long. An hour later, dressed in jeans and a black sweatshirt, he popped through the door, looking guilty. In his hand he carried a bag.

Krystal greeted him joyfully, and Dan swung her up into his arms. They all moved into the living room and sat on the sofa. Dan eyed Vicki. "Get annoyed with me if you want."

"About what?"

"I heard what you said about the tide of gifts, but I brought one, anyway."

Vicki, inexplicably relieved that he had shown up

and put Krys's concerns to rest, merely laughed. "What did you do?"

"Don't hate me forever." He reached for the bag and pulled out a stuffed gray-and-white wolf, just a small one, but suitable for carrying around. He handed it to Krys. "Your very first wolf."

She squealed in pleasure and said thank-you before crawling into Dan's lap, holding her new treasure.

"It's beautiful," Vicki said, admiring the wolf, and happy with Krys's reaction. Apparently, whatever had troubled her was gone now. Vicki didn't want to think about that.

"Not easy to find," Dan remarked. "Ranchers don't care for the wolves at all, and we've got a pack up on Thunder Mountain. It's not the kind of thing most people around here would want to buy."

Vicki had read about the problems, the concern on the part of ranchers that wolves presented a threat to livestock. She got it, but didn't say any more about it. She was the newbie here, and reading up on something didn't make her an expert.

"I like wolfs," Krys said.

"Wolves," Vicki corrected gently. "I know, it seems dumb, but that's the way it is."

Krys giggled and admired her new toy while leaning against Dan's chest. "This is a wolfie," she announced.

"Fair enough," Vicki agreed. She glanced at Dan and saw him looking down at Krys with a slightly wistful smile. Clearly, he was enjoying having her on his lap, and enjoyed her pleasure in the wolf, but Vicki could only imagine what other thoughts must be running through his head. Perhaps he was thinking about the daughter he might have had.

Between the two of them, she guessed she was by far the luckier.

He suggested they play a game, and Krys ran to get one. When she came back downstairs, she was carrying the children's version of Scrabble. Vicki felt a little surprised. Krys hadn't shown much interest in it lately.

"Wow, that's heavy," Dan said. "I'm not the world's best speller. Are you sure you want to play with me?"

"Mommy will fix it if you're wrong."

With that assurance they adjourned to the dining room. With a new player in the mix, Krys seemed to have regained her liking of the game, and often laughed delightedly when Dan made an obvious mistake and Vicki fixed it. She suspected most of those mistakes were on purpose, but Krys had a lot of fun. In fact, they all did.

But eventually Krys tired and needed to go to bed. Dan remained downstairs while mother and daughter followed the nightly ritual. At least Krys didn't want to hear Bartholomew Cubbins again, but instead chose a very elementary Dr. Seuss book she could mostly read herself.

Afterward, Vicki went back downstairs. Dan had made coffee and waited in the kitchen, offering her a cup as soon as she appeared.

All of a sudden, she felt nervous. Lena was gone, Krys was already sleeping and Vicki was utterly alone with a man she found incredibly attractive. A man who had kissed her not once but twice, which kind of indicated he was interested.

Slowly, she sat at the table and wrapped her hands around her mug.

"What's wrong?" Dan asked, studying her. "Krystal?"

She shook her head quickly. "She's fine. Sound

asleep already. I wish I could drift off as fast as she does."

He smiled. "Clear conscience."

A quiet laugh escaped Vicki. "Maybe so." But she didn't feel like laughing, not really. Part of her wanted to take advantage of this rare privacy, and part of her was terrified of it.

Words burst out of her. "I'm getting awfully tired of being a responsible adult."

His smile widened a shade. "I can certainly believe it. You need to make some room for yourself, Vicki. I understand how many obligations you have, and I'm not suggesting you run off for a wild weekend and leave Krys behind. But you need to find something to do just for your own enjoyment."

She was sure he was right. The problem was the only thing she wanted to enjoy right now was being in a man's arms again, the world banished by the wonder of lovemaking. Worse, the only arms she wanted around her were Dan's.

"Maybe I should go," he said presently. "You're looking skittish, and I get the feeling I'm the problem."

"Reading minds again?" she asked, even though he was exactly right.

"Reading faces," he said. He pushed his mug aside and reached for both her hands, holding them gently. "We both know what's going on here. We're attracted. You don't want it. In fairness, I'm having a few qualms myself. There's been nobody since Callie, and I feel a little guilty about how much I want you. Just a bit guilty. Well, if I can feel guilt after five years, it's got to be worse for you."

Talk about blunt. Vicki's cheeks flamed, and she wanted desperately to break their gaze, but she couldn't.

Those warm gray eyes held her as surely as a spell. "It's not just that," she said, astonished at the way her voice had thickened. Her heart began a steady throbbing, whether from fear or anticipation, she couldn't have guessed. Once again heavy heat pooled between her thighs.

"Well, I'm sure it doesn't help that I'm a cop." He sighed, released her hands and went to dump his coffee in the sink and rinse his cup. He paused by her chair, touching her shoulder briefly. "I'll see you tomorrow. I've got two games in the afternoon, but otherwise... we'll see."

Then he was walking to the front door. A crazy desperation filled her. Before her mind and fears could take charge, she jumped up, answering a deeper need that refused to be denied.

"Dan!" She reached the foyer. "Don't go."

He hesitated with his hand on the doorknob, looking back at her. "Vicki, I'd never forgive myself if I hurt you."

"I'm... You..." She couldn't find the words. "Oh, for Pete's sake, just stay, unless you want to go." Heading into the living room, she plopped down on the couch and folded her arms.

What the hell was she doing? Better yet, what had gotten into her? She couldn't believe the weird way she was acting. Fearful, irritable and hungry all rolled up in one. What did she expect from the man? Clearly, she had problems, and he was simply trying not to make them worse.

Although really, he should have thought of all that before he'd kissed her and held her the other night. Pandora's box was now wide-open, and she couldn't decide which of the world's troubles were emerging from it. If troubles they were.

She heard Dan's step. He came into the living room and sat right beside her on the couch. Their shoulders brushed, but he didn't try to embrace her.

"Talk to me if you can," he suggested.

"I'm confused!" That at least was true.

"I gathered that." He sighed. "You know, some things ought to be as easy as rolling off a log. Too bad there seem to be brambles everywhere."

A great description. She relaxed a hair, but didn't shift position. Her folded arms said she was closed off, and she knew it. But she didn't feel any need to open up. Not yet. Not when a whirlwind seemed to have taken possession of her senses.

Minutes ticked by while she sorted through her personal morass and tried to pick out what was really important. Krystal, of course, but even Vicki knew she couldn't continue to make her daughter the center of her life indefinitely. Krys was growing up. In a few years the last person she was going to want to hang with all the time was her mother. She'd make friends, find activities, expand her horizons.

So Vicki needed to do some fixing of her own. Life would move on, and she'd come here to make it happen. If anything was holding her back, it was her.

"Dan?"

"Yeah?"

"I can't figure it out."

"What, exactly?"

"Me. The more I try to figure things out, the messier they get. I swore I'd never get involved with a cop again. Well, look at me now."

"We're just friends."

At that she unfolded her arms and twisted to face him. "That makes it better how? You think I'd care any less if you didn't come home tomorrow night?"

"Whoa." His eyes widened a bit. "What are you saying?"

"Obviously, I care about you. You've become a good friend. Krys cares about you. It's not like it wouldn't be a blip on the emotional radar if you disappeared."

He frowned. "But I don't have to make it worse."

"Worse is a matter of degree, and you don't have to do anything. This isn't about anything you've done. It's about me and my crazy, mixed-up feelings. Sure, I get it. Anyone could walk out that door and never come back. My God, it was only a week ago that I nearly lost Krys."

He nodded, studying her intently, but evidently deciding to let her ramble on without interruption.

That was the problem, though—she was rambling around in her own confusion. He couldn't sort it out for her, and she was doing a lousy job of it herself.

"I want you," she admitted finally. It was possibly the one thing she was sure about, apart from her daughter. Blunt, bold, concealing nothing of her inner turmoil, but useless in sorting herself out. Only one thing she could figure out, that she wanted this man?

"But?"

"I don't know. I'm afraid. I told you that. Not of you, but of your damn job. Maybe that's unreasonable. You tried to tell me that, and you're probably right, but how do you argue with feelings?"

"You can't," he agreed. His face grew shadowed, but only for an instant. Once again, he listened attentively.

"Like the other night, when you risked your life to save Krystal. That's the kind of man you are. It was the kind of man Hal was. He didn't have to get involved in that store robbery. He was off duty. He could have ducked with everyone else and called 911. Instead, he chose to confront the robber. He wasn't even wearing his vest. Why would he be? He went to the store for milk. For *milk*!"

Dan nodded, and at last looped his arm loosely around her shoulder.

"But I get it intellectually," she ranted on. "Oh, yes, I get it. The store manager could have been shot. An ordinary customer could have died. Hal's being a cop didn't necessarily have anything to do with the outcome. Ordinary people get killed every day doing ordinary things. But tell that to my heart."

"You're angry with him."

"Yes, I am! I'm furious! He never gave one thought to his daughter when he acted."

"Or to you," Dan said quietly.

"Or to me." She lost her steam, and her voice became small. "Nobody else entered his head. Just like nothing entered your head when you saw Krystal in danger. Heroes. God deliver me."

"Damn, woman," Dan said, sounding bemused and a bit startled. "I'd have done what anyone would. You were trying to get there yourself."

"But I'm her *mother*. It's programmed into me. What's programmed into you, Dan Casey?"

"The same thing that's programmed into you," he said quietly. "Tell me you wouldn't have tried to save any child, even one you didn't know. Because if you do, I won't believe you. That's not heroic. It's human."

Even in her distressed state, Vicki had to admit he was making sense. Would she have chased *any* child? Probably. But that didn't resolve the entire issue. She didn't make traffic stops, or report to domestic disturbances, two of the most dangerous things any cop could do.

On the other hand, how many Austin police officers had died during the time she had known Hal? Only him. And before that? Even Hal had dismissed it, much as Dan did. She couldn't remember how long it had been, according to Hal, but it had been a while. Maybe she'd exaggerated the dangers.

But she had faced them up close and personal. No arguing with that.

Dan's arm tightened around her shoulders. "You can't sort it all out at once," he said finally. "It'll come with time."

"You'd have the experience to know," she admitted. She turned her head and let it rest against his shoulder. "What I'm doing makes about as much sense as you never finding another woman to love because something bad might happen."

"Well, I haven't exactly been looking." Not until this blue-eyed beauty had popped her head out a door, looking tired, dusty and very much alone. "But I'm not a kid anymore. When the time is right, the person is right…" He shrugged. She felt the movement beneath her ear.

"It used to be so easy," she murmured.

"It's still easy. It just hurts more. But there's only one thing to do, and we've both been doing it—taking one step at a time. Day in and day out. Just take the next step. You took a huge one coming here. So I guess, much as it may terrify you, that you still have some hope."

"Hope?"

"For a better future." He tightened his arm around her, turning it into a hug. "You haven't given up, Vicki. I don't think it's in you. I mean, you could have stayed in the cocoon in Austin, surrounded by people you know and care about. It would have been easy. Instead, you decided you needed to build a different future. That requires hope."

"Or desperation," she said with something between amusement and bitterness. Everything inside her seemed to have been tossed into a blender somehow. She'd focused on two things for a year: grief and Krystal. Moving here had shifted her focus in some essential way. She no longer had just two major things to deal with. Now she had longings she wasn't prepared for, and a friend named Dan who drew her as strongly as anything in her life ever had.

The right man with the wrong job. Damn! She wondered if she might be crazy, making the same mistake over again when she ought to have learned.

But had she learned the right lesson or the wrong lesson? Danged if she knew.

"Love hurts sometimes," Dan said. "We both know that. But I wouldn't have missed a single moment with Callie to have avoided the pain. Maybe you're not ready to feel that way yet, but I hope you get there."

Maybe that's why everything inside Vicki felt all mixed up. Maybe she *was* transitioning, changing. She believed she had needed to, believed it enough that she had uprooted her daughter and moved far away from all the reminders.

Well, except for a certain man who wore a uniform that reminded her. That probably wasn't fair to either herself or Dan, to categorize him by a badge. But the fear still lingered, a miasma she couldn't quite blow away.

"Nothing has to be settled right now," he reminded

her. "Big changes require lots of time. I just want you to know something."

She tipped her head to see his face. "Yes?"

"I want you, too. I can't set eyes on you without getting hot and heavy. So if you ever decide to risk it…"

She caught her breath. She knew what he was doing. She'd exposed herself to him, and now he was giving her the same in return, so she wouldn't feel stupid and vulnerable. But apart from that, she realized how much she liked hearing him say it. Warmth drizzled through her again, trying to drive out all the doubts, creating an ache inside her that was huge. *Wanting* barely scratched the surface of the needs he awoke in her.

This ought to be between the two of them, but she doubted it would be that simple. There was Krystal to consider, and the likelihood she would come to care even more deeply for Dan.

That still frightened Vicki. If they moved into a romantic relationship and it didn't work, how could they carry on as friends if they broke up? How would that affect Krystal? Her daughter's attachment to Dan was already painfully clear. To risk anything that would sever that connection…

Vicki leaned forward, out of Dan's embrace, and put her face in her hands. Her body was racked with unanswered needs and longings, so hungry for this man it almost hurt. Every cell seemed to have wakened to possibilities, to the anticipation of pleasure, and except for one little girl, she'd probably dive in headfirst without another thought.

She might be acting unreasonably about the cop thing, or maybe not, but her fears for Krys were well-founded.

Finally, Vicki lifted her head. "Dan, whatever happens, you'd still be friends with Krys?"

"I'm surprised you need to ask. That girl has wormed into my heart in a very special way. It'd take a restraining order to stop me from being her friend." He paused. "I'll still be friends with you, too, Vicki. No matter what. It *is* possible."

"As long as I don't turn into a raging shrew."

He sounded truly curious. "You? Do you ever do that?"

"I never have, but there's always a first time."

He laughed. "I'll believe it when I see it."

She envied how comfortable he seemed with all this. He was an accepting man, she realized. Rarely if ever criticizing, seeming to take people as they came. With the possible exception of Junior Casson, but that was different.

"Were you always like this?" she asked.

"Like what?"

"So calm and accepting. So relaxed. I've just put you through the weirdest conversation, and you seem comfortable. Wouldn't most guys be heading for the hills by now?"

"I can't speak for most guys. I have no desire to head for the hills. And if I'm accepting, maybe it's because I've had to learn to accept myself since Callie became sick. But remember how I suggested that you need something in life just for yourself, Vicki. I'm not saying it's me, but you need something you can look forward to. You handle responsibility well, but doesn't there have to be something else?"

"Do you get that from your coaching and baseball?"

"Some of it, yes. It started as a way to keep busy, but

now I love it. I look forward to the practices and games. This winter it'll be basketball."

"So it's not exactly selfish. You're helping others at the same time."

He gave a quiet laugh. "It's mostly selfish. I enjoy it too much to think of it any other way. Just like I enjoy an occasional poker game, going to the movies, hanging out at Mahoney's with a few friends and visiting with the three of you."

She was touched that he included them in his list of things he enjoyed. Especially since she hadn't always been fun or easy to deal with. "When Krys gets into kindergarten next year—"

He stopped her, touching her lips lightly with a finger. "No putting it off for a year. Maybe it would be good for Krys to know you enjoy something besides being a mommy. That you get some me time." He paused. "Not my place to say, I guess."

"Oh, it's your place. Why not? You've practically become family for her and me. I respect your judgment, anyway."

"But I've never been a parent." He arched a brow. "I've found that parents don't like advice from people who've never done the job."

She had to laugh, however weak it sounded. "They don't like it from teachers, either."

"Pity. There's a world of wisdom available from some folks."

Vicki leaned back and his arm surrounded her again, making her feel good, and this time it helped her relax a bit. Oh, her hunger for him was still present, but he offered something else, something amazingly close to solace.

Whatever came, she no longer doubted that she had found a great friend in Dan Casey.

Eventually, conversation moved to lighter subjects, matters that didn't leave her drained from struggling with them. Remembering Hal's hyperkinetic nature, she recalled how she had loved the excitement he always seemed to bring with him. Now, however, she was discovering a new experience, the experience of being able to enjoy just relaxing with someone. It was peaceful, and not at all boring. Comfortable and friendly.

"Are you going to be all right alone here tonight?" Dan asked. "I know you're used to having your own place. I just wondered if this being a different house might make you feel differently. So far Lena has always been here at night."

Vicki hadn't even considered it. It hadn't been looming in front of her like some daunting task. Her instinct was to say she'd be fine, but then she wondered. It *was* a different house, much bigger than any she had lived in before. Getting used to being alone after Hal's death had given her some difficult moments, even though he'd worked plenty of night shifts. Things seemed differen in the dark, and even familiar noises could take on whole new quality. She wasn't familiar with this hou yet, and without Lena nearby, or Krys filling the pl with her energy and chatter, Vicki wondered if it going to feel like an echoing cavern.

"Why did you have to mention that?" she ask wasn't even thinking about it."

"Sorry." But then he laughed. "I wasn't tr scare you. It's just that I need my bed soon. I early half day tomorrow, followed by two gan I'd rather you think about it before you're all

and pacing the floor because something disturbs you. I can camp on this couch easily enough."

"You wouldn't sleep well," she argued, even though the idea appealed to her.

"Wanna bet? I go out like a light."

"I don't know, Dan. I appreciate the offer, but I need to get used to this sooner or later."

"True." He stood. "Then I'll just head on home. But if anything makes you nervous, call me. I sleep with the phone beside my bed. For obvious reasons."

She looked at him standing there, and felt desire drowning her again. How could any man make jeans and a black sweatshirt look so good? It's not as if he'd dressed to show off, but even a sweatshirt couldn't conceal powerful shoulders, and the jeans accentuated his narrow, hard hips. She longed to run her hands up under that shirt and learn the feel of his skin, and if his muscles would ripple at her touch. Such long legs, too. She bet he'd look great in shorts. Or naked.

He sighed. "If you keep looking at me like that I *will* be spending the night here."

Her heart leaped, then crashed immediately. He turned for the door. "Conversation to be continued at a later date, when you're *really* ready. See you tomorrow."

He'd almost reached the door when she couldn't stand it. Forgetting everything else, she jumped up. "Dan!"

He turned, saw her hurrying toward him. He opened his mouth to ask a question, then apparently saw the answer on her face.

"Vicki…" He sounded almost cautionary, but she kept hurrying toward him and at last his arms closed around her, his mouth covered hers and everything inside her washed away in an explosion of passion. One

thing for herself? This was it. She cast all thought of risks and ramifications aside, needing this more than she had needed anything in a very long time. The hunger had been dancing around the edge of her awareness almost from the start. Now it consumed her, a fire gone wild. She ached. She yearned. Every cell in her awoke, crying for his touches, demanding satisfaction.

His tongue plunged into her mouth, tasting her with almost as much desperation as a starving man tasted food. When at last he tore his mouth away, they were both dragging in air as if there wasn't enough of it in the universe.

"Be sure," he said hoarsely. "Just be sure."

Her voice emerged in a rusty-sounding whisper. "I am if you are."

He seemed to have no doubts at all. Astonishing her, he swept her up in his arms. "Krystal," he said thickly.

Vicki hadn't thought of that, and for one instant it almost killed her desire. What if her daughter heard them, or came in? "My room is down the hall." In this old house, sounds didn't carry room to room if the doors were closed.

That seemed to settle it for him. He carried her up the wide staircase, a remnant of better times, while she looped an arm around his shoulders and clung. She could feel the power of the muscles that carried her, and a renewed thrill raced through her. With each step, the throbbing ache within her deepened.

Passion ruled her now, and she didn't have even a flicker of doubt, or a concern that she might be making a big mistake. She needed what Dan was offering, and he seemed to want it, too. The rest could wait.

As he set her on her feet beside the bed, and kissed her again, she felt all the flutters, nervousness and excitement of a first time. Even though she'd been married four years and had borne a child, right then she felt sixteen and caught in the enchantment of an utterly new experience, one she wanted with breathless anticipation.

After releasing her mouth so that they could both breathe again, Dan trailed kisses along her jaw. His breath, warm and a bit ragged, entered her ear, causing her to shiver with delight.

"You nervous?" he asked.

"Plenty."

"Me, too."

His admission ignited a spark in her. She tipped her head almost coquettishly for the first time in forever, and gave him a sidelong glance. "Are we going to hold a meeting or just jump each other's bones?"

"I forgot the roses and chocolate," he said, laughter in his voice. "So jump it is."

All of a sudden Vicki realized that she felt free, truly free, for the first time in forever. Reaching out, she began to tug his sweatshirt up with all the eagerness of a kid opening a present. This was *her* present. A special hour or two just for her. The sweatshirt went flying at last, and she stared at his chest in the moonlight that bathed the room. Her heart hammered, her blood pounded until it was loud in her ears. Every cell seemed suspended in a moment of almost painful anticipation.

"Who made you so beautiful?" she breathed, running her hands over his pecs, her palms finding the nubs of his small nipples. So absorbed was she in admiring him, in feeling his warm skin and the way his muscles moved and quivered beneath her touch, that she hardly noticed when her own T-shirt and bra vanished into some dark corner in the room.

"You're exquisite," he said hoarsely. "Perfect." His

hands cupped her breasts, at first just holding them. But then his thumbs began to torture her nipples, each brush and gentle pinch sending ribbons of fresh fire through her.

She ached, oh, how she ached, and her entire body screamed for him to enter her, now, now...now. Demands rose in her, speechless but no less powerful. There was only one answer to the pounding hunger in her, and it was Dan deep inside her. She became an aching emptiness that only he could fill.

He took her mouth in another kiss, plunging his tongue into her as he himself would, soon. She began to move in rhythm with his strokes, even as he played with her nipples, until she was clinging to his shoulders and arching backward, trying to bring her hips closer to his.

The room spun. Almost as soon as she felt her back hit the bed, her shoes and jeans vanished. She lay naked in the moonlight and he towered over her, drinking her in, the very touch of his gaze fueling her passion as surely as the touch of his hands and mouth.

He stripped quickly, and soon hovered over her on the bed. Her legs parted, her need to welcome him so strong that she didn't want to waste any more time.

He knelt until he had rolled a condom onto his full erection, then seemed almost to hesitate. She couldn't stand it another second. Half rising, she grabbed his shoulders and pulled him down on her. Moments later he slipped inside her and she let out a groan of sheer delight.

At last!

The passion that drove them was impatient. It swept them up and away so swiftly that in no time at all, Vicki felt herself teetering on the painful yet glorious brink of completion. Part of her wanted to hover there forever, but with one more stroke he pushed her over, and an instant later she felt the shudder of completion take him.

A million fireworks exploded inside her. The world vanished. All that remained was the man who held her.

Chapter 9

Dan didn't want to move. He didn't care if he never moved again. He could have died a happy man wrapped in Vicki's delightful body.

But as always, awareness returned. He had to withdraw, get to the bathroom, take care of necessary matters. He hated reality for a few seconds.

He stirred and kissed her gently. "Be right back."

He pulled on his jeans and sweatshirt in case Krys came out of her room, then headed to the hall bath. He washed quickly, then just as quickly returned to the bedroom. Vicki still lay naked and uncovered, silvered by moonlight, looking like a faerie. But she, too, had returned to earth. She lifted a foot and wagged it at him.

"Socks. We forgot about socks." Then she giggled.

The sound made him smile, and filled him with pleasure. So far, so good. He sat on the edge of the bed, sprinkling kisses on her face, then grasping her hand.

Her expression changed. "Are you bailing?"

"Absolutely not. I'm admiring you. I liked that big Cheshire grin on your face, so put it back."

Another giggle escaped her. "Wow," she said quietly, and rolled on her side, wrapping one arm around his hips.

"Wow," he agreed. He supposed he ought to say something about how he'd be slower next time, that he didn't usually make love with all the finesse of a horse racing back to the barn. But then he skipped it. If she allowed them another time together, he'd have a chance to show her.

She squirmed some more until her cheek rested on his denim-covered thigh. He couldn't resist stroking her silky shoulder. "Dan."

"Yeah?"

"Just saying your name. I like it. I like everything about you."

He didn't mention the badge that was causing her so much concern. He didn't want to disrupt the beauty that suffused the room, filled both of them. That showered its blessings in the argent moonlight.

He squeezed her shoulder. "Can I get you anything? Food, beverage?"

She sighed and sat up with clear reluctance. "You said you needed sleep tonight."

"Believe me, I can go on short sleep for one night. Trying to throw me out?"

"Not hardly." She pressed her face to his shoulder and inhaled his wonderful scent. "Unfortunately, the world doesn't go on vacation. I need to put something on. What if Krys comes looking for me? She's still doing that some nights."

Reluctantly, Dan stood, acknowledging the justice of

her concern. They could explain this a whole bunch of ways to her daughter. He was fully dressed, her mom could hide under sheets... But why run the risk? The last thing he ever wanted to do was create any kind of problem for that little girl. Kids, he'd noticed, seemed to have built-in lie detectors, and evasions rarely satisfied them.

Vicki rose and pulled on her clothes again. He watched with enjoyment, then redirected his own attention long enough to put on his shoes. They went downstairs holding hands, and into the kitchen to make fresh coffee. If coffee ever started keeping him up at night, he didn't know what he'd do. Staff of life and all that.

Vicki pulled out some banana bread and cut a few thick slabs. "I hope it's not stale," she said. "I made it a couple of days ago."

He pronounced it perfect and he meant it. "It's not too sweet."

"That's because I let the bananas do all the sweetening. Kids get enough sugar without me adding to it."

He and Callie had often done this, sitting together at their kitchen table for a late-night snack. His mind traveled back over the years, and he could almost hear her voice again, reminding him of the promise she'd extracted from him.

"Callie made me promise something."

Dan felt Vicki's gaze on him, and wondered if he had just achieved the world's highest score for bad timing. He had made love to this woman only a short time ago, and now he was talking about Callie? He ought to quit right now before he really messed things up.

But Vicki's hand covered his. "What did she make you promise?"

"That I wouldn't turn into a lonely, crusty old widower. She said I wasn't built to be crusty."

"I'd agree with her," Vicki answered softly.

"Anyway, she was pretty definite about it. She said we'd had our time together, that we were damn lucky to have had it, and she made me promise to start living again."

"She was a very loving woman."

"Yes. She was." He sighed, passed his hand over his eyes. Tears, long gone, didn't return now. He guessed he'd made some peace at last. "I was listening to her, and I promised, but at the time I was thinking if this is life, I don't want much more of it."

"Oh, Dan…"

But he could hear that Vicki understood perfectly what he meant. Of course she would. Her loss had come more swiftly, but the piper got paid all the same. Mountains of grief, guilt and anger.

"Anyway, I thought of that because Callie and I used to do this—sit up late at the kitchen table and have coffee with something sweet."

Vicki hesitated, then asked, "Would you prefer to sit in the other room?"

"No." He shook his head a bit. "No, I was just realizing… I guess I've made peace. It's okay. It's very much okay."

He looked at her then, wondering how she'd take that. She hadn't had nearly as much time as he. Of course, peace came in its own good time. No calendar dictated it.

"I think," she said after a few minutes, "that I had it easier than you. No lingering, painful illness. Just a swift end."

"But unexpected," he reminded her. "That had to be hard."

"Of course. But I had Krystal. That made me lucky. When I least wanted to carry on, I had to. Most of the time when I just wanted to go wallow, I couldn't. And I was rarely alone because of her. I had a focus beyond Hal's loss. And I had a piece of him. She looks a little like him. Well, you saw his photo up in her room, didn't you? There was a time when I couldn't look at her without seeing his face. Now I mostly see Krys, and I guess that's a good thing."

"Probably."

"She can't become a monument to her father. Not in my mind most of all. So did Callie have any directions about how you were to live the rest of your life?"

That surprised a laugh from him and returned comfort to the room. "Actually, no. She did tell me once that she'd haunt me mercilessly if I didn't get on with life."

"Has she been around?"

"Sometimes I feel as if she's close." He shrugged one shoulder. "Maybe I imagine it."

"I feel Hal, too. I'm not so sure it's imagination." Their fingers twined, and they shared a moment of deep understanding. "It's like a whisper of feeling. A sense. Sometimes it's almost so strong I'm convinced that if I just had ears to hear or eyes to see, he'd be right there. I know how that sounds, like wishful thinking, but it feels so real. Then it's gone, like it never happened." She looked down at their clasped hands. "It doesn't happen so often anymore."

"For me, either."

They shared another look of understanding.

"I guess," Vicki said, "that I'm moving on. It sounds awful, but it's necessary. Callie was right about that. That's why I moved up here. Time to get on with the rest of it, whatever it is. I'd like you to stay tonight, Dan. But you need some sleep. I get it. So…"

Before she could finish, they heard Krystal coming downstairs. Vicki gave Dan a wry look before withdrawing her hand. "What did I tell you?"

"I think kids have radar."

"It's entirely possible."

Clad in her pink, ruffled nightgown with pink bunny slippers on her feet, Krys stumbled sleepily into the kitchen.

"Something wrong, honey?"

"Hungry."

Vicki widened her eyes comically. "Really? After that big burger?"

Krys smiled sleepily. "I didn't eat it all," she reminded her mother. Then, as naturally as if she'd been doing it forever, she held out her arms to Dan. He swung her up into his lap so she faced the table.

"I see some banana bread," he said. "Want some?"

"Yummy," Krys answered. Her head drooped against his shoulder.

Vicki jumped up and went to get another slice. She put the plate and a fork in front of her daughter.

"Dan?" Krys said.

"Yes, pumpkin?"

"Don't go away tonight."

The words jolted him. She'd said them once before to him, but now he wondered how often Vicki had been hearing them. Their eyes locked over her daughter's head. He could see the concern on Vicki's face, but he wasn't at all sure how to handle this.

Vicki was gnawing her lower lip. He waited for her guidance on how she wanted to proceed. She surprised him, because this time she addressed the question directly.

"Why don't you want Dan to go home, Krys? It's just next door and we'll see him tomorrow."

"I like Dan," she answered simply. Krys seemed more awake, and she sat up, reaching for her pumpkin bread.

"We all like Dan," Vicki agreed. "But you're going back to bed soon, and he needs to go home to sleep."

"He can sleep here," she stated promptly, then filled her mouth with pumpkin bread.

"How come?" Vicki asked. "Why is it better if he stays here?"

"'Cuz I know he's okay."

Dan felt a shaft of guilt that made his entire chest hurt. Had he made things worse for this child by injecting himself into her life? But being friends with Lena, he couldn't have avoided it, except by being less nice. He wasn't that kind of person, and he had quickly come to love Krystal. So what now? He looked almost desperately at Vicki, who was frowning faintly.

"Time for therapy," she murmured.

"What's that?" Krys asked.

Vicki didn't answer and Krys finished her snack. Then she threw her arms around Dan before slipping off his lap. "Take me to bed," she demanded.

So Dan, with a nod from Vicki, did exactly that, wondering what kind of hell he'd stirred up for Vicki and Krystal.

Vicki waited downstairs, pacing from the kitchen across the foyer, through the living room and back again. There was no question what was going on with Krystal now, and it wasn't just the move. She was grasping the fact that the father she barely remembered had gone away and he wasn't okay anymore.

Understanding had been inevitable. Maybe her anxiety was, as well. Maybe this was perfectly normal coping, but Vicki felt desperate for a second opinion. She'd unleashed something with this move. Or maybe it would have happened, anyway. How the hell could she know?

But it seemed to be Dan that Krys was worrying about. Not her friends back in Austin, not Lena going away for a weekend. Krys's concern seemed specifically focused on Dan and her mother. This was no generalized anxiety. The child seemed worried about just two people.

Inevitably, Vicki wondered if seeing Dan in uniform had exacerbated the problem. But then in fairness she had to admit that it had started the first night they'd been here, just as she was leaving Krys's bedroom. If anything had stirred it up, it had been the move. It had just reached out to include Dan, as well.

Vicki heard him coming down the stairs. "Sound asleep," he said as he reached the bottom. "Vicki—"

She waved her hand. "This isn't about you. It started the day we moved here. Maybe it just needs to happen. Sooner or later she had to deal with the fact that Hal would never come back. Maybe she's just getting to a point where she can adequately express her fear."

"Maybe." He hesitated. "Was she worried about Lena going for the weekend?"

"She never mentioned it."

"Then I'm a problem."

Vicki rounded on him, trying to keep her voice low so as not to wake Krystal. "You're not the problem. The problem is a murdering SOB who took that girl's father away. The problem is me moving her halfway across the country. She's learning that sometimes things go away for good. The question is how to deal with it, because much as it stinks, Dan, it's reality. It's life. Everything goes away eventually. You and I know that. Now she does, too."

Vicki resumed pacing. He finally got out of her way by sitting on the bottom steps. "Talk to me," he said quietly.

"I worked for years with kids near her age. I saw it all the time. They have a full complement of emotions to deal with. Anyone who dismisses a child's feelings is a fool. They're real. They're huge. The problem is that a child doesn't have the means of expressing them completely. Or sometimes even a way to identify them."

"And a therapist can do that? Better than you?"

"A good one with training, of course. I'm a teacher. That's a whole different bailiwick." She settled at last on a chair in the kitchen with a fresh cup of coffee. He joined her. "A therapist would get her to act out the things she can't put into words. Dealing with them in nonthreatening ways could be helpful."

"Then I guess that's what you need to do. I know we have some psychologists in town, but I can't evaluate them."

Vicki put her elbows on the table and her chin in her hand. "You need your sleep. I'm perfectly capable of worrying on my own."

"Hey," he said. "You don't have to worry alone, and if you think I'm walking out of here after everything that's happened, you're crazy. I'm staying. Live with it."

She gave him a wan smile. "Okay." Then she closed her eyes. "I may be making too much of this. It wouldn't be the first time. I was thinking that sooner or later she was going to deal with her loss in some way, and I guess this is it."

"But you're sure I'm not making it worse?"

Vicki's eyes popped open. "No, you're not. She's

worrying about me, too. What are you and I supposed to do? Desert her? Hardly. She's afraid of losing *us*. That's what we need to deal with, and the only way to make it worse is to withdraw in some way."

"Okay." He nodded. "But then there's you. I shouldn't have made love to you. You already told me your feelings about cops, and I should have kept a safe distance. Damn it, Vicki, you've got enough on your plate to worry about without adding me to the equation."

"Too late, cowboy."

"Ah, hell, how often do I have to hint to you that this isn't a dangerous job? Do you have a computer? Look up the ten most dangerous jobs. Cops don't even make the list. You'd have more to worry about if I were a logger."

"I'm starting to realize that," she admitted. "Gut emotional reactions don't give way easily to reason, though."

"No," he agreed with a sigh.

Just then thunder rumbled loudly, vibrating the entire house. Both of them instinctively looked up.

"With any luck," Dan said, "we'll be rained out tomorrow."

She eyed him curiously, noting again how sexy he was. Even now, in the midst of all this concern about Krys, she was noting that. Broad shoulders, strong face, warm eyes… God, she had the bug bad. She'd have liked nothing more than to forget everything in his arms right now. She dragged her thoughts back into line. "You want the games to be canceled?"

"Now I do. I don't want to be away from you two that long. That's me talking, not Krys, by the way. I'm in danger of developing some separation anxiety of my own over you girls."

If she hadn't been in such a confused and worried

state, Vicki might have laughed. It was such a sweet admission for him to make, though. "Thank you, Dan."

Thunder rolled again, and the house shook once more. Dan pulled out his cell phone, tapped it a couple times. "Bad weather but no tornado warning. Thunderstorms through tomorrow afternoon."

"There go the games."

"The fields will turn to mud if we try to play." He set his phone on the table. "Assuming it rains. And we can't play if there's any danger of lightning."

Almost as if the heavens heard him, they opened up. Even from the ground floor, the rain sounded loud and heavy.

"Question answered," Vicki said.

"Yeah. By the way, a cop is three times more likely to get struck by lightning than die in the line of duty."

Her head jerked a little. Why had he said that? But she knew why. Oh, yes, she knew. He was trying to reach past her emotional resistance to his profession. Gently, persistently, he just kept working at it.

After their lovemaking, she had begun to think resistance was futile. She wanted him again. And then again. At no foreseeable time did she want Dan to back out of her life. She guessed that meant she was already in trouble.

"I told Krys I was going to sleep on the couch. I hope that was okay."

"Of course." Vicki decided that she had to put an end to this evening now. She had a great deal of thinking to do, all because she'd made love with him, and because of Krys's reaction to his leaving.

Vicki would be surprised if she slept at all.

In the morning, the storm showed no sign of abating. The games were officially postponed. Dan took over the kitchen, making pancakes and chatting with Krys as she sat at the table, coloring industriously. She was currently fascinated by coloring books that featured tropical fish.

Vicki doubted that nature, for all its love of color, had created anything like what Krystal produced. At least the colors were bright and cheerful, she thought as she admired the two that Krys had already completed.

At some point Dan must have darted back to his place, because he'd exchanged last night's sweatshirt for a green one.

Soon a platter piled with small pancakes sat in the middle of the table. Vicki helped Krys with the butter and syrup, then helped herself. Dan poured more coffee and joined them.

Such a perfectly normal scene, Vicki thought. Like an ordinary family sitting around a breakfast table. But last night had blown up her illusions. She was getting seriously involved with a man who was a cop, and Krys had attached herself to him like a limpet. Worst of all, Vicki's own uneasiness about herself had been completely swamped by her concerns about her daughter.

She felt a momentary burst of resentment, then banished it. Sure, it would be nice if she could just revel in memories of what she and Dan had shared last night, if she could just look forward to spending the day and another night with him, acting like giddy kids in the first throes of a relationship.

But that wasn't going to happen, and she felt shame for resenting it even for a moment. She wasn't a kid any longer, and she had a daughter who needed to be her top priority at all times. But Vicki was also human, as her all-too-frequent mistakes made abundantly clear. She had committed herself and her daughter to a path that might not have been the wisest choice.

But back in Austin, even with all the concerned friends, she had felt a deep emptiness inside. At first she had put it down to missing Hal, but as time passed she'd realized she desperately needed to try to find a normal life. She had a lot of years ahead of her, and much as she missed Hal, living them out as his widow forever wasn't going to satisfy anything else inside her. She needed other things, a life that didn't exist only in the past, or in the immediate moment when something needed her attention. She needed a future to look forward to, beyond watching her daughter grow up.

Was that a crime? Of course not, but sometimes her emotions made her feel like a traitor. Then she wondered why. The life she had once planned with Hal was gone. All those desires needed to be replaced somehow.

She watched Dan and Krys laughing about something, and felt an ache for all she had lost, but also felt the beauty of the moment. Krys moved ahead almost fearlessly, making new connections, coming to care for new people. She wasn't afraid of putting her heart out there. But she did fear losses.

Vicki took a hard look at herself and wondered if she was less courageous than a four-year-old. Krys had left everything behind, too, when they moved here. And to this day Vicki honestly didn't know how much Krys missed her father. Or how much she remembered him, apart from photographs. Surely some of her sense of security had been affected, but Vicki wondered if the move up here, which had started all those pleas for people not to go away, might be the real source of Krys's anxiety. It was recent, a fresh wound, and might be the whole problem.

Yet Krys had never asked to go back to Austin. Overall, she seemed to be happy here. And Vicki was spinning in circles, wondering what she could do about any of this now.

Dan leaned toward Krys. "I need to go home and shower and change. Is that okay?"

Vicki held her breath. Then, to her amazement, Krys nodded. "Okay."

Dan smiled. "I won't be long, pumpkin."

"We'll do the dishes," Vicki announced—cheerfully, she hoped. Had they just crossed a hurdle? Would it last?

"Save some for me." Dan grinned. "I made quite a mess."

"Ah, but you cooked," Vicki retorted, managing a smile of sorts.

Dan walked out, the front door closed behind him, and Vicki felt herself on tenterhooks again. But Krystal didn't react negatively at all. She slid off her chair and carried the first plate to the sink. "Let's go, Mommy."

Dan took far longer than was necessary for a shower and change. Vicki wondered if he was testing the waters...or if he needed some escape. Certainly, he hadn't had a moment to do things his way since walking in here yesterday. He needed some space. Who wouldn't?

But the thought made her glum, even though she scolded herself for being unreasonable. The man had a life. He had things to do. No reason she and Krys should just take over his every waking moment, apart from his job.

Then she wondered if he'd gotten a call. At once her heart slipped into high gear. Could he be responding to a dangerous situation right now? What if he never came back?

She glanced at the clock. It really hadn't been that

long. She was overreacting and being unfair, all at once. Krys had resumed her coloring, and asked if purple and orange went together.

"If you want them to," Vicki answered a bit absently.

Finally, the phone rang. She jumped to answer it. "Hey," said Dan's warm voice. "Sorry, but I have to go into work. It should be only a couple of hours."

Vicki glanced at the clock, setting a timer in herself even though she knew it was foolish. "Okay." She bit back the question about whether it was dangerous.

"Want me to explain to Krys?"

"She seems okay right now. Coloring."

"Leave well enough alone. Be back as soon as I can."

She hung up and looked at her daughter. "Dan had to go to work for a little while."

Krys nodded, and Vicki felt a huge wave of relief, as no crises or disturbances seemed to ensue. The only thing that drew Krys out of her preoccupation was loud rumbling from the sky.

"I don't like thunder," she said decisively.

"Really? I do." Vicki sat with her at the table.

Krys eyed her. "Crazy" was her pronouncement, and despite fears that were determined to nibble at Vicki, she had to laugh.

"Maybe I am," she agreed. Lately, she was wondering if that was a serious possibility.

At noon, Dan still hadn't returned. By then Vicki was trying to keep a leash on major anxiety. When the phone rang, she flew to pick it up.

"Hi," said the familiar voice of Janine Dalrymple. "Can I come over and steal Krys?"

Her mind had been so far away that Vicki blinked and had to replay the question in her head. "Steal her?"

"The only thing more tiring than two four-year-olds

having a good time together is one of them creating trouble out of boredom," Janine said wryly. "Help? I'll pick up Krys and they can have some playtime over here for a few hours."

Krys wanted to go. Vicki knew a moment's surprise, then wondered why. Of course Krys wanted to play with Peggy. Her daughter showed no signs of wanting to check out on normal life. What she did show was separation anxiety, but only sometimes. Vicki guessed she'd wait and see for a while before hunting for a therapist. If the problem didn't ease, or if it grew, she'd take action, but right now a lot of this could be explained by the move. Whatever bugged Krys from time to time, it certainly wasn't bugging her today.

So a half hour later, Krys left with Peggy and Janine, bouncing happily as she went out the door.

Which left Vicki alone with a clock. A couple hours? It had already been four.

The nightmare slammed her—the nightmare of Hal's delayed return from the convenience store, followed later, much later, by the arrival of the department chaplain and a couple of Hal's friends. The News.

She paced almost insanely, arguing with herself. The job had just taken longer than expected. Dan was no kid, having to report in every time he got delayed. She was overreacting. Nothing had happened.

But deep inside, she didn't believe it. She couldn't. Something terrible was wrong.

Chapter 10

Janine called at four. "If you don't mind, I'm keeping Krys for the night. The girls are happy and have already built a tent in the living room they want to sleep in. If Krys has any problem or gets homesick, I'll call you and bring her home."

Vicki's instinct was to say no. She wanted Krys at her side right now. She needed to touch her, see her, be sure she was all right. The need grew proportionately with her fears about Dan.

But she caught herself, tried to speak calmly with Krys, and when she realized her daughter really wanted to spend the night, she agreed. It was a good step for her.

Even if it was hell for Vicki.

All the day's stress overwhelmed her, exhausting her. Finally numb, she collapsed on the couch, trying so hard not to think about what the next knock on the door might bring.

Starkly, she faced the fact that if something had happened to Dan it was going to hurt every bit as much as her loss of Hal. No amount of arguing with herself could change that.

She faced something else in those long hours, too. She faced the loss of Hal, and the near loss of Krys to a maniac driver, and accepted at last that it was impossible to care without taking the risks that went with it. Nobody could escape that.

But understanding didn't ease her fretfulness. Loving meant risking, and now Vicki faced her demons all over again.

Numerous times she thought of calling Dan just to be sure he was okay, but stopped herself. Hal had long ago explained that calls while he was working might distract him at exactly the wrong moment.

But when Dan had called that morning, he'd made it sound so much as if this would be routine. A couple hours. They were well past that and then some.

Anxiety made her skin crawl, and inside she could feel herself bracing for the blow of bad news. What the hell had she been thinking, letting another cop into her heart?

She had known him such a short time. How had he come to mean so much? And now, with Krystal so engaged, there was no way to back out of this. It had happened, and this rock was rolling all the way down to the bottom of the hill.

Vicki almost hated herself as she watched the minutes tick by, so slowly that time seemed nearly to stop. She'd dropped her guard and done the very thing she had vowed never to do again. How had she been so stupid? The anticipated pain was already shredding her.

Then she heard the front door open. She stood up,

ready for disaster, but instead saw Dan. He was still in uniform, and the sight almost made her sick. A cop. A damn cop.

"Vicki?" Evidently, he could read something on her face. He paused on the threshold of the living room, hands at his side, worry creasing his brow.

"You...you..." Words failed her and she flew at him. His hands caught her elbows, but that didn't stop her from pounding his chest. "I was scared," she cried, the entire day's worry pouring out of her. "So scared! Where the hell were you?"

He caught her hands, stopping her blows. "Easy," he said quietly.

"Easy? How can I be easy? Damn you, I've been waiting for news and..." She choked and tears began to flood her cheeks.

"I'm sorry," he said, keeping his voice quiet. "I'm sorry. I was out of phone range and it went on longer..."

"You could have died and I wouldn't even have known!"

He wrapped his arms around her, pinning her arms to his sides, turning into a strong but gentle straitjacket. "I was safe. We were looking for a lost little girl..."

"That makes me feel better how?" But her tears renewed, and along with them came hiccups. Then, with shocking abruptness, she realized she was acting like a wild woman. The shock froze her and everything within her.

Strong arms surrounded her protectively, and at last, at long last, the tension seeped out of her. Reason made a steady return. Still crying, but more quietly, Vicki sagged in Dan's arms and rested her head on his chest. He was here. He was safe.

"It's okay," he murmured repeatedly. "It's okay. Next time things run over, I'll make sure you get a call."

That made her feel foolish. She had no claim on this man, certainly not one that justified a leash on him. Fear had ripped her for hours, and now all she could feel was painful relief. She felt shredded inside, but reason returned. She drew ragged breaths, seeking her voice, finding it. Rustily, she said, "I'm sorry."

"No need. But where's Krys?"

Vicki heard the concern in Dan's voice and it struck her that she had given no thought to what *he* might fear. Could she have been any more selfish? She sucked in more air. "She's fine. She went to Peggy's for the night."

"That's a relief," he admitted. Loosening his hold on her, he raised a hand to stroke Vicki's hair. "All day long I wondered what you were dealing with when I didn't get back."

"Now you know," she said brokenly. "Krys is fine and I'm falling to pieces. Sorry."

"Don't be."

He shifted his hold and lifted her from her feet, carrying her to the couch, where he sat with her on his lap. For a long time, he simply cradled her, scattering kisses on her head, stroking her arm, letting the storm pass.

Eventually, when her heart stopped aching, she said, "I went off the deep end."

"I can't imagine why."

She scrubbed her face with her sleeve, then leaned back a bit to look at him. Oddly, or so it seemed to her, he looked fairly happy. "You mad at me?" she asked.

"For what? I knew you had to be worrying. I was afraid Krys was freaking out, and I couldn't even get a satellite connection with my radio. We were in the woods, hunting for this girl, and the storm...well, it killed our comms. We were reduced to tracking each other with whistles."

"Did you find her?"

"The dogs did. God knows how with all this rain, but they did. Poor kid, she was hypothermic, nearly blue. She's in the hospital now, but I hear she'll be okay."

"Thank God."

"Yeah. Thank God. Now let's stop worrying about her and talk about you."

Vicki shook her head and burrowed her face into his shoulder. "I went off the deep end, as I said. I'm not proud of it."

"You shouldn't be ashamed, either. Although next time you want to pound your fists on my chest, could you avoid the badge and the name plate?" He sounded amused.

She jerked back. "I hurt you? I hurt you. Let me see."

He shook his head. "Just some small bruises. Kinda painful when it was happening, though."

She felt so ashamed. But that didn't stop her from reaching for his shirt buttons. Unfortunately, he had a T-shirt underneath. "Damn it," she said.

He laughed. "Really, do you see any blood? I'm fine."

"Dan…"

He shifted her off his lap. "Okay, okay. Need to get rid of this damn gun belt, anyway." He pulled it off, placing it on a table, then shucked both his shirts. "See, I'm whole."

But she could see the red spots where she had hammered the clasps into him. "I'm so sorry," she whispered. "I never hit anybody before. I'm so ashamed, Dan."

"Cut it out. I'm kind of flattered that you cared that much. And believe me, I know what you were thinking."

"I left thinking behind hours ago," she admitted. She scrubbed her face again, trying to get rid of the last stickiness from her tears.

He squatted in front of her, clasping her hands. "I need to go over to my place to change. My pants are still full of burrs. And I don't want my gun in this house whenever Krys comes back. At home I can lock it up. Do you want to come with me or will you be okay for a little while?"

She wanted to go with him. So far she'd never seen his house. On the other hand, she needed to prove something to herself and to him, that she could be okay when he was away. That she wasn't going to be a constant burden demanding to know his whereabouts every minute of the day.

"You go," she said. "I think I'll clean up, too."

He leaned forward and kissed her. "Not long this time, I promise."

Back at his own place, Dan locked his gun belt in the armored box he kept for just that purpose, then put it back on the high shelf. It felt good to get out of his wet clothes, and he spent some time pulling burrs out of his pants. Then he tossed them aside, deciding that could wait. He needed to get back to Vicki.

And if today had taught him one thing, it was that his need for her was pretty strong. Being away from her, busy though he had been, had been tough. He'd missed her, and worried about her and Krys damn near every second.

He'd hoped he'd come back to find everything was okay, but he hadn't. Evidently Krys was fine, but her mother had had a major freak-out. He couldn't blame her for that, not given what had happened with Hal.

But as he stepped into the shower, Dan realized that

he could no longer just let things between them drift along. He knew she was resistant to his job, so he hadn't really pressed her in any way, but today had written an entirely different story.

Not only had he missed the woman all day long, but apparently she'd been anxious enough about him to turn into a wild woman when she saw he was safe. She must have been pumped on adrenaline and fear the entire day. They had to talk about that, because unless she could deal with this, they'd have to part ways.

The thought speared him painfully. He knew how much he cared about her, but he couldn't do this to her repeatedly. That would be selfish. Maybe he'd been selfish from the outset. She'd told him about her worries during her marriage to Hal, and he'd been smug enough to wonder if she'd exaggerated them in the aftermath of his death. Well, Hal had died, and Vicki clearly bore the scars of that trauma. How they were going to get past that, he didn't know.

He showered in hot water, then toweled himself briskly, glad to feel warm again. It wasn't a cold day, just a cool one, but the rain hadn't helped. At last, in fresh jeans and a wool shirt, he pulled on a jacket and headed next door. Dread dogged his steps, because the two of them had something to work out, and they couldn't let it drag on. It wouldn't be fair to any of them.

He let himself in, and smelled coffee from the kitchen. Like a hound, he followed the aroma and found Vicki seated at the table, with a mug in front of her and a coffee cake. She was freshly showered, with her hair beginning to curl all over her head.

"You must be starved," she said brightly. "I can make us dinner shortly."

But he wasn't deceived. She might be smiling and

acting as if nothing had happened, but they both knew better. Something had happened, all right, and it was momentous. Just how momentous remained to be seen.

He grabbed a mug of coffee and sat next to her. "The first time I saw you," he said, "you peeked out the door to see who Krys was talking to."

"I remember." Vicki smiled faintly.

"You looked tired, but that wasn't what struck me."

"No?"

"No. I thought you were one of the most beautiful women I'd ever seen."

She caught her breath, then her smile widened. "Wow."

He wondered if he was going to make a mess of this. His heart began to beat more heavily, and for the first time in a long time he felt fear. Not the fear that sometimes happened on the job. Not the fear he'd felt for that little girl today. No, this was personal. This was Dan Casey's happiness on the line.

"Vicki, I can't do this again to you. Today, I mean. I put you through hell. No one has the right to do that. But I'm a cop. I'll continue to be a cop. This job is part of me. It's in my blood."

She nodded, her smile fading. "I didn't ask you to quit."

"No, you never did. But I understand why you don't like it, and if I didn't get it before, I sure as hell got it this afternoon."

He thought she flushed faintly, but he couldn't be sure. "I'm sorry," she said again.

"Don't keep apologizing. This is reality, and that's part of it. You were terrified, and I can't blame you for that. But neither of us is going to change, so maybe it would be best if I just kind of eased away. I'll still be friends with Krys. I love her to death. But no matter how hard I try, there are going to be days like this. I can ask the dispatcher to give you a call if I'm gone longer than expected, and explain what's going on, when I can't reach you, but this is a big county and there are plenty of places where communications fail. So there *will* be days like this again. I don't have the right to ask that of you."

She nodded and looked down into her mug. Now his heart was sinking. This was it, and today he'd faced the fact that losing her was going to be as hard as losing Callie.

Vicki was quiet for so long, he wondered if he should just get up and leave. But then she sighed and reached out her hand. He took it and their fingers twined.

"I was terrified today," she admitted. "Then I acted like a madwoman when I found out you were okay. That makes no sense, does it?"

"Actually, it does. But go on." His heart was already hurting.

"The thing is, Dan, what difference does it make if you walk away for good, or die?"

The question caught him sideways. He was still trying to be sure he understood when she continued speaking.

"However I lose you, it's going to be hell," she said. "I figured that out. And I figured out that you were right when you once told me that you wouldn't have traded a single minute with Callie to avoid the pain. I wouldn't give up a single minute with Hal. So why should I give up a single moment with you? If you want me, that is. Because loss is inevitable for everyone. The end comes. And I finally realized that what matters is the journey. A week, a month, fifty years. It's the journey, not the end."

She lifted her gaze, meeting his. "I don't want to trade any moments with you to avoid what could happen tomorrow or what might never happen."

His grip on her hand tightened. "You're sure?"

"I had plenty of time today to relive hell. I may have to do it again. But... I don't want to lose you, and certainly not for that reason."

His voice cracked a little as he said, "I love you, Vicki. I am so hugely in love with you. You can handle that?"

She smiled. "I hope so, because terror taught me a lesson today. I'm so in love with you that it hurts. I don't want to live without you."

He watched the joy grow on her face, and felt the answer in his own heart. "Just promise you won't hide your fears from me," he asked. "That would be bad for both of us. I can handle it if you can."

"Okay." But she was still glowing. He hoped he never caused that glow to vanish. But another need was growing in him.

"I want to take you upstairs," he said. "Make love to you until neither of us can move."

"Oh, yes," she breathed, leaning toward him. Then she startled him by straightening. "Krys. I'd better phone her and make sure she still wants to spend the night. Otherwise she might call when..."

Vicki's blush enchanted him and heightened his hunger for her. "Call," he said, much as he didn't want to wait to sweep her to bed, where he could show her in the best way possible how much he adored her.

So Vicki got the phone and soon was speaking to Krys. She had to hold the receiver away from her ear, and even Dan could hear the excitement and words tripping over each other. Then Vicki handed the phone to him.

"Hey, pumpkin," he said warmly. "How's it going?" He wound up laughing as he listened to Krys talking about tents and blankets, and a movie and...well, pretty soon he lost track of it all. It was wonderful just to hear her so happy.

When he said goodbye, there were no words about him not going away. Relief swelled his heart even more.

Thunder rumbled hollowly as he led Vicki upstairs. There was no moonlight tonight, so she turned on the small lamp beside her bed. In its golden glow, they made love slowly, learning each other as they hadn't the last time, savoring every touch and kiss and newly discovered delight.

She was perfect, he thought, and he ran his hands along her, from her breasts to her thighs. Perfect. He wouldn't have changed one thing about her, not even the mole he found on her hip. Her hands traced his contours in the same way, building the fire between them until everything vanished.

When he entered her, he knew he'd come home. And when he toppled over the summit with her, the explosion seemed to sear him, wiping away old scars and leaving him whole again.

They slept fitfully that night, making love lazily or desperately as the mood struck. But finally Vicki awoke from a dreamless sleep to see the sunlight of a new day filling her room.

"Good morning."

She turned a bit and found Dan watching her with a smile. She stretched and smiled back.

"You keep doing that and we're going to still be here when Krys gets back."

She sat up. "Krys!"

"Janine's bringing her in a few minutes. I was trying to decide whether to let you sleep, but the fact is, if I answer the door, the whole town is going to be talking. Which isn't a big deal, if you want to marry me."

Her breath lodged in her throat. Joy exploded in her chest like a million fireworks. "Is that a proposal?"

"Seems like," he said. "You don't have to answer right now. Just think about it."

Then he swung out of the bed and began to toss clothes to her. "I guess there's another lady I need to ask, too. Assuming you say yes."

Her hands were shaking as she donned the jeans and blue T-shirt he'd found for her. He pulled on what he'd worn last night. How could she not say yes? Of course she was going to say yes. She couldn't imagine life without Dan anymore. Her heart overflowed with happiness, and as long as Krys didn't have a problem...

Vicki looked at Dan. "I've got to ask Krys first." Not that she really wondered how Krys would react. Her attachment to Dan was as plain as a neon sign.

He nodded. "I guess that's an indirect yes from you." Then he grinned.

Vicki struggled with the zipper on her jeans. "I can't believe I didn't hear the phone."

"I can. You were zonked. If I weren't programmed to wake up from a coma at the sound of the phone, I'd have missed it, too."

He grabbed her and spun her around quickly, saying, "I never thought I'd be this happy again." He gave her a quick kiss before turning toward the stairs. "Mmm," he said. "Trouble's brewing if we stay here. Let's go."

She was laughing as she hurried downstairs. She could hear Janine's car pulling into the drive.

"I'll make coffee," Dan said.

Vicki answered the door and found Janine standing there with Krys, who was pulling her small overnight suitcase.

"They had a wonderful time," Janine said. "I don't think they slept two winks."

"Want to come in for coffee?"

"Another time. I've got one very tired Peggy, and I'm hoping that when I get home we can both have a nap. We'll do this again soon."

Krystal entered the foyer with somewhat less energy than usual. Vicki waved at Janine as she pulled away, then closed the door and looked at her daughter, taking in the obvious signs of fatigue. "Good fun, huh?"

"Yup," Krys answered. Her T-shirt looked rumpled from being slept in, and her hair was only partly brushed. Her eyelids drooped a little before suddenly widening. Then she cocked her head, dropped the handle of her suitcase and beelined for the kitchen. "Dan!"

When Vicki entered the room, she saw Krys in Dan's arms as he stood at the counter. He held out one arm, inviting her into the hug.

Nothing could be more perfect, Vicki thought as she leaned into him and hugged her little girl. Somehow one move and one man had brought her a joy she had thought she would never know again. The painful past seemed to recede more with each moment.

Krys looped one arm around Dan's neck and the other around Vicki's. "I was lonesome for you."

"I was lonesome for you, too," Vicki said.

"Me, too," Dan agreed. "But you had a lot of fun?"

"Yup." Krys beamed. "Peggy's great. She still has a daddy and he's funny."

Vicki's heart lurched. She looked at Dan and found

him watching her. He seemed not to want to step on her toes or something. That had to change.

"Let's sit on the sofa," Vicki said. "Dan and I want to ask you something important."

Soon they were sitting with Krys between them. She looked from one to the other. "Was I bad?"

"Heavens, no!" Vicki said. "You weren't bad at all. This is about something else."

"Good."

But how to begin this conversation? Once again she sent a silent appeal to Dan. He tilted his head a bit, as if he were reluctant to start, but realized the duty had fallen to him.

"Krys?"

She turned to him.

"I want to marry your mother. Do you like that idea?"

Krys surprised Vicki. "Does Mommy want to marry you?"

"Yes," Vicki said. "I do."

"Does that mean Dan will be my daddy?"

Vicki's heart nearly stopped. Her throat jammed up, leaving her unable to speak. Dan reached out and lifted Krys onto his lap. "I will be your daddy if that's what you want. Is it?"

Krys didn't hesitate a beat. "Yup," she said decisively. "You're a good daddy."

"Wow," Dan murmured. "Um, just wow."

Krys then looked at Vicki with a tired but happy smile. "I picked him, Mommy."

Vicki guessed she had. She dissolved into laughter, and Dan joined her.

"So can I have a baby brother or sister, too?"

Dan's and Vicki's gazes locked. "That's entirely possible," they both said at the same moment.

"And I want to be a flower girl."

Dan hugged her tight. "You're going to be one very special flower girl."

"Good." Then, between one breath and the next, she dozed off in Dan's arms.

Vicki felt tears of happiness prickle her eyes, and thought Dan's eyes shone, as well.

"That was easy," he murmured.

"Well," said Vicki, "she picked you." And then she added something that seemed as important to her as all the mountains and valleys she had traveled since moving here. "And I guess I picked you, too."

He smiled, adjusting Krys on his lap so he could draw Vicki up against him and hug her. "I am one hell of a lucky guy."

Vicki smiled, truly happy, content and at peace for the first time in forever. The shadows would return sometimes, and storms might come, but she no longer feared them. They would weather them as they'd weathered everything else, but this time they'd get through them together.

A bright new future had begun.

Epilogue

They were married just before Christmas in Good Shepherd Church. Krystal got to be a flower girl, and at her insistence, so did Peggy. The little girls scattered bright red petals down the aisle ahead of Vicki, who walked on the arm of her late husband's best friend, Bill Hanton. Her attention was fixed on Dan, resplendent in a blue suit. She herself wore blue velvet, rather than the traditional white. Dan loved her in blue.

The pews were filled with her new friends, a lot of deputies and their families, some teachers, Lena's friends. Many of Hal's old friends from Austin had made the trip, too, resplendent in their dress uniforms, prepared to provide an honor guard a little later. This time Vicki was happy to see the blue wall gathered around her, and they looked as thrilled for her as she was.

Inside her, still a secret from everyone but Dan, a new child was growing. Ahead of her lay her new life, and she was being ushered there by Hal's closest friend. Joy filled her heart to overflowing.

When Bill placed her hand in Dan's, she felt almost as if it was a changing of the guard. Dan broke tradition a bit, drawing Krys to stand between him and Vicki.

Lena, grinning from ear to ear, stood as maid of honor for her, and gave her a little nudge as if to say "You go, girl."

Krys had gone to therapy, but hadn't needed much of it. Not for months now had she expressed any anxiety over anyone leaving. Vicki felt she had overcome the worst of her own fears, and faced the future with excitement and pleasure.

"I love you," Dan whispered to her, just before the minister began the ceremony.

"I love you, too."

Smiling, they faced the pastor, ready to embark on a new journey.

* * * * *

Though her name is frequently on bestseller lists, **Allison Leigh**'s high point as a writer is hearing from readers that they laughed, cried or lost sleep while reading her books. She credits her family with great patience for the time she's parked at her computer, and for blessing her with the kind of love she wants her readers to share with the characters living in the pages of her books. Contact her at allisonleigh.com.

Books by Allison Leigh

Harlequin Special Edition

Return to the Double C

A Weaver Proposal
A Weaver Vow
A Weaver Beginning
A Weaver Christmas Gift
One Night in Weaver...
The BFF Bride
A Child Under His Tree
Yuletide Baby Bargain
Show Me a Hero
The Rancher's Christmas Promise
A Promise to Keep

The Fortunes of Texas: The Rulebreakers

Fortune's Homecoming

The Fortunes of Texas: The Secret Fortunes

Wild West Fortune

Visit the Author Profile page at Harlequin.com for more titles.

SARAH AND
THE SHERIFF

Allison Leigh

For my parents,
who've celebrated more than
forty-nine years together.
You are my inspiration.

Prologue

She hadn't thought things could get any worse.

Twenty-one years old.

Pregnant with no husband in the wings. No fiancé, of course. And a boyfriend? Oh, please.

Sarah wanted to laugh over that one, and might have if she hadn't felt so horrible.

Laughing might have drawn attention to herself, anyway. And attention was the last thing she wanted, considering she was practically hiding in the thick of an oleander bush that was as tall as she was.

She brushed at the pink blossoms tickling her arm, shifting her position. The bride was handing off her spray of deep red roses to her attendant and Sarah nearly jumped out of her skin when a voice spoke behind her.

"I love weddings."

She looked at the small, wizened woman who'd toddled up beside her. If she'd noticed anything odd about

Sarah's position, virtually hiding in a bush, she said nothing. "Don't you, dear?"

Feeling stupid—nothing new there, either—Sarah managed a shrug and a noncommittal smile.

Again, the woman didn't seem to take any notice. She just peered around the bushes of the Malibu garden in which they stood, toward the bridal couple standing about fifty yards away. "They have weddings at this spot pretty regularly. I can certainly understand why, though, with the Pacific Ocean in the background and the garden here. It's a lovely setting."

"Mmm-hmm."

"Of course, in my day—" the woman's voice dropped, confidentially "—choosing to get married out of doors usually meant the bride was going to be having an early baby. Premature, but not really premature." Her face wrinkled even more as she continued her study. "Times are different nowadays. And the bride obviously has already *had* her baby. Looks like a tiny mite, being held like that against the daddy's shoulder. Wonder if it is a boy or a girl?"

Sarah couldn't manage even a shrug. "Boy." The word felt raw against her throat. The reality of that boy baby had felt raw in her soul since she'd learned of his existence a few weeks earlier. "And not so tiny. He's nearly nine months old already."

"Really? You know the couple? Why aren't you sitting with the rest of the guests?"

Sarah wished she'd kept quiet. "I didn't expect to make the wedding," she murmured.

"Are you a friend of the bride or the groom?"

"Groom," she said. "Acquaintances." Which was a lie.

One didn't make love with acquaintances.

They didn't fool themselves into thinking they loved an acquaintance.

The explanation was good enough for the woman, though. "Ahh. Well, that baby will probably grow up as handsome as his daddy there," the woman mused. "My husband was tall and dark like that. Italian." Her wrinkles deepened again with a surprisingly impish smile. "Passionate."

Sarah forced her lips to curve.

"Bride's gown is pretty, too. Nothing I'd want to see my granddaughter wearing, mind you, but still pretty."

The gown *was* pretty. Sophisticated. Sleeveless and reaching just past her knees. It wasn't even white, but a sort of pinkish oyster-like hue that seemed to reflect the glow of the sun as it hung on the horizon over the ocean.

"What do you do, dear?"

Sarah swallowed. "I'm an intern at the L.A. office of Frowley-Hughes."

The woman looked blank.

"It's a brokerage firm."

"Ahh. Financial stuff." Seemingly satisfied, the woman turned her focus back to the wedding party. "I taught school. Until my own children started coming along."

Sarah managed not to press her hand against her abdomen. She knew it was still flat beneath her T-shirt and jeans, but she was painfully aware that state would end soon enough. "How many did you have?"

"Four. And now I have eleven grandchildren. They're scattered all over, though. Don't come out to see their old grandma here in California too often."

Sarah felt a swift longing. "My family is mostly in Wyoming."

"Long way from here."

"Yes." Her gaze settled on the groom once more. "A long way."

"Maybe someday you'll have a beachside wedding. You'd be a beautiful bride. Such wonderful long hair you have."

Sarah's throat tightened. The memory of his hands tangling in her hair taunted her. "Thank you. But I don't have any plans to get married."

The woman smiled and waved her hand. "Forgive me, but you're just young. You wait. You'll want a husband and children at some point. I can tell. Oh, look." She nodded toward the wedding party again. "They're doing the rings now. Such a beautiful couple," she said again, her voice a satisfied sigh.

The bride did look beautiful.

The groom did look handsome.

And the baby—well, the baby was a baby. Sarah couldn't blame a baby.

She couldn't blame that lovely bride, either.

But the groom?

Oh, she could certainly blame him, all right.

But the person she blamed the most?

That would be herself.

She turned away, pushing the oleander branches out of her way, being careful not to let them snap back and hit the other woman.

"Don't you want to watch the rest of the wedding?"

Sarah shook her head gently. "No. I've seen enough."

More than enough.

Only problem was, she'd seen it all too late. Much too late.

And though Sarah had thought things couldn't get any worse, it was only a matter of months before she learned that they *could*.

Chapter 1

The first time Sarah saw the name on her class roster, she felt shock unlike anything she'd felt in years roll through her.

Elijah Scalise.

Not that daunting of a name, really. It surely suited the dark-haired eight-year-old boy who'd soon be joining her third-grade class. She had made a point of not looking at the boy's picture, even though she was perfectly aware that there was one. It was framed in a plain gold frame that sat on his grandmother's desk in the classroom right next to Sarah's classroom. Genna Scalise often talked about her grandson, Eli.

Sarah hadn't expected to ever be the boy's teacher, though.

She set aside the roster on her desk and went to the window that overlooked the playground. Frost still clung to the exterior corners and she could feel the coolness of the pane radiating from it. Outside, the bell hadn't yet rung and children were clambering over the swings and jungle gym. Winter scarves flew in the breeze and boots crunched over the crispy skiff of snow scattered across the playground.

Despite the cold, they were enjoying the last few minutes of freedom before they had to settle down into their seats. Until they broke for recess in a few hours, that was.

Nothing like feeling carefree.

She couldn't remember the last time she'd felt as carefree as they looked.

Which wasn't strictly true. She could probably pick the exact date on the calendar when she'd stopped feeling carefree.

Her gaze slid to the class roster.

"So, why didn't you tell me the news?" The chipper female voice drew her attention to the doorway of her classroom.

"Hey, Dee. What news?"

"About the new deputy." Deirdre Crowder was the sixth-grade teacher and at five-foot-nothing, she was about as big as a minute. Her blue eyes were mischievous. "He works for *your* uncle, girl, but you could have shared the wealth. A new, single man suddenly in town and all that. If it were the week before Christmas rather than Thanksgiving, I'd consider him to be our very own Christmas present!"

Sarah now had years of practice under her belt at keeping her true thoughts to herself. "Go for it," she said with a smile. "He's my new student's father. And you know I don't get involved with my kids' fathers."

Dee's eyebrows lifted as she sauntered into the room. Her shoulder-length blond hair seemed to crackle with the energy that kept it curled in loose ringlets. "I may have only come to Weaver a year ago, but as far as I can tell, you don't get *involved* with anyone. What's with you?" She joined Sarah at the window. "If I had your looks I'd be dating every available man in town."

"There is nothing wrong with your looks," Sarah countered. She'd heard Dee's opinion plenty in the months since school had begun in August. "Deputy Tommy Potter thinks they're about perfect."

"Oh, Tommy." Dee shook her head, dismissively. "Unless he was going to arrest me for something, or wants to spread a little gossip, that boy moves about as slow as molasses in winter. He has no gumption." She pushed up the sleeves of her bright red sweater and pointed out the window. "Since it might as well be winter, with all that snow on the ground, you can just imagine the snail's pace I'm talking about."

Sarah's lips curved. "You're the one who moved to a small town, Dee. Could have stayed in Cheyenne where the pickings were more varied."

Dee pressed her nose against the cold windowpane, looking not much older than the children playing outside. "Have you met him? The new deputy, I mean? I heard he comes from Weaver."

If Sarah hadn't been prepared to see that name on her class roster, she definitely wasn't prepared to discuss her new student's father. "He left Weaver a long time ago."

"Yeah, but you *did* know him, right? Most everyone in Weaver seems to know everyone else."

"Maybe by sight," Sarah allowed. Though the Clay family had its history with the Scalise family—history that had nothing to do with her experience with him. "Talk to Genna," she suggested. "She's his mother.

She could tell you everything you ever wanted to know about Max."

Her throat tightened.

Max.

At the mention of Genna, the most senior teacher at Weaver Elementary, Dee turned her back on the window. "How's she healing up, anyway?"

"Fine, last I heard." Sarah felt a little guilty that she didn't know more. That she hadn't made a more concerted effort to visit Genna herself. After all, they were coworkers and had been since Sarah began teaching at Weaver Elementary nearly six years ago. Genna was a friend of her mother's. Her aunts!

"What was she doing skiing at her age, anyway? It's no wonder she broke some bones."

"Anyone can have a skiing accident, even someone who's barely twenty-five," Sarah said pointedly.

Dee grinned impishly and rolled her eyes. But Sarah was spared her comment when the bell rang, sharp and shrill.

"To the salt mine," Dee said, heading for the classroom door. "Want to head over to Classic Charms one night this week? See if Tara's got anything new in?"

Sarah nodded. The children outside had scattered like leaves on the wind when the bell rang, and now she could hear footsteps ringing on the tile floor in the corridor. "Sure."

Classic Charms was the newest shop to open its doors in Weaver, though it had eschewed the new shopping center area for a location right on Main Street.

Dee swiveled, deftly avoiding a collision with the first trio of kids bolting into Sarah's classroom.

Sarah began passing out the workbooks she'd corrected over the weekend as the tables slowly filled. She had seventeen kids in her class this year.

Correction.

Eighteen, now.

They sat two to a table, usually, though she had enough room for them to all sit separately if need be. Some years were like that. This year though, had so far been peaceful.

"Thanks, Miz Clay." Bright-eyed Chrissy Tanner beamed up at her as she accepted her workbook. "Are we having science today?"

"It's Monday, isn't it?" she asked lightly and continued passing through the room. Her attention, though, kept straying to the door.

Sooner or later, Eli would be there. Her gaze flicked to the wide-faced clock affixed high on the wall and noted he'd have three minutes before he'd be tardy. Not that she'd enforce that rule with a brand-new student on his very first day. She wasn't *that* much a stickler for the rules.

The thought struck her as incredibly ironic.

The last workbook delivered, she walked back through the tables, heading to the front of the classroom where she picked up her chalk and finished writing out the day's lesson plan on the blackboard. The sound of chatter and laughter and scraping chairs filled the room.

It was familiar and normal.

Ordinarily those sounds, this classroom, felt safe to Sarah.

But not today.

Would *he* bring Eli?

Between her fingers, the chalk snapped into pieces. Squelching an impatient sound, she picked them off the floor, and rapidly finished writing as the final bell rang.

No Eli Scalise.

As she'd done every morning at the beginning of the school day, she moved across the room and closed the door. Regardless of her feelings about her new student and his presence—or lack of it—she had a class to teach.

She turned back to her students, raising her voice enough to get everyone's attention. "How many of you saw the double-rainbow yesterday?"

A bunch of hands shot up into the air.

And the lessons of the day began.

"Why do I gotta go to school?"

"Because."

Eli sighed mightily. "But you said we were going to go back to California."

"Not for months yet."

"So?"

Max Scalise pulled open the passenger door of the SUV he'd been assigned by Sawyer Clay, the sheriff. They were already late, thanks to a conference call he'd had to take about a recent case of his. "In."

His son, Eli, made a face, but tossed his brown-bag lunch and dark blue backpack inside before climbing up on the seat.

"Fasten the belt."

The request earned Max another pulled face. He shut the door and headed around to the driver's side. As he went, his eyes automatically scanned the area around them.

But there was nothing out of the ordinary. Just bare-branched trees. Winter-dry lawns not quite covered by snow. A few houses lined neatly along the street, all of them closed up tight against the chill. Only one of them had smoke coming from the chimney—his mother's house that they'd just left.

Genna was as comfortably situated as she could get in the family room, where Max had lit the fire in the fireplace as she'd requested. She had her heavy cast propped on pillows, a stack of magazines, a pot of her favorite tea, the television remote and a cordless phone.

Outside the houses, though, there were no particular signs of life.

His breath puffed out around his head in white rings and cold air snuck beneath the collar of his dark brown departmental jacket.

God, he hated the cold.

He climbed in the truck.

"I could'a stayed in California with Grandma Helene," Eli continued the minute Max's rear hit the seat.

"What's wrong with your grandmother here?" He made a U-turn and headed down the short hop to Main Street.

Eli hunched his shoulders. The coat he wore was a little too big for him. Max had picked up the cold-weather gear on their way to the airport. There hadn't been a lot of time for fine fitting. "Nuthin'," his son muttered. "But she always visited us out *there*. How come we gotta come here this time?"

"You happen to notice that big old cast on Grandma's leg?" Max drove past the station house and turned once again, onto the street leading to the school. It took all of three minutes, maybe, given the significant distance.

The closer they got to the brick building that hadn't changed a helluva lot since the days when Max had run the halls, the more morose Eli became. If his boy slouched any more in his seat, he'd hang himself on the seatbelt.

"Look at the bright side," Max said. "You won't be bored."

Eli's eyes—as dark blue as Jennifer's had been—rolled. "Rather be bored back home than bored in there." He jerked his chin toward the building.

Max pulled into the parking lot and stopped near the main entrance. "Don't roll your eyes." Donna, the school secretary, had told him when he'd faxed in the registration forms from California that the office was just inside the main front doors. A different location than he'd remembered from his days there.

"Do they have an after-school program?"

Eli was used to one in California—two supervised hours of sports and games that had never managed to produce completed homework the way it should have.

"No."

Eli heaved a sigh. "I *hate* it here."

Unfortunately, Max couldn't say much to change his son's opinion. Not when he remembered all too clearly feeling exactly the same way. He reached over and caught Eli behind the head, tousling his hair. "It's only for a few months. Until Grandma's all healed up and can go back to teaching school." By then, hopefully, Max would have finished the job *he'd* been assigned. But Max didn't tell Eli that. He wasn't about to tell anyone in Weaver what his true purpose was there.

Someone was funneling meth through Weaver. It was coming out of Arizona by way of Colorado and heading north after Weaver, even—occasionally—on a locally contracted semi. But only occasionally.

The transports seemed to be wide and varied and Max's job was to determine who was organizing the local hub.

It was a job he'd managed to avoid being assigned

until his mom broke her leg two weeks earlier. She'd needed help. His boss had been putting on the pressure. So here they were. Father and son and neither one too thrilled about it.

"I'm already late, you know." Eli dragged his backpack over his shoulder. It rustled against his slick coat. "On my first day. The teacher'll probably be mad for the rest of the year."

"I seriously doubt it," Max drawled. His son had inherited his mother's dramatic streak, as well.

"Is it a lady? Or a man?"

"Who?"

Eli started to roll his eyes again, but stopped at a look from Max. "The teach. I liked Mr. Frederick. He was cool."

"I have no idea."

Eli made a sound. "You didn't *ask*?"

Max felt a pang of guilt. He'd been more preoccupied with this unexpected—and unappealing—assignment than with the identity of Eli's temporary teacher. Max had only had a few days to take care of the school paperwork, as it was. But Eli was right about one thing. They were late. Both of them.

The sheriff had expected Max at the station nearly thirty minutes ago.

Great way to start off, Scalise.

He caught Eli's jacket and nudged his son around the corner into the office when he spotted the sign.

A young woman he didn't recognize smiled at them the moment they came into her view. "The new student," she said cheerfully. "Welcome."

Max heard the gritty sigh that came out of Eli and hoped he was the only one who heard it. He didn't need Eli having trouble at this school. He needed everything to go as smoothly as possible. With no distractions, Max could finish his investigation as quickly as possible, and they could get the hell back out of Dodge. As soon as his mother could get back in the classroom.

Weaver held no great memories for him.

He was just as anxious to leave it again as Eli was. Telling his boy that, though, was *not* going to happen.

"Deputy Scalise—" the girl at the desk had risen "—I'm Donna. It's nice to meet you in person. You, too, Eli. I'll just let Principal Gage know you're here."

"He already knows." A balding man approached from behind them, hand outstretched. "Max. Good to see you. Been a long time."

"Joe." He shook the principal's hand. "Still can't believe you're head honcho here." Joe Gage had been a hellion of the highest order back when they'd been kids. "Guess they don't hold a little thing like blowing up the science room against a man."

"Guess not. They made you a deputy, and you were in that room with me."

"Whoa, Dad." Eli sounded impressed.

The principal chuckled. "Come on. I'll take you down to Eli's class." He looked at the boy as they stepped into the corridor once more. "Miss Clay. You'll like her."

Max's boot heels scraped the hard floor. Clay. Another name from the past.

Well, why not?

The Clay family had plenty of members—seemed to him there'd been a teacher among them.

For a moment, he wished he'd been more inclined to listen to his mother's talk of Weaver over the years. But she knew his reasons for not wanting to hear about the town well enough. Weaver was where Max's father betrayed everyone they knew. It was where Tony Scalise had abandoned them. And on her visits to see him and Eli, she barely mentioned details about her life back home. Mostly because it generally led to an argument between them.

Max had wanted Genna to leave a long time ago. To join him in California.

For reasons that still escaped him, she'd been just as determined to stay.

The principal stopped in front of a closed classroom door. Through the big square window that comprised the top half of the door, he could see the rows of tables—situated in a sort of half circle—all occupied by kids about Eli's size. At the head of the class, he caught a glimpse of the teacher. Slender as a reed, dressed in emerald green from head to toe. A little taller than average and definitely young, he noted. Her arms waved around her as she spun in a circle, almost as if she were acting out some play.

Max started to smile.

Then the teacher stopped, facing the door with its generous window head-on. Through the glass, her sky-blue eyes met his.

He felt the impact like a sucker punch to the kidneys.

He'd only known one woman with eyes that particular shade.

The principal pushed open the door. "Pardon the interruption, Miss Clay," he said, ushering Eli inside. "This is your new student, Eli Scalise. Eli, this is Miss Clay."

Max stood rooted to the floor outside the doorway.

Sarah.

She was no longer looking at him with those eyes that were as translucent as the Wyoming winter sky, but at Eli.

Her smile was warm. Slightly crooked. And it made

Max wonder if he'd imagined the frigid way she'd looked at him through the window.

"Eli," she greeted. "Come on in. Take off your coat. Can't have you roasting to death on your first day here." She gestured at the line of coats hanging on pegs. "We do our roasting only on Wednesdays."

Eli shot Max a studiously bored look. But Max still saw the twitch of Eli's lips.

A good sign. Maybe he wouldn't have to worry about Eli, after all.

He looked back at Sarah again.

What the hell was she doing here? A teacher of all things. When they'd been involved—

He cut off the thought.

She gave him no more attention than she gave the principal as she showed Eli where to sit, and after assuring herself that he had the usual school supplies, she moved back to the front of the class. Without a glance their way, she picked up right where she'd left off. "Okay, so if the tornado is spinning to the right," she turned on her heels and the braid she'd woven her hair into swayed out from her spine.

Max started when Joe Gage headed out of the classroom and pulled the door closed, cutting off whatever else Professor Sarah was imparting. "She's a good teacher," Joe said. "Strict. But she really cares about her kids."

Max headed back up the corridor with Joe. "How long has she been here?"

"This will be her sixth year. So, Donna tells me you've already completed all the paperwork for Eli. You put your mom down as his caretaker? Is Genna up to that?"

He could have asked a dozen questions about Sarah Clay.

He asked none.

"Eli doesn't need a lot of care. He's pretty independent. He'll do as much taking care of her as she does him." He didn't like feeling as though he had to explain himself. "With the job I might not always be available. You know. If Eli got sick or something, my mother can make decisions about him."

"Fine, fine." Joe accepted the explanation without a qualm. "I'll be glad when Genna can make it back to work here. So, I know Eli lost his mother a year or so back. I'm sorry to hear it. Anything else in your personal life that he's dealing with that we might need to know?"

Max shrugged. "He's annoyed as hell that I took him out of his regular school to come here."

Joe smiled. "That's not too surprising." He stopped outside the office. "Any questions *you* have?"

None that he intended to ask Joe Gage. He shook his head and stuck out his hand. "Good to see you again."

"Deputy." Donna waved at him from her desk. "The sheriff just called here looking for you."

Not surprising. "I'm on my way over to the station house."

"I'll let him know for you," she offered.

"Don't worry about Eli," Joe told him. "He's in good hands."

Sarah Clay's hands, Max thought, as he headed out to his SUV.

It might have been seven years, but he still remembered the feel of those particular hands.

He climbed in the truck, and started it up, only to notice the brown bag sitting on the floor. Eli's lunch.

Dammit.

He grabbed it and strode back inside, right on past

the office, around two corners, to the third door. He knocked on the window.

Once again, inside the classroom, Sarah stopped and looked at him.

The glass protected him from the fallout of that glacial look. He definitely hadn't imagined it, then.

She moved across the room and opened the door. "What is it, Deputy?"

He held up the lunch sack. "Eli forgot this."

Her eyes seemed to focus somewhere around his left ear. She snatched the bag from his fingers and turned away.

He started to say her name.

But the door closed in his face.

Chapter 2

By the end of the day, Sarah felt as if she'd been through the wringer. She didn't have to look hard for the reason why, either.

Not when he sat in the chair next to her desk, a sullen expression on his young face. The rest of the students had already been dismissed for the day.

She pushed aside the stack of papers on her desk and folded her hands together on the surface, leaning toward him. All day, she'd been searching for some physical resemblance between him and his father, and it annoyed her to no end.

Unlike Max, who was as dark as Lucifer, his son was blond-haired and blue-eyed and had the appearance of an angel. But he'd been an absolute terror.

Nevertheless, she was determined to keep her voice calm and friendly. "Eli, you've had a lot of changes in your life lately. And I know that starting at a new school can be difficult. Why don't you tell me what your days were like at your last school?"

"Better 'n here," he said.

She held back a sigh. She'd be phoning his last school as soon as possible. "Better how?"

"We had *real* desks, for one thing."

She looked at the tables. The only difference between a desk and the table was the storage, which was taken care of by cubbies that were affixed to each side of the table. "Do you prefer sitting at your own table?"

He lifted one shoulder, not answering.

"If you do, then all you have to do is say so. We both know that you won't be sitting next to Jonathan tomorrow."

"He's a tool." His expression indicated what a condemnation that was.

"He's a student in my class, the same as you are and doesn't deserve to be picked on all afternoon by anyone."

"I wasn't picking on him."

She lifted her eyebrows. "Really?"

"I don't care what he said."

"Actually, Jonathan didn't say anything. He didn't have to. Eli, I saw you poking at him. You were messing with his papers. You even hid his lunch from him. And then on the playground after lunch, you deliberately hit him with the ball. So, what gives?"

"He didn't dodge fast 'nuff or he wouldn't have got hit."

"This isn't the best way to start off here, you know."

"So call my dad and tell him that."

She had no desire whatsoever to speak to his father. Just seeing Max in person for a brief five minutes had been more than enough for her. "Let's make a deal, shall we? Tomorrow is a brand-new day. We'll all start fresh. *Or,* we can add your name to the list on the board." She gestured to the corner of the board where two other names were already written. "You know how that works. The first time, you get your name on the board. The second time, you get a check mark and a visit to the principal. If you get another check mark, you're out of my class." Something that had never once occurred, but it was the commonly accepted practice at her school.

Eli looked glum. "That was Mr. Frederick's rule, too."

"Mr. Frederick was your last teacher? Did you think that system was unfair?"

The boy lifted his shoulder again, not looking at her.

She propped her chin on her palm. "I want you to enjoy class, Eli. It's no fun for any of us if one of our class members is miserable. But the fact of it is, if you're caught trying to deliberately hurt another student, there's not going to be *anything* I can do to help you. Principal Gage has very clear rules about behavior. What you did on the playground today was wrong."

"The ball hardly hit him."

"Only because he wasn't standing still. And don't act as if you were playing a game of dodgeball, because I know you weren't."

His face scrunched up, like he'd swallowed something bitter. "Sorry," he mumbled.

"It's Jonathan who deserves the apology. You can use my phone here to call him, if you'd like."

His lips parted. "*Now?*"

She could almost have let herself be amused by his appalled expression. "No time like the present. And I'll bet that Jonathan is home by now since he lives just around the corner." She plopped the phone on the corner of her desk in front of Eli and pulled out the phone list. "Ready?"

Eli morosely picked up the phone and dialed the number that she recited.

Deciding to give him at least the illusion of some privacy, she rose and moved away from her desk, crossing the room to straighten the art supplies still scattered across the counter. The students had been painting Thanksgiving turkeys that afternoon.

Behind her, she heard Eli deliver his apology. Short. Brief. About what she'd expected.

But at least he'd offered it.

She hadn't been sure he would, given his mutinous attitude that afternoon.

She tapped the ends of her handful of paintbrushes on the counter, then dropped them into the canning jar where they fanned out like some arty bouquet. She turned around to face Eli and caught him surreptitiously swiping his cheek.

Tension and irritation drained out of her the same way it always did when it came to working with kids.

Evidently, Eli—son of Max Scalise or not—was no exception.

"Remember that tomorrow is a brand-new day," she said to him. "All fresh. Right?"

He didn't exactly jump up and down in agreement. But he didn't roll his eyes, either.

"Come on. I'll walk you out. Is—is your dad supposed to pick you up?"

He shook his head. "I gotta walk."

This time she didn't hold back the urge to smile slightly. He made walking sound like a fate worse than death. "To your grandmother's house?"

"To the station house."

"Well, that's even closer." She pushed a mammoth amount of papers and books into her oversized book bag and grabbed her own coat off the hook. "Have you met the sheriff yet?"

Eli shook his head.

"He's not too scary," Sarah confided. "He's my uncle."

At that, the boy looked slightly interested. He hitched his backpack over his shoulder and followed her into the hallway. "You got relatives here?"

"Lots and lots. Can't swing a cat without hitting a member of the Clay family."

"Gross. Who'd wanna swing a cat?"

She chuckled. "Well, nobody, I guess."

"*There* you are."

Her chuckle caught in her throat at the sight of Max standing in the middle of the corridor. His dark, slashing brows were drawn together over his eyes. They varied from brown to green, depending on his mood. Currently, they looked green and far from happy.

She looked down at Eli beside her. "Guess you won't have to make that walk after all."

The corner of his lips turned down. "Think I was better off if I'd'a had to," he muttered.

She curled her fingers around the webbed strap of her book bag to keep from tousling his hair. Terror or not, there was something about the boy that got to her.

Not that most kids didn't, she hurriedly reminded herself.

"You're late," Max said. His voice hadn't changed. It was still deep. Still slightly abrupt. As if he spoke only because he had to.

"Only about ten minutes. He had some questions

we needed to take care of," Sarah said, answering before Eli could. The boy shot her a surprised look that she ignored.

Max's eyes narrowed. He still had the longest lashes she'd ever seen on a man. Long and thick, and as darkly colored as the hair on his head. "What kind of questions?"

She decided to let Eli handle that one.

"About, uh, sports," he finally said.

Max looked suspicious. "Truck's in the parking lot," he said after a moment. "Go wait for me."

Eli gave that little shrug of his and headed down the hall. "See ya tomorrow, Miz Clay."

"See you, Eli." Her hand was strangling the web strap. "Deputy." She barely looked at Max as she turned on her heel, intending to head out the other way. She could wend her way through the school to a different exit.

"Sarah—"

Every nerve she possessed tightened. She felt it from the prickling in her scalp to the curling in her toes. And though she would have liked to keep walking—no, she would have *loved* to keep walking—she stopped and looked at him over her shoulder.

After all, he *was* the parent of her newest student. She would have to deal with him on that level no matter what her personal feelings were.

"Yes?"

His lips compressed for a moment. "I...how are you?"

She didn't know what she might have expected him to say, but it definitely hadn't been that. "Busy," she said evenly. "Did you need to discuss something about Eli?"

"I'm sorry he was late this morning. It won't happen again."

"Okay." When it seemed as if he had nothing further to say, she started to turn again.

"I didn't expect to see you here."

Which meant she'd never been a hot topic of conversation between him and his mother, since she'd been working with Genna for some time now. "I can say the same thing about you."

She felt certain that she imagined the flicker in his eyes at that. Wishful thinking on her part that he might feel something, anything, about what had happened all those years ago. He'd made his feelings then perfectly clear, even though he'd never been perfectly clear about anything else.

And darnitall, that fact *still* stung even though she'd made herself believe that it was all water beneath the bridge.

She shifted the weight of her book bag to her other shoulder. "Coming down a little in the world, aren't you? From detective to deputy?"

"The job meets my needs for now."

She didn't want to know *what* his needs might be. "Then you have my congratulations." Her tone said the contrary, however. "Excuse me. I have things I need to do." She turned again and strode down the corridor, the click of her shoes sounding brisk and hollow.

Max's hands curled as he watched the bounce of that long, thick braid as Sarah strode away from him.

He didn't make the mistake of speaking her name again.

She hated him.

Well, could he blame her?

When it came to Sarah Clay, he pretty much hated himself, too.

God, but he still couldn't believe she was here. In Weaver.

Aware that Eli was still waiting for him, he headed out to the SUV. His son was fiddling with the scanner when he climbed in the truck.

"She tell ya?" Eli sat back in his seat as Max reset the equipment.

Great. Tell me what? He started driving away from the school. "What do you think?"

His son heaved a sigh, obviously assuming the worst. "Figures. I was only kidding with the guy. How was I supposed to know his glasses would fly off like they did? At least they didn't break or nothing, though."

He gave his son a hard look, thinking he was glad Eli was more open than his teacher evidently was. "Did you apologize?"

"Yes. I used Miz Clay's phone in the classroom."

"Good. Don't do it again."

"How come you came to get me?"

"I told you. You were late. I was worried."

Eli rolled his eyes. "What for? This place is dinky. I mean, geez, Dad. There's not even a real mall!"

"Missing those afternoons you liked to spend shopping, is that it?"

His son snorted. They both knew that Eli loathed shopping. That was one trait he had gotten from Max.

He drove past the station where he'd go back on duty after Eli was settled with Genna. He drummed the steering wheel. "So, what's your teacher like?"

"Besides a rat fink?"

Max let out an impatient breath. "She didn't tell me anything, pal. You did that all on your own."

"Geez." Eli's head hit the back of the seat. He looked out the window. "She's all right, I guess." He was silent for a moment. "She kinda reminds me of Mom."

Max let that revelation finish rocking. Since Jen had died of cancer almost fourteen months earlier, Eli rarely mentioned her of his own volition. "In what way?"

"I dunno. What's for supper?"

"Grandma's cooking."

"I thought we were here to take care of *her*."

"We are. But she's pretty bored sitting around all day letting her broken leg heal. She's not used to that much inactivity."

"Can *we* go skiing sometime?"

Max wanted to tell his son they could. He didn't want Eli to be miserable the entire time they were in Weaver. "We'll see." Most everything would depend on how well the case went.

"Do ya even know how to ski?"

"Smart aleck. Yeah, I know."

"Well, you just lived in California all my life."

"All your life, bud. Not all of mine."

"What about horses? Can we go riding horses sometime?"

Max suppressed a grimace. He and horses had never particularly gotten along. "We'll see."

"Did you know Miz Clay?"

The question, innocence and curiosity combined, burned. "Yeah. I knew her."

"Did you, like, go to school with her?"

"No. She's a lot younger than me."

"Well, yeah. 'Cuz you're old and she's still pretty."

A bark of laughter came out of him. Miz Clay *was* still pretty. Beautiful, in fact; all that youthful dewiness she'd possessed at twenty-one had given way to the kind of timeless looks that would last all of her life. "That's why I keep you around, Elijah. To keep me humble."

His son smiled faintly. "She says you can't swing a cat without hitting someone from her family. Was she your girlfriend?"

He pulled to a sudden stop in his mother's driveway and the tires skidded a few inches. He needed to get out the snowblower, and soon. "Just because she's female doesn't mean she was my girlfriend. I just told you. She's a lot younger than me."

"How much younger?"

God, give him patience. "I don't know. A lot." Liar.

"Five years?"

As if a paltry five years mattered. "Twelve."

"Geez. You *are* old. Not like Grandma old, but still—"

"Enough. I'm not so old that I can't beat your butt inside the house."

Eli grinned and set off at a run, his backpack swaying wildly from his narrow shoulders.

Max jogged along behind him. At least one thing had gone right that day. Eli was smiling.

Just before his son bolted up the front porch, Max put on the speed and flew past him to open the storm door first.

"Dad!"

He shrugged and went inside. "Wipe your boots," he reminded. He pulled his radio off his belt and set it on the hall table and tossed his jacket on the coatrack. "Hey, Ma."

Genna Scalise was sixty years old and looked a good ten years less. Her hair was still dark, her face virtually unlined. And she was currently trying to poke one end of an unfolded wire hanger beneath the thigh-high edge of her cast. "Turn the heat off under the pasta."

"Don't poke yourself to death." He went into the kitchen and turned off the stove burner. The churning water in the pot immediately stopped bubbling. The second pot on the stove held his mother's homemade sauce. "Smells great, but I thought you said you were just going to throw together a casserole or something." He went back in the family room and took the hanger from her frustrated hands. "Here. Try this." He handed over the long-handled bamboo back scratcher that he'd picked up at the new supermarket on the far side of town.

Her eyes lit as if he'd just told her she was going to have a second grandchild. She threaded the long piece beneath the edge of her cast and tilted back her head, blissfully. "Oh, you're a good boy, Max."

Eli snickered.

"How was school?"

"I got homework," the boy said by way of answering her. "Vocabulary."

"Well, horrors." She smiled. "Get a start on it before we have dinner." She withdrew the scratcher and set it on the couch, then held up her arms to Max. "Help me up, honey, so I can finish that."

He lifted her slender form off the couch. From above, he could hear Eli moving around upstairs. Doing his homework, hopefully. "When you said you wanted to cook today, I didn't think you meant making homemade pasta."

"What other kind of pasta is there?" She patted his cheek and reached for her crutches.

He followed her slow progress back into the kitchen. He wasn't used to seeing his mother have to struggle; he didn't like it. But he knew she didn't want him constantly helping her, either, considering they'd already had a few skirmishes on that score since his and Eli's arrival a few days earlier. "Why didn't you tell me Sarah Clay would be Eli's teacher?"

Balancing herself, she sat down on the high stool that Max had put in the kitchen for her. She gave him a sidelong look. "I didn't think about it. I assumed that you knew. Is there something wrong with her? She's a fine teacher."

He shook his head. He was hardly going to tell his mother about it.

She sighed and set down her long wooden spoon. "What happened with your father and the Clays was a very long time ago. The only one it still bothers seems to be you."

What happened with Max and Sarah was a long time ago, too, yet it still felt like yesterday. "Last I heard, she was studying finance. Didn't expect to find her here teaching third grade."

"I like her." Genna pointed the spoon. "Hand me the strainer."

He shook his head and drained the pasta himself. "You're supposed to be resting, Ma, not cooking up a storm like this."

"Consider it good planning. We'll have leftovers for a week."

He heard the crackle of his radio and went out to get it. He listened to the dispatch, answered, and stuck his head back in the kitchen. "Gotta go. You okay with Eli?"

She waved her wooden spoon. "Of course. Be careful, now."

He yelled up the stairs for Eli to mind his grandmother, and hustled out to the SUV.

The drive to the Double-C Ranch wasn't an unfamiliar one, though it had been a helluva long time since Max had made it. The ranch was the largest and most successful spread in the vicinity. It was owned by the Clays, though as far as Max knew, Sawyer—the sheriff—had never taken an active part in running it. That was the job of Matthew Clay.

Sarah's father.

He turned in through the gate and a short while later stopped in the curved drive behind Sawyer's cruiser. He could count on his hands the number of times he'd been to the Double-C. The last time, he'd been barely fifteen and his father had been caught red-handed stealing Double-C cattle.

It was still burned in his memory.

He climbed out of his truck, nodding at Sawyer, who was leaning against one of the stone columns on the front porch. "Matthew," he greeted the second man.

Sarah's father ambled down the steps, sticking his hand out. "Max. Good to see you again."

Max returned the greeting, looking past the man to his new boss. "What's up?"

"Thought it best to discuss things away from the station."

Max looked from Sawyer to his brother.

"He's aware of the situation," the older man said. "Let's walk."

"You're surprised," Matthew observed as they headed away from the house, cutting across the drive toward a sweeping, open area unoccupied by anything but a stand of mighty trees.

Max didn't like feeling out of control. Sawyer might be the sheriff, but the investigation was *Max's*. "It was my understanding that nobody but my superior and the sheriff knew what I was really doing here."

"Matt's noticed another discrepancy among his

trucking records," Sawyer told him. "This time on a shipment of stock heading to Minnesota."

"How recent?"

"Couple weeks." Matt settled his cowboy hat deeper over his forehead. "When I talked to Sawyer about it, he admitted the other thing that's been going on." His face was grim. "Bad business. Kind of thing I don't want to see going on in Weaver."

"Drug trafficking shouldn't be going on *anywhere*," Max said flatly. For five years, he'd been serving on a special task force investigating distribution cells that were cropping up in small towns. The less traditional locations were highly difficult to pinpoint.

"You're right about that," Sawyer agreed. "Seems as if Weaver is just one more small town to become involved lately." He tilted his head back, studying the sun that hung low on the horizon. It wasn't quite evening yet, but the temperature was already dropping. "Much as I hate to admit it, we need help. That's why I didn't oppose your assignment here."

It wasn't exactly news to Max since he'd have done just about anything to get out of this particular assignment. But he was here now. He'd do his job.

He was a special agent with the DEA and it was one thing that he was usually pretty good at.

"I'm going to need the details about your discrepancies," he told Matthew.

The other man pulled an envelope out of his down vest and handed it over. "Copies and my notes."

Max didn't bother opening it now. He shoved it into his own pocket. "Anything else?"

"Matthew!"

All three men turned at the hail from the house.

"Supper's on!"

For a moment, Max thought the woman on the porch was Sarah. She bore an uncanny resemblance. But when she turned and went back inside, he didn't see that waist-length braid.

"Care to stay?" Matt offered. "My wife, Jaimie, is a pretty fine cook."

"Another reason why I'm out here," Sawyer admitted. "Bec—my wife—is in Boston on some medical symposium all this week. Been getting tired of my own cooking."

"Appreciate the offer," Max said. "But I need to get back to town."

"At least come in and say hello or Jaimie'll bug me from now until spring. Everyone in the county wants to greet the new deputy."

"Sure, until they start remembering the days when I lived here," Max countered. His father, Tony, might have been the criminal, but Max hadn't exactly been an altar boy. Getting friendly with the folks of Weaver was *not* in his plan. He was just there to do a job.

In that way, at least, he could make one thing right with the Clay family.

But after that, he and Eli would be gone.

Still, Max could read Sawyer's expression well enough. The steely-eyed sheriff expected Max to act neighborly.

"I'd be pleased to say hello," he said, feeling a tinge of what Eli must have been feeling when Max had lectured him on behaving well.

Matthew wasn't entirely fooled, as far as Max could tell, as they headed toward the house. They skirted the front porch entirely, going around, instead, to the rear of the house. They went in through the mudroom, and then into the cheery, bright kitchen.

"Don't get excited, Red, 'cause he's not staying," Matthew said as they entered. "But this here's Sawyer's new right-hand man, Max Scalise."

Jaimie rubbed her hands down the front of the apron tied around her slender waist. "Of course. I remember you as a boy, Max." She took his hand in hers, shaking it warmly. "Genna talks of you often. She always has such fun sharing pictures from her trips out to see you and Eli. I know she must be so pleased that you're back in Weaver. How is her leg coming along?"

"More slowly than she'd like."

"Mom, I still can't find the lace—" Sarah entered the kitchen from the doorway opposite Max, and practically skidded to a halt. "Tablecloths," she finished. "What're *you* doing here?"

"Just picking up some paperwork from the sheriff," Max said into the silence that her abrupt question caused. "Nice to see you again, Miss Clay." He looked at Jaimie, who was eyeing him and her daughter with curiosity. "And it was nice to see you, too, ma'am."

"Give your mother my regards," Jaimie told him as he stepped toward the mudroom again.

"I'll do that. Sheriff. Matthew. See you later."

He was almost at his SUV when he heard footsteps on the gravel drive behind him.

"Max." Her voice was sharp.

The memory of that voice, husky with sleep, with passion, hovered in the back of his mind. He ought to have memories just as clear about Jennifer.

But he didn't.

He opened the SUV door and tossed the envelope from Matthew inside on the seat. "Don't worry, Sarah," he said, his voice flat. "I'm not *trying* to run into you every time we turn around."

She'd taken time only long enough to grab a sweater, and she held it wrapped tight around her shoulders. Tendrils of reddish-blond hair had worked loose from her braid and drifted against her neck. "Believe me," she said, her tone stiff, "I didn't once think that you *were*." She worked her hand out from beneath the sweater. She held an ivory envelope. "It's an invitation for your mother to my cousin's wedding."

He took the envelope, deliberately brushing her fingers with his.

The action was a double-edged sword, though.

She surrendered the envelope as if it burned her, and the jolt he'd felt left more than his fingertips feeling numb. "Ever heard of postage stamps?"

She didn't look amused. "Most of the invites are being hand-delivered because the wedding is so soon. Friday after Thanksgiving. We're all helping out with getting them delivered. Since your mom's in the same quilting group as Leandra's mother, they wanted her to have an invitation."

"Leandra?"

"My cousin. She's marrying Evan Taggart."

He remembered their names, of course. Taggart had grown up to become the local vet. Leandra was yet another one of the Clays and, he remembered, Sarah's favorite cousin. If he wasn't mistaken, he thought the vet had been on some television show Leandra had been involved with. More proof that Weaver wasn't quite so "small town" as it once was. "I'll make sure she gets it." He tapped the envelope against his palm. "Eli told me what he did today."

She pulled the dark blue sweater more tightly around her shoulders, and said nothing.

He exhaled, feeling impatience swell inside him. "Dammit, Sarah, at least *say* something."

Her ivory face could have been carved from ice. "Be careful driving back to Weaver. Road gets slick at night sometimes."

Then she turned on her heel, and for the third time that day, she walked away from him.

Chapter 3

Despite Sarah's hopes, days two, three and four of Eli Scalise were just as bad—or worse—than day one.

He didn't hit another student with a dodge ball, but he was still miles away from the model of behavior. A conversation with his previous school had told her that this was *not* the norm where Eli was concerned.

By Thursday, she knew she had to speak with Max about it. She hated the fact that several times throughout the day, she put off calling him. It showed her cowardice.

And since she was supposed to be *thoroughly* over the man, what did she have to be afraid of?

For another ten minutes or so, her students would still be in the cafeteria, practicing their part in the holiday program they'd present in less than a month. And Sarah had done enough dithering.

Nerves all nicely inflated, she snatched up the phone

and dialed the sheriff's office. But Pamela Rasmussen, her uncle's newest dispatcher, told her that Max was out on a call.

"I can get a message to him if it's urgent. His son's okay, isn't he?"

Okay was a subjective term, Sarah thought. "It's not urgent. I'd appreciate you asking him to give me a call when he's free, though."

"Sure, Sarah. No prob. So, how are Leandra's wedding plans coming together?"

"Rapidly." Sarah was Leandra's maid of honor. "She's got so much going on with the start-up of Fresh Horizons that we're all doing as much as we can to take some of the wedding details off her shoulders." Fresh Horizons was Leandra's newly planned speech, physical and occupational therapy program. It would be located at her parents' horse farm, so they could utilize hippotherapy as a treatment strategy.

"Wouldn't mind taking the honeymoon off her shoulders," Pam said with a laugh. "Think Evan Taggart was one of the last hot bachelors around here. Everyone else seems too young for us. Or too old."

Sarah had an unwanted image of Max shoot into her brain. She knew he'd turned forty that year. His August birthday was just another one of those details about the man that she couldn't seem to get out of her head. "Hadn't really thought about it," Sarah lied. "Thanks for leaving the message, Pam. Gotta run."

"You betcha."

She quickly hung up, then nearly jumped out of her skin when the phone rang right beneath her hand where it still rested on the receiver. She snatched it up. "Sarah Clay."

"Sounding sort of tense there, Sarah."

Her breath eked out. "Brody. What's wrong?"

"Nada. Kid's fine."

She looked toward the classroom door. She could hear footsteps outside in the corridor. "Then what are you calling me here for?" She made it a point not to blur the lines between her real life and her other job. It's the reason she'd been as successful at keeping that other duty under wraps as she had been.

Not even her family knew about it.

"Megan needs more schoolwork. She's already blown through the materials you left."

She wasn't surprised. Her few encounters with Megan Paine had told her the girl was exceptionally bright. "Maybe you should just register her for classes." Her associate, Brody Paine, hadn't been entirely thrilled with the idea of homeschooling Megan. Presenting the child as his daughter while under his protection was one thing. Trying to keep the girl up on her schoolwork was another. Not even two months of it had made the man more comfortable with the situation.

"My daughter's not ready for that. She is still adjusting to her mother's death."

Sarah's nerves tightened a little. That was the cover, but she wasn't used to Brody using it when it was only the two of them. Which probably meant that Brody wasn't confident the school's line was secure.

The man was notoriously paranoid when it came to things like that.

"I see. You know best, I'm sure." Sarah wasn't so sure Brody was right on the school attendance, but she wasn't going to argue with him. He was a trained agent.

She was just a...go between.

It was a position she'd sort of fallen into.

The only good thing to have come out of her time in

California. When Coleman Black had approached her, she'd been swayed by his passionate explanation of how a person like her was needed by the agency. She'd believed she'd been abandoned by Max and had just lost their child. She'd needed to *count*. To matter to this world in ways that had nothing to do with her family, with anyone else but her.

She and Brody had already discussed the matter at length. Who would expect Megan to be in Weaver, after all? That's what made Sarah's involvement these past years with the agency work so beautifully. Their charges—children who, for one reason or another needed more protection than could be provided through traditional avenues—could be hidden in plain sight. In Megan's case, her parents, Simon and Debra Devereaux—both mid-level politicians—had been brutally killed earlier that year. Hollins-Winword had become involved when other means to protect Megan—the only witness—had continually failed. The sight line of Weaver was pretty much off the radar unless you were a local rancher or worked for CeeVid, her uncle Tristan's gaming software design company.

Nine times now, she'd arranged the houses when Hollins-Winword contacted her.

Another agent—never the same one—came in with their assignment for a while, and then moved on when it was time. She never knew where the children went, only that they'd been found a permanent safe haven.

This time, the agent was Brody Paine. And it was his opinion that ruled, whether she considered him paranoid or not.

The footsteps outside in the hall sounded louder. "I'll pull some more work together for her. Want me to drive it out to you?" The safe house where Brody was staying with Megan was located about fifteen miles out of town. Located midway between nothing and more nothing.

"I'll pick it up sometime tomorrow."

She frowned a little, not liking the alarm that was forming inside her. "Brody—"

"Appreciate your help, Sarah. You're a good teacher." He severed the connection.

She slowly replaced the receiver. When she lifted her gaze to the doorway, though, Max Scalise stood there. The sight so surprised her that she actually gasped.

"Didn't mean to startle you."

Denying she had been would be foolish. She drew her hand back from the telephone and eyed him. "What are you doing here?"

His eyebrows rose a little. He wore the typical uniform of brown jacket and pants, his radio and badge hanging off his heavy belt that could also sport a weapon and a half-dozen other items, but currently didn't.

She realized her gaze had focused on his lean hips though, and looked back at his face.

"You left *me* a message, remember?"

"Barely five minutes ago. I didn't expect you to show up here."

He closed the remaining distance between them and picked up the gleaming porcelain apple that she'd been given by a student at the end of last year. "What'd you want to see me about?"

She hadn't wanted to *see* him at all. "Eli cheated on his math test today."

His gaze sharpened on her face. "Eli doesn't cheat."

She pushed back from her chair and stood. Sitting there while he towered over her desk just put her at too much of a disadvantage. "Well, he did today. And he did yesterday. During the spelling test. He also tried to turn in another student's homework as his own."

A muscle flexed in his jaw, making the angular line even more noticeable. It was only one in the afternoon, yet he already had a blur of a five o'clock shadow. "He doesn't *need* to cheat," he said flatly.

According to her conversation with Eli's last school, that had been the story, too. Eli's grades hadn't been as high as they could be, but they'd been solid. "Maybe not, but that doesn't mean he didn't do it." She pulled out a slightly wrinkled piece of notebook paper and pointed at the corner where pencil marks had clearly been erased and overwritten with Eli's name.

"Any kid could have done that."

She exhaled and reminded herself that Max wasn't the first parent who didn't want to acknowledge some imperfection about their child. "Any kid didn't. Eli did."

He tossed the paper back on the desk. "Look, I know his first day here wasn't the best. But he's promised me that every day since he's been on his best behavior."

"And you believe him, unquestioningly?"

"He's my son."

She pressed her lips together for a moment. How well she knew that. "Yes, and it doesn't change the facts," she finally said, and hated that the words sounded husky. She cleared her throat. "Why don't we three meet together, later. After school. And we can talk about it then."

"I don't have time after school." He replaced the apple on the desk. "Maybe Eli would be better off with a different teacher."

Her fingers curled. "I'm the *only* third grade teacher here."

For the first time, he showed some sign of frustration. He pushed his long fingers through his short hair, leaving the black-brown strands rumpled. "Damn small town," he muttered.

Defensiveness swelled inside her. "You're the one who came back here, Max. Lord only knows why, after all this time." She felt the warmth in her cheeks and knew they probably looked red.

"I came for my mother's sake."

The dam of discretion she ordinarily possessed had sprung a leak, though. "How admirable of you. It's been once in…how long? Twenty years?" The last time he'd been in Weaver, she'd been all of six years old.

His lips tightened. "Twenty-two years, actually."

"Like I said." Her lips twisted. "Admirable."

"I'm not here to argue with you, Sarah. What happened in California between you and me was a long time ago."

Seven years. Four months. A handful of days. "If you think I'm holding the fact that you dumped me against your son, you're *way* off the mark."

"I didn't dump you."

She gave a short, humorless laugh. "That's exactly what you did. But it doesn't matter anymore. I never even think about it." *Liar, liar, pants on fire.*

"Then why the hell are you so angry?"

Her lips parted, but no answer came. She'd gotten over angry a very, very long time ago. But the hurt?

That was a much harder row to hoe. Chock-full of boulders and stone-hard dirt.

"Maybe I just don't understand why my uncle thought you'd be a good choice for deputy," she finally said.

His well-shaped lips thinned. "I am not my father."

"No, he just rustled Double-C cattle. You rustled—" She broke off, her face flushing again.

"Rustled what?" He planted his hands on the desk that stood between them and leaned over it. "You?"

She would have backed up if there hadn't been a wall right behind her. "There's not anything in Weaver that'll hold your interest for long. I think you'll get bored stiff catching the occasional speeder and settling disputes between Norma Cleaver and her neighbor over her dog barking at night, and you'll take off again, leaving my uncle to find yet *another* deputy."

"I think your uncle is capable of deciding whether or not that's a problem for him."

"I just don't like knowing my family is going to be disappointed by you."

He stifled an oath. "Jesus, Sarah. We saw each other for less than a month. Does it occur to you that you might be overreacting?"

Anger wasn't beyond her, after all. It curled low and deep inside her like a hot ember.

Mirroring his position, she pressed her hands against the edge of the desk and leaned forward. Close enough to see the individual lashes tangling around his green-brown eyes. To see that the faint crow's-feet beside those eyes had deepened and that an errant strand of silver threaded through his thick, lustrous hair, right above his left temple. "Dumping me was one thing. Lying to me was another."

"What, exactly, did I lie about?" he asked, his expression suddenly unreadable.

She could hear the roar of kids coming down the hall. Chorus practice was definitely over. "I'm not interested in giving you a list, Max. What would be the point? You know your own lies better than anyone." She pushed the homework page that Eli had swiped at him. "Talk to your *son*," she said evenly, "about his behavior in school. We need to get this straightened out for his sake."

"Eli never had trouble in a class until now."

Meaning this was her fault?

She didn't reply. If she did, she'd lose her temper for certain.

Chrissy Tanner was the first student to round the classroom door, closely followed by several more, and Sarah was heartily glad to see them.

When Eli skidded around the corner, his eyeballs about bulged out of his head at the sight of his father standing there. He gave Sarah a furtive look as he gave his father a "yo" in greeting and headed to his lone table.

Max looked back at Sarah. The radio at his hip was crackling and he reached for it, automatically turning down the volume. "We'll finish this later."

It sounded more like a threat than a promise of parental concern.

And the problem was, Sarah didn't know *what* they were to finish discussing. The problems with Eli, or the past.

Once Max departed though, Sarah enjoyed one benefit from his unexpected appearance in her classroom. Eli didn't do one thing to earn a second glance from her for the remainder of the afternoon. He even offered to help clean up the counters after their science experiment.

She handed him the sponge. "Don't make me regret this," she murmured.

He gave her an angelic smile that she wanted to trust.

And aside from flicking water at Chrissy when she began telling him that he was sponging *all wrong*, he behaved.

In the end, as she was driving out to her aunt Emily's place later that evening, she decided to look on the afternoon as a success.

By the time she arrived at the horse farm that bordered a portion of the Double-C, Sarah was more than ready to put thoughts of both the Scalise men out of her head. And the evening of wedding planning with Leandra would surely provide enough distraction to do just that.

She didn't bother knocking on the door at the Clay Farm house. She'd grown up running in and out of Leandra's house just as comfortably as Lee had run in and out of the big house at the Double-C. The kitchen was empty and she headed through to the soaring great room. There, she hit pay dirt.

Leandra was standing on a chair, long folds of delicate fabric flowing around her legs while her fiancé's mother, Jolie Taggart, crouched around the hem, studying it closely.

"Looks serious," Sarah said.

Leandra shot her a harried look. "I never should have thought it was a good idea to wear a wedding gown. Who am I kidding? I've already done the whole white wedding thing. People are going to think we're ridiculous."

"The only thing people are going to think is that they wish they were as lucky as you, getting married to the person you love."

Leandra had come back to Weaver only a few months ago to shoot a television show featuring their old friend, Evan Taggart, who was the local veterinarian. The show had been a success, but even more successful was the love they'd managed to find along the way.

"And besides, you're not wearing white," Sarah pointed out. "You're wearing yellow."

"Hint of Buttercup," Emily Clay corrected blithely. She sat to one side with Sarah's mother, Jaimie, watching the fitting. "And if you'd wanted to elope with Evan, you've had ample time to do so."

"Well, thanks for the sympathy, Mom." But Leandra was smiling faintly, even though she was dragging her fingers through her short, wispy hair. She turned her gaze on Sarah. "I'm telling you. When you get married, just pick the shortest route between you and the preacher, and forget all this folderol."

"I'd need a date with a man first before I could entertain such lofty notions as marriage." Sarah dropped the box of soft gold bows that she'd picked up in town on the floor beside her mother and aunt. "We just need to attach the flower sprays with hot glue. Glue guns are in the box, too," she told them, then looked back at Leandra. "And you're just stressing because you're trying to do too many things at once. Put together a wedding in about a month's time and take care of all the details for Fresh Horizons."

"Speaking of which—" Leandra jumped on the topic "—I wondered if you'd mind helping me look through the resumes of all the therapists that I've received."

Sarah immediately started to nod, only to stop and eye her cousin suspiciously. "How many are there?"

Leandra lifted her shoulders, looking innocent.

Sarah was reminded of Eli's habit of making that sort of shrug, accompanied by that sort of look. Usually, when she'd pretty much caught him red-handed at something. "That many, huh?"

"Yeah. Nice problem to have, though, right? We figured it would be hard to find a therapist willing to come to Weaver to staff the program. Even though our focus will be the use of hippotherapy—I mean this *is* a horse farm, and we've got the best pick of animals to train for it—there could well be situations when hippotherapy isn't the strategy that the therapist will want to use." Animation lit her cousin's features as she lifted her arms to her side. "Anyway, we've got a *huge* stack of resumes to go through. It's great."

"Keep still, honey," Jolie said around a mouthful of stickpins.

Leandra lowered her arms. "Sorry."

"Good thing your future mother-in-law is better with a needle than I am," Emily observed, grinning. She, like Jaimie, held a margarita glass in her hand.

Jolie carefully placed another pin. "Never fixed a wedding gown that was six inches too long before, though." She looked up at Leandra, smiling. "And stressful or not, my son will fall in love with you all over again when he sees you in this."

Sarah sank down in an oversized leather chair and stretched her legs out in front of her. "The sooner you settle on a therapist, the sooner we can get the brochures out to the schools and agencies in the area. I was at a meeting recently and three other teachers had families that they *know* will be interested in your program." She glanced around and saw no evidence of a child around. "Where's Hannah, anyway?" Hannah was Evan's niece, for whom he had guardianship, and was Leandra's inspiration for realizing that Weaver and the area surrounding it needed more specialized services available for children with developmental and physical disabilities. She'd felt so strongly about it that she'd even given up her hard-won promotion on the television series.

"With Evan. They went to Braden to see her grand-parents for a few hours."

"I'm glad Sharon stopped fighting Evan on Hannah's guardianship." Jolie stuck her unused pins into a red pincushion and sat back to study her efforts with Leandra's hem. "Poor woman has lost her daughter—poor Darian, too—but neither one of them are up to the task of dealing with Hannah's autism."

Sarah was watching Leandra's face. She'd lost a daughter, too, only Emi had been a toddler. Sharon and Darian's daughter, Katy, had been serving in the military and up until recently, they'd been caring for Katy's four-year-old daughter, Hannah. "How's Hannah adjusted to you moving to Evan's place?" She was concerned for the little girl, but she was also concerned for her cousin, who'd blamed herself for the loss of Emi.

Leandra's gaze, when it met Sarah's, told her she understood exactly what Sarah meant. "We're all adjusting just fine." Her lips curved. "And Evan's learning what it's like to be outnumbered by females under his own roof."

"Don't think he's suffering too badly," Jolie observed, looking amused. "You can take off the dress, honey, but watch the pins."

Leandra gingerly stepped off the chair, holding the long folds up and baring the thick red-and-black argyle socks she was wearing.

"Nice fashion touch there."

Leandra rolled her eyes. "Give me a break. This is the first winter I've spent in Wyoming in a long time. It's *cold!*"

The rest of them just laughed.

"Come help me get out of this thing," Leandra bid as she passed Sarah. Jolie had pushed herself off the floor and was helping herself to the pitcher of margaritas that Emily and Jaimie were already sampling. Sarah rose and followed her cousin out of the great room and up the stairs to Leandra's childhood bedroom. Little had changed there since they'd been teenagers. Except the posters of Leandra's favorite rock star were gone.

"So—" Leandra said, the moment they closed the door "—how's it going with Eli? More to the point, how is it going with Max?"

"There's *nothing* going with Max." Sarah began unfastening the long, *long* line of pearl-like buttons stretching from Leandra's nape to below her waist. "I thought these things were just for looks," she said. "You know, to hide a sensible zipper or something that won't take a week to unfasten."

"But you've seen him since Eli's first day at school, right?"

Her cousin knew that she'd run into Max at her folks' place, because Sarah had told her. And her cousin also knew why it mattered, because Leandra was the only one Sarah had ever told about her ill-fated affair with the man. She was the only one who'd known about Sarah's pregnancy.

About the miscarriage that followed.

"He came by the school today," she admitted. "To discuss Eli."

"And?"

"And nothing." She slipped a few more buttons free. "I think you can step out of the dress now."

Her cousin did a little shimmy and pushed the fabric down over her slender hips. Sarah took the dress and held it up while Leandra pulled on a dark brown velvety sweat suit. "This dress is so beautiful," she murmured.

Leandra took the dress and carefully laid it aside

on the foot of the bed. Then she took Sarah's hands in hers. "*Talk* to me."

"There's nothing to talk about. Truly." She squeezed her cousin's fingers, then headed for the door. "Come on. Margaritas and glue guns are waiting."

"You know, you were the one who kept telling me I needed to talk about Emi."

"You did need to talk about her. But there's a world of difference between that and what happened between Max and me."

"You were in love with the man."

Sarah wrapped her fingers around the doorknob. "I *thought* I was," she corrected. "A big difference."

Leandra just looked concerned. She picked up her wedding gown. "Is it?"

"Look, don't worry about me. I'm a big girl. Eli is the only challenge I have where the Scalise family is concerned."

Leandra followed her into the hallway and toward the stairs. Her gown rustled softly as they walked. "Then you won't be bothered at all by knowing that your mom has invited Genna Scalise and Max and Eli over for Thanksgiving dinner next Thursday."

Sarah stopped dead at the head of the stairs. "What? How do you know that?"

"Before you got here, your mom and mine and Jolie were all talking about Thanksgiving dinner. The only place with a large enough dining room to seat *everyone* and still be inside, is at the big house."

"Which has what to do with Max?"

Leandra looked knowing. "Sounding a little perturbed considering his presence isn't bugging the life out of you."

"Leandra—"

Her cousin looked slightly repentant. "Sawyer really likes Max, Sarah."

"I assumed he must or he wouldn't have hired him." She didn't like the increasingly dry feeling in her mouth.

"Did you know that Sawyer is thinking about retiring? He and Dad were talking about it the other day."

For as long as Sarah could remember, her uncle had been sheriff of Weaver. He was as popular as he was effective. "No, but it doesn't seem unreasonable, given how long he's served. But what does that have— Oh, no. *No*." She shook her head. "If Sawyer thinks Max might be a good replacement, he's way off base."

They heard a low, melodious chime and Leandra looked down the staircase. The foyer below was empty, but they could hear peals of female laughter coming from the great room, and footsteps heading toward the front door. "You want to go to Sawyer and tell him just why you feel that way?" She lifted her brows, waiting for a moment. "I didn't think so."

"And since Sawyer thinks he can groom Max to be his replacement, he invited them all for Thanksgiving dinner. Just one big happy—" Sarah's throat tightened "—family."

"That's what it looks like to me." Voices from the foyer floated up to them. "I figured you might want a heads-up." Leandra started down the steps when people came into view, only to stop short. "Evan!" She suddenly turned to Sarah and thrust the gown into her arms. "Bad luck. Bad luck. We don't need any bad luck." Then she hurried down the staircase to hug her fiancé.

Sarah would have laughed at the sudden comedy of the moment if she hadn't also noticed the other man who'd entered behind Evan.

Max.

Dealing with him because of Eli was difficult enough.

So why did he have to keep popping up everywhere *else* she turned, too?

And why, if she'd put him in the past the way she kept telling herself, did that fact bother her quite so much?

Chapter 4

From his position at the base of the wide, curving staircase, Max could see the color drain right out of Sarah's face when she looked down and saw him.

Once again, when it came to Sarah, his timing couldn't have been worse.

She stood there, clutching a hank of buttery colored fabric that streamed down around her legs. Given the other woman's panicked reaction, he supposed it must be a wedding dress. He could remember Jennifer having a similar reaction when E.J. had seen the wedding dress she was to have worn for *their* wedding.

The bad luck that had struck there, though, hadn't been caused at all by Jennifer.

That had been Max's doing.

He looked at the petite blonde who was eyeing him speculatively. She looked vaguely familiar, which meant he'd either known her as a girl, or she was kin to the rest of the Clays. Probably both.

Emily Clay was smiling at him. "Max, you might not remember my daughter, Leandra. Honey, this is Max Scalise." Her brown gaze turned back to him. "We've been talking about you this evening, I'm afraid. So if your ears have been ringing, blame us."

Max stuck out his hand toward Leandra. The favorite cousin. Did she know about his past with Sarah? "Nice to see you again." When he'd left Weaver, he'd been eighteen and she'd have been just as young a girl as Sarah had been. But he remembered Sarah talking about her cousin when they'd known each other in California.

Known.

What a pitiful word to describe those few brief, memorable weeks.

Leandra shook his hand, but it was brief. She didn't return his greeting, though she managed a cordial enough smile.

Oh yeah, he thought silently. Favorite cousin knew chapter and verse just what had occurred between Sarah and him.

"We drove up at the same time," Evan said, breaking the infinitesimal lull that marked Leandra's silence.

The small, dark-haired girl who'd insisted on ringing the doorbell stood half-hiding behind Evan's legs, not looking at Max at all. Hannah, the other man had introduced while they'd been out on the porch.

Cute kid. Definitely shy. Looked a lot like her uncle.

Max had already checked out Evan Taggart, though the sheriff had discounted him as being involved with the trafficking. But Max liked to form his own opinions. The guy did seem like a straight shooter, though. Max even knew about Taggart's recently awarded guardianship of his niece.

"I'm here to see Jefferson." Max focused on Emily.

"Right. He mentioned that you'd phoned." She showed no hesitation in the way her daughter had, but tucked her hand under his arm and drew him farther into the house. "He's downstairs, I think. Took shelter there in the face of too much wedding talk."

Max couldn't help himself.

He glanced up toward Sarah, still standing there like a statue above them all, her reddish hair a gilded crown that flowed down past her shoulders.

When his gaze met hers, though, she turned on her heel and retreated up the two steps she'd managed to descend. A moment later, he heard a door close.

Her walking away from him was becoming a seriously irritating habit.

Emily ushered him down to the basement that really wasn't like any basement that Max had ever experienced. There was no sight of a washer and dryer, no furnace, no jumble of old bicycles and discarded furniture. Instead, there was the crackle of a fire burning in a stone fireplace, oversized leather couches and chairs scattered around it, and a big-screen television that took up a good portion of one wall.

"Max." Jefferson Clay greeted him with a brief nod. Not an unfriendly one, though. Just to the point, the way Max remembered. "Come on in. I've pulled the records you asked me to."

"I know you won't mind, so I'll excuse myself," Emily said. "Margaritas are calling." She sent Max a friendly smile and headed back toward the stairs. "We have plenty to share once you're finished here."

Jefferson's gaze followed his wife's departure for a

moment before he returned his attention to Max. He led the way into another room—clearly an office, though in Max's opinion, the furnishings were a helluva lot nicer than what filled the sheriff's office. Those leaned more toward scarred metal desks and chairs right out of the 60s. Functional was the kindest description there.

The other man lifted a manila folder that contained at least a half-inch of papers off the massive teak desk. "Fortunately, my wife is the accountant in the family," Jefferson said. "Because personally, I hate paperwork. All the trucking records are here. What are you looking for particularly?"

"A common thread." Max took the folder. In the past few days, he'd talked with nearly all of Sawyer's brothers about the investigation.

"Good luck finding it," Jefferson said. "I've been through it all and didn't see anything amiss. But maybe fresh eyes are what's needed."

Max grimaced wryly. "Been a long time since I've considered much of anything about myself to be particularly fresh."

Jefferson's lip quirked. "I hear you there. But I'll still suggest you wait another passel of years before you say that. How's Genna healing up?"

"Too slowly to suit her." He tapped the folder. "Appreciate the hard copies." Max hadn't wanted faxes going in or out of the station house. He wasn't going to do anything to raise questions about what he was doing that he didn't want raised. "I'll make sure you get them back."

"Shred 'em," Jefferson said. "I've got the originals." He leaned back against the desk, crossing one boot over the other at the ankles. He looked casual. Interested. Friendly.

Like most of the Clays had.

Except Sarah.

He hadn't really expected warmth from any of the Clays after what his father had done. He wouldn't have blamed them if they'd wanted nothing to do with Tony Scalise's son. But Sarah—*that* had nothing to do with Tony and everything to do with Max.

"You're settling in again all right here?" Jefferson asked.

The question came out of nowhere. As unexpectedly as Sawyer's insistence that Max and his family join the Clays for Thanksgiving. If it hadn't been for Genna and Eli, Max would have happily declined. But his mother and son deserved *some* sort of Thanksgiving celebration. "Except for freezing my ass off," Max answered smoothly. He wasn't particularly joking.

Jefferson's lips quirked again with faint amusement. But it didn't really extend to his eyes. "Most folks figure coming home is always an easy thing to do."

Another unexpected observation. Only Max knew that in his day, Jefferson had spent a fair period of time away from Weaver, himself. "I'm not 'home' in that sense," Max corrected easily. "This is just an assignment."

The older man eyed Max for a silent moment. Then he nodded. Whether in agreement or acceptance or amusement, Max couldn't tell.

Not that it mattered, anyway.

"Appreciate this." He tapped the folder. "I'll let you get back to enjoying your evening now."

Jefferson didn't argue and they headed back upstairs. Emily spotted them before Max could make for the door, though. "You have to come in and have something to drink."

"Afraid margaritas are not on the menu for me, ma'am. I'm on duty." Not technically, but he didn't figure anyone there would argue the point.

Particularly Sarah, who was sitting on the floor, surrounded by a dozen intricately shaped bows. She had warily tracked him from the moment he entered the room.

"We've got coffee, too," Emily assured. "Come on. I can't send you back out in this temperature without putting something warm inside you. Did you know it's ten degrees colder than it normally is this time of year?"

Despite himself, Max smiled. The woman was hospitality in motion.

From her niece, Sarah, though, he could practically feel the waves of animosity directed toward him.

And since he'd always been an ornery cuss, he changed his mind about leaving. "Feel's more like twenty degrees," he told Emily. "And coffee would be welcome. Thank you."

At his hip, his radio crackled with a call being sent to one of the other deputies on duty. He turned down the volume a little more.

There were plenty of places to sit in the great room. It probably wasn't the smartest thing he'd ever done in his life, but he took the seat closest to where Sarah was sitting on the rug.

Her long jeans-clad legs were folded cross-legged, and she had her head bent over one of the bows and some flowery-looking thing that reminded him a little of the weeds that grew wild in the culverts.

Against the white sweater she wore, her shining hair looked more red than blond. It was nearly as long as it had been seven years ago.

There was no way she could be unaware of him in

the seat barely two feet away from her knee, but she didn't look up at him.

"Here you go, Max." Emily handed him a thick white mug full of steaming brew. "Sugar? Cream?"

"Black's fine, thanks."

She gave him another smile.

His mother had always claimed that the Clay family was fair and generous. Before he'd left Weaver, he'd never allowed himself to acknowledge whether or not that was true.

"Excuse me." Sarah reached past him for the box sitting beside his chair. She still didn't look at him, though, as she withdrew another bow.

Not the smartest thing he'd ever done, he thought again. Something that had always been a problem where Sarah was concerned. "What are you doing?"

Her gaze flicked to the other occupants of the room. Leandra sat with her own collection of bows. Beside her, Hannah was running a toy car up and down her leg. Evan and Jefferson were talking about some horse and the three older women were chattering away a mile a minute, probably running on margarita fuel.

"More to the point—" her voice was low as she looked back at the items in her lap "—what are *you* doing?"

"Drinking coffee." He lifted the mug. "You're probably familiar with the act, despite that." He nodded toward the half-full margarita glass by her side.

"Where's Eli?"

"At home. With his grandmother. That a problem for you?"

The fine line of her jaw flexed slightly. She glanced around again. "Not as long as he's doing his *own* homework." Her voice was dulcet. "And you know good and well I'm not talking about coffee." She picked up the small glue gun beside her and dabbed melted glue on the bow, then stuck the flowery piece in it and set it aside with the growing stack of glued-up bows.

He sat forward, his arms resting on his thighs. This close to her, he could smell the fragrance of that long, beautiful hair.

It used to smell like lemons.

Now, he couldn't put his finger on the scent, but it was soft, womanly and seductive.

Damned heady, too.

He wrapped his fingers around the mug. He kept his voice low. For her ears only. "You hate all your old lovers with this much passion, Sarah?" He had no business wondering how many there might have been. No business caring.

He wondered anyway.

Cared anyway.

She snatched up another bow. "Only the ones who lie as easily as they breathe."

"I didn't lie to you."

She snorted softly and squirted glue out on the bow. Slapped a flower on it, then cursed softly, lifting her finger to her lips to blow on it.

"Did you burn yourself?"

"Seems to be my problem when you're in the vicinity." Her cheeks colored and she focused on her finger, peeling off the strings of glue that clung to it.

"You knew I tried to stay away from you." God, he'd tried. But she'd been the only fresh, unsullied person in his life back then. Everything else had been going to hell, but Sarah had been... Sarah.

He could still remember the day he'd walked into Frowley-Hughes and came face-to-face with a woman who'd made him nearly forget his own name. Then when he'd learned *hers*—that she was one of those little Clay kids from back home, all grown up—he'd hung around to catch her after work. Just to make sure she didn't blow his cover.

And he'd been too damn weak to resist basking in her.

For just a while. Until the responsibilities in his life couldn't be ignored, couldn't be put off any longer.

But after he'd ended it, he'd never forgotten her.

Nor forgiven himself.

She'd gone still. "You should have tried harder," she finally said, her voice nearly inaudible. Then she yanked on the electric cord plugging the glue gun into an outlet behind his chair and rose, gathering up her materials. "Leandra, I've gotta run. I'll take these home and finish them up later."

"But—" Leandra started to rise, but Sarah was already hustling out of the room, a box of bows bumping against her slender hip.

Max watched her go. He set his unfinished coffee on the side table next to her unfinished margarita and quickly bid his own goodbyes. He didn't even care if the rest thought his departure after Sarah's had anything to do with her.

She wasn't twenty-one anymore, after all.

But by the time he made it out to his SUV, Sarah was already gone.

He yanked open the door, cursing under his breath. He tossed the manila folder inside and climbed behind the wheel. Going after her would be *beyond* stupid.

She'd made her feelings more than plain. She had no affection for him lingering inside her. No soft and sweet memories of the time they'd spent together when he'd been a narcotics detective and she'd been a finance intern.

When he'd learned that he could be just as content sitting beside her on a beach towel as he could be burying himself inside her sweet warmth.

She'd been left with something completely opposite. So much so that she couldn't even seem to separate her feelings about Max from Eli.

The gravel crunched beneath his wheels as he headed away from Emily and Jefferson's place. A few snowflakes hit his windshield.

Going after her would be pointless.

Out of habit, he called in his location. He would be the last one called if something came up. The sheriff didn't want Max tied up with dozens of mundane calls when he had higher priorities. But he also had to respond to enough calls to keep up appearances.

At the gate, he turned on the highway heading toward Weaver. He flipped the heater up another notch.

The highway was empty, the pavement stretching out in front of his vehicle in a dark, snaking path, illuminated by nothing except his headlights where snowflakes danced in the beams. There were no city lights. No high-rises. No billboards.

Except for the unexpected sprawl of growth Weaver had experienced, nothing about the place had really changed since Max left it all those years ago.

He saw the small blue sedan before long. Driving well within the speed limit. Obeying all the rules of the road.

She'd always been a little rule-follower.

Conscientious and conservative and cool, despite the red in her hair.

His foot gained some weight and the SUV inexorably began closing the distance between them. He turned on his beacon and pulled up behind the sedan when she slowed and veered off to the side of the road.

Once parked, she didn't wait inside her car, though, the way she should have. She shoved open the door, stepped out onto the soft shoulder and strode toward him, meeting him halfway.

"Are you out of your mind?" She shocked the hell out of him when she pushed her hands against his chest and shoved him. "You nearly scared the life out of me!"

He steadied himself easily enough. "Assaulting an officer, Miz Clay?" He peered into her face, brilliantly illuminated by his strobes.

Oh, yeah. He was a stupid damn fool is what he was.

"Give me a break." She glared at him.

"Have you been drinking, ma'am?"

She crossed her arms tightly over her chest, which only drew his attention to the fact that she hadn't pulled on her coat, but stood there in the light snowfall wearing narrow jeans and that white cable-knit sweater. "You're abusing your authority here, Max. Think that's wise for the future sheriff of Weaver?"

He jerked his head back. "What the hell are you talking about?"

She sniffed. "As if you didn't know. So—" she tossed her arms out dramatically "—am I being stopped for drinking half a margarita, the audacity of suggesting your son cheated today, or am I being stopped for my monumentally bad judgment to have fallen for your line seven years ago?"

"I never gave you a *line*." His voice was tight. "And I'm sorry that you were hurt when I broke it off. You knew it would happen though, because I told you it couldn't last. I told you and you insisted that it didn't matter, that the only thing that mattered was the here and now. And dammit to hell, I *knew* better than to believe you really felt that way. You were hardly more than a kid." Annoyed that he'd stopped her, annoyed that he was there in Wyoming in the first place, annoyed that he still wanted the woman, he turned away from her.

It was either that or kiss her.

He was an idiot, but he wasn't that much of one.

"I wasn't a kid."

"Fine." He looked back at her. "You weren't. You were a legal adult. Yet in comparison to me, you were a babe in the woods. And the hell of it is, if *anyone* fell for someone's line, it was probably me. Because I fooled myself into thinking that you *weren't* going to get burned in the end."

She was still staring at him as if he possessed three heads. "It wasn't a line, you stupid jerk. It was the way I felt. *I* didn't lie to you!"

"Meaning that I did?" Showing none of the control he was ordinarily famous for, he grabbed her shoulders, ignoring the squeaky gasp she made, and hauled her two inches from his nose. "Stop tossing out accusations like that. What exactly did I lie about, Sarah? *What?*"

She was trembling.

From cold or from his appalling behavior, he didn't know.

He only knew that, once again, every action he took when it came to Sarah was the wrong one.

He exhaled roughly. Deliberately set her back on her heels and started to let her go.

"You didn't tell me about Eli. And you didn't tell me that barely two weeks after you *broke it off* with me, you were marrying his *mother.*"

He hadn't fooled himself into believing that Sarah

didn't know he'd been married, but he damn sure didn't expect her to know it had happened right after he'd stopped seeing her. "Dammit, Sarah, my marriage to Jen was—"

"Don't!" Her voice rose. "Just don't. I might have been foolish enough to fall into your bed, Max, but do you honestly think I'd have done that if you'd told me you were engaged to be married? That you were already involved with someone else? That you had a child with her?" Her voice broke over the last and she shrugged out of his hold.

"I saw you, you know. On your wedding day. I stood by a bush and watched you exchange vows with her, while you held your son against your shoulder. There wasn't a single thing seven years ago that you *didn't* lie about, Max. From start, when you pretended to be a client at Frowley-Hughes, to finish."

She knew good and well that he'd been conducting an investigation at Frowley. He'd only told her to keep from blowing his cover. They might not have had much to do with one another in Weaver before he'd left, given their age differences, but she damn sure knew who he was.

His father had been convicted of rustling cattle from her father's ranch, for God's sake.

"I was on an assignment."

"And you were worried I might spill the beans," she snapped back. "You could have just asked me to keep quiet. You didn't have to pretend you—" She caught her hair in one hand, keeping it from blowing across her face. The snowfall was beginning to gain momentum. "Forget it. Just forget it. It's old news anyway. Water under the bridge." She reached for her car door. "Now, *Deputy*, do you mind if I get back in my car and drive away? Or are you going to haul me in on some trumped-up excuse?"

Pretend what? That he'd loved her? "I didn't pretend that I loved you." His voice was quiet, but it still carried to her. "And I wasn't engaged to Jennifer when I was with you. When I was with you, I was *only* with you. I can explain it all."

Her shoulders stiffened. The fingers clutching her thick, wind-tossed hair, tightened. "Save it. I don't even care anymore."

"Is that so? *Now* who is lying?"

She didn't answer. And after a silent moment that stretched on too long, she yanked open her car door and climbed inside.

A moment later, she set the car in gear, and pulled off the shoulder, back onto the empty, snow-dusted highway.

Max brushed a snowflake off his face, watching the red taillights until he could no longer see them. Then he climbed back in the SUV.

He'd known coming back to Weaver would be a mistake.

He just hadn't realized that mistake would include the ones that he'd already made—and continued to make—with Sarah Clay.

Chapter 5

By Saturday morning, the stack of bows in Sarah's living room were finished. She'd also finished tying pretty ribbons around a couple hundred little net packets of birdseed, and had addressed nearly that many place cards with gold calligraphy. She'd even printed up the signs to be used for the upcoming fundraiser boutique at her school that she was in charge of, and made lists of all the merchants she needed to contact for donations.

She'd done all that, taught school and even had time to spring clean her house—even though spring seemed eons away given the snow that had been falling since the evening she'd spent at Clay Farm. She'd done her laundry. She'd done her manicure. Her pedicure. She'd written up her lesson plans from now until the end of the school year.

What she hadn't done was sleep.

Not Thursday night.

Not Friday night.

How could she when every time she closed her eyes, every time she felt herself falling asleep, she couldn't keep her guard up against thoughts of Max?

Now, it was Saturday morning.

Snow was mounded up against her front door and drifts were piled in her driveway. The few cars that had been parked on the street were unrecognizable because of the snow covering the tops of them.

There was not one single thing Sarah could do inside her house to keep herself busy. Not unless she started stripping wallpaper from her kitchen walls.

She recognized that giving Max that much power over her was really beyond pathetic, and she knew it was time to get away from the house. She bundled up in coat and scarf, went out the back door that was fortunately not blocked by a snow drift, and slowly made her way down the street.

It was still early. Only a few people were starting to emerge from their warm cocoons with snow shovels or snowblowers in hand. The sky was an unearthly white-blue, perfectly devoid of clouds. The air, so cold it burned if she inhaled too deeply. Even though it wasn't a far walk to Ruby's Café—just a few miles down to the end of her street and around the corner a ways—she was huffing by the time she made it there.

It was a relief to see a car parked outside on the street. She hadn't entirely been certain the place would be open, given the snow.

Inside, Evan Taggart's little sister, Tabby, was putting coffee in the filter and her smile was rueful as she greeted Sarah. "It may be just you and me here this morning," she said. "Justine's never late, but she is this morning." Justine Leoni was the granddaughter of Ruby Leoni, the café's founder, and now ran the place.

"Half the town is probably blocked in by snow." Sarah unwound the scarf around her head and hung it over the back of one of the stools at the counter. She dragged off her coat and shook out her hair, then slipped onto the stool. "How's school going?"

Tabby was a senior in high school. She was smart and bright and as shiny as a new tack.

She made Sarah—short of sleep and feeling generally stressed out—feel older than the hills.

Tabby was nodding. Smiling. "Good. Glad we have a break for Thanksgiving next week, though."

"Been looking at colleges yet?"

"I want to study abroad. My parents—well, my mom mostly—is having a fit about it."

Sarah could well imagine. "My folks weren't thrilled when I went out to California, either." But they hadn't tried to stop her.

She almost wished that they had.

But it was pointless wishing over the past. She'd learned that a long time ago, when she hadn't even been left with the baby she'd realized too late that she'd desperately wanted.

"It's just because they'll miss you," Sarah told the girl. "They'll get used to the idea. Give them time. And it doesn't hurt to have some alternatives in your mind, as well. You might be the one to change your mind." Goodness knows she certainly had. She still couldn't fathom why she'd ever thought she'd be happy in finance when she was so satisfied now working with children.

"Oh, I know. I've already taken my entrance exams. I have applications in at several universities." The teenager flipped over a mug in front of Sarah. "Coffee will be a few minutes, yet. You want me to toss something on the grill for you?"

The idea of eating wasn't overly appealing. "Just some toast."

"Sure thing. Here." Tabby handed over the small remote control for the minuscule television that sat behind the counter. "If you want some noise. I'll be in the back for a few minutes." She popped some bread into the toaster and went through the swinging double doors that led to the kitchen.

Sarah wasn't opposed to sitting in the quiet café, listening to the sounds of Tabby getting the place ready for the day. But she hit the power button, anyway. The television came on. Morning news from the station in Cheyenne.

Above average snowfall all across the state.

She propped her chin on her hand and closed her eyes, letting the soft drone of the weather report flow over her. When she heard the toaster pop, she went around the counter and plopped the toast on a plate. Found a few pats of butter in the cooler and returned to her stool.

But once she'd buttered the toast, it held little interest. She took a few bites anyway. Going without any real sleep was one thing. Going without food for another meal was going to lead to her passing out.

The sound of the door opening behind her preceded a rush of cold air that invaded the comforting warmth of the diner. She looked over her shoulder and smiled when she saw her uncle. "Sawyer. You're out and about awfully early."

He yanked off his lined gloves as he made his way between the empty tables to the counter. He dropped a kiss on her cheek. "Could say the same about you,

squirt." He took the stool beside her and began working out of his shearling coat. "It's barely daylight yet."

"Toast was calling me." She lifted one of the half-
eaten slices and took another bite. "Is Rebecca still out
of town?"

"Comes back tomorrow." He jerked his chin toward
the swinging doors. "Justine back there?"

"Tabby."

He grunted a little. "Sent the snowplow out Justine's
way. She'll be in soon enough, I 'spect. That coffee
been on long?"

Sarah hid a smile and went around the counter again.
She poured her uncle a mug of coffee, but handed him
a saucer as well. Sure enough, he balanced the nearly
flat saucer with the fingers of one hand and poured the
steaming hot brew into it. She was still blowing on the
coffee in her mug when he'd drunk down half of his,
thanks to the way it cooled rapidly in the saucer.

"How's the new boy in your class doing? Eli?"

If it weren't for Sarah's history with Eli's father, she
wouldn't have thought twice about Sawyer's interest.
The man pretty much knew everything that went on in
town. As a result, she forced herself to respond naturally.

"Settling in." A huge example of misinformation.
Eli wasn't settling in well at all. Nor had he been in
school the previous day. When she'd questioned the
office about his absence, she'd learned only that his
grandmother had called him in. "Hear anything from
Ryan yet?"

Ryan was Sawyer and Rebecca's oldest. He was also
the oldest of all of Sarah's cousins, and for the past few
months, he'd been out of touch with the family.

Since Ryan served in the navy, it was a significant

worry. Whatever assignment he'd been on was classified. They didn't even know what part of the world he was in.

Sawyer shook his graying head. "It's been five months now."

Sarah hid a sigh. She squeezed her uncle's hand. "He'll come home."

"Yeah." He lifted the saucer and refilled it. His expression was grim and she knew that worry about Ryan was taking its toll.

She also knew that he'd think it unnatural for her not to ask about the newest member of *his* department. "What about Max Scalise? He settling in?"

Sawyer merely nodded. Which made Sarah wonder if his response was as truthful as hers had been about Eli.

"You gonna eat that toast, or look at it?" he asked.

She happily slid the plate toward him.

Then Tabby reappeared and Justine walked in with another rush of cold air. "Sarah. Sheriff," she greeted as she headed around the counter. "Thanks for the digging out this morning. Snow was halfway up my house." She poured herself some coffee and pressed open one of the swinging doors. "Breakfast's on me this morning, if you're taking."

"I am. How long before you've got some cinnamon rolls?"

The woman grinned. "Give me twenty."

"Ten," Tabby corrected. "I've already got 'em in the oven."

"Good girl," Sawyer said, feelingly.

"Your new deputy is on his way in, too," Justine said. "He was pulling into the parking lot right behind me. You still wanting hot rolls for the school's boutique, Sarah?"

Sarah had stiffened. "As many as you can bake up," she told Justine. She wasn't up to an encounter with Max just yet, particularly when she hadn't yet recovered from the last one. She dropped a few dollars on the counter for her toast and coffee, then reached for her scarf and flipped it around her neck.

"Leaving already?" Sawyer shot her a curious look.

"You know how it is with a wedding approaching. Maid of honor's work is never done." She gave him a quick hug and headed to the door, pulling on her coat as she went.

Max entered, just as she reached it, and she gave him a brusque nod. "Deputy. Hope Eli is all right." What she really wanted to ask was if he'd kept his son out of class because he really thought she was such a rotten teacher.

"Might be coming down with a cold," he said.

She fumbled with her coat buttons, very aware of their small audience. "If he's out more than a few days, I can send home some schoolwork so he doesn't fall behind." She finally fit the button in place, and flipped her hair out of her collar. "Otherwise, I guess I'll see y'all on Thanksgiving." She reached for the door, but he beat her to it, his hand brushing hers on the crash bar.

"Sarah." His voice was low. "Don't keep walking away from me."

"Have a nice day." She pushed through, anyway. The only reason her eyes were suddenly stinging, she assured herself, was because of the bitter cold.

A few cars were slowly driving down Main Street, where Ruby's was located, and she returned a wave or two as she hustled across the street once they'd passed. When she arrived at her little house across the street from the snowy park a short while later, she wasn't sure if she was surprised or not that Max hadn't followed her.

Not that she'd wanted him to.

Lord, no.

She went in through the back again, because—naturally—the snow blocking the front hadn't magically disappeared. She bypassed the neat piles of completed wedding projects sitting on every available surface in her kitchen, and went into her excruciatingly clean living room.

And then she just stood there, not knowing *what* to do.

Everywhere she turned these days, Max was there. She raked her fingers through her hair and thought about screaming, but that would just prove that she really was losing her mind where Max Scalise was concerned.

She changed into heavier boots and went out to her garage, found her snow shovel, and carried it around to the front. At least attacking the snowdrifts would keep her hands busy. Once she finished that, she'd drive out and check on Brody and Megan. Deliver some more classroom materials for the girl. Maybe some craft projects or something.

She almost smiled at the picture in her head of Brody Paine helping out the eight-year-old girl with the Thanksgiving turkeys that Sarah's class had made out of magazines the prior week. The guy didn't strike her as the artsy type.

She cleared the drift that blocked her front door, scraped the snow off her few porch steps, and was halfway down the front walk when she heard his voice.

"You need a snowblower."

Max had followed, after all.

Seven years ago, she'd have given everything for him to come after her. To turn around and tell her that

he'd changed his mind. That he'd been wrong. That he
didn't have to end things with her.

But that had been seven years ago. Now, she just
wanted him to leave her alone. She dug the shovel's
sharp edge into the snow and hefted another load to
the side where, in the spring and summer, plants would
bloom alongside the walkway in glorious profusion.
"Who says I don't have one?" She kept her eyes on the
snow as she scraped up another shovelful.

"Why use a shovel if you do?" His black boots
crunched on the snow and came into view.

She dumped the snow on his feet. "Sorry," she said
without feeling an ounce apologetic. "You're in my
way."

He shook off the clumps of sticking snow. "You
didn't return my phone call yesterday."

"Was it about Eli?"

She knew it wasn't because his message said only
"Let me explain about Jennifer."

"You know it wasn't."

She gave him a brief, pointed look, and wielded the
shovel once more. "Unless you're here to talk about
Eli, we have *nothing* to say." A few more scrapes and
she'd be able to move on to the driveway. If her arms
and shoulders held out that long when they were already protesting.

"Fine. I talked to him about the tests."

She exhaled. Beneath her layers of flannel and knit
and wool, she was beginning to sweat. "Let me guess.
He told you he didn't cheat."

"Right."

"Shocking." Her tone was arid. She pushed the shovel
along the cement walkway and it scraped loudly as she
cleared away the last several inches of snow.

"He's never lied to me before."

She stomped across the yard toward the driveway. It would take her considerably longer to clear it than the walkway, and the snowblower's appeal was growing. Not that she'd drag it out now, after he'd made a point of mentioning it. She knew that was pretty much cutting off her nose to spite her face, but didn't care.

"You're my son's teacher, Sarah. You have to talk to me."

She tossed the shovel onto the ground where the thick layer of snow cushioned it, and turned to face him, her hands on her hips. "To listen to you, *I'm* your son's problem! You don't want to hear what I have to say when it comes to Eli. You've already made up your mind."

"Sort of like you've already made up your mind about me and what happened between us."

Her lips parted. She was breathless from shoveling, *not* from his presence. "You've got to be kidding me. That's like comparing apples and oranges. For heaven's sake, I'm trying to *help* Eli. And you're just…just sticking your head in the snow!"

He strode across the lawn, leaving fresh footprints alongside hers in the pristine smoothness. "Goddammit, Sarah. I was *not* with Jennifer when I was with you."

She stared at him, wanting to deny the emotion suddenly bubbling over inside her, and being completely unable to do so. "Really." She stomped past him, crossing the yard yet again. "Come with me." She didn't wait to see if he followed as she stormed up the newly cleared steps and porch.

She yanked open the door and went inside, heading straight through to her kitchen. "Look." She pointed at the pile of bows for the ceremony, the favors for the reception. "That's just the stuff I've done in the past few weeks for Leandra's and Evan's wedding. They've been planning it since October, and it's taken most of the family to pull it together in this short amount of time."

Her throat started tightening. "So don't *tell* me that you weren't involved with Jennifer when we were together. I told you. I *saw* the wedding, myself. Events like that don't get pulled together in less than two weeks. I would imagine that you'd had to reserve that particular spot about a year in advance! Am I right? Well?"

His jaw hooked to one side. She couldn't read the expression in his brown-green eyes, but she figured she knew the answer, anyway.

"Of course I'm right." Her voice sounded hoarse. "That wedding probably took six months to plan."

"About nine," he said finally.

She didn't think it would hurt. Not when she was already prepared for the answer; not when she'd reasoned it out for herself all those years ago.

Yet it felt as if she'd been kicked in the stomach.

She reached her hand back for the counter behind her, needing to hold on to something steady. Something concrete.

He yanked off his gloves and shoved them in the pockets of his close-fitted brown coat. "There are things you don't know about it, Sarah. Things I couldn't say. Couldn't tell you."

She just shook her head. "Please, Max. Just go. I can't—I can't keep running into you and going through this. It's over and done."

"But it's not done." He stepped closer. "I wish to God it was."

She took a step back. Bumped into the counter. "Max. Don't."

He drew his dark eyebrows together in a frown.

"Don't what, Sarah? Don't remember? Don't lay awake at night, still to this day, and want you? Or don't worry that your judgment when it comes to my son might be skewed because you hate me that much?"

"I don't *hate* you." She pushed the words out. How much easier it would be if she did.

He took another step toward her. "But you don't trust me."

She couldn't take a breath without inhaling him. The crispy coolness that clung to his coat. The warmth of his breath. "It doesn't matter whether or not I trust you," she managed. "You're just one of my students' parents."

"Liar." His thick enviable lashes dropped and her lips tingled as if his gaze had actually brushed against them. "I'm your first lover, Sarah."

She tossed back her head, pride stiffening her resolve. "So I should be quivering in my boots now? Do you really think that you've been such a...a *monument* in my life, after just those few weeks we were involved? I could have had dozens of lovers since you. Ones that I tossed aside as easily as you did me."

"There was no tossing and it sure in hell wasn't easy." His brooding gaze met hers. "And I don't think there have been dozens."

She made a scoffing sound. "It's hardly any of your business now, is it." It wasn't a question.

His head tilted to one side. "How many?" His voice was soft. Impossibly gentle.

"Go to hell."

"Been there. How many, Sarah?"

"How many lovers have *you* had, Max? How often were you unfaithful to Jennifer?"

"That wasn't what our marriage was about."

She lifted her brows, feeling shocked. "Well, how very modern and sophisticated of you both."

His lips tightened a little. "We married because of Eli."

"Oh, well, that makes it all okay then." Her voice cracked. "Did you tell your wife that you had a girlfriend practically up until the week you were saying your vows to each other?"

"She knew about you."

For some reason, that made the edge of pain cutting inside her even sharper.

"She must have been the forgiving type. Unlike me."

"That's not what I meant."

"Then what *did* you mean, Max? You told her about me after you'd put your ring on her finger? After your honeymoon? After your first anniversary? Or your fifth?" Her eyes burned. "You didn't just go through a wedding, Max. You had a marriage. And until she... she died, you were still together. I wasn't the one who mattered. She was. Your son was. I was just a...blip."

He looked pained and his fingers, when they touched her cheek, weren't steady.

Or maybe that was just because she was shaking. From head to toe.

"You were the one I loved, Sarah." His fingers smoothed down her cheek. Traced her jaw. "That was never a lie."

She had to steel herself not to sink against him. Not to let herself fall into that seductive chasm of believing every word that came out of those perfectly sculpted lips. "Did you regret marrying her?"

"Do you want me to lie now?" He let out a harsh sigh. "I had Elijah to consider. Jennifer was his mother. No. I didn't regret marrying her."

"You loved her."

He let out a sigh. "Eventually. Yeah."

She closed her eyes. Painful or not, at least he had been honest about that. "What do you want from me, Max?"

"I wish to God I knew," he murmured. His finger brushed over her lower lip. Just the slightest of grazing.

She very nearly stopped breathing. She angled her head away, looking up at him again. "I don't get involved with fathers of my students."

"Seven years ago, you told me you didn't get involved with Frowley-Hughes' clients."

"I should have stuck to my conviction."

"Probably." His hand slid back along her jaw, cradling her face.

"And you weren't really a client. I'm not going to get involved with you again."

He lowered his head. His words brushed across her lips like a physical caress. "We're already involved. We have been since the afternoon you talked me into sharing a picnic with you on the beach."

"The picnic was your idea."

"Yeah, so maybe it was." He closed the last few inches between them, covering her mouth with his.

Chapter 6

He tasted of coffee and minty toothpaste.

And Sarah opened her mouth to Max, kissing him back because she couldn't stop herself.

But before she could remember all the reasons why she shouldn't be standing in her kitchen kissing Max Scalise—and they were supposed to be hovering right there in her mind at the ready—he was lifting his head.

She felt like her brain was operating on only half a cylinder when he pulled his radio off his hip and responded.

Naturally. She'd been losing her mind and he'd been perfectly capable of hearing his radio.

She covered her eyes with her hand for a moment. Then brushed her fingers through her hair. Gathering her composure took effort.

"I have to go."

Her lips twisted. "Of course you do. It's what I've

been wanting you to do all along." He wouldn't be leaving just her house, either. Before long, he'd leave Weaver, as well.

She knew it down in her bones.

Max Scalise and the town of Weaver were not destined to grow old together, any more than she had been destined for something other than heartache where he was concerned.

His lips twisted. "Yeah. I noticed that when you were kissing me back."

She felt her face flush. "Look. We're going to have to find a way to be...civil to one another. I don't want my family wondering why—" She broke off and tried again. "They don't know anything about what happened in California. I want to keep it that way."

"Your cousin knows, though. Leandra. Doesn't she?"

She winced. Leandra knew far more than he could possibly realize. "She and Evan will be heading out on their honeymoon in less than a week."

His gaze flicked to the phone that hung on the wall when it suddenly rang. "Early caller."

"That's ironic coming from you, don't you think? Considering you're standing here in my kitchen at this hour?" She snatched up the telephone. "Hello?"

"Meet me. Two hours." The call severed. And though the voice had been abrupt, she still recognized the caller.

Brody Paine.

Aware of Max watching her, she hung up. "Wrong number."

She was lying, Max thought. *Why?*

But he had his own duties to take care of. Ones he wouldn't shirk.

If there was one thing Max knew about, it was taking responsibility for things.

There were only two people in Max's life that he'd failed. And one of them had just lied, for unfathomable reasons, about the phone call she'd just received.

Indulging his curiosity would have to wait, though. "I'll let you know about Eli's schoolwork if he's not feeling better by Monday."

"Fair enough." Her voice was careful.

Because she didn't want to spar with him over his son's supposed cheating? She sidled past him in the small kitchen and walked through the living room where the delicate, feminine furniture looked almost as if it would break should he sit on it.

Not that he was likely to get an invitation from her to do any such thing, particularly after he'd kissed her the way he had.

She waited at the door, going through the motions of showing him out, without uttering another peep. The second he was out on the porch, the door shut behind him with a click. "Here's your hat. What's your hurry?" he murmured under his breath, and headed out to his SUV, parked at the curb.

A few hours later, he had just arrived at the new supermarket on the far side of town to deal with a fender bender when he saw the familiar little blue sedan barrel into the parking lot.

He scratched his name on the report and climbed out of his warm vehicle to deal with the annoyed drivers involved in the minor accident. Sarah's blue sedan was still parked in the lot when he finished, and he hooked his radio on his belt, heading toward the entrance of the store.

Inside, the place was fairly bustling. Clerks were stocking special holiday displays, and Christmas music was coming from the speakers. The store hadn't been there when Max had lived in Weaver. It was one of the additions to come after Tristan Clay started up that video game business of his. CeeVid.

Eli had quite a few of the games in his collection.

As proof of its modernism, there was even a small coffee counter near the entrance of the supermarket. The coffee was hot and strong and he bought himself a tall cup of it as he hung around, watching the shoppers.

He garnered as many curious looks as he did friendly smiles, and his coffee was about a third down when he spotted Sarah entering one of the checkout lines behind a tall brown-haired guy and a thin girl who looked about Eli's age.

Sarah wasn't paying much attention to the man—who was unloading his basket for the clerk. But she was giving the girl plenty of it, seeming to be talking a mile a minute. When the guy had paid for his two plastic bags of purchases, Sarah put down her bag of—Max angled his head, trying to see better—flour. It had sure taken her a while to choose one large bag of flour.

She was giving a friendly wave to the girl, who was following the guy right past Max.

He wasn't sure, at first, what made him take second stock of the man as he took the girl's hand in his and left the store. Maybe it was the way the guy seemed to be cataloging his environment as thoroughly as Max was.

From his position near the sliding glass entrance, Max watched the two cross the parking lot. They got into a late-model short bed, parked two spots down from Sarah's sedan.

"What are you doing here?"

He looked back at Sarah. There was probably something wrong in the way he took perverse pleasure in her annoyance. "Drinking my coffee, ma'am."

Her lips firmed and she sniffed. "Too bad they don't sell donuts at the coffee counter, too."

His lips twitched. "Never been one for donuts. Used to leave that for E.J."

Surprise lifted her eyebrows. "You didn't used to mention your partner so easily."

"His death was seven years ago."

"Yeah." She settled her heavy bag on her other hip. "I remember."

He'd have been surprised if she hadn't, considering how messed up he'd been about it. Aside from the departmental shrink he'd been forced to see, Sarah was the only one with whom he'd been able to voluntarily talk about it.

Admitting to her that his partner had caught a bullet during what should have been a routine follow-up on an investigative lead that Max had uncovered hadn't been easy, though. And he'd never been able to admit to her that he'd felt bound to help the ones E.J. had left behind—Jen and Eli.

He jerked his chin toward the bag. "Find yourself in sudden need of flour, did you?"

Her lashes swept down. "I'm making cookies for Thanksgiving dinner, and then for the holiday boutique my school is having next weekend. It's a fundraiser."

"What kind?"

"The money-raising kind," she drawled. "Want to donate something? We sell Christmas decorations and craft projects and all sorts of things. Sell raffle tickets, even. Just got a donation for a weekend stay in Cheyenne's best hotel."

"What kind of cookies?"

"Why? Are you the cookie police now, too?"

"Just curious. Since I'll be sitting down at the same dinner table as you on Thanksgiving."

"You could have declined the invitation, you know."

"And either have to drive somewhere to pick up a decent meal for that day, or poison my own family with my cooking attempts?" He shook his head, belying just how much he'd wanted to get out of it. "No thanks. My favorite is peanut butter, by the way."

Her lips twisted. "I'll be sure to make oatmeal-raisin, then."

He caught himself from grinning. And when she turned around to acknowledge someone calling her name, he thought he caught her fighting one, as well.

She waved to the two boys and their harried-looking mother, then turned back to Max. "Students of mine from last year. Twins. They were a handful in class. Still can't imagine what they're like at home."

"Double the trouble. Who was the guy in line?"

Again, she looked away. "What guy?"

"The one in front of you. With the little girl."

"Oh. Him. They're new in town."

"How recent?"

She shook her head, shrugging. "I don't know. A few months. He's some sort of freelance writer, I think. Doesn't come into town much."

"The girl go to your school?"

"Megan? Not yet." She shifted the flour sack again. "Her dad—Brody—told me that his wife died this past summer. He says that Megan's not ready for school, so he's homeschooling her. That's how I know him. I've, um, given him some school materials for her."

He drained the rest of his coffee and dropped the cup in the trash bin behind him. "Something going on between the two of you?"

Her cheeks went red. "With who? Brody?"

"Yeah." He reached for the bag. "Twenty pounds of flour seems a lot for cookies."

"I make a lot of cookies and *no*, there's nothing going on between me and Brody Paine. For heaven's sake, I barely know the man." She surrendered the bag to him and sailed out the sliding door.

"There was a time when you barely knew me."

She glared at him. "Consider that to be the foolishness of a twenty-one-year-old." She walked quickly to her car, flipping the collar of her coat up around her neck.

She was tall, but he was a good half-foot taller and he kept up with her easily. "You never did answer me before, Sarah."

She yanked open her unlocked car door, making him think in the back of his mind that she needed a lecture about vehicle safety. She didn't pretend not to understand what he was referring to. "I told you that my love life was none of your business." She grabbed the flour from him and heaved it inside her car. A small puff of white powder shot out of the bag. She muttered an oath and slid behind the wheel, swiping her hand over the passenger seat.

He stepped in the way of the door, preventing her from closing it on him and he leaned down. "Are you involved with someone now?"

She fumbled with her keys, trying to fit one into the ignition. "What if I am? Will that give you reason enough to leave me alone?"

"The only thing that would do that would be a wedding ring on your finger, and I don't happen to see one." With every passing hour, he seemed to be increasingly glad for that fact.

She finally succeeded with the key, and cranked the engine over. "Move away, then, so I can go buy myself one."

The corner of his lips lifted.

She let out an exasperated sigh and rolled her eyes. "Go bug someone else, Deputy. I have things to do."

"Cookies to bake. Peanut butter."

She put the car into gear and he hastily stepped away from the door. But he still saw the triumphant grin she gave when she pulled the door shut and finished backing out of the parking spot.

A moment later, she was buzzing down the row of cars and turning out onto the highway.

He strode to his unit and climbed behind the wheel. Then he pulled out his cell phone and dialed the sheriff's personal line. "Brody Paine," he said, when Sawyer answered. "I need to know everything there is to know about him."

"Been staying at the old Holley place for a few months. Got a girl he homeschools. Lost his wife recently."

Max added his own comments to the sheriff's. "Where'd he come from? We need the whole story." He described the vehicle he'd seen them use.

"On it." The sheriff hung up.

Max sat there, drumming his fingers on the steering wheel as he watched the comings and goings in the parking lot. The idea that he might one day be investigating drug trafficking in Weaver, of all places, would never have occurred to him even ten years ago.

Now, he knew differently.

Across the United States, small towns were falling prey at an alarming rate. Weaver was merely the latest where he'd been sent. And given his history with the town, he'd been awarded the assignment of uncovering the means that were being used. He hadn't stopped fighting the assignment, though, until his mother ended up in a cast from hip to toe. Send another agent, he'd said, until then. Only there hadn't been another agent available—not in the task force that was already stretched too thin.

His cell phone buzzed. "Scalise."

"Looks like he's off the grid," Sawyer said. "No registrations, no banking, nothing. How'd he cross your path?"

"He didn't." Not yet, anyway. But if there was one thing Max knew, it was that Brody Paine was either on one side of the law, or the other. And no matter what Sarah claimed, there was *something* going on between them.

On Monday, Eli Scalise was back in class.

With a vengeance.

It didn't seem to matter what tack Sarah took with the boy; he was bound and determined to cause mischief.

Oh, he was good at it. She never caught him flagrantly in the act. She didn't actually *see* him smear glue on Chrissy's desk chair. She didn't actually *see* him exchange the lunch meat in Jonathan's sandwich with rubber erasers. She didn't actually *see* him do anything. But by the afternoon recess, her students were practically at each other's throats.

Finally, knowing she was being chicken in not contacting Max, during the kids' chorus practice, she called Eli's grandmother, Genna, and told her the problem.

Genna was shocked. "Max hasn't said a word to me."

Sarah didn't consider that much of a surprise. But she didn't exactly want to get into the reasons why Max thought her judgment was off the mark where Eli was concerned.

"Has he had trouble adjusting to his mother's death?" It wasn't something that had really occurred to her until Brody's panicked call that weekend. Megan, whose real parents had been killed recently, had been giving him fits, yet when she'd met them at their agreed-upon place—the supermarket through which everyone in town eventually passed—she'd seemed perfectly fine and typically quiet to Sarah.

"He did, at first," Genna said. "Jennifer's cancer was so sudden. But Max had him in counseling. I don't think Eli handled the loss in any unusual way, or that he put off grieving his mother. It was over a year ago now."

Sarah sighed. Maybe it *was* something about her that Eli was taking exception to. "Maybe if I talk to Eli outside of the classroom, I might make some headway. I'll call Max and ask if I can bring Eli home today."

"No need to call Max. He's expecting Eli to come straight to the house after school today. I'll let him know. Perhaps I should talk to Eli."

"Then he'll think I've ratted him out to his grandmother."

Genna made a soft sound. "Well, you have, dear. You do what you need to do, though, Sarah. You have excellent judgment when it comes to your students."

The vote of confidence was more than Sarah had expected. "Thanks, Genna."

"Any time. Let me know how things progress, won't you? Max can be somewhat…closemouthed."

Sarah could well imagine that. "I will. And thanks, again." She hung up.

So, she'd have a short while with Eli outside of the school environment.

What was she going to do with the time?

She wasn't any closer to the answer by the end of the day, when the final bell rang.

"Eli, I'd like you to wait, please."

He shot her a wary look, his backpack halfway to his shoulders. "My grandma's expecting me."

"I know she is. I've spoken with her already."

His lips pursed. He dropped the backpack into the cubby attached to his table and flopped down on his seat. His gaze followed the other children who were making their typical mad dash home for the day.

Sarah waited until the classroom was empty and utterly silent. She didn't look at Eli. She just picked up the erasers that Jonathan had pulled out of his sandwich, and walked over to Eli's desk where she set the items. Sadly, for poor Jonathan's sake, one of the erasers had teeth marks in it.

"I believe these are yours."

He wrinkled his nose, picking up the eraser with the bite taken out of it. "Gross."

"I think so." She returned to her desk and began packing up her book bag. "Fasten your coat. We're going."

"Where?" His tone was suspicious.

As well it might be, given his behavior. "Home."

"You're not keeping me after school?"

"I'm going to walk you home."

His jaw dropped a full inch. "But why?"

"Take a guess," she said dryly.

He groaned a little. He zipped up his parka, though, and shouldered his backpack. "I didn't mean to hurt anyone," he said.

She pulled on her coat, but tossed her scarf into her book bag. Since the snowstorm that had hit, the weather had climbed back up to a more tolerable and usual temperature.

Eli shuffled along beside her as they left the school building. "Don't you got a car?" he asked when she didn't turn toward the parking lot.

"Have a car," she corrected. "And yes, I do. Though I don't need it for coming to school." She pointed across the school yard. "I live over there. Across the street from the park. Students aren't the only ones who walk to school."

"Weird." He squinted, as if the idea had never before occurred to him. And coming from southern California where everyone seemed to drive a car even if it was only for a block, she supposed it might not have.

Slipping the strap of her bag over her shoulder, she pushed her bare hands into the pockets of her coat. "Do you like Thanksgiving time?"

He shrugged. "S'okay."

"It's my favorite holiday."

"More than Christmas?" He kicked his shoe against a mound of snow, scattering it.

"Yup."

"But all you do is sit around and eat and watch football."

"Yes. I can see how it would seem that way." She pointed. "Let's sit on the swings for a sec."

"You're a teacher. Swings are for the kids."

"Well, as it happens, I've been using those swings since I was younger than you." Her voice was droll. "So I reserve the right to still use them when I feel the urge."

He shook his head as if he found her increasingly odd.

She dropped her book bag on a patch of gravel where the snow had melted away, then slipped onto one of the swings. The cold, metal chains screeched at the movement.

She managed not to wince.

Eli, however, found the sound fascinating, for he took possession of the swing next to her and made a point of swinging back and forth, causing a similar noise.

"So, I suppose you know what I want to talk with you about."

He didn't stop swinging. "I guess."

"Eli, I want to help you. I really do. I don't want to see you expelled from school. My goodness, you've only just arrived here."

He didn't reply and she hid a sigh. "You know, your dad thinks that I'm the problem. And if he's right, I'd *like* to make things better." She tipped her toe against the snowy ground, pushing the swing back several inches. The cold chains groaned again.

"That's 'cause you gotta. It's your job."

"Actually—" she lifted her toe and let the swing glide forward "—if I were sticking to the rules of my job, you'd have already been at least suspended."

"Then how come I'm not?"

She dug in her toe again. Pushed back until her toe barely reached the ground. Swayed forward once more. "I don't know. I guess I kind of like you."

"Better 'n the other kids?"

"I like all of my students," she assured him diplomatically. "What was your mom like?"

At that, he shot her a surprised look. "Why?"

"I'm curious."

"*Why*?"

"Because you're my student and I'm interested." *Because your father was married to her.* But she couldn't say that, could she? And she was having enough trouble trying to get to the bottom of Eli's issues without her own emotions being added into the mix.

He let out a sigh much too large for a boy of his size and despite herself, her heart squeezed.

"She smelled good," he said finally. "Like…like summer days."

She let her swing go still.

"Grandma Helene doesn't smell like Mom did," he went on.

Jennifer's mother, Sarah deduced. "Do you see a lot of your grandma Helene?"

"I guess. I spent the nights there when Dad had to work. My grandma here's cool, though. She cooks. Even with her broken leg and all. Grandma 'Lene just orders takeout. Not that there's something wrong with take-out. Mom ordered it a lot, too. You know. 'Cause my dad worked a lot. Before we came here, he usually had to travel a lot of different places."

Sarah moistened her lips. "I imagine you must miss your mother a lot."

His lashes lowered, avoiding her gaze. He pushed the swing a little higher.

"Eli, if I ask you a question, will you be honest answering me?"

His knees bent as the swing sailed backward. "What?"

She watched him swing forward again, and stood from her own swing. When his swing pelted backward, she stepped in the path, and caught the chains when he plowed forward, stopping him midair.

"Cool," he breathed.

She held him there until his eyes met hers. Not necessarily an easy task, because the wiry boy was heavier than she'd have thought. "Do you dislike me for some reason?"

A shadow came and went in his blue eyes. "No." His voice was low.

She believed him.

But not until that moment had she let herself acknowledge how concerned she'd been that his actions *were* about her.

She let out a soft sigh. "Okay." She stepped out of the way, and the swing dipped forward, finishing its arc.

"How come you haven't turned me in to the principal?" His voice was barely audible as he dug his feet into the ground, trying to pick up speed once more.

She eyed him. He straightened his legs as the swing went forward, and put his entire body into it as he swung backward. "Would you have preferred it if I had?"

"Least my dad couldn't ignore that." He suddenly let loose of the chains and sailed out of the swing, jumping to the ground. He landed on his feet, but barely.

"Eli!" She ran over to him, grabbing his shoulders. "Are you trying to give me a heart attack, too?" She crouched beside him, balanced on her heels. "Did you hurt yourself?"

He just shook his head. "I'm fine. All I did was jump."

She looked up to the clear sky. All he'd done was jump, same as she used to do when she'd been a kid, same as she'd seen dozens of other children do. Somehow, it had never made her heart simply stop before, though. "Right. So what do you mean about your dad?"

The faint breeze plucked at the fine blond strands of his hair. "When my mom was around, he used to yell when I got into trouble." He chewed at his lip. "She said it's 'cause he loved me."

"And now?"

He lifted his shoulder. "And now he doesn't care."

"Oh, Eli." She managed not to hug him, though she suddenly wanted to. Badly. "Of course your dad cares."

"He only dragged me here with him 'cause he had to."

"I'm sure he has you with him because he wants you with him."

The boy rolled his eyes. But she caught the glisten in them and knew the uncaring act was completely and totally feigned. "He *is* only here for a while," Eli admitted. "We're going back home when Grandma's leg is better. He said so."

The revelation shouldn't have been a shock for Sarah, yet it still settled inside her, dark and unpalatable.

"What the *hell* do you think you're doing?"

She jerked and very nearly fell off her heels as the harsh question accosted them.

Max was striding toward them. She could see his SUV parked on the street.

She gave Eli's shoulder a slight squeeze, and pushed herself to her feet. "Max."

He barely spared Eli a glance. "Get in the truck, Eli." He waited until his son was well on his way toward the vehicle before he spoke again. "Care to explain yourself, Sarah?" His voice was tight. Abrupt.

And his eyes were like shards of green glass.

Anger, she hadn't expected. "Eli and I were talking."

"Ever think that you should have consulted his father before you took off with him?"

Her lips parted. She made a point of looking around the wide open grounds of the park. "I hardly consider this *taking off*."

"When you don't have my permission, I don't care

if you were just stepping off the parking lot curb at the school."

She winced. "Max, come on. This isn't the big bad city here."

He snorted. "And you think that makes it all right?"

She could have argued. Could have told him that she'd cleared it with his mother—who had his authority yet, to answer for Eli when it came to school matters—but she could see the boy's face from where she was standing.

He'd stopped midway to the SUV and was watching them, worry written in every line.

"No," she said quietly. "You're right, Max. I should have spoken with you first. My apologies."

His eyes narrowed, as if he didn't quite know how to take her abrupt agreement.

She walked over to the swings and picked up her book bag.

When she looked at him once again, this time it was Max who was walking away from her.

Chapter 7

When her doorbell rang later that night, Sarah considered not answering.

But if she didn't, word would get around town quickly enough that she hadn't been under her own roof to answer her door at eleven o'clock at night.

Knowing Weaver's grapevine, she'd soon be battling rumors of a wild, probably lascivious, nightlife.

So she didn't ignore the bell.

She went to the front door and peeked behind the curtained window beside it.

She didn't need the circle of light from the porch light to recognize Max standing on her doorstep.

"Go away, Max." She also didn't need the rumor mill gearing up over the presence of Max Scalise at her house at this hour, either.

Nor was she over the sting of his accusations where Eli was concerned.

"Come on, Sarah. Open up."

"Why?"

She saw him tilt his head back. He exhaled into the cold air, creating a cloud around his head. "Because it's bloody freezing out here."

"Doesn't sound like a good enough reason to me."

He focused on the window where she stood. "So I can eat some crow, all right?"

She pressed her lips together, and pulled open the door.

A draft of cold air slid inside, making her shiver.

He stepped in, his gaze traveling first over her pink flannel robe, then to the chain lock that she very clearly hadn't needed to unfasten. "Start locking your doors," he said flatly. "This one *and* your car."

The day she needed to lock her doors in Weaver was the day something precious would be lost. She closed the door and pressed her back against it, crossing her arms over the chest of her thick robe. "I don't see you spitting out any feathers, Max."

He pulled off his coat, and when she didn't offer to take it, tossed it over the back of her wing chair. Beneath the coat, he wore an aging gray sweatshirt with LAPD printed on the front of it.

Hardly regulation for Weaver, but then the boss man wasn't exactly known for wearing a uniform, either. In fact, Sawyer rarely wore one.

"I overreacted," he said abruptly. "I'm sorry."

The thing was, she wasn't hugely upset that he'd overreacted. Stung, yes. More importantly, though, she was concerned with *why* he'd been so upset. "You were worried about Eli. And you didn't know he was with me," she surmised, watching him closely. "Did you?"

He ran his fingers through his hair, leaving it in short, disheveled black waves. "No."

"Why were you looking for him, anyway? Your mother said you expected him to head straight for the house after school, rather than the station. You were on duty, weren't you?"

"I wanted to tell him I was gonna sign him up for horseback riding lessons."

She raised her eyebrows. "And that necessitated a special trip to school?"

"He's been bugging me about it since we came to town. We got into it this morning before I dropped him off at school. I left knowing he was upset and I didn't want to wait any longer."

She steeled herself against softening too easily. "As I recall, you don't much care for horses."

He made a noise. "They don't much care for me, is more to the point."

"Then I'll take Eli out riding. Thanksgiving. After dinner. We have plenty of horses at the *C*. You needn't go out and pay for lessons for Eli." She had an idea of what he earned as a deputy sheriff. It wasn't paltry, but paying for something when he didn't have to seemed silly to her. She was a teacher and supported herself. She couldn't pay for too many unnecessary things, either.

"We'll see."

She might not be a parent herself, but she certainly knew what *that* usually meant. *No.*

She decided to let the matter rest. Thanksgiving Day would be there, soon enough, anyway. It would be a simple matter to include a little riding.

"Why would you think someone would take off with your son? Weaver hasn't changed that much since I was a kid. Since *you* were a kid. It's larger, true, but we're still just a small Wyoming town. Everyone watches out for everyone else. Or have you really forgotten that?"

"You haven't seen the kind of crap that happens to people that I have. Whether you recognize it or not, Weaver is not the same town that it used to be," he said evenly. "And I haven't forgotten *anything* about this place."

Which left her wondering what else he *wasn't* telling her.

"I suppose you spoke with your mother."

His lips twisted. "I believe the proper description would be that *she* spoke to me."

"Mmm."

He shook his head and looked at the chintz couch, as if he wanted to sit on it, but was half-afraid to. "She called me Massimo," he muttered. "Believe me. That is *never* a good thing."

She unfolded her arms. Okay. He'd come and apologized for taking a strip off her hide when he'd been worried about the whereabouts of Eli. She should tell him to go.

"You want something to drink?" She nearly slapped her hand over her mouth, but the invitation was already out there.

He angled a look her way. Slightly less surprised than she, herself, felt. "What are you offering?"

Evidently, her head on a platter. "Coffee. Hot chocolate." Her voice was abrupt. She'd never known him to drink tea, but then she hadn't known him for all that long.

Just long enough to color everything she'd done in her life ever since.

She pushed her hands in her pockets, crossing her fingers that he'd decline.

"Coffee'd be good."

So much for childish superstitions. She pulled her hands free. "If I didn't come from a family of avid coffee drinkers, I'd be shocked at wanting some at this hour." She pushed away from the door, excruciatingly aware of her state of undress in the face of his softly faded jeans and sweatshirt.

"Sit. The couch won't fall apart," she assured. "It's covered with chintz, not made of it."

She went into the kitchen, not waiting to see if he sat, or not. She deftly filled the coffeemaker and flipped it on, then stood there staring at the liquid that immediately began dripping into the glass carafe and debated whether or not she should change into some clothes.

If she did, he'd undoubtedly think she'd done so because of him.

Which was true.

She let out a breath, and pulled the sash of her robe tighter around her waist. She was already covered from her neck to her toes, and *those* were covered with fuzzy socks.

It doesn't matter what you're wearing. The voice inside her head was stern. *He's only here because of Eli.*

She fiddled with her sash again. Tapped her fingers against the counter, and willed the carafe to fill more quickly.

"Didn't your aunt once live in this house?"

She whirled. The hem of her robe flew out, baring her knee and she yanked the pink fabric closed. "What?"

His gaze slowly lifted to her face, which felt on fire by the time he reached it. "Your aunt lived here, didn't she?"

"Um, yes. Hope, back before she married my uncle

Tristan. He's the one that, um, keeps me supplied in those." She waved her hand absently at the cutting-edge computer sitting on the small secretary desk opposite the stove. Her uncle actually kept the school supplied with computer equipment. The advantages of knowing a man who'd earned a fortune in the business. "And then Belle lived here for a while before she married Cage Buchanan. The place was occasionally rented out to someone outside the family, but not very often."

"Hope. I remember her. Ruby Leoni was her grand-mother."

"Great-grandmother, actually. Justine is Hope's mother, not her sister." Evidently, in their day, that revelation had been a bit of a shock.

The coffeepot gave a reassuring gurgle that she recognized as the end of its work, and she grabbed a mug, filled it, and thrust it at him. "There you go."

"Aren't you having any?"

She moistened her lips. Shook her head. It was all she could do not to grab her robe even more tightly around herself. But she figured she already looked uptight enough.

His long fingers curled around the white mug as he studied the liquid. The light overhead picked out the silver strand over his left temple. "What made you turn to teaching?"

She swallowed. That was territory she didn't want to discuss. Not when it was all tangled up with their history. "I missed my family too much. *And* Weaver," she said, which was a good portion of the truth, though not all of it. "Besides which, there's not much call for investment advisors here. For teachers, though?" She managed a faint smile. "Big need for teachers."

Standing there in her minuscule kitchen where he

seemed to occupy more than his fair share of the space was making her a little crazy. She slipped past him and headed back into the living room, and took the only single seat there—the wing chair.

He could have the couch all to himself.

Only he didn't head to the couch. He carried his mug in one long-fingered hand as he stopped in the short hallway and studied the framed family pictures that hung on the wall. "Whenever I thought about you, I pictured you living in some glass high-rise, married to another stock jockey."

Her mouth went dry and she wished that she hadn't been so quick to decide against the coffee. She'd convinced herself that he'd *never* thought about her. Not once.

"Are you, um, really happy being a deputy sheriff?"

"I'm here, aren't I?" He lifted the mug to his mouth again.

She recognized well enough that he hadn't actually answered her question. He probably had his reasons for hiding the temporary status Eli had told her about, even if she didn't agree with them.

Max continued looking at the pictures, eventually pointing to one. "Who's the little kid with Leandra?"

"That was her daughter, Emi. Emily, actually, but we all called her Emi."

"Called?"

"She died several years ago."

He blew out a breath. "Must've been hell."

"Yes." He'd had his share of losses, so he'd certainly know.

"And now she's marrying Taggart. He's raising that niece of his?"

"Why do I feel like you already know that he is?"

"You know Weaver. Full of gossip."

"Yes, and the next round tomorrow morning will probably be about why your unit is parked in front of my house at this hour of the night."

He finally turned away from the photographs. "Maybe we should give them something to really talk about."

She stilled.

He smiled faintly, though his eyes were dark and inscrutable. "I'm kidding."

"Ha ha."

His lips twisted and a small dimple briefly showed itself in his lean, shadowy cheek.

She deliberately looked away.

"Other gossip around here says you don't go out much."

"Who told you that?"

He grinned slightly. "Tommy Potter, actually. For a deputy, the guy gossips more than any female I've ever known. So?" He finally sat down on the small couch. The feminine fabric contrasted sharply with his masculinity.

"You know how gossip works. Sometimes accurate. Sometimes not." *Why* had she invited him in for coffee? She flicked the long edge of her robe back over her knee which it kept wanting to reveal. A glance at him told her he was perfectly aware of that fact, too. "Gossip about *you* says that you had to come back here because you couldn't find a job anywhere else." Her voice was tart.

"Like you said. Sometimes accurate. Sometimes not."

Frustration nipped at her. "You rarely answer a question straight out, do you?"

Unlike her, he wasn't frustrated, but amused. His lips twitched. "You didn't *ask* a question."

"It was implied."

He smiled. His teeth were straight. White.

And it dawned on her that she hadn't seen him smile, truly smile, since he'd returned to Weaver.

She pulled in a breath that felt a little too shaky. It wasn't fair, the effect the man had. It gave him far too much of an advantage. "Eli." Focus on Eli.

"What about him?"

She flushed. She needed to remember to guard her tongue better. "He...what else is he interested in? Besides horses, I mean."

"Video games, sports and generally making his old man crazy. Once that boy gets an idea between his teeth, he's a dog with a bone."

She pressed her hands together, sitting forward. "Yeah. About that. He, um, well, you know, when he and I were in the park, we were talking and—" She broke off and stood. There was too much nervous energy flowing in her veins to stay still.

"And what?"

She pushed her hands in the side pockets of her robe, only to pull them out again. "Can you believe me when I tell you that I'm... I'm not taking out the past on your son? Eli is so bright. He's imaginative. Creative. He's everything I—" *wanted* "—I like to see in a child. But he *has* been cheating and acting up in class. Badly. And I understand that's out of character for him, so it's hard for you to believe, but—"

"He told me."

She blinked, off balanced by the admission. "He did?" She brushed her hair away from her cheek. "Did he say *why*?"

"He doesn't have to. He's pissed that I moved him here." He sat forward, settling his mug on the coffee table. "So, that's my fault, too."

She closed her eyes for a moment, then moved around the oval edge of the coffee table and sat on the couch, angling toward him. "He's got it in his head that you don't love him, Max."

"No way," he immediately dismissed the idea. "Most everything I've done in this life has been for Eli."

And she'd nursed a broken heart because of it, knowing that Max had chosen Jennifer and their son over her. That the morning after they'd made love for the last time, he'd simply disappeared from her life.

She'd had to track him down, only to learn from a talkative member of his department that he had a son and a fiancée in the wings.

"*You* know that," she said huskily. "Eli, however, has lost sight of it."

His eyes, those changeable eyes of his, focused harder on her face and it felt as if he were looking right through her, seeing directly through all the walls she'd so carefully built against him. "He told you this? Today. In the park. That's what you were doing. Asking my son if he thought I loved him."

"No, I did not ask him that," she said evenly. "I was *trying* to get to the bottom of his behavior in my class. He figures that since you didn't get after him for any of it, that you no longer care about him."

"Where the hell did he get that idea?"

She lifted her palms. "That'll be for you to work out with him. I just thought you should know where his head is at." She dragged her robe back over her knee and pushed off the couch, restlessly moving away from it. "Look, it's late. And you're probably on duty early in the morning and I've got a meeting before school starts, so—"

"Eli isn't mine."

She hadn't heard right. That's what she got for going short of sleep for too many nights. "I beg your pardon?"

He unfolded himself from the couch, too, facing her. His jaw was tight. "I'm not Eli's biological father."

Her lips moved, but no words came. Nothing. Her head had simply gone blank. And her legs felt curiously rubbery. She moved, and when her knee knocked into the wing chair, she sat down on it. "I...see," she finally said. Her tongue felt thick.

"I doubt it." Now he looked the restless one as his long legs ate up the cozy confines of her living room. "He's E.J.'s."

She pressed her fingers against her lips, focusing hard on the two botanical prints framed on the wall above the couch.

"Sarah—"

She dropped her hand, shaking her head sharply. "Why are you telling me this now?" Now, when it didn't matter? Now, when she'd finally put everything—*everything*—behind her?

"I just wanted you to know." He shoved his hand through his hair again. "So that you would at least understand *that*."

But she didn't understand. And the more he told her, the more unclear everything became. "When did you find out?" she asked slowly.

"I knew from the start. Jennifer and I weren't—she was E.J.'s girl."

"You never mentioned her to me back then. Not when you told me about your partner. About his death."

"I know." His gaze was dark. Shadowed. "I should have."

She winced. "So, you *did* have plans to marry her when we...when you and I..." She couldn't make herself finish.

"I knew what I had to do. Yeah. I hadn't convinced Jennifer of it yet, though." He paused. "That came later. After you."

There was a burning deep behind her eyes. "And the fancy wedding on the beach?"

"Was supposed to have been for her and E.J. She hadn't cancelled all of the arrangements, and it was a pretty easy matter to just use them. Not because she wanted to, but her mother, Helene, was pretty gung ho about her daughter being properly married. Didn't matter so much to Helene *who* the groom was, as long as there was one." His restless pacing ceased for a moment. "I never slept with her."

"Ever?"

He hesitated, looking even more grim. "Yeah, well, later. After we'd been married a while. We were friends, Jen and me. We both lost E.J., though she never blamed me for it. Never understood that it was my lead he was following. If anyone should have been shot, it was me. But she never understood that. In the end, we had a marriage that we both wanted to make work."

"You loved her." She'd figured she'd had a masochistic streak since she'd stood hiding in a bush to watch him wed another woman even after he'd already broken it off with her.

Now she knew the streak had never really gone away.

"Yes. But not at first. Not like that."

Her throat felt like a vise was clamping it shut. She didn't have to ask if he'd grieved her death when she could see it written on his face. "Then why did you *marry* her?"

"I told you. Because of Eli. If it weren't for me, his real dad wouldn't have died, okay? I was E.J.'s partner; I should have had his back."

"Instead, you just had his girlfriend."

He grimaced. "Dammit, Sarah, I told you. It wasn't like that." He scrubbed his hand down his face. "When E.J. was killed, he and Jen already had the wedding planned. That was practically a miracle in itself because they'd had their problems. But they'd worked them out. And they'd put off the wedding as long as they had because Eli was in and out of the hospital back then. He was premature."

He reached the doorway to the kitchen. Turned around and prowled back. "Then, when E.J. was shot, Jen was devastated. She sort of lost it for a while. She was a hairdresser and her insurance benefits were minimal at best; they'd already been pretty much used up with Eli's expenses to that point. Her mom helped where she could, but she had her limits, too.

"E.J. sure in hell hadn't expected to die." His voice roughened. "He hadn't changed his life insurance over to Jen from his ex-wife's name and when he was gone, Jen and Eli were out in the cold. She couldn't even get survivor's support for Eli, because when he was born, she and E.J. were fighting so she didn't put his name on the birth certificate."

"But Eli *was* his son, despite what the piece of paper said. Surely there was some means of—"

"The only means were me," he said flatly. "Believe me. I looked into every other alternative. I'd already been on the force for a while by then. My insurance benefits were completely available, but only to members of my own family. So, I talked Jen into marrying me. After a year or so, I adopted Eli legally as well."

She blinked. A tear slid past her lashes and burned down her cheek. "Why didn't you tell me all of this then?"

"It wouldn't have changed anything. They were the decisions I had to make."

"Then why...why me? Why get involved with me at all? There was nothing forcing your hand there, Max." And she hated it that she was still looking for something deeper, some reassurance that she hadn't imagined the connection they'd had, something that would tell her that she hadn't been an utter and complete fool.

His pacing brought him closer. "I didn't say they were easy decisions. And you—you were the one thing in my life during that month that *wasn't* all messed up. I wasn't the reason you didn't have the man you loved, I wasn't the reason your baby had no father."

She trembled, feeling a sudden wave of nausea.

"It was selfish of me and I knew it at the time, which was why I told you that first day on the beach that there was no place for us to go. No future."

She'd invited him to that beach picnic. Had wheedled an agreement out of him, because even her virginal twenty-one-year-old self had recognized the look in his eyes when he'd looked at her. He'd confided that he was working a case, and she'd made sure she was there every time he had an appointment with his supposed financial advisor. She'd chased after him until she'd caught him. And when he'd talked about there being no future, she'd confidently assured him that she didn't *care* about the future.

She'd believed his reticence where she was concerned had only been because of what his father had once done to her family.

All she'd cared about was the present. And sharing it with him. Confident in her arrogant innocence that the future would take care of itself.

It had, but in ways she'd never anticipated.

She looked down at her hands, twisted together in her lap until her knuckles looked white. "Does Eli know?"

"That I adopted him? Yeah. He's always known."

"And h-his health issues? What about them?"

"He had a bunch of surgeries. Respiratory stuff primarily. He still has a tendency toward bronchitis that I try to watch out for. But mostly, the older he got, the stronger he became." He stopped next to the chair and bent his knees, crouching beside her.

Her heart stuttered when he covered her twisted hands with his.

He was silent for a long moment. His thumb slowly stroked the sharp ridge of her knuckles.

"Everything I've done since before he was a year old has been for Elijah."

And everything she'd accused him of hadn't been wrong. She hadn't gotten his reasons right, but the end results were still the same.

He'd chosen someone else.

Sarah had still lost their child.

"It's late," she whispered. Seven years too late. "You should go."

In the gentle light of the lamp sitting on the side table beside her chair, his eyes looked so deeply brown they might have been black.

"I'm sorry," he murmured.

Her vision blurred. She pressed her lips together and slowly pulled her hands from beneath his.

"So am I."

Chapter 8

"Happy Thanksgiving!" Assigned to door duty at the Double-C, Sarah stepped out of the way while Max helped his mother maneuver her weighty cast through the wide doorway. "It's good to see you, Genna."

If she concentrated on Max's mother, maybe she'd get through the afternoon without embarrassing herself too badly.

"You too, dear." Genna leaned forward and caught Sarah in a quick hug. "Eli is bringing pies from the car, so beware." She balanced on one crutch while Max helped her work out of her coat. She was dressed in a pretty red sweater and skirt that reached down toward the ankle of her cast.

"Max." Sarah kept her smile in place as she took the coat from him, and waited for him to hand her his own, as well.

It was the first time she'd seen him since that night

he'd come to her house. And even though she'd had two and a half days to prepare for the moment, she still found herself entirely *un*prepared.

"Happy Thanksgiving," he murmured. His hands brushed hers as he handed over his shearling coat. His expression wasn't exactly relaxed, either.

If anything, he looked *very* uncomfortable standing there in his dark gray trousers and ivory fisherman's sweater.

More handsome than any man she'd ever seen. But uncomfortable nevertheless.

She clutched the coats to her chest. "Everyone is in the living room. Go on in. Make yourself at home, but beware. Squire is playing bartender, already." Squire Clay was her grandfather. Still standing almost as straight and tall as his five sons, he was opinionated, interfering, and grew more lovably irascible by the year.

She was crazy about the man.

But all affection aside, she knew he could have a heavy hand when it came to pouring a drink.

Genna tucked her crutches more firmly beneath her arms and smiled. "Well, frankly, a drink sounds good to me." She winked, looking younger than her years, and planted the rubber tips of her crutches to begin working her way through the foyer.

"And that's why I get to be designated driver," Max murmured, but at least he'd managed a smile of his own.

A smile that her attention snagged on and they stood there alone, next to the open door for a silent moment that dragged on too long.

He started to lift his hand.

She swallowed and deliberately looked out the doorway that she hadn't yet closed.

From the side of her vision she saw his hand lower, his fingers curling.

Outside, Eli was slowly making his way through the numerous vehicles congesting the circular drive. His tongue was caught between his teeth as he balanced a pie on each hand.

She couldn't keep silence up the entire afternoon. "Maybe I should help him."

"This is a point of manly pride for him." Max's arm brushed hers as he looked out, too.

For a moment, she let herself wonder if he'd made the contact deliberately. "Manly pride," she repeated, amused despite herself. "Carrying *pies*?"

"Give him a break. He's eight. And he made those pies with his grandmother. He's not gonna drop 'em."

Eli still had to make it up the half-dozen shallow stone steps to the front door, though. "But—"

"Relax." Max's hand dropped on the back of her neck and even through her turtleneck sweater, she felt singed.

Definitely deliberate.

"He knows to be on his best behavior here," Max said.

She shifted and his hand slid down her spine, then fell away as she looked up at him. "*Here?* What's that supposed to mean?" The Double-C had raised up her father and uncles, then her and her brother and myriad of cousins. It was hardly going to fall in the face of one, sometimes mischievous boy.

"We're Scalises," he said. "This is Clay territory."

As if that should explain it all.

But Eli had made it up the steps by then and any chance she had for a response was lost. "Miss Clay," he lifted the pie tins triumphantly. "Pumpkin and chocolate because Grandma says no self-respecting woman wouldn't prefer chocolate pie over *squash*."

Sarah smiled and caught the pumpkin pie before it could slip off his flattened palm. "She's right, of course."

"Good job." Max took the chocolate one, and lifted the pumpkin out of her hand. "Your hands are already full," he murmured. "Where should I put them?"

"Um, the kitchen. Through there—"

"Unless it's moved, I remember." He walked out of the foyer and turned to the hall leading to the kitchen that was located at the very rear of the house.

"My dad's been here before, huh?"

"Mmm-hmm. He used to come here sometimes with *his* dad." Though he'd stopped doing that when Tony was arrested. Sarah had been little more than a toddler, then. "You want to give me your coat there?"

He shrugged out of his slick parka and thrust it into her hands. "Dad said you might give me a ride on a horse."

"I just might." Her gaze traveled over his clothing. "But you look quite handsome there in those clothes. Did you bring some grubbies to change into?"

His blond hair was slicked back, still wet from being washed. "Jeans. Dad, too." He looked up at her, as if debating. Then he leaned closer. "I got grounded," he whispered. "For a whole week. 'Cept for today, he said, 'cause it's a holiday."

Never had she heard a boy so happy to be punished. She hid a smile. "I'm glad it didn't include today," she admitted.

"Me, too." His voice was fervent. "You know what else? My dad hates horses. But he said he'd maybe ride."

She couldn't help herself. She brushed her fingers

through his damp hair, rumpling it a little. "Sounds great."

Eli nodded and peered around her toward the living room. "There's a lotta people here, huh?"

"Mmm-hmm. Pretty much my entire family."

His eyebrows climbed upward. "Holy cra…cow," he finished, looking innocent. "I only got my dad and my two grandmas. What do you do at *Christmastime?*"

She laughed and took his hand in hers. "We draw names out of a hat to see who we'll get a gift for," she said, and watched his expression fall a little at that. "Come in and meet everyone."

His eyes nearly bugged out of his head when they walked into the merry confusion of the living room. Every piece of furniture, plus chairs that had been dragged in from the dining room, seemed occupied. "Where's my grandma?" he asked.

He was looking at a sea of strangers. She pointed to the couch where Genna was flanked by two of her aunts. "Go ahead," she encouraged.

Sure enough, he made a beeline for her familiar face.

"Cute kid."

Sarah glanced over at her cousin, J.D., who'd flown in from Georgia along with her sister, Angeline, just that morning. "He is."

"That blond hair, he sort of blends right in with the Clays." Her eyes laughed. "Like I do." She wiggled her head and her blond waves danced. Her humor stemmed from the fact that, while blond, she wasn't a Clay by birth.

"He's Genna's grandson. Eli."

"Right. The hunky deputy's boy." J.D. grinned. "Come on, Sarah. You don't think we haven't already heard all about the new pickin's in Weaver? Even if he is getting long in the tooth."

Sarah flushed. "Good grief, J.D., you sound just like Squire. Maybe you're spending too much time with those expensive racehorses of yours."

Her cousin tucked her arm through Sarah's. "Wish they were *my* racehorses," she corrected, "rather than the ones I work with. Then I could retire in a style I'd like to become accustomed to."

"Excuse me, ladies."

J.D. whirled around at Max's voice coming from behind them, taking Sarah with her. "And there he is in person." She stuck out her hand. "I'm J.D. and I remember you, but it seemed like you were a hell of a lot taller."

Max's lips twitched. "Probably because you were a tad shorter back then."

J.D. cocked her head, considering. "Quite possibly. So, how's it feel coming home again? You've been playing out in the waves off California for a spell, haven't you?"

"More or less." His dimple flashed and he turned his attention to Sarah. "And returning has its advantages. Did you make those peanut butter cookies I saw in there?"

Sarah shrugged, feeling suddenly flushed.

"Dad!"

He looked past them to where Eli was boisterously trying to draw his attention. "Pardon me. I'm being paged." He entered the fray, making his way toward Eli.

He really was clearly devoted to Eli. And knowing what she did now, Sarah found herself floundering in a whole new set of emotions. Ones not necessarily mired in the past. Ones that seemed very new and even more frightening.

"Mercy, mercy. He could use those long teeth on me any day." J.D. sighed dramatically. "Lord, but he's a pretty one, isn't he?"

"He's not long in the tooth," Sarah defended. "He's—" She broke off, recognizing the glint in her cousin's eyes that told her she'd walked right into J.D.'s snare.

"I thought so," J.D. whispered, amused. "Hey. Go for it. Celibacy isn't all that it's cracked up to be, and I can testify to it."

"And since when have you been without a man dangling from your fingertips for your amusement?"

J.D. rolled her eyes. "Believe me, you don't want to know how long."

"Honey," Jaimie called to Sarah, "can you check the potatoes for me?"

Sarah nodded, and turned back toward the kitchen. Within minutes, not only was she joined by J.D., but Angeline, Leandra and Lucy—in from New York where she made her living as a ballerina—as well.

They were an eclectic group. J.D. in her blue jeans and white T-shirt that suited her whipcord frame. Angeline in a smoothly tailored ivory suit that disguised her hourglass figure. Leandra—the most petite of them all—wore a sheer, patterned dress that she'd probably found in some funky antique store. Then there was Lucy, who was Cage and Belle's eldest, and generally accepted to be the most elegant of them all. She was living up to expectations in a pencil-slim black dress that only made her look more blond and ethereal.

As different as they all were though, they were family.

Sarah stuck a fork in the enormous boiling pot of potatoes. They were almost tender. She set the fork on the counter and turned to face the crowd.

"Well," J.D. demanded.

Sarah's gaze met Leandra's. She shrugged a little. "Who can control them?"

"Well, nothing." Sarah turned on the oven light and peered in at the turkey that was roasting and sending its delectable aroma throughout the big house.

"Come on," J.D. wheedled. "Everyone in this house knows that man was at *your* house a few nights ago. That particular nugget has kept the phone lines around Weaver buzzing, I'll bet."

"He's Eli's father. My student. We were just discussing him."

J.D. snorted softly. "That ain't all he is, sugar pie. Just one look at those red cheeks of yours is enough to tell us that."

"It's *hot* in here with all the ovens and burners going."

Even Angeline—an E.M.T. who was usually the most serious one of them all—looked amused. "Since when do you conduct parent-teacher conferences at your house at midnight?"

"It wasn't midnight. It was eleven."

"Squire would say to pull the other leg, 'cause it's got bells on," Lucy countered.

Sarah exhaled, exasperated. "What do you want me to say? That we had wild monkey sex or something?"

"Works for me," J.D. said, laughing. "Personally, that's my favorite kind."

"Favorite kind of what?" Gloria, who'd been married to Squire for most of their lives, stood in the doorway, her eyebrow arched.

J.D. muffled her laughter with her hand.

Gloria just shook her head a little, apparently recognizing that she wasn't going to get an answer. "I swear. You girls are every bit as bad as your fathers once were. And you—" she pinned her amused gaze on Lucy "—obviously let my Belle rub off too much on you."

"I tried, Mom." Belle was poking her dark head around her mother, trying to see into the spacious kitchen. "Anyone seen Nikki around?" Nikki was Belle's twin sister.

"I think she went upstairs to rest for a few minutes before dinner."

Belle turned her gaze upwards as if she could see to the bedrooms there. "Can't believe she's *pregnant*. Forty-four years old. What were she and Alex thinking?"

"Sometimes thinking doesn't have much to do with conceiving," J.D. said abruptly. "I think it's great. I mean, why not? They're happy about it, and we should all be in as good a shape as Nikki is."

"Your sister will be fine." Gloria patted Belle's cheek. "Now, if you're all just going to stand in here kibitzing, then put your hands to good use, and bring some of those trays of appetizers out. And *not* the ones for the wedding reception tomorrow." She turned on her heel and disappeared once more.

"Only this family would have a huge family holiday dinner one day followed by a wedding the next," J.D. muttered, yanking open one side of the enormous stainless steel refrigerator. "So which trays—oh. They're even labeled. Good gravy. Someone's sure organized around here." She began pulling out an assortment of trays, handing them off to anyone who stuck out their hands. Then she took one herself, and nudged the door closed with her slender hip, and headed back into the living room.

Sarah was left in the empty kitchen with Leandra.

"They didn't hear anything from me," Leandra assured.

"I know." Sarah let out a breath. "It's this town. Everyone talks about everything."

"So, how *are* you?"

"Fine." She had no intention of recounting Max's revelations there. "What about you? Nerves calming down yet?"

Leandra nodded. "Actually, they are." Her brown eyes were shining. "I can't wait to marry Evan."

"That's good, 'cause you've got—" Sarah glanced at the clock on the wall "—less than twenty-four hours of singleness left."

"And I'm happily counting off every minute," Leandra assured. "So, do I still need to dislike the man? Because I have to admit, it's not so easy now that he's here in person. He's even helped Evan out with some stuff at the clinic."

"Of course you don't have to dislike him," Sarah said briskly. "Now, go. Take this dip in there. It goes with the veggies that Angel was carrying."

"Yes, Miss Clay," Leandra said in a singsong voice. She took the crystal bowl and sailed out of the kitchen.

Sarah let out a breath.

She could get through the afternoon.

She really could.

"No. I really can't."

Sarah propped her hands on her hips and eyed Max. "You mean you *won't*."

"Same results." He eyed the enormous horse standing placidly a few feet away. "I'm allergic," he said.

She snorted. "Lies like that'll make your nose grow a foot."

"Come on, Dad." Eli was already in the saddle atop Pokey, one of the gentlest mounts the Double-C possessed. He was rocking back and forth in the saddle, clearly anxious to get moving. "You said you'd think about it."

Pokey turned her head toward Sarah and Max, her large brown eyes gentle.

"Even Pokey wants you to saddle up," Sarah encouraged.

"I told you. Horses don't much like me. I'll watch y'all from here," Max said. Like Sarah and his son, he'd changed into jeans after they'd finished the monstrously huge and decadent meal.

She wasn't sure which she found more appealing.

Max dressed in fine wool, looking urbane and dangerous, or Max dressed in faded blue jeans, looking casual and dangerous.

Either way, *dangerous* was the word she clearly needed to be remembering.

She circled the reins with her leather-gloved hands and urged Donner closer. The horse she'd chosen for Max took a few steps. The reins jingled. The saddle creaked.

The sky overhead was turning gray, and they had maybe another hour or two of light left. "*Why* do you think horses don't much like you? Honestly, I thought it was practically a requirement of Weaver citizenship to know how to ride."

"I didn't say I didn't know *how*." He leaned back against the fence rail.

"When did you ride horses, Dad?" Eli asked. "You never said. How come?"

"I rode horses with my dad," Max finally said. His voice was even, but Sarah could tell that the admission hadn't been one he'd particularly wanted to make.

And, she suspected, he stepped forward and took the reins from Sarah's hand mostly because he didn't want to encourage any more questions from Eli about Tony Scalise. He reached his foot up to the stirrup and grimacing, pulled himself up onto Donner's back.

"Cool," Eli breathed.

Max gave Sarah a wry look. "Yeah, I might need traction after this and he thinks it's cool."

"Push your heels down," Sarah instructed, struggling against the appeal that the man possessed. Max wasn't wearing cowboy boots, but his heavy-treaded shoes possessed a heel of sorts. "Okay." She tapped his shin. "Pull out your foot. I need to let out the stirrups a notch." Her head nearly brushed his leg as she worked the buckle, giving him a little more length. "Try that."

Max stuck his toe through the stirrup again and tried to ignore the proximity of her shining head to his thigh. He could think of about a dozen things he'd rather do than sit on top of an infernal horse—including having a root canal or spending even more hours secretly investigating the backgrounds of every member of the sheriff's department. There was nothing unusual in that job; he'd just never found it quite so distasteful before, looking into the lives of people with whom he was working.

But there was definitely something to watching Sarah moving around him, making sure everything was just so.

"Much better," she said and went around the horse

to adjust the other side. She angled a look up at him. "Did you get thrown once or something?"

"Being thrown would have been easier for my ego to take," he admitted. "I was stepped on."

Her eyebrows rose. "Seriously? What happened? Were you hurt? How old were you?"

"'Bout twelve. And hell yeah, it hurt. Damn horse stood on my foot and stayed there for about a month of Sundays. Only ended up with a few broken toes, though," he admitted.

She looked sympathetic and amused all at once. "Where were you?"

"I was working with my dad on the weekends, like I usually did."

"He was a farrier, wasn't he?"

"Yeah." Farrier and convicted rustler. The kind of father every son could be proud of.

Her eyes seemed to mirror the gray of the sky. "So how long has it been since you've been *on* a horse, rather than the other way around?"

"I was fifteen," he muttered. He'd managed to avoid riding completely after his father's arrest and conviction.

She let out a silent whistle. "Wow. We won't go out for very long then. Don't want you getting saddle sore."

"Not from riding a horse, anyway," he murmured.

Her cheeks went red. She avoided looking at him, and checked his hold on the reins. Satisfied that he wasn't completely inept, she headed to her own horse and swung up in the saddle with economic grace. She clicked her tongue, and the beast turned as obediently as a dog, until she was next to Eli. "Okay, kiddo. Remember what I told you about holding the reins?"

Eli nodded. His tongue was caught between his teeth, so great was his concentration.

Watching the young woman patiently explain the basic points of riding to his son, Max shifted and the leather beneath him creaked.

It was an old, nearly forgotten sound.

Just then, though, it wasn't an unwelcome one.

He looked back toward the big, rambling house where Sarah had grown up. She'd been just a toddler when everything Max believed about his father had been shot to hell. When Tony had shown himself to be a thief—and he'd done it while Max sat waiting for him in the truck.

"Earth to Massimo."

He looked back to see both Sarah and Eli watching him, clearly waiting. "Yeah?"

"Ready?" Sarah held up the reins in her left hand.

"No, but that hasn't stopped either one of you from nagging me up onto this nag."

Sarah made a face, but her eyes were sparkling. "Show some good sportsmanship here."

"Speaking of sports, you realize there is a perfectly good football game on that big ol' television your dad has in that house over there?"

"Da-ad," Eli said.

"Fine." He laid the rein against the horse's neck, and sure enough, the animal obediently moved, heading away from the rein. That was one thing that hadn't changed about the Double-C. The horses that the Clays maintained were well trained and responsive as hell.

"We're just going to ride out to the hole and back," Sarah said, bringing up the rear after Eli. "Just keep going straight out from here, Max."

He lifted his hand in acknowledgment. "Straight ahead, Donner."

The horse plodded along and Max looked out over the widespread snow-covered land, beyond the barns and other outbuildings. Mountains in the distance looked blue against the gray sky. A long line of trees stretched toward the horizon, planted to break the incessant wind.

When he'd left Weaver, he'd vowed never to return. Yet here he was.

"What's the hole?" he heard Eli ask behind him.

"The swimming hole," Sarah said. "It's a small lake a few miles out from the big house. We swim there all the time when the weather's warm."

"Not today, though, huh?"

She laughed. "No, Eli. Not today."

Max shifted in his saddle, settling into the horse's rocking rhythm. Sarah's laughter floated on the air. It seemed to curl around him, and for the first time in a long while he didn't feel quite so cold inside.

Chapter 9

"Here." Jaimie Clay pushed several plastic containers of food into Max's hands. "You have to take home leftovers. A requirement of eating Thanksgiving Day dinner with us."

"That, and if we used up every refrigerator this family possesses, we wouldn't have room for all the leftovers," Sarah said, smiling crookedly.

Max handed off the containers to Eli, whom he'd had to practically tear away from Hannah. The little girl was half his age, and somewhat remote with nearly everyone—a result of her autism, he assumed. But she'd glommed onto Eli the moment they'd reentered the big house after putting up the horses from their ride.

Not that Eli had seemed to mind. Aside from him, Hannah was the only other youngster present; the other young people were all at least of driving age.

"Take those to Grandma in the truck," he told his son.

Eli nodded and turned away, jumping down the steps, only to stop midway. He turned and looked back. "Thanks for letting us come to dinner," he said. "It was real nice of you."

"You're very welcome," Jaimie said, smiling. "It was real nice of you to come and join us." Her green gaze followed Eli down the rest of the stairs and back through the throng of vehicles that gleamed under the illumination from the porch light. "Your son is delightful, Max." She squeezed his arm. "Now, we'll see you tomorrow at the wedding, won't we?"

"Think I'm on duty, ma'am."

"Ma'am. Oh, save me from that, please. Call me Jaimie. And if you won't tell Sawyer that you need to be available for our big do, then I will." She glanced back toward the house when someone called her name. "Sarah, you talk to the man." Smiling again, she went back into the house, closing the heavy door behind her.

Which left Max standing alone under the porch light with Sarah.

She'd pulled an oversized plaid jacket over her shoulders. Her hair hung loose over her shoulders, the ends lifting in the whispering breeze, like beckoning fingers.

And he could have sworn he saw a twitch of the lace curtains hanging in the enormous window that overlooked the front of the house. "Are we being watched?"

She didn't look back at the window. "Probably. Couldn't begin to tell you by whom, though. Any one of those people in there is capable of it." She leaned her shoulder against the pillar closest to the steps. "Don't let my mother make you feel pressured to come to the wedding," she said. "If you're busy or…whatever." Her voice trailed away.

"Would you prefer it if I didn't show up?" Aside from

a few awkward moments, the day had gone better than Max had expected. During the horse ride, she'd even seemed to enjoy herself, though she'd kept her attention mostly on Eli.

"I'm just part of the wedding party," she said blithely. "It's nothing to do with me."

He snorted softly. "Bull."

Her lips firmed. "Your mother's planning to be there. Go with her if you want. If you don't…well, don't go."

He turned his back on the lacy window, blocking Sarah from the view as well. "I want to know what *you* want, Sarah."

Her lashes dipped. "Max—"

"Yes or no. Toss a coin if you have to."

She sucked in her lower lip for a moment, leaving it with a soft shine that seemed to catch the light as much as it did his gaze. Her fingertips were pressed lightly against her throat. "Yes," she finally whispered.

He felt like he'd just cleared a fifty-foot hurdle. "Eli had a good time today. So did my mother." Because he didn't really give a good damn about who was watching from behind the curtains, he touched those flirting tendrils of hair.

Silky. Just like he remembered.

Her lips parted and he heard her soft breath.

"I had a good time today, too," he admitted.

"Good." Her voice was husky.

He looked beyond her. The SUV was running, the exhaust making clouds in the colder air. His mother sat waiting in the front seat. Eli in the rear.

Some things should be simple. Like standing on a porch, bidding your goodbyes to a pretty girl after a nice day.

But nothing was simple about Weaver, nor about Sarah. Not then. Not now.

He let her hair slip free of his fingers. "See you tomorrow."

She nodded, and he felt her wide-eyed gaze on him as he went down the steps to the SUV.

"I now pronounce you husband and wife."

Cheers filled the cozy church as the minister made the announcement. Smiles wreathed his weathered face as he continued, though they held nothing on the smiles the bride and groom were giving each other. Leandra, in her buttercup-colored gown, looked like a breath of spring next to her tall, tux-clad, black-haired groom.

"Ladies and gentlemen, it's now my pleasure to introduce to you Dr. and Mrs. Evan Taggart."

Sarah didn't bother hiding the tears in her eyes when Leandra turned and took her bouquet of lush lilacs back from her. A moment later, the couple was heading up the center aisle toward the exit of the crowded church.

Leandra's brother, Axel, had served as best man. He grinned and gave Sarah a wink as they moved next to each other to continue the recessional. "Now we can get on with the partying, right?"

She chuckled, nodding. But her gaze kept wandering over the congregation who were now all on their feet.

Max's face wasn't among them.

He hadn't come, after all.

And the disappointment of that fact ran alarmingly deep.

The church wasn't really large enough to hold all of the people who'd turned out to see the nuptials. Those who hadn't made it inside, stood crowded around outside, despite the crisp, cold evening. Before Leandra went out the wide-opened doors, she stopped and collected the thickly lined cape that matched her gown and swung it around her shoulders.

Tabby, who was the other bridesmaid, followed closely behind Sarah with Sarah's little brother, Derek. Though, at twenty-four he was nowhere near as little as eighteen-year-old Tabitha, and Sarah gave him a pointed look when she saw his appreciative gaze lingering on Tabby as she handed the younger girl the cape that matched her lilac-colored dress.

"Thanks." Tabby swung it around herself and managed to look even more striking with her black hair against the lovely wool. "Probably looks better than the parka I have in my car." She grinned and without a second glance at Derek, headed out toward her own buddies—primarily Caleb Buchanan and April Reed.

"Put your eyeballs back in your head, Derek," Sarah murmured. "She's too young for you."

"She's eighteen, isn't she?" But Derek didn't seem unduly crushed. Particularly when two women that Sarah couldn't quite place rushed up to him, ostensibly to keep him warm as they pressed themselves against him.

Leandra and Evan were already shaking hands and greeting people. They had decided that Hannah would be too upset by the crush of unfamiliar people; she was already at the home of her grandmother, Sharon, who would be watching her until Leandra and Evan returned from their brief honeymoon. As soon as the bridal couple could break free of the people crowding around them, they'd all head to Clay Farm, where the reception was being held.

"When you gonna let your old man walk you down the aisle?" An arm suddenly came around her shoulders.

Sarah leaned her head against her father and smiled. "Think there was a day when I wanted to marry you, but mom told me you were already taken. Afraid finding someone up to that par has been difficult."

His eyes crinkled. He brushed his lips over her forehead. "The par is off the charts because of you," he assured. "So, what's going on between you and Scalise?"

She stilled. "Nothing."

"You sure?" His eyes were sharp as they focused on her face. "Didn't seem that way yesterday out at the big house."

"You've said that about nearly every unattached man who's come into my vicinity since I was five," she reminded him, keeping her voice light. "I remember when I was in high school, you used to sit on the porch cleaning your shotgun when it was time for one of my dates to pick me up."

"Worked, didn't it?" He looked unrepentant.

"Too well. Half of my class was afraid of you."

"As it should be with a pretty girl's father." His lips twitched. "But now, well, you know your mother's making noises about grandbabies. Says it's been too long since we've had little ones running around the house."

"Don't let him kid you." Jaimie came up beside them. "He wants to hear the patter of little feet just as much as I do."

"Come on, Red, don't blow my cover here."

"Oh, you love it." Jaimie reached up and lightly kissed his lips. "Now, come on. We can't dawdle around here. People will be heading out to the farm and I promised Emily we'd be there to greet folks since they'll be tied up here for a while with the receiving line."

"You riding out with us?" Matthew looked at Sarah.

She shook her head. "I'm going to make sure we

don't forget any of Leandra's things behind in the bride's room. Plus there are some wedding presents I still need to load in my car. I'll be along as soon as I can, though."

Satisfied, her parents moved off.

Sarah's gaze traveled over the throng once again.

Still no Max.

She slowly worked her way through the crowd, exchanging greetings as she went, until she made it to the parking lot where cars were already jammed, trying to get out of the single exit.

The only sheriff's department vehicle around was her uncle's.

And then, because she felt foolish standing in the parking lot for no discernable reason, she went to her car and unlocked the trunk. Gifts of every size and shape were already inside. Despite Leandra and Evan's request for no gifts, people were still bringing them anyway.

Leaving the trunk wide, she went in through the rear entrance of the church and began loading up the gifts that people had left in the narthex. Some of her cousins eventually appeared, helping, and before long, the gifts were all packed, the parking lot was nearly cleared, and there was hardly anything left for her to do at the church. Leandra and Evan departed and Sarah sent everyone else on ahead to the farm.

She went back inside the church, making one last pass, even though she'd already gathered up every last gift, every last flower petal. Now, all she found was one forgotten gold, silken bow with the wild heather attached.

She picked it up, twirling it between her fingers.

The sun was still above the horizon, and it cast its angled beam through the stained glass window behind the pulpit, throwing the colored panes into sharp relief.

The church was small, and probably half of her relatives had been married or baptized in it.

There was even a time when Sarah had dreamed of walking down the center aisle, carrying her own bouquet of wildflowers.

She shook her head at the sentimental thought. She had a teaching career that she thoroughly enjoyed and a calling in her role with Hollins-Winword that she believed in. She no longer had the notion that "happily ever after" existed for everyone.

If it did, she'd have a child only a little younger than Eli.

Instead, all she had was her involvement with other peoples' children.

"Guess I missed the vows."

Her fingers tightened around the bow, crushing the heather. She slowly turned on her heel.

Max stood at the narthex doors. He wore a black suit, but his dark red tie was unknotted, hanging loosely around the neck of his white shirt. "So, a funny thing happened on the way to the church," he said.

She managed a faint smile. "I think that only works when you're the groom who is late."

He tilted his head in acknowledgment and slowly headed into the sanctuary. When he reached the last row of pews, he dropped his hand on the wooden arm. "I saw your car in the lot outside."

"I was just, um, seeing if we'd forgotten anything." She lifted her shoulders a little, and held up the bow. "This is it."

His fingers grazed over the next pew as he slowly continued toward her. "I *was* headed here."

"The tie was my clue."

His lip twitched. "Yeah." He pulled one end and it

slid out from beneath his collar. He rolled the tie in a ball and tucked it in his pocket. "Something came up that I had to take care of."

"Your mom didn't make it," she said, hoping he would elaborate.

"She was tired after yesterday. Her leg was giving her fits. Eli stayed home with her."

She waited, but he said no more about what had kept *him* away.

"Nice dress."

Feeling self-conscious, she swept her hand down the lilac gown. "This old thing? Just something I found in the back of my closet."

His gaze worked its way up to her face. "You look good in anything."

Her fingers tightened on the bow. It crinkled softly.

"And in nothing," he finished.

She stared at him, unable to think of a suitable response to save her soul.

But his gaze went past her to the pulpit and the high stained glass windows she'd been studying. "Lightning's probably gonna strike me down now."

She moistened her lips. "Well. This *is* a church."

"Except I do think God knows about what goes on between men and women."

She couldn't argue that particular point. "I, um, need to go."

"The reception?"

She nodded and started to turn, lifting her long skirt with one hand.

"Save me a dance."

She stopped. The dress swished as she shot him a quick look. "You're going?"

He didn't stop his approach, closing the distance between them to only two pews width. "I was invited, wasn't I?"

"Yes, of course," she said slowly.

"Then don't look so surprised."

"Everything about you lately surprises me."

He finally stopped when the toes of his black shoes were brushing the hem of her dress. "That makes two of us."

He must have shaved again since morning, she thought dimly. Because his lean cheeks were still smooth, no hint of five o'clock shadow.

"Max—"

He drew his dark eyebrows together when she said nothing more. "Sarah."

She swallowed. She didn't know what to make of the man. For that matter, she didn't know what to make of herself. She was supposed to have him all neatly boxed up and categorized.

He reached up and she nearly jumped.

But all he did was draw a small spray of baby's breath from where it was tucked in her hair. He brushed the tiny, delicate white blossoms down her cheek. "You need your car there?"

"Hmm? Oh. Yes. G-gifts are in the trunk."

His lashes drooped until there was nothing showing of his eyes but a narrow, brown gleam. "I'll follow you, then."

She managed a nod. "Right. Okay." She turned on her heel, feeling absurdly unsteady, and made her way through the back of the church to the door there.

When she looked back, Max was not following her.

But when she climbed behind the wheel of her car, trembling as if it were thirty degrees below the zero mark rather than above it, she saw him sitting in his SUV, idling in the street.

She flipped on her heater and headed out of town toward the farm.

Max didn't budge from her rearview mirror the entire while.

When they arrived, the sun had nearly set and there was an even larger crowd hanging out beneath the enormous tent that had been erected directly in front of the house. Dozens of propane heaters were burning, keeping the cold mostly at bay. A country-western band was situated on the wide, rambling porch, already playing.

Sarah pulled her car around to the rear of the house, but there was simply no hope of parking very close. Not with that many vehicles.

Max parked beside her and when she opened her trunk, he nudged her toward the house. "I'll get 'em," he said. "You just want them inside the house?"

She nodded, still hovering.

He lifted his eyebrows. "You'd rather hoof all these inside yourself?"

"No."

"Then go. I'll find you."

She went. Straight into the house and to the first empty bathroom she could find, where she closed the door and leaned back against it, shaking like a leaf.

But hiding in the bathroom at her cousin's wedding reception was hardly the mark of a controlled woman, and eventually, she had to force herself to leave the temporary sanctuary. She tightened the sparkling clip that was holding her wavy hair more or less under control at the back of her head and the remaining sprig of baby's breath fell free.

She moistened her lips, picking it up.

Oh, Sarah. Keep your head, girl.

She dropped the tiny spray in the trash and quickly splashed water over her wrists. Then she yanked open the door to brave the world.

J.D. stood there in the hallway, a sly smile on her face. "Hiding out?"

Sarah made a face and swept past her cousin. "Not in this lifetime."

J.D. laughed and took possession of the powder room. "Sell it somewhere else, honey."

There were people everywhere Sarah turned as she made her way back downstairs. She stopped in the kitchen, only to be shooed out by her aunts Maggie and Hope, who had the place well under their control.

She finally pulled her cape around herself and went back outside.

And despite the hundred or so people who were crowded under the tent, she spotted Max immediately. Standing next to the table where an enormous barrel was holding bottles stored in ice, he was holding one of the beer bottles and talking with Sawyer.

She wondered if it was only in Wyoming that people could drink icy beer outside on a winter day.

The lead singer of the band was talking, introducing the new bride and groom, who were occupying the center of the wooden dance floor that was set up in the middle of the linen-draped tables. A moment later, they began playing again and Sarah dragged her gaze away from Max to watch her cousin dance with her brand-new husband.

Within minutes, the couple's parents had joined them on the dance floor.

Angeline came up beside Sarah. "Pretty romantic,"

she said with a soft smile. "Remember when we were little and took turns playing bride?"

"I think our veil was usually one of the dish towels from the kitchen that we held on with hair bands."

"Come on, sis. I'll dance with you." Casey joined them. He, too, held a beer bottle in one hand.

Angeline just eyed her not-so-little brother. "Since when do *you* know how to dance?"

"Hey. I've learned all sorts of things that you don't know about." He grabbed her hand and pulled her unceremoniously toward the dance floor.

The prickling at Sarah's nape told her Max had come up behind her before he spoke. "You've got a nice family," he said. "Here." He handed her a glass.

She looked at it.

"It's grapefruit juice," he said. "Only juice. Kept Squire away from it, though he was plenty willing to spike it if that's the way you want it."

Sarah took the glass. "This is fine. Thank you." She sipped at it. The last thing she needed was to add alcohol to her already shaky resistance.

"How many *are* there of you?" His arm brushed her shoulder as he lifted his bottle for a drink. "That dance floor's nearly full and I don't think anyone but your family is on it."

"Let's see. Starting with Gloria and Squire—" she mentally counted "—more than thirty, actually. We could do a head count, actually. Ryan's the only one not here."

"Sawyer's boy."

"Yes." Though Ryan was thirty-three and hardly a boy. That wasn't keeping the entire family from worrying about him, though, as his absence continued.

"Well. Come on."

Her fingers felt slippery on the glass. "Where?"

"So cautious," he murmured. "When did that happen?"

She didn't answer and he made a soft noise. "More things to hold me accountable for." He took the glass out of her hand and set it on a bare space on the table behind them. "The dance floor," he said. "Think there's a rule somewhere that says the maid of honor has to be on the dance floor." He held out one hand, palm upward.

She looked at the square palm. The long fingers.

And even though she was afraid she was making the biggest mistake she'd made in recent years, she slowly settled her hand on top of his.

Chapter 10

Later, Sarah could hardly recall any details of the reception. It was a blur of sparkling lights and music and voices. And at the center of it was Max.

Max, who kept her locked in his arms on the dance floor just long enough to drive her slightly insane before he'd surrendered her back to her maid-of-honor-type duties. Tasks that she must have managed, though as she was driving her car home hours later, she couldn't even remember.

Still, she had the bridal bouquet sitting on the seat beside her.

Somehow or other, she'd ended up catching the thing when Leandra had tossed it.

And after the cake and toasts there had been more dancing, during which the magnetic focus of her personal compass had been called away on some sheriff's department matter.

Max's departure had been just as well.

Things were getting just too foggy where he was concerned.

"Distance is a good thing," she said aloud, then laughed a little at her own absurdity. She flipped on the radio station and turned the heater up a notch. The temperature had magically held out for the wedding and reception, but according to Sarah's dad, another snowfall was on its way.

And everyone knew that Matthew Clay had a nose for snow.

The familiar road swept out before her in an unending lazy arc and she reached out with one hand, brushing her palm over the soft petals of the bouquet. Suddenly the car lurched and she jerked the wheel, sucking in a gasp as she bumped over the shoulder.

The car rocked to a jolting halt and she winced as her seatbelt forcibly restrained *her* rocking, as well.

She pressed her head back against the headrest, catching her breath. The bouquet had tumbled onto the floor, but that seemed the only casualty of her precipitous stop. The engine was still running; a jazzy sax was still crooning on the radio station; the heater was still blowing out warm air; the headlights were still beaming out over the road—albeit at a lopsided angle thanks to the car's position.

She unclipped her safety belt and climbed out of the car and the cause of her problem was immediately apparent in the sight of her tire, laying in pieces still on the highway. "Great." She pulled her cape closer around herself and climbed back in the warmth of the car.

She had a spare in the trunk, of course, but the idea of changing it held about as much appeal as sticking her head in a vat of motor oil. Calling a road service would be fine, only it was about two in the morning. By the time somebody made it out to assist her, she could have the spare on herself.

Only a day earlier she'd had an extra pair of jeans in the car that she could have slipped into. But she'd emptied it of all unnecessary items to make room for wedding paraphernalia. Grumbling under her breath, she turned the steering wheel until her tires were straight again, and hit the button to pop open the trunk. Then, she got back out on the shoulder, pulled on her cape, fastening it snuggly around her neck, and went to the rear of the car to unearth the jack and lug wrench.

She had the lug nuts loosened and the car up on the jack when headlights swept over her. She squinted into them, unable to see beyond the glare, but wasn't surprised when the vehicle pulled over to the side of the road behind hers.

That's what people did in those parts.

She lifted her hand in acknowledgment as the driver climbed from the vehicle, and kept twisting the jack, lifting the car another inch.

"Now there's a sight," a familiar voice said.

She squinted into the light again, surprised. "Brody? Is that you?"

"In the flesh." The man walked up beside her and crouched down next to the car. "Having fun?"

She snorted softly. "Barrels of it."

"Here." He nudged her hands out of the way on the jack.

She was happy enough to scoot out of the way. "Where's Megan?"

"Sound asleep in her bed," he assured. "Had to take care of another matter this evening. An associate of ours is with her."

An associate. She rolled her eyes at the term. In minutes, the tall near-stranger had the tire off and was fitting the spare in place. "So, you always get dressed up to change tires on the highway in the dead of night?"

"Doesn't everyone?"

He laughed softly and let down the jack. The car's weight settled once more on all four tires and he tightened the nuts. "Okay, kiddo. You're good to go." He dropped the remains of her ruined tire in her trunk, tossed in the jack and wrench after it, and closed the trunk.

"Thanks. You came by at the perfect time."

"Well." He leaned down and twitched her ankle-length cape. "Nearly."

Sure enough, she had a lovely black mark crossing the front. But at least it had occurred after the reception rather than before.

"You gonna be okay now?"

She nodded. "Of course. These are my stomping grounds, remember?"

"That's what I hear." He lifted a hand and was striding back to his vehicle when another set of lights swept over them.

This time, Sarah recognized the vehicle immediately.

Particularly when he turned on the light bar atop the SUV, and red and blue lights slowly flashed over them.

"What's going on?" Max asked, approaching.

He looked very much in deputy mode, she thought vaguely. He neared Brody and the two men gave each other a sizing measure.

Sarah shivered and pulled her cloak closer around her. "I had a flat tire," she said and her voice sounded loud in the night air. "He stopped to help me change it."

"And you would be?"

Brody stuck out his hand. "Brody Paine," he said shortly.

Max ignored the hand and kept walking toward Sarah. "You all right?"

"Of course." She thought she heard Brody cover a snicker with a cough. For a high-priced agent he was hardly subtle.

"I'm gonna head out, since you're in such good hands," Brody told Sarah. "That all right with you, *Officer?*"

Max's head slowly turned and he gave the man a long look. "You can go," he finally said.

Sarah pressed her lips together, not sure if she was amused or irritated at the display of testosterone flying between the two males. She turned and climbed into her car, cranking the engine over.

The air that shot out of her heater vents was lamentably cold, though. It would take a while to heat up again. She leaned over and caught the bouquet off the floor, setting it back on the seat.

Max knocked on her window and she rolled it down. Brody's pickup was moving back onto the highway, giving them a wide berth before picking up speed.

"Supermarket guy also performs roadside assistance, does he?"

She stiffened a little. "They do around small towns like Weaver."

"Kind of coincidental."

She flapped her hands. "It's a small town! Now, do you mind if I get moving? It's cold and late."

"Not at all."

He stepped back from the car and she rolled up the window.

Her hands were shaking.

It was as if the man who'd moved with her on the dance floor had never existed.

She punched the gas a little harder than necessary, and her car shot off the shoulder with a spurt of dirt and gravel. In her rearview mirror, the emergency lights atop Max's vehicle were doused and a moment later, his headlights were beaming into the mirror.

She adjusted it so the lights weren't blinding her, and continued driving into Weaver. When she passed the sheriff's station, she fully expected him to pull into the lot beside it, but those headlights of his stayed steady and strong in her rearview mirror.

He followed her right up to her house, pulling around in the back where she parked near the door.

"You needn't have followed me all the way here," she said, climbing out of her car. "As you can see, the car was just fine once the tire was changed. *I'm* just fine."

He joined her on the steps leading into the kitchen and cursed under his breath when he twisted the knob and found it unlocked. "What'd I tell you about your locks?"

She brushed past him and went inside, unwinding her cape as she went. She left it sitting on the washing machine and slapped on the wall switch as she passed it, throwing the kitchen into bright light. "Interestingly enough, I can choose whether to lock my doors or not." She rounded on him, her hands on her hips. "What are you doing?"

"My job," he said, his lips twisting. "Watching out for the citizens of Weaver. Do you have any idea how dangerous it is to stop on the road like that? Particularly at this hour?"

She lifted her eyebrows. "You happen to notice that I had a *flat?* What was I supposed to do? Drive the rest

of the way into town on my rim? And Brody Paine was
just being a good Samaritan. You didn't need to act so
suspicious of him."

"Honey, I'm suspicious of any man who comes
around you."

Her lips parted. Annoyance clogged her veins, making her face feel hot. "Just because we shared a few
dances tonight doesn't mean you can—"

Her words caught in her throat as he grabbed her
shoulders and pulled her close. "I'm going to kiss you,"
he said flatly. "Say no, if you really mean it, and I'm
out of here."

He waited, his gaze darkly brown.

She opened her mouth. But the word *no* simply did
not emerge, though every logical, functioning brain cell
she possessed was screaming at her to say the word.

"That's what I thought," he muttered, and lowered
his head.

She barely had time to draw breath before his mouth
covered hers.

Hot. Desperate.

She wasn't sure if that stemmed from him or from
her. All she knew was the taste of him.

Familiar, yet new.

And it was a lot more enticing than those logical
cells in her brain.

His hand caught her face when he finally lifted his
head. His breathing was rough.

Hers was no better.

"I'm sorry," he muttered. "Sorry."

She touched the tip of her tongue to her lips that felt
swollen and tingling. "Really?"

His jaw cocked. She saw the edges of his teeth come
together. "No. Not really."

Her hands snaked up around his neck, fingers sliding through his thick hair. "Thank goodness," she whispered and pressed her mouth to his jaw. She slowly touched the tip of her tongue against the rough stubble there.

His hands caught her waist again, fingers flexing. "I didn't intend this."

Such horribly, horribly familiar words when they came from him.

And still she ignored the common sense that cried out for her to run.

Run far.

Run fast.

But most of all…run.

"Yet here we are," she said huskily. "Again."

His hands slid up her spine. "You can always say no, Sarah. I'm a bastard, but I don't push that line. You want me to go, I will." He looked pained. "I won't like it, but I will."

What was worse? Being miserable that she'd sent him away? Or being afraid of letting him stay?

"I want you to go," she whispered huskily.

A muscle worked in his jaw. He slowly drew his hands away from her back.

She felt cold.

He headed for the kitchen door. "Lock this after me," he said evenly.

She swallowed.

His hand closed over the knob.

He was really going to leave.

She crossed the room, stopping him with her hand atop his. "Max. Wait."

He let out a harsh breath. "I'm a little short of control here, Sarah."

She slowly slid between him and the door, facing him. She dragged his hand to her mouth and pressed her lips to his palm. "Sometimes control is overrated."

He pulled his hand away, pressing it flat against the door above her head. His gaze was fierce as he studied her for a long, tight moment.

Then he lowered his head until his lips grazed her earlobe. "I've never stopped wanting you."

She let out a shaky breath, her eyelids suddenly feeling heavy. Her fingers climbed up his chest, slid over the solidness of his shoulder, still clad in the suit coat he'd worn for the wedding. Found his neck and kept sliding until they tangled in his thick, thick hair. "Max—"

He tilted his head back against her touch, like a big, dangerous cat. His gaze burned over her face and he reached for the single narrow strap of her dress, tugging it down over her shoulder.

She tucked her tongue between her teeth, biting down to keep from moaning right out loud.

His fingers traveled over her bare shoulder, slipping behind to slowly walk down her spine. "Where's the zipper?"

She could hardly breathe. She drew his hand back over the front of her shoulder, nearly seeing double as his palm brushed over her breast, but she didn't stop, continuing to guide him beneath her arm to the hidden zipper in the side of her dress.

He slowly drew it down and the fabric fell away, revealing the strapless corset she wore beneath.

He made a strangled sound.

She felt her skin flush, from head to toe. "It was the only thing I could find to wear under this dress that didn't leave a line showing."

He laughed gruffly. "Believe me, darlin', I'm not

complaining. Just would've been good to have some warning. I think I might be having a heart attack here."

Flushing even harder, she pushed out from beneath his arm, only he caught her from behind, hauling her right back to him.

His lips covered the point of her shoulder. "Don't go running scared now, Sarah."

"Who said I was scared?"

His palm flattened against her abdomen and he slowly, deliberately nudged her dress over her hips.

It fell in a pool of lilac silk around her ankles.

"Maybe I am," he murmured, his words a caress against her skin.

"What have *you* got to be scared about?" She tried not to groan when his hand crept upward, brushing against her breasts, snugly confined within the ivory fabric.

"Same thing as always where you're concerned." His fingertips dragged along the straight edge where corset gave way to soft flesh. "Forgetting everything else that suddenly seems less important."

"And that's bad."

His palm flattened against her collarbone, fingers nudging her head back against his shoulder. "That's dangerous," he murmured. He turned her head until his mouth touched hers. He slowly sucked in her lower lip, then released it.

She twisted around to face him, only to realize her feet were still caught in the folds of the dress. She kicked at it, trying to step free.

"Definitely a heart attack," he muttered, falling down to his knees. He caught her ankle in one hand and lifted her foot from the fabric.

She grabbed his shoulders, as much unbalanced by

his hand on her ankles as she was by him lifting her
foot.

When he pulled the dress from beneath her other
foot, he didn't rise, though. His fingers slowly slid along
the very narrow strap that circled her ankles until he
found the minuscule buckle.

She held her breath, watching him as he carefully
worked the strap free and turned to the other one.

"Lift."

She raised her foot again and he slid the fancy pump
free.

Suddenly a good three inches shorter, she almost
wished for the artificial height back. Something about
being closer in height to him had given her a foolish
sense of confidence that was now completely, frighteningly absent.

His hands drifted up the backs of her calves. Her
thighs. Skimmed over the garters holding up the fine
weave of her nude hose, and far more easily than she'd
fastened them earlier that day, he released them.

His head tilted slightly, looking up at her as his hands
continued upward, settling around her waist.

J.D. didn't have it even half-right.

Max wasn't pretty.

He was the most beautiful man Sarah had ever seen
in her life.

Still.

Her throat suddenly tightened and her eyes burned.
She slowly brushed back the lock of hair that had fallen
over his forehead. She ran her knuckles down his cheek.
Leaned over and gently pressed her mouth to his, softly
rubbing until he made a low growl and caught her head
in his hands, deepening the kiss. She pulled back, feeling as if her nerves were ready to pop out from be-

neath her skin. She looped her fingers through his, and straightened again, pulling.

He rose and she silently led him out of the blinding bright kitchen into the dark hall to her bedroom at the end of the hall.

She hadn't closed the blinds entirely and the moonlight outside shined through them, casting stripes of dim light over her bed.

She didn't stop until her knees brushed the wedding-ring quilt covering the top of it and she turned her back toward him. "It fastens in the back," she told him softly.

His fingers brushed her nape, but he didn't immediately search out the lacings holding the corset tight against her torso. Instead, he fumbled with the clasp holding her hair back.

Waves tumbled free and he ran his fingers through them, slowly spreading the length forward over her shoulders.

Her knees felt weak. She reached back, catching hold of whatever she could reach—his suit coat.

And finally his knuckles brushed against her spine as he worked the lacings loose. He pulled the fine cord completely free, and tossed it aside.

The corset fell forward and she caught it in her hands, pressing it against her breasts as he turned her to face him. "Sit back," he murmured.

Her shaking legs were only too happy to comply. She sat on the side of the bed and sucked in a harsh breath when he tucked his fingertips beneath the lace band at the top of her hose and slowly rolled them down and off her feet.

They landed somewhere near the corset lacing.

Watching her in the dim light, he pulled off his suit coat. Kicked off his shoes and worked loose the buttons on his shirt. Only when he reached for the buckle of his belt did he pause.

Even then, she knew he was giving her a chance to change her mind.

And in that moment, the fear that was almost as great as the desire, slid away.

This was the only man she'd ever wanted to share herself with. And no amount of reasoning seemed able to change that fact.

She slowly lowered the corset and felt her nipples draw up, even more rigid beneath his gaze. The stiff ivory garment fell from her fingertips to the floor and she reached for him, pushing his hands away to unfasten the belt herself. When she'd finished with that, she worked his zipper down, and as if she'd done it a hundred times rather than a handful, she stripped his clothes from him in one smooth stroke.

Her hands grazed over his hard abdomen, up his chest where the smooth skin gave way to the soft crinkle of dark swirls of hair. When she reached his shoulders, she tugged him down. His name was a murmur on her lips.

The stripes of moonlight seemed to undulate over his body as he settled beside her. "I haven't done this in a long while." His voice was gruff. Hushed.

A soft ache spread through her. She slid her thigh over his and leaned over him, her breasts nestling against that warm, hard chest. Everything inside her wept for him.

She pressed her lips against his. "I haven't done this since *you*," she admitted.

He let out a long, slow breath. His hands glided up her waist. Her spine. Tangled in her hair.

And then all semblance of patience snapped. He

dragged her beneath him, his mouth on hers. His hands raced over her. Tempting. Taunting. Finding.

And when she couldn't stand another second of waiting, couldn't stand another moment of his tormenting, seductive touch without *more*, he knew it, and settled against her, filling her, for she was as impatient as he. And when she heard him groan her name, when she felt herself splintering apart, he swallowed the sobs that she couldn't hold back.

And she knew that once again she'd never be the same.

Chapter 11

After, with Max's arm thrown over her shoulders, holding her snugly against him, Sarah slept.

Deeply. Soundly.

Not even the strident ringing of her telephone penetrated at first. Maybe it wouldn't have at all, if Max hadn't muttered something under his breath and pulled that warm, heavy, wonderfully shaped arm away from her.

She managed to pry open her eyes a fraction.

Sunlight had replaced the bars of soft moonlight.

Her wedding-ring quilt was tangled around their legs. They were sharing one pillow—the other two had ended up on the floor somewhere along the way. She could see them resting carelessly on the floor near the doorway.

"Phone's ringing." His voice was rusty with sleep.

"Why?" She closed her eyes again, turning toward

him as he rolled onto his back and instinctively fitted herself against his side.

His hand dropped onto her shoulder, his fingers lazily tracing circles over it. "You'd have to answer it to know that."

"Mmm." Her foot slid over his shin. Her knee brushed his hair-roughened thigh. So many textures. So many sensations.

He gave a rough chuckle and tumbled her onto her back as he rolled over, lifting his head, looking around the bedroom. "Where's your phone?"

It was still ringing. "In the kitchen."

"Why isn't it in here?"

She slid her hands around his waist as he climbed over her. "Because I don't want it waking me *up*," she said pointedly. "Let it ring. The machine will pick up."

He dropped a kiss on her forehead, and kept moving, right off the bed.

She shivered and dragged the quilt more closely around her as he walked, naked and bold as brass, out of her bedroom and down the hall. A second later, she heard him answer the phone. "It's 7 a.m.," he greeted the caller. "It better be important."

She pressed her head into the pillow, cringing. Sensibility was slow in coming, but she knew that a man answering her phone was definitely going to cause some talk.

She heard his footsteps padding back along the hall and stop when he reached the bedroom.

"If that's my mother or father," she mumbled from the pillow she'd pressed to her face, "we are *both* in big trouble."

He didn't answer and she lowered the pillow.

His dark brows were pulled down low over his brow.

He ought to have not looked as fierce as he did considering he was standing there as naked as the day he was born, albeit far more grown than an innocent babe. And even though now was not the time—judging from his black expression—to be wallowing breathlessly in the sheer, masculine beauty of him, she couldn't help it.

"It's not your parents," he said flatly.

She moistened her lips. "Who—"

"Your knight-errant."

"What?"

"Brody Paine." He grabbed his pants and started pulling them on.

"He's probably calling about schoolwork for Megan," she said hurriedly.

His lips twisted. "Most people consider this a holiday weekend and the sun's barely up."

"You've got no reason to sound suspicious." She shoved back her heavy hair and slid off the bed, snatching up the first thing her hand came in contact with, which happened to be her corset.

His gaze followed her movements, fastening on the garment in her hands. "Sure about that?"

Her lips tightened and she dropped the corset, grabbing his white shirt, instead. She pulled it around her shoulders, clutching it together at her waist and sailed past him.

Worry was tightening her stomach, which didn't make keeping up the front against him any easier. She hurried into the kitchen and snatched up the receiver where it was resting on the table. "Brody? This is Sarah."

"He standing there listening?"

She didn't have to glance over her shoulder to know that Max was standing in the doorway because she could practically feel his gaze boring a hole between her shoulder blades. "Sure," she answered brightly.

"We got a problem."

Her stomach tightened even more. "Oh?"

"Roberta—the agent who spelled me last night—has got some fricking bug. She's been puking all morning. I've got something I need to see to. Megan needs someone to stay with her."

"I—well, I suppose I could. For how long?"

"Just today. I should be back tonight. If I'm not, we'll get more backup here by then."

"Could Megan come here?"

He sighed, sounding completely frustrated. "That's not exactly protocol."

As far as Sarah had ever been able to determine, there really wasn't a strict protocol about much of anything where Hollins-Winword was concerned. What the agency's concern was, was safety. Personal safety. Corporate safety. National and international safety. She was just a very small cog in one small facet. "It'll be fine," she assured, even though she really wasn't confident of any such thing.

She *was* concerned that Megan might slip on the cover story if they ran into anyone in town—and given the explosion of relatives around because of the holiday and the wedding, it was likely that Sarah would be encountering someone. And she was definitely concerned that Max was already suspicious where Brody was concerned.

It was ridiculous, of course.

The man had no reason to be suspicious.

Except that Brody Paine isn't who you've said he is, and your involvement with him isn't coincidental at all.

She swatted away the irksome truth.

Max had been used to a certain level of excitement when it came to his work. Weaver couldn't possibly come close to the challenges that had been presented to him in Los Angeles. He was looking for shadows that weren't there.

She heard Brody curse under his breath. "Fine. She can stay there. But keep it to yourself."

"Yeah. That'll work," she said dryly. She was supposed to be driving around to pick up donations for the upcoming holiday boutique. "Bring her when you're ready." She hung up the phone and turned to face Max.

He'd pulled on his trousers, but hadn't fastened the button, and they hung low on his hips, exposing the fine line of hair arrowing downward from his navel. His arms were crossed over his bare chest, and his biceps bulged.

It was distracting just to look at the man. He might joke about feeling old, but in her opinion, he looked hard, fit and impossibly perfect. "I'm going to mind Megan Paine for the rest of the day," she told him. "Her dad's in a bind."

"So he calls you."

"I'm probably one of the few people he knows around here, because of Megan's schoolwork," she dismissed. "Want coffee?" She headed toward the coffeemaker sitting on the counter next to the stove.

What Max wanted was an answer to the reason she kept avoiding his eyes. And he wanted to keep her away from Brody Paine. Not only because he'd seen the way the guy looked at Sarah, but because the man was a complete unknown. Despite Max's efforts to learn something—anything—about him, Brody Paine remained totally off the grid.

Given the timing of his arrival in town and the reason for Max even being there in the first place, it was a coincidence he didn't like.

Brody Paine could *easily* be connected even though Max had yet to find proof.

"I don't like him," he told her.

She laughed slightly as she filled the coffee filter. "Brody? For pity's sake, Max, I've told you. There's nothing between us."

"Keep it that way."

She pushed the filter in place and jabbed the power button with a little too much enthusiasm. Her eyes were the color of a frozen-over lake when they turned his way. "Excuse me?"

He dropped his arms and moved next to her at the counter. She was no longer clutching his shirt together between her breasts and it had fallen open, revealing a wedge of smooth, satiny skin that had the blood warming in his veins. "There's something wrong where that guy is concerned and I want you to stay away from him."

She shoved the canister holding the coffee grounds back against the others that matched it. "Are you that bored with Weaver already that you're conjuring up drug dealers and murderers? Or are you just afraid that he might try to get me into bed?"

"He'd be a damn fool not to try that. And, as it happens, there's nothing all that boring about Weaver."

She looked disbelieving. "You're telling me you're satisfied stopping a speeder now and then and writing up reports for fender benders in the shopping center's parking lot? Please. You thrived on the hunt, Max. I might have been naive about everything else when I ran into you in California at Frowley-Hughes, but even I recognized *that*. Before we know it, you'll be heading on, looking for something a *lot* more interesting than what Weaver's got to offer."

Getting into an argument wasn't going to solve anything, particularly when she was right about one thing—he *did* have plans to move on. Plans that, by the day, were becoming annoyingly murky. "Trust me on this, Sarah. I'm asking you. Please. Stay away from him."

Her lashes lowered. The high color in her cheeks slowly retreated. "I've already agreed to watch Megan for him. What's one afternoon? She's a sweet little girl who's lost everything that mattered to her."

"Except dear ol' dad."

"Except Brody," she agreed. The coffeemaker hissed softly between them. "I wouldn't turn my back on Eli," she pointed out after a moment. "I won't do that with Megan, either."

"What's he got to do that's so important he can't take care of his kid?"

"I have no idea." She pulled down two white mugs from the cupboard above her head and rested her palms over the tops of them, giving him a look. "You've left Eli alone with your mother and you've been here all night since we...since we—"

He circled her narrow wrist with his fingers and lifted her hand. Her fingers curled downward and he pressed his index finger over her pulse, feeling the beat. "That's different. I let my mom know where I was."

"You don't know that it's different. You're just assuming that Brody doesn't have a perfectly valid reason for needing someone to watch Megan."

"Your pulse is racing."

She moistened her lips, looking wry and pained at the same time. "Pardon me. I'm not so used to having a half-naked man in my kitchen."

He lifted her wrist until it was above her head and slowly revolved her until she was facing him, her back pressed against the counter top. Her other arm was free and the sleeve of his too-large shirt was falling loosely off her shoulder. "You meant it then. That there hasn't been anyone."

She bent that arm, crossing it over her chest and halting the descent of his shirt. "Did *you* mean it?"

That he hadn't been with a woman since Jennifer? Admitting it in the cold light of morning was a far sight more difficult than it had been in the dark, drugging warmth of Sarah's inviting bed. "Yeah."

Her lips softened and the icy-lake blue thawed. "I'm sorry you and Eli had to go through losing her. Nobody should have to lose anyone to cancer."

"She knew about you. She felt badly about everything. Told me that I needed to get in touch with you."

She was silent, absorbing that. The long line of her lovely throat worked. "But you didn't."

"I couldn't," he corrected. He closed his fingers around the bottom of his shirt that she was pretending to wear and slowly pulled on it. It began sliding downward between her bent arm and her breast. "Walking away once was all I could manage."

Her eyes hadn't merely thawed. They glimmered. Sheer. Wet. "Don't tell me things you don't mean, Max. I can take nearly anything but that."

"I mean every word." He continued pulling the bottom of the shirt. Beneath her arm, the swell of her breast was revealed. He kept up the pressure, slowly and inexorably drawing the shirt aside, until her nipple, tight and raspberry sweet, peeked free above her forearm. "Now you. Did you mean it?"

The coffeepot behind her gurgled and sighed its last drops of brew.

Her gaze lifted to his. "The men I've occasionally dated—I, we haven't—" She broke off, her cheeks flushing. "There's only been you," she finished huskily.

It humbled him, he realized, hearing her confirm it.

He slid his arm beneath the shirt, circling her waist, fingers spreading over the gentle flare of hip. He lifted her and she gasped as he settled her on the counter's edge.

He dropped his head, finding that taunting nipple with his lips and dragged the shirt from her, tossing it away.

She let out a shuddering sigh, her fingers flexing, kneading against his shoulders. His hands slid along her smooth thighs, slipping between, nudging them apart, making room for himself.

"Max, oh *God*—we're in my kitchen!"

"And I'm starving," he said against her.

The skin of her inner thighs was the smoothest thing he'd ever felt in his life.

The down at the apex the softest.

The flesh the sweetest.

She jerked when he touched her there. Tasted her there. Her hands scrambled against the flat countertop, finding no purchase, and knocked into his shoulders, and finally settled into his hair, holding him to her. She moaned, shuddering. Quivering. And finally, too quickly, too slowly—convulsing.

He looked up at her. Her lips, soft and rosy, parted as she dragged in long breaths. Her eyes still had tears in them, but they seemed to gleam with a deep blue flame. Her reddish-blond hair licked down her back and he could actually see her heart beating through her pale, delicate skin.

Her gaze tangled with his, and watching her, never breaking that contact, he kissed the flat belly and felt it spasm beneath his lips. He kissed the valley between her breasts and felt her heartbeat pound against him.

And when he reached her lips, they were moving, chanting his name again and again.

He would never get enough of this woman.

He pulled her off the counter and her legs came around his hips and he turned to go to the bedroom.

It was Saturday, he reasoned with the few remaining reasonable cells functioning in his brain.

His son was taken care of by his grandmother. He wasn't on deputy duty because Tommy Potter had offered to take the shift. The guy was always wanting extra shifts. This time Max had taken him up on it and he was glad.

He could spend the entire day making love to—

"The doorbell's ringing," Sarah muttered against his mouth. "Oh, good grief, they're already here!" She was suddenly pushing against Max, swinging her legs free.

He either had to let her go, or they'd both end up in a tangle on the hall floor. All he caught was a glimpse of her shapely, nude derriere as she scrambled, practically on all fours, into her bedroom at the end of the short hall.

The door slammed shut.

Leaving him standing there, hard, and alone.

"Dammit." He could have said a lot worse as he saw Brody Paine peering around the side of the window next to the door, trying to see through the curtains hanging there. Thank God, Max knew it was a lot harder to see *into* the house, than it was to see out of it.

He strode into the kitchen and swiped up his shirt, yanking it over his shoulders and fastening the bottom few buttons. Then he grabbed open the door, and glared at the man standing on the porch.

Brody's gaze went over Max's state of undress. "Sarah here?" His voice was mild, but he did sort of step in front of the skinny girl hovering behind him.

Max turned away. Annoyed, horny, suspicious, and quite possibly jealous didn't make for a welcoming demeanor. "Sarah," he barked.

"I'm here, I'm here." She was skidding back into the room on stocking feet, having thrown on a deep blue sweat suit that looked like it was made for lounging on the cover of a fashion magazine rather than for working up an actual sweat.

She was dragging her hair back into a ponytail holder and if there was any sign of the woman who'd just come apart in his hands on her kitchen counter, he'd be damned if he could see it.

Avoiding his eyes, she hurried past him to the door and pushed the storm door wide. "Hi, Megan. Brody. Come on in."

Max stomped down the hall to the bedroom and slammed the door behind him.

Yeah, he was acting about as mature as Eli, but at the moment, he didn't give a flying flip.

He pulled on his shoes and socks. Sarah was obviously going to be busy watching over the girl.

And Max—like it or not—had a job to do.

Brody was heading *somewhere* that day.

Max was going to find out exactly where.

And then, maybe, he could close the file on Weaver.

For some reason, that possibility was losing its appeal.

He pushed off the tumbled bed and slowly picked up the pillows that had fallen to the floor. He pressed one to his face.

It smelled of Sarah.

He set both pillows on the bed and left the room.

Sarah and Brody were facing each other, the full distance of the living room between them.

Megan was hovering behind her father, misery practically screaming from her narrow shoulders, clad in a knitted sweater that looked about a full size too large. Her dishwater blond hair hung lank alongside her solemn face and her too-big brown eyes followed every movement Max made.

He picked up his coat that he didn't even remember leaving on the couch. He eyed Sarah for a moment. "Remember the locks."

She nibbled her lip. Nodded.

Ignoring Brody altogether, Max left, going out through the back door.

Who the hell was he kidding?

He knew why closing the case and getting out of Weaver didn't fill him with joy any longer.

And she was inside that tiny house, lying her sweet tush off to him about what she was doing.

Chapter 12

"Come on, Megan. Why don't you try on this one?" Sarah held up the vividly colored blouse she'd plucked off the rack.

They were in Classic Charms, Sarah's favorite shop on Main Street. It had been there for less than a year, but even in that time had gained a rapid popularity, carrying an eclectic mix of clothing, furniture, and various bric-a-brac.

On the weekend following Thanksgiving, it was doing a pretty brisk business, too, and Sarah had been about at her wit's end thinking of something to entertain Megan.

They'd already driven around collecting the items for the school boutique, which was probably more than Brody would have approved of. Driving over to the mall in Braden would have undoubtedly sent him over the edge when she'd have to tell him, and the shopping center on the other side of town held little appeal to Sarah.

But browsing down Main? When she'd proposed the idea to Megan, the girl had agreed, almost as if she'd believed she had no choice. Probably because everything that had happened in her young life lately had definitely *not* been her choice.

The girl was so excruciatingly sad it was heartbreaking.

"What do you think?" Sarah waggled the padded hanger and the purple-and-blue tie-dyed fabric seemed to shimmer a little. "It'd look great with your coloring."

Megan's lashes barely lifted long enough for her to look at the blouse. She'd hardly spoken five sentences all morning.

Not that she was rude. Inordinately polite, if anything. "I'm sorry, Miss Clay. But I don't have money."

Sarah tossed the blouse over her arm and crouched down in front of Megan. "Well, I do," she countered gently. "And I *love* to shop, but my closet is chock-full already. This is a gift from me. So all you have to decide is if you like the colors." She looked at the clothing rack—which was actually an old-fashioned phone booth with pipes sticking out of it at all sorts of odd angles. "Or do you prefer something else?"

Megan's fingers lightly touched the fabric, as if she couldn't quite resist. She finally leaned forward a little and lowered her voice. "Mr. Brody doesn't take me out shopping," she said, almost inaudibly.

"I'm not Mr. Brody," Sarah whispered back. She squeezed Megan's thin shoulder.

If Sarah accomplished anything that day, she was going to get a smile out of this girl.

And, it kept her mind off the fact that when Max had

left her house that morning, he'd said nothing whatsoever about calling her. Or seeing her.

She, of course, hadn't wanted to make an issue about it in front of Brody, and had cowardly said absolutely nothing.

She'd just watched Max walk out her door.

It had been a dismaying moment of déjà vu.

"Well? Want to try it on? Tara has a dressing room behind the counter there. I'll wait right outside the curtain," she promised.

The girl nibbled her lip again. Then shyly nodded.

Triumphant, Sarah straightened. She took Megan's hand and they walked to the back of the shop. She handed over the top to Megan and pulled back the long curtain that afforded complete privacy for the single changing room. "You have to show me," she told Megan. "When you have it on. No switching back to your sweater before I get to see."

Megan ducked her chin. She nodded and pulled the curtain down.

Sarah hummed under her breath along with the Christmas carols that were playing on the shop's sound system. Maybe she'd take Megan out to the *C*. The girl might like a horse ride as much as Eli had.

In fact, maybe Eli would like another lesson and she could kill two birds with one stone.

The expression made her mentally wince given how Megan's parents had died.

Was it any wonder the child was skittish? She was an exceptionally smart girl. She knew the sort of danger she'd been in before they'd brought her to Weaver.

Sighing a little, Sarah toyed with the pens that were stored in a milk-glass vase next to the vintage cash register and whirled back around when she heard Megan whisper her name.

"Oh, Megan. Look at you! That is *so* pretty. Do you like it?"

Megan looked at herself in the tall mirror that lined one side of the dressing room. She nodded before casting a worried look at Sarah. "Can I try on some others?"

"Honey, you can try on everything here right down to lampshades on your head if you like."

Megan's lips lifted just a hair. She walked back to the rack of clothes and studied them carefully.

Tara Browning, the shop owner, walked behind the cash register and smiled at Sarah. "Getting a start on Christmas shopping?"

"I suppose I should be," she admitted.

Would Max still be in Weaver by then? Christmas was four weeks away.

Turning off the thought proved difficult, so Sarah joined Megan at the rack. Only every garment that she pulled out and held up to her own chest had her wondering how Max would like it.

She stopped looking, and sat down experimentally on the wide, nubby couch that, according to the hand-lettered signs, could be ordered in three-dozen other fabrics. She was watching the glass door that opened out onto Main Street, and smiled when she saw Eli come into view, followed closely by Genna Scalise.

The woman definitely had the whole crutch thing down.

Sarah rose and crossed the shop. "I was just thinking about you," she said to Eli.

Genna pulled her long knitted scarf off her head and unbuttoned her coat. "Seems to be going around," she replied. "Eli's talked nonstop about you and the day we had at your family's place. I still can't tell you how much we enjoyed it."

"We were all glad to have you," Sarah assured. From the corner of her eye, she watched Megan go into the changing room again. "So, is the Christmas shopping season calling to you, too?"

Genna nodded. "Have a few gifts to pick up. Don't know *what* to get my son. Ever since Tony, he's had it in his head that he should only get *me* gifts, doesn't want to take any in return." She finished working out of her coat, and Sarah took it from her, laying it over the back of a bar stool that was doing double duty as a plant stand. "I've also been hearing nothing but talk around town today about Leandra and Evan's wedding yesterday. I was sorry to miss it. Have they left for a honeymoon?"

"Last night. Five days in balmy Mexico."

Genna's eyes twinkled. "Sounds lovely. Max and Jennifer went to Mexico after they were married."

Sarah waited for the pang, but when it came, it was not as sharp as it once would have been. "It's a popular place. I'd better check on Megan's progress. Oh." She turned back to Genna. "If Eli's interested, I thought he might like to go riding again today. I'm going to take Megan, too. They might enjoy meeting each other and I *know* they'll both enjoy the horses. I'm thinking maybe around two or three?"

"I can't seem to place her," Genna said, looking beyond Sarah to the girl.

"She and her dad are staying out at the Holley place. Haven't been in town too long."

"Oh, of course. He's the writer." Seeming satisfied she'd placed them, she looked at Sarah again. "I'm sure Eli would love to go with you. Particularly since Max is out of town for a few days. But I'm sure he told *you* that." She looked pleased at the idea.

Sarah tucked her tongue between her teeth for a moment, feeling her face flush. Naturally Genna knew that Max hadn't come home last night. But Sarah *hadn't* known that Max had left town. "Right," she baldly lied.

Genna was already crossing the shop, heading for a display of delicate Christmas ornaments. "I don't know what case he's working on, but he's sure putting in some ridiculous hours." She picked up a translucent green bulb. "Pretty, isn't it?"

"Yes." But Sarah wasn't really looking at the ornament. She was too busy telling herself that Max's abrupt disappearance was nothing to worry about.

She'd hear from him.

She would.

The self-assurance was definitely wearing thin by midweek. By the *end* of the week, it was bare threads. Only the fact that Eli was still coming to class every day—and primarily behaving himself—assured her that Max hadn't just gone from Weaver for good.

So, when he suddenly appeared the morning of the holiday boutique being held in the auditorium at her school, acting as if nothing was amiss, she told herself her irritation was justified.

"Where do you want the rolls, Sarah?" Justine Leoni drew back Sarah's attention from Max's unexpected entrance. She was carrying an enormous, flat bakery box that smelled delicious. She had three more boxes stacked on a rolling cart behind her.

Ignore Max. Sarah gestured to the tables to one side of the auditorium. "All the food'll be over there. Need some help?"

Justine waved off the offer, and deftly maneuvered the cart, even with her full hands.

Sarah's gaze started straying toward the doorway and Max once again.

More irritated with herself than anyone, including him, she snatched up one of the fresh wreaths that she hadn't finished hanging around the room, and headed for the ladder where she'd left it, directly opposite the doorway. She looped the wreath over her arm and started up the rungs. The soothing fragrance of the fresh balsam surrounded her.

"Looks like somebody shook up a bottle of fizzy Christmas soda and let it explode in here," Max said, below her.

She kept her eye on the light fixture from which she was hanging the wreath. "Hello to you, too." She twisted the floral wire on the back of the wreath together and looped it over the light.

The wreath settled neatly against the wall and she adjusted the bright red bow at the bottom of it.

"Eli told me he put my name on a list last week to help out at this shindig."

She'd passed out the sign-up sheet on Monday. "Don't worry, Max." She descended the ladder, her gaze skimming over him. He wore jeans and a leather bomber jacket and aside from smelling dismayingly good, she thought he looked tired. "Plenty of other parents are coming to help."

He slanted a look at her. "Meaning what?"

She reached the floor. "Meaning you don't have to feel obligated." The ladder folded together with a loud snap and she tilted it against her shoulder to drag it over to the last light fixture.

He grabbed the ladder, and would have lifted it right

out from her hands if she hadn't held on. "Who says anything about obligation? Maybe I want to be here."

She recognized that fighting over the ladder would be silly so she let go of it. "Right."

"Where's this coming from?"

"You're clearly a busy man." Her voice was dulcet.

"Yes, I am. Yet I have the distinct feeling that those words aren't a satisfactory excuse. You're angry."

She picked up the last wreath. "Put the ladder there, if you're so determined to help."

He set the ladder in place. Spread the legs of it. "Sarah—"

She could feel her eyes burning and felt like she was all of sixteen years old, and had been jilted for a school dance. Either she was an adult, or she wasn't.

She set the wreath over a ladder rung and looked at him. "Why didn't you tell me you were leaving town?"

"It was work stuff."

Her lips twisted. "Yes. I believe I *heard* that. It would have been nice to hear it from you. But, you know, it was a necessary reminder for me."

His lips were tight. "About what?"

"Not to get used to you being around."

He stifled an oath. "I'm not going anywhere."

She lifted her eyebrows. "Really? That's not what Eli thinks. He specifically shared with me how you've told him you're only here until your mother is healed up. He told me and I still—" She broke off, realizing her voice was rising. She picked up the wreath again. "I still slept with you," she said for his ears only. "My mistake."

He grabbed the sides of the ladder as she started up it. "This is *not* seven years ago, Sarah. Nothing is the same as it was then."

She rapidly stuck the wreath in place and quickly

descended the ladder once more. He was right about that. The feelings she had for him now seemed frighteningly new. "Only thing that has changed is geography," she lied.

"That and the propensity you've acquired for keeping secrets."

Her lips parted. "*Secrets?*" She darted a look around them, hoping they weren't drawing more attention. She still had to live in Weaver once he went on his way. "Compared to you, my life is an open book!"

"Really." He jerked his chin, his gaze moving past her. "Then what the hell are you doing with him?"

She turned to see what he was looking at and wanted to groan out loud at the sight of Brody Paine.

Of all times for him to take her up on her regular invitations to include Megan in at least one of the school functions. "Get your mind out of the gutter," she told Max stiffly, and crossed the room to greet Megan.

The girl was wearing the colorful tie-dyed blouse and looked even happier than she had the afternoon that Sarah had taken her and Eli riding. "I like the shirt, Meggie."

The girl's cheeks colored, seeming pleased. "Thank you." She tugged on Brody's arm. "Can I go see Eli… Dad?" She managed to tack on that last.

Brody nodded. His eyes tracked the child's progress as she crossed the room to where Eli was hanging over a chair, watching Dee Crowder set up the Pin the Beard on the Santa game.

"So, Brody. What spurred this nice surprise?"

Brody pushed his hands in the pockets of his jeans. If Sarah weren't so entirely consumed with a certain black-haired deputy, she might be more inclined to appreciate the view he presented.

Brody Paine *was* a good-looking man. And judging by the arch looks Dee was sending toward Sarah, that fact was definitely being noticed.

"They're pulling me from this gig," he murmured. "About one more week."

Dismay filled her. "Already? But—but what happens with Megan?"

He lifted his shoulder. "The guy who did her parents is finally taken care of. And you know the drill. Everyone moves on—no more contact."

She did know the drill. She just had never particularly liked it. Now, with Megan, she liked it even less. She wasn't ready to see the girl disappear from their lives. "Can't you at least stay with her through the holidays? For heaven's sake, she deserves a little consistency."

"I don't call those shots, Sarah." A hint of sympathy crossed his face. "And you're not supposed to get so involved that you lose your objectivity, either."

She huffed, crossing her arms and looking away. If she'd been objective, she never would have agreed to be part of Hollins-Winword in the first place.

Across the room, Dee had now enlisted Megan and Eli. They were helping her pin up the big Santa posters and both the children seemed to be having a grand time from the looks of it. "I want to talk to Coleman Black," Sarah said abruptly.

Brody's expression changed. "So would a lot of people, doll. Doesn't mean it'll happen."

She gave him a hard look.

He made a face. "Ask your uncle. Get better luck through him than me."

"My *uncle?*"

"Tristan. He's—well *hell*." His expression was almost comical with surprise. "You don't know, do you?"

She'd never liked feeling in the dark. "Know what?" she asked warily.

"Tell *him* who you want to see," Brody said simply. Then he lifted his arms as if to end that particular topic. "So, I'm here. Not gonna drag Megan away now. Even I'm not that callous. Where do you want me to work?" He looked around. "I assume you *do* want me to work."

She exhaled, feeling completely off-kilter. Her uncle Tristan designed video games. What could he possibly have to do with Hollins-Winword? "I need someone to sell raffle tickets," she said.

He looked disgusted. But, when she plunked an enormous roll of tickets in his hands, he didn't decline.

Then she turned and faced Max.

Just one more man to deal with, she told herself.

Only Max wasn't just anything, and no matter how many times she tried to tell herself that, she couldn't make herself buy it.

He was leaning against the side of a long table, openly watching her exchange with Brody, and as she headed toward him, she couldn't help noticing again how tired he looked. There were dark circles beneath his changeable eyes, and the lines fanning out from the corners seemed deeper than usual.

"He's volunteering," she told him evenly.

"I thought only school parents were doing that."

"Maybe he *is* a school parent. You don't know everything that's gone on this past week."

"Megan would be in Eli's class and Eli didn't say squat about her, other than to talk about how you took them both riding at your folks' place. As you told me once, you *are* the only third-grade teacher here."

"You can do trash duty."

Unfortunately, the terse assignment only seemed to amuse him. His lips stretched. "Yes, ma'am. I'm here to serve."

Her teeth clamped together and she turned away, heading toward a cluster of parents who'd arrived and were waiting for direction.

Fortunately, Sarah didn't have much time to worry about Max after that. Not when there was a line of people waiting at the door the moment they officially opened their auditorium-sized boutique. Things didn't start to settle down until just before they were ready to close their doors at the end of the day, and Sarah had a chance to sit down and man a table herself.

It was the first break she'd had all day.

Within minutes, Max was emptying a trash can behind her table, whistling tunelessly along with the Christmas carols being played on the school's sound system, and Brody was sitting down beside her. He plopped a big paper bag on the floor between them. It was filled nearly to overflowing with the ticket halves from which the drawings would be taken at the end of the day. "Sold 'em all," he announced.

"Maybe you missed your calling," she murmured, amazed.

"Speaking of which," Max said, his voice annoyingly smooth, "what is it that you write?"

Sarah rested her elbows on the table and pressed her hands to her cheeks. She was tired enough to let the two men battle whatever pissing contest they had going on between them.

"Technical reports," Brody said easily. "Nothing anybody ever remembers me for, I'm afraid, but it pays the bills."

She made herself smile when Tommy Potter ambled over to the table and started picking through the arrangement of homemade wrapping paper and gift tags. "How're you doing, Tommy?"

The deputy shrugged. "Fair enough." He picked up a plastic baggie filled with gold tags on which Sarah herself had calligraphed the greetings. "Max, you want to trade shifts again tomorrow? I could use the extra time in the old paycheck this month."

"Sorry. Can't." Max whipped a fresh bag inside the barrel. "Try Dave." Dave Ruiz was the third deputy, Sarah knew, though he spent more time in the Braden office than in Weaver.

"No problem. Will do." Tommy flipped open his wallet and handed over some bills. "Thanks, Sarah. Nice turnout you're having here. Good job."

She gave him his change. "Thanks. Stop and visit Dee on your way out, why don't you?"

He seemed to flush a little, and ducked his chin, mumbling something inaudible before ambling away again.

"Only time that guy mumbles is when it comes to a pretty woman," Max murmured. "Can't shut the guy up when we're at the station house."

"He's shy," Sarah excused.

"And I think we'll be outta here." Brody leaned back in the metal folding chair to stretch. "Gotta feed Megan something other than peanut brittle and Christmas cookies."

"Brody—bring her to the holiday pageant at least. It's just next week. Thursday evening."

His smile was sympathetic, but noncommittal. "We'll see."

She hadn't liked that phrase as a girl and nothing had changed since.

The moment Brody vacated the seat beside her, Max assumed it. His arm brushed against hers as he folded his hands on top of the nearly empty table.

She shifted, putting a few more inches between them. Across the room, Brody had collected Megan and the girl turned, sending a wave in her direction.

Sarah's heart squeezed. She lifted her hand.

"What's wrong? You look like you're never going to see her again."

She dropped her hand, her cheeks heating. "Not at all. She's a nice girl. She's lost a lot in her life. You know what it's like for a child to lose a parent."

"She looks a damn sight more animated than she did last week," he admitted. "Think Eli's got a crush on her or something the way he jabbers on about her." He idly picked up the last of the baggies filled with tags. "He's no writer."

"You're like a dog with a bone."

"Been compared to worse things. What do you want to bet me that you know what he *is?*"

She snatched up the bag of raffle tickets. "Time for the drawing."

He stretched out one leg, settling deeper into the folding chair. "I'm not going anywhere."

"Yet." She didn't wait for his reaction as she headed to the small stage and the microphone there. "All right, ladies and gents, time for the big moment. I need someone up here for a little help, though."

A bunch of hands flew up in the air, mostly belonging to students of the school. She pointed out several whom she knew to be first-graders and they all raced up to her, jockeying for position. She held the bag where they could reach in. "Dig deep now, and pull out just one ticket."

Fierce expressions of concentration crossed their young faces as one by one they drew and Sarah read off the numbers for the prizes—everything from free meals and massages to a cord of chopped firewood to a weekend trip to Las Vegas. The last prize—considered by some to be the granddaddy of them all—was a year's worth of Sunday breakfasts at Ruby's.

Sarah joggled the bag, smiling over the catcalls to mix the tickets even more, and took the ticket that emerged courtesy of the last young ticket-puller. She held it up and read off the numbers, watching the crowd. And when Max rose and began making his way forward, she managed to keep her smile in place. He worked through the back-slapping congratulations and came up beside her on the stage where she held the envelope holding the certificate Justine had generously donated.

Sarah flicked off the microphone. "I'm sure Justine won't mind if you give the prize to your mother," she murmured as she handed over the envelope.

His fingers brushed hers. "Why would I do that?"

"A year's a long time." She picked up the bag and held it against her chest, turning to flip on the microphone and thank everyone for their support.

When she was finished, Max followed her off the little stage. "A year's not so long, depending on who you spend it with."

She swallowed, her heart giving an odd lurch. "Eli *does* make time fly. Excuse me. I have to collect all the money now." She turned and practically raced away from him.

But she knew she was really racing away from the longing to believe he actually meant her.

Chapter 13

After the school event, Sarah dropped the money they'd collected in the night depository at the bank and headed home.

But she couldn't relax. Not after Max's presence all that day. Not after what he'd said.

But he hadn't suggested seeing her that evening, hadn't done anything but collect Eli and head out after he'd hauled bag after bag of trash to the containers behind the school building.

She made a few phone calls. Leandra, who was back from her honeymoon with Evan and so distracted that Sarah was half-afraid of just what she'd interrupted with her phone call. Her cousin, Lucy, who had a flight out to New York the following morning. She even tried her uncle Tristan's number, only Justin—their youngest—told her that his folks had gone out of town for the day.

When she found herself dialing Genna Scalise's

number, she quickly hung up the phone. Chasing after Max was something she would *not* do. Not again. No amount of explaining the past could change her feelings on that score.

But as she was pulling out the box of Christmas decorations in preparation for decorating her *own* place, her gaze kept falling on the recent purchases she'd made at Classic Charms. She'd gone back to the shop and had picked up every single item that Megan had seemed to like. They were already wrapped in festive Christmas packages.

Only Megan would be gone before Christmas.

For all Sarah knew, Max could well be gone by then, too, no matter *how* many free breakfasts he'd won at Ruby's.

Knowing that Max was at the root of her restlessness didn't stop Sarah from doing at least one concrete, productive thing.

She gathered up Megan's gifts and loaded them in the front seat of her car. The late hour didn't prevent her from driving out to the Holley place. She knew Brody and Megan would be there. She just didn't know for how many more *days* they'd be there.

The graded road out to the old farmhouse was passable. It had been snowplowed, but time and use had worn deep ruts that she wasn't entirely successful in avoiding. So she bumped along the miles and was particularly grateful when the single light burning on the front porch came into sight.

Though it was nearing ten o'clock when she arrived, she hadn't even doused her headlights before several more lights around the house flashed on, startling her for a moment.

Security lights, she realized. Probably motionau-
tomated.

She parked her car and gathered up the items she'd
brought for Megan and headed toward the porch.

Well into the darkness, Max watched the front door
of the farmhouse open even before Sarah could knock.
Brody Paine looked out, casting a quick look around,
then practically pulled Sarah inside.

The door closed.

"What the hell is my niece doing here?" Beside Max,
Sawyer's mild voice was belied by the tension suddenly
emanating from him.

Max knew how the man felt. "Good question."
They'd had the Holley place under surveillance for
more than a week, ever since an unusual money flow
had been traced to Paine, the timing of which coincided
too neatly with a major drug ring bust that had been
made in Arizona that week. Then, another package of
meth had been discovered just that morning on a trailer
belonging to Jefferson Clay.

There'd been no unusual activity around the property
though, until that afternoon, when a stranger had arrived in a Hummer bearing a false registration. He'd left
after less than an hour, and the tail Max had assigned to
the vehicle reported that it was left in the parking lot of
the Cheyenne airport. Unfortunately, the driver of the
Hummer had been lost inside the airport.

Unfathomable to Max, but stuff happened.

"I prefer good answers," Sawyer countered. Max
knew the sheriff wasn't entirely convinced of Brody's
involvement. "What was she carrying?"

"Looked like Christmas presents to me," Max murmured, knowing perfectly well that the other man had

seen the same gift-wrapped boxes. "Maybe they're for Megan. Sarah seems attached to the kid. But I know one thing—" he pushed open the door of the vehicle "—I'm going to find out." He checked his weapon, and yanked his coat on, shoving his radio in the side pocket.

"No warrant, yet," Sawyer reminded. "This may be your show, son, but I wouldn't want anyone slipping through legal technicalities."

Max didn't either. "I'm just a jealous boyfriend," he assured smoothly, and started toward the house. Unfortunately, the explanation was more true than not.

He heard Sawyer swear under his breath and the man who eschewed guns slowly reached for the rifle hanging in the rack behind his head.

Max didn't particularly like guns, either. Hell, if the truth be known, he was pretty sick to death of them.

Beneath his boots, the gravel—half muddy, half covered with frozen-crisp snow—sounded loud in the still night. He passed Sarah's car, looking in the windows, seeing nothing but a box sitting on the back seat, containing leftovers he recognized from the school sale.

The security lights positioned with military precision around the house were still on. Feeling itchy with exposure, Max rapidly covered the distance to the house, heading up the steps. The door held little resistance to a well-aimed boot, and he almost could hear Sawyer cursing from the vehicle two hundred yards away.

His eyes took in the two figures that turned toward him when the doorjamb splintered. He was hitting the floor, his weapon drawn before Sarah's face could become more than a blur as Brody roughly shoved her aside and trained his own Glock at Max's head.

The other guy was as wide open as Max was—neither had any cover in the sparsely furnished room.

Sarah's startled scream echoed inside his head, but Max didn't take his eyes off Brody. "Put it down," he warned grimly.

"Max." Sarah was scrambling to her feet. "You don't know what you're doing!"

"Stay out of the way—"

"Stay back—"

Both men spoke at the same time.

She ignored both of them. "I won't stay back!" Max wasn't sure if Brody looked more pained than Max felt when she stubbornly stepped right between them.

"Thought you told me he was no threat," Brody said. His voice was cold.

She flapped her arms. "He's not." She glared at Max. "What *are* you doing?"

"My job," he snapped. "Now get out of here. Sawyer's outside. You can explain yourself later."

Her brows rose, nearly disappearing beneath the hair that had tumbled across her forehead. "Explain *myself?*"

Max's weapon didn't waver. He had sweat crawling down his spine, and there'd come a time when he'd probably puke his guts out at the panic he was feeling, seeing Sarah blocking Paine.

"I don't have to explain myself to you, Max Scalise!"

"Oh, fun," Brody drawled, looking suddenly amused. "A lovers' spat."

"Be quiet." Sarah whirled on him. "And put that thing away." She sounded just like Max's first-grade teacher. Only Mrs. Krantz had seemed older than the hills and had scared the bejabbers out of him.

"Him first," Brody said, gesturing with his handgun.

Sarah propped her hands on her hips. "Honestly, Brody, is this how you always do business?"

"It is when some fool crashes through my door in the middle of the friggin' night."

"What business?" The question gritted from between Max's clenched teeth.

A sudden blur of motion launched itself into the room, aiming straight for Sarah.

Max's aim shifted.

"Don't even try," Brody said icily, all semblance of amusement gone. He looked as if he'd just as soon shoot Max as breathe.

Megan was clutching Sarah's legs, mute and clearly terrified. He could see her shaking right through the red flannel nightgown she wore.

Sarah bent over the girl, hugging her and smoothing back the tumbled hair. "It's all right," she soothed. "Nobody's getting hurt." But when she angled a look at Max, her gaze was furious. "There's a perfectly reasonable explanation." She spoke slowly, her gaze taking in both men as if she were speaking to the village idiots.

Brody's expression was stony, and huffing a little, Sarah looked toward Max. "Isn't there?"

Megan hadn't budged her head from Sarah's belly.

"You tell me. Give me a perfectly reasonable explanation why your phone records show you've been in contact with Paine's cell phone since before he even *came* to Weaver."

Her lips parted. "You've been checking my phone records?"

"I've been trying to check *his*," he corrected tightly. Only they'd been extremely difficult to obtain. "What a delightful surprise that, in that process, I kept coming across *your* number."

Her lips looked white. "I... I know Brody professionally, all right? That's all."

"*What* profession?"

"Not the oldest one," she snapped, "So stop giving me a look like I just announced I'm a call girl."

Brody snickered and she shot him a deadly look.

"He's part of an investigation," he said finally.

"*He* is standing right here," Brody inserted blandly.

Sarah ignored him. "Investigation of what?"

"Drug trafficking."

At that, Brody suddenly lowered his weapon and raised his other hand. "Whoa. I think we got a problem here."

"Damn straight." Max didn't trust that casual grip on the Glock. "Put it on the floor and step away."

Sarah looked completely bewildered as Brody slowly complied. He set the gun near Sarah and Megan's feet and backed away.

"That's far enough. Sarah, push the gun over here."

She made a face, but nudged the toe of her brown boot against the weapon. She didn't let go of Megan.

Max snatched up the weapon and unloaded it. He heard the scrape of a shoe and swung his arm around, taking aim at the doorway, but the sight of Sawyer had him lowering his weapon.

"Uncle Sawyer." Sarah sounded painfully relieved. "Thank goodness. We *need* a voice of sanity here."

Whether he regularly carried a weapon or not, Sawyer carried the rifle with ease. "Just a jealous boyfriend?" His voice was dry, giving no real clue to what he really thought.

Max could guess though. Nothing like a royal FUBAR.

"Boyfriend." Sarah sniffed. "Not likely."

"You prefer the word *lover?*" Max drawled.

She flushed and leaned over Megan, whispering to

the girl. After a moment, the child unclenched her iron-tight grip and slipped over to Brody.

The man tucked her behind him, and though the motion was protective, it hardly seemed paternal to Max.

Sawyer sighed. "I'm too old for this crap," he muttered. "Sarah, get the girl there dressed. Seems we need to take a trip to the station house. Get some questions answered."

"With all due respect, Sheriff," Brody said, "you're barking up the wrong tree if you think I'm moving dope."

Sawyer didn't look any more convinced than Max felt. "Sarah," he prompted sharply.

Looking shaken, she ushered the girl out of the room.

"Now." Sawyer looked back at Brody. "Face on the floor. Something tells me you know the position."

Brody snorted and started to laugh, but it died when Max leveled his gun at him. Swearing under his breath, he dropped to the floor, arms and legs spread.

Max knelt over him, taking a little too much joy as he held the man down with his knee to his spine. He frisked the guy, found nothing but a small cell phone in his pocket, and snapped cuffs around his wrists. Then he grabbed Brody's arm and hauled him to his feet.

Sarah, entering the room again with Megan—now dressed in jeans and a sweatshirt instead of that long flannel nightgown—gasped at the sight. "This is all wrong," she said.

"Then we'll get it straightened out," Sawyer said wearily. "Can I trust you to drive yourself and the girl to the station?"

Her shoulders snapped back. She looked insulted. "Of course." Her gaze sent frosty daggers at Max as she picked up her coat from the threadbare couch and pulled it on. But her voice was gentle when she told Megan to get her coat, as well. As soon as the girl pulled it on, Sarah took her hand and they went out the front door.

"All right," Sawyer said. "Let's move it."

Megan was sitting on a molded chair across the room from Sarah. Exhaustion showed in the dark circles beneath her eyes, but she wouldn't let herself fall asleep, even though they'd been sitting in the sheriff's office for over an hour.

Max, Brody and Sawyer had disappeared down the hallway shortly after they'd arrived. Sawyer had merely told Sarah to stay put.

So she had. She'd stayed, and she'd fretted, and she'd fumed and then fretted some more and watched the clock on the wall slowly tick past midnight. Across the room from them, the dispatcher, Pamela, was doing a decent job of not looking too curious as she answered an occasional call and paged through a magazine.

Sarah was on the verge of going down that hallway beyond Pamela and finding her uncle herself when the blinds over the front door swayed and it opened.

Her uncle, Tristan, entered.

He took one look at her and frowned, but there was no surprise in his expression. "Well." he stopped in front of her, and the overhead light picked out a few silver hairs among his deep gold hair. "Seems there's more going on under my nose than I knew about."

She stood. "Tristan, what's happening? What's Max doing?" She hadn't forgotten Brody's implication that she could reach Coleman Black via her uncle.

He gave Megan a sidelong look. She'd folded her arms around herself and was not looking at anyone.

She'd even stopped responding to Sarah's efforts at conversation.

"Pamela—you can keep an eye on Megan?"

The woman nodded at Tristan. She sent a smile in Megan's direction.

It wasn't returned, and Sarah's stomach tightened. She badly wanted to get the girl out of there.

Tristan took Sarah's arm. "Come with me."

She thought, at first, that he was taking her back to the office where Max had disappeared. Instead, he ushered her into an empty office and closed the door.

He gave her a long look and seemed to sigh. "Sit down, Sarah."

"I don't want to sit. I want to know *what* is going on." She wanted to see Max. Not that she knew what she'd say to the man when she did.

He shoved his fingers through his hair. "A damned mess, far as I can tell." He pulled out one of the two chairs at the scarred Formica-topped table and sat down. "Max's investigation evidently crossed wires with Brody's assignment to protect the Devereaux kid."

She stiffened. "How did you know Megan's real name?"

His lips twisted. "Because you're not the only Clay family member that Coleman Black has tapped for Hollins-Winword. He seems to treat this family like his personal garden for growing agents."

She reached for the other chair, sitting weakly down on it.

"If I'd known what he'd done, I'd have stopped it, though. How long have you been involved?"

"Seven years." Her voice was faint.

"Someone—say, an aging white-haired guy—just

one day strikes up a conversation with you and, says 'Oh by the way, want to be a spy?'"

She jerked. "I'm not a spy." The idea was ludicrous. "I just…set up a safe house here in the area now and then. That's all. And it's perfectly legal."

Tristan's lips twisted. "Your part is," he agreed. "And I'm glad to know that's the extent of your involvement. Because H.W. can tiptoe along some murky lines in the whole *legal* regard."

Her stomach clenched. "If I'm not the first in the family, then who—"

"Jefferson. Daniel. They're both out of it now. Me?" He looked up at the ceiling and sighed faintly. "Let's just say that I'm not always as smart as they are."

"You've been here in Weaver running CeeVid my entire life."

"Close enough. You know the computer biz, squirt. Always a way to keep your fingers in pies that most people don't even know exist."

She shook her head, finding the entire situation unfathomable. Jefferson raised horses. And Daniel worked with her father at the C and had built more than half the new houses on the other side of town. "But—"

The door to the office creaked open and Max appeared.

He looked weary as he eyed the older man. "Great. You, too, huh?"

Tristan unfolded himself from the seat. He clapped Max on the shoulder. "Sorry, man. If I'd have known where your investigation was heading, I could have steered you clear of Paine. Saved you some wasted effort. Now, I'm gonna have to fess up to Sawyer that I didn't get out of the game a long time ago when he thought I did."

"Uncle Sawyer knows, too?"

Tristan's lips twitched. "Hell, squirt, he's the big brother of us all. Yeah. He knows." He dropped a kiss on her forehead and knuckled her head like she was ten years old. "Keep your chin up," he murmured. "Sun always rises in the morning." And with that, he left the office.

Alone with Max, Sarah closed her hands over the back of the metal chair. "You really thought that I could be involved with drugs?"

He reached behind himself and pushed the door closed. "What I believed was that you might not *know* what you were involved with," he countered grimly. "Which is why I would have appreciated it if you'd have stopped with the evasions and just told me the bloody truth about your relationship with Paine."

"There is no relationship."

A muscle ticked in his jaw. "Association, then."

"I didn't think there was anything to tell! All he was doing was protecting that little girl. And for heaven's sake, Max. My uncle surely never thought for a minute that I'd be involved in something illegal. Much less drugs!"

"It wasn't your uncle that suspected it, Sarah. It was *my* boss."

She winced. "Sawyer is your boss." But her stomach, that she'd already thought couldn't sink any lower, was seeming to puddle around her ankles.

Max stared at her from across the width of the table. "Sawyer was cooperating with the special DEA task force I'm on."

The width between them was suddenly miles wider than an old-fashioned Formica table.

Her grip on the back of the chair felt slippery. The

ticking of yet another industrial-looking clock on the wall sounded loud and distinct. He wasn't only a cop anymore. He was DEA. "You're working undercover again," she realized aloud. Her voice sounded muddy and dull.

He nodded once.

She swallowed, trying to clear the knot in her throat. "Déjà vu, indeed. Only this time, you didn't clue me in to that particular truth." Before, it had been his situation with Jennifer and Eli that he'd kept to himself.

"You haven't exactly been an open book either, darlin'."

"Does anyone besides Sawyer know why you're really here? Before now, I mean."

"No."

That was something, she supposed. She hadn't been the *only* one he'd kept in the dark.

"How'd you get involved with Hollins-Winword, anyway?"

Her palms hurt from pressing so hard against the chair back. She slowly straightened her fingers and let go. "What does it matter?"

He exhaled roughly. "Because, dammit, everything *about* you matters."

"And you sound so happy about that."

He suddenly raised the chair in front of him a foot and slammed it back down on the linoleum floor.

She winced.

He let go of the chair, shoving it against the table. "What should I *be* happy about, Sarah? The fact that you don't trust me enough to tell me the truth when I ask for it? Or that my one damn lead turns out to be a dead end the size of a mountain?"

"I've never heard anything about drugs being transported through Weaver. I mean, we have the occasional person busted for marijuana, but—"

"—Ten pounds of methamphetamine were found in Montana last month on a truck hauling Double-C cattle. This morning, Jefferson confiscated another ten that he found in a trailer he was sending out."

She swayed. "And you think my *family* is involved?"

"No."

"God. At least there's that."

"Other than the trucks, we couldn't find a link to your family."

Her hands trembled as she pushed back her hair. "Which means that you actually *looked* for a link."

His gaze didn't flinch. "It's my job, Sarah."

Her eyes burned. She pressed her lips together. "And was *I* part of the job, too?"

"No."

She felt like crying. "Where's Brody?"

His lips tightened again. "Making arrangements for Megan."

She suddenly headed for the door.

"Where are you going?"

"Presumably I'm not under arrest?" She barely waited for his annoyed shake of his head. "Then I'm going to tell Brody that I want Megan to go home with me."

He blocked the door, though. "Your concern is admirable, Sarah, but you're not even the girl's teacher. She probably should be placed with someone who's already raising children."

She winced. "I'd be *raising* my child if I hadn't miscarried him." Her voice was thick. "Now *move* away from the door or I swear, Max, the next thing my uncle will be doing is putting me in a cell for assaulting his fake deputy."

Chapter 14

"I'm sorry, Sarah." Brody was inflexible. She'd found him in her uncle's office, sitting behind Sawyer's desk. "You can't take Megan."

"Why not?"

"Because she's already been placed with a perfectly nice family in Quebec."

"*Quebec!* But that's not even in the country."

"I don't make the arrangements."

"Then who does? Coleman Black?"

Brody shook his head. "He doesn't get involved at that level."

"Tristan. He'll help me."

"He can try. But for now, I've got to take her."

She brushed her hands down her face. "This is a nightmare."

"Only because you've lost your objectivity."

"Thanks for the reminder, Brody. That's *ever* so helpful." But her voice was thick with tears as she turned out of the office. Brody followed.

Megan was still in the lobby where she'd been left. At the sight of Sarah, she slipped off the chair, looking small and defenseless. "It's okay, Miss Clay," she whispered. "Mr. Brody's doing what he has to."

The tears Sarah had been fighting slipped past her lashes, burning hot. The sight of Max handing a file over to Pamela didn't help any. She knelt down and put her arms around Megan's thin shoulders.

How quickly she'd let the girl under her skin. "You can call me. Or write."

Megan hugged her back. "I don't think they'll allow that." She stepped back, her chin trembling. "Thank you for my blouse. It's the nicest thing anyone's given me since…since—" She broke off, looking down at her feet.

Brody muttered something under his breath and surprised everyone when he picked Megan up. "Come on, kid, before we're all crying in our soup." He tossed Megan's coat around her shoulders and carried her out of the sheriff's office. Megan's solemn eyes looked over his shoulder. She lifted her fingertips.

And the door closed behind them as they disappeared into the night.

Sarah covered her face.

When arms surrounded her, she turned against Max and let the tears come even though it was *him* who held her.

Maybe because it *was* Max who held her.

His hands smoothed down her back. "I'll take you home."

The word just made Sarah cry harder.

He finally let go of her long enough to push a wad of tissues in her hand and wrap her coat around her shoulders pretty much the same way Brody had done with Megan. Then he nudged her outside and into the SUV he'd left parked outside the door.

When he parked behind her house, her tears had slowed, leaving her feeling numb and empty.

Not even the tight-lipped expression he got when he pushed open her unlocked back door made an impression on her. She tossed her coat on the kitchen table and walked through the darkened house, dropping down on her bed.

A moment later, the mattress dipped as Max sat beside her. "Sarah—"

"Go home, Max."

He was silent for a long moment. "The baby was mine." His voice was low.

She pressed her cheek against the pillow. "Yes."

He let out a long sigh. "When did it happen?"

She rolled onto her back, staring up at the ceiling. Once again, narrow swaths of moonlight shined through the tilted blinds. "I was five months along. It was a boy." She looked sideways at him.

In the dim light, she could see a dark gleam in his eyes and it made her ache inside.

When he finally spoke, his voice sounded hollow, rusty. "What happened?"

"Cervical incompetence." The words were clipped. "By the time we knew, it was too late."

"Why didn't you tell me before?"

"When?" She swallowed. "Should I have run up and interrupted your wedding to Jennifer? Or maybe when you showed up here in Weaver, I should have just blurted it out."

He was silent.

She threw her arm over her eyes. She was so tired. "Leandra is the only one who knew."

"Not even your parents?"

"They'd have worried themselves sick."

"That's a parent's right," he said huskily.

Her eyes burned all over again. "Please go, Max. I can't take any more tonight."

He slowly pushed himself to his feet. But he didn't move to the door. Instead, he moved to the foot of the bed and lifted her foot, slowly pulling off her boot. He set it on the floor beside the bed.

She swiped her cheeks.

He pulled off the other boot and set it next to the first.

Then he unfolded the blanket at the end of the bed and slowly drew it over her. His hand shook as he smoothed it over her hair. "I'm sorry. There're so many reasons that I'm sorry."

She should be out of tears, but they still filled her eyes.

He walked to the doorway. Stopped once more and looked back at her. "You wanted the baby?"

"Yes." She closed her eyes.

"I'm sorry," he said again.

But when she opened her eyes again, he was already gone. "I wanted you, too," she whispered.

Max drove back to the sheriff's station. He found Sawyer, looking tired and worn, leaning back in his chair behind his desk. The man's eyes tracked his entrance and watched silently as Max dropped the keys to the SUV on the desk, followed by his badge, the sheriff's ID, and his radio.

Then the sheriff eyed the display laying across his desk. "Sure you want to do that?"

Max wasn't sure about much of anything, anymore. "Yeah."

"Shame," Sawyer murmured. "Was hoping you might find a reason to stick around this time."

"Think I've done enough damage."

"Because you followed a lead that didn't pan out?"

It was a gross simplification of all that Max had—and hadn't—done. "The task force will send another special agent. I'll make sure he gets the background checks I was nearly finished with. At least *those* I didn't screw up. Only ones left are *you* and Tommy." He turned and walked out the door.

When daylight rolled around a few hours later, he was still awake, sitting in his mother's kitchen. Bundled in a thick robe as she hobbled into the kitchen without aid of her crutches, Genna stopped short at the sight of him. "I didn't even realize you were here, Max. I didn't hear your truck come home last night."

He'd walked from the station to his mother's place.

Evidently, he wasn't the only one capable of walking. "Where are your crutches?"

She looked innocent. "In my bedroom. Why?"

"Thought you couldn't manage without them."

She tossed up her hands. "Eh, what can I say?" She sat down at the table across from him. "So I'm healing better than I let on. I'm not so feeble as you thought."

"I never thought you were feeble."

Her eyebrows lifted. "And now you know for certain I'm not." She lifted her hands. "What can I say? After more than twenty years, I wanted my family here with me for a while."

"We can't stay, though, Ma. Eli and I will be leaving."

Her lips tightened. "You disappoint me, Massimo."

He exhaled. "Get in line. Coming here was a mistake. I knew it and I came anyway."

"Because you thought I needed you?"

"Something wrong with that? Just come away with us. Back to California. You can live with us or I'll find you a place of your own. Whatever you want. To this day I don't understand why you want to stay in Weaver after what happened here."

She just shook her dark head. "What I want is for my son to stop running from *his* home."

His lips twisted. "So I'm more like Dad than either of us like to admit."

"Oh, *now* you mention your father? You go for years never mentioning his name as if *you* have something to be ashamed of, rather than him." She reached across the table and as if he were still twelve and guilty of cow-tipping, closed his chin in her surprisingly strong fingers. "What happened tonight?"

"I screwed up."

She stared into his face, then sat back in her seat. "Then make it right. You're *not* your father, Max. He never once wanted to really make things right."

"He abandoned us."

She tsked. "Tony would've come back here in a second if I'd have let him. But why would I let him? He betrayed us. I know you thought the sun rose and set on his head. But he lied, he cheated, he stole. Getting caught like he did was just the last straw and I finally found some backbone to make him stay away. Something I *should* have done long before things got so bad. He was no husband and no father I wanted raising you."

"I was practically grown by the time he was sent up."

"You were fifteen," she dismissed. "A baby." She tapped her hand on the table. "So...did you lie? Cheat?

Steal? Did you do all these things deliberately, not caring who you harmed? Of course you didn't. You're a grown man, Massimo. You don't want to be like your father, then you don't be like him. You think you messed up, you make it right."

"Some things can't be made right, Ma."

"So you face it and you apologize and you move forward." She shook her head again, her voice tart, but her eyes were as soft as they'd always been. "Your whole life you've been making things right for other people. You're forty years old now. It's time to start making things right for you. Sarah loves you. Stay. Don't give up."

"I didn't say anything about Sarah, Ma."

"You don't have to. I've seen your eyes when you look at her. You never looked at anyone else that way. And I've seen her face when she talks of you. Why do you think I haven't boxed your ears for having your truck parked outside her house at all hours?"

He felt his face flush. Trust a mother to make a guy want to hang his head even more than it was already hanging. "Little old for ear-boxing," he said.

She just eyed him. "Want to test that theory?"

Amazingly, after the miserable night, the miserable day, the miserable years, he felt a smile tug his lips. He pushed out of the seat, feeling stiff from sitting there so long. He pressed a kiss to her forehead and headed from the room. "Think I'll pass."

"I knew I raised a smart boy."

Upstairs, Max looked in on Eli. He was sleeping face down on the mattress, one foot stuck out from beneath the quilt. Max pulled up the quilt and tucked it over his son's toes.

Eli mumbled and stuck his foot right back out, like it

was searching for freedom. He rolled over and blinked blearily. "Am I late for school?"

Max sat down, nudging the boy over. "It's Sunday."

That seemed an even worse fate than it being a school day. "Grandma's gonna make me go to church."

"There are worse things." He eyed his boy. He was so much like Jennifer. "How would you feel if we *didn't* go back to California?"

Eli squinted. "Ever?"

"Not forever. We'd visit Grandma Helene, of course."

"You wanna live here? For good? Are you gonna marry Sarah? 'Cause she's my teacher, you know, and that's well—it might be kinda gross."

Max was pretty sure that marrying Sarah wouldn't be the foregone conclusion that Eli seemed to think.

"What makes you think I want to marry her?"

"'Cause you're all kissy with her. Grandma says you're in love."

Max jerked a little. "She does, huh? It, uh, doesn't mean I didn't love your mom."

'I know. Grandma says that, too."

Grandma says a lot, Max thought.

"So, would that really bother you? If Sarah were... in our lives?"

Eli rolled back over onto his face. "If it keeps her from making me stand next to Chrissy Tanner in the pageant, I guess it's okay."

It was about the last thing in the world that Sarah wanted to do that morning, but she dragged herself into the shower, dried her hair and slapped on enough makeup to hide the circles under her eyes, pulled on a knitted tube of a dress, and took herself to church.

If she didn't, she knew her parents would just come

calling afterward to find out why she hadn't joined them as she usually did.

She would have driven, but her car was still parked at the sheriff's station. So, she pulled on her low-heeled leather boots and walked.

They were singing the first hymn when she finally got there, and she pulled off her coat and slipped through the narthex doors, quietly sliding into the pew beside her parents. Her mother gave her a glance, then a second sharper one, before she handed over the opened hymnal she'd been holding.

Sarah stared hard at the page, and tried to pretend she was unaware of her mother's eagle-eyed once-over. By the time the service ended nearly an hour later, she thought she might have passed Jaimie's muster. But as they all filed out of the sanctuary, Sarah felt a finger latch in the back of her collar. "Not so fast, honey," Jaimie said. She had a smile on her face as she nodded and greeted everyone around them—more than a few of whom were part of the family. She even urged Sarah's father on ahead. "We'll be along in a minute, Matthew."

But Sarah didn't mistake the look in her mother's eyes for casual interest.

Jaimie waited until their pew was empty, before she spoke. Even then she kept her voice low. "I had an interesting conversation with Darla Rasmussen this morning. Why do I have to hear from her that you spent hours at the sheriff's station last night?"

"Pamela Rasmussen better learn to keep her mouth shut around her mother or Sawyer's going to put her out of her job."

"Don't hedge, Sarah."

She tugged down the close-fitting sleeves of her

dress. "It was all a misunderstanding, okay? I accidentally got in the middle of an investigation of Max's."

"Mmm. Well, I can imagine what investigation that is, given what your father has told me. So if it was all a misunderstanding, why do you have circles under your eyes that even I could back a pickup truck into?" It was well known that Jaimie didn't have the best of judgment when it came to driving pickups.

"I'm just tired. After the sale yesterday." *Was it only yesterday?* "And the week I've got coming up with the pageant. It's always busy this time of year for me."

"Sarah!" Eli was weaving his way through the departing people like a salmon going upstream. He finally stopped next to her, and seemed to be vibrating with energy. Maybe that was why his shirt was half untucked, and he had a cowlick standing up at the back of his head. "I can call you that now, right?" He shot Jaimie a look. "Oh, hi, Mrs. Clay."

Jaimie's lips twitched. "Hello, Eli."

"Where's your grandma?"

He looked back at Sarah. "She's out there talking to *everybody*. I don't know how come. We see them every week."

Jaimie covered her mouth, hiding her chuckle. She shot Sarah a look though, one that said their discussion wasn't finished. "I'll leave you in Mr. Scalise's fine hands, here, Sarah."

Eli grinned and held up his palms. "They're even clean."

Despite herself, Sarah smiled. She sat on the wooden arm of the pew and watched her mother walk away. "Didn't want to come to church, huh?"

Eli shook his head fervently. "Well, it's okay once we're here. But I had to get up early and everything."

Sarah nibbled the inside of her lip. "I-is your dad here, too?" She would surely have known if Max had been present in the church.

Eli shook his head. "He's at the office. So, do I get to call you Sarah? All the guys in class are gonna be *so* ticked."

It ought to have alarmed her some to see how much he relished the idea.

But Eli was nothing if not an energizing factor in the classroom. And no matter what had happened between his father and her, she was crazy about the kid. "Well, I think Miss Clay will still be good in the classroom," she said. "But, yes, you may call me Sarah in private."

He gave a choking laugh. "That's a good one." His head swiveled when he heard his name being called. "That's Grandma. Gotta go." He darted off again, his shirttail flapping.

Sarah pressed her hands to her stomach. She had no objectivity where Elijah Scalise was concerned, either.

The church was nearly empty. She picked up her coat and pulled it on, and headed out the rear door rather than facing the gauntlet of people standing around out front drinking their hot coffee while they critiqued the worship service and traded gossip.

Walking back home didn't take long, and she went in through the kitchen, only to stop short at the sight of Max sitting at her kitchen table.

She slowly unwound her scarf, trying to will her heart back into some normal rhythm. "What are you doing here?"

"Proving what happens when you don't lock your doors. Anyone can get in."

She slid out of her coat. She didn't want to recognize that he looked even more tired than she had before

424   *Sarah and the Sheriff*

she'd used up half a tube of concealer. "Taking your deputy duties a little seriously, aren't you? Oh, that's right. You're not really a deputy."

"I'm a deputy all right." He pulled out his badge and flipped it on the table. "What I'm not is a special agent with the DEA. I resigned this morning."

She stared at the badge on the table. It reflected the sunlight coming from the window, seeming to wink up at her. "Why?"

"Because we're staying in Weaver. Eli and me."

Her coat was a bundle against her waist as she hugged it to herself. "So that's what he was going on about at church."

Max's gaze sharpened. "You saw him?"

"I saw half the town," she countered. "Or so it seemed."

"What'd he say?"

"He wanted to know if he could call me Sarah from now on."

"That's *all* he said?"

Sarah lifted her shoulders. "Pretty much. What else should he have said?"

"Nothing." He pushed to his feet, looking oddly restless. "I just wanted to tell you. That we're not leaving Weaver."

"Okay."

"Just like that...okay."

She wasn't sure how long she could keep up the façade. "What else do you want me to say? You're staying. For now. I get it."

"Not *for now*. For good."

The knot in her chest felt like it was choking her. Slowly. Painfully. "Right."

He exhaled. "You don't believe me."

"You're not going to be happy being a deputy for long."

"Maybe I won't be. Maybe I'll be the sheriff, and serve out a term that's as long as Sawyer's has been."

"You won't win if you run against him."

"I will win, because he'll be the one telling the voters to elect me."

Beneath cover of the coat, her fingernails dug into her palms. "What about your case? The trafficking case?"

"It's still open. I'll just be on the local side of the investigation now."

She pressed her lips together. "Why now?"

"Don't you know?" He stopped in front of her. Tucked his knuckles under her chin and nudged her face upward. "Because Weaver is where *you* are."

She swallowed with an effort. "I don't need you feeling sorry for me, Max."

"That's good, because I don't." His thumb brushed over her cheek. "I feel sorry about *everything* that's happened. But you're talking about pity. And that I don't feel. Except maybe for Chrissy Tanner because Eli definitely has a bee in his bonnet when it comes to her." His half-hearted attempt at humor died. "I'm sorry for what you lost. I'm sorry that I didn't even know what we'd lost, until now. I'm sorry that I wasn't there for you. But I'm here now. And I'm not going anywhere again. Not unless I have to follow you somewhere else. And I will."

Her knees felt weak. "The past is over, Max. You don't have to do this, trying to make up for it. It's done."

"There's no way I can make up for what happened in the past," he said quietly. "And maybe it's done, but neither one of us will ever forget it happened. Maybe you'll understand in time that I would have cut off my arm to keep from hurting you as badly as I did. But my staying here now isn't about what happened then. It's about us. Now. Here." He lowered his head, brushing his lips over hers. Softly. Gently.

She shuddered, steeling herself against him. Against letting herself believe.

Before, she'd barely comprehended how much she could love this man, and her heart had been shattered.

Now, she did comprehend it. She knew, truly knew, what kind of man he was. The depth of caring that he possessed. She knew, and she loved him all the more for it.

And she knew that when he moved on, this time it would destroy her.

"It's about us from here on out," he said softly. "I love you, Sarah. I want to spend my life with you." He dragged the coat out from between them and closed his warm hands over her cold ones. "Will you marry me?"

She bit her lip. Looked into the eyes that were brown and green and so beautiful they made her want to weep.

She slowly pulled her hands free.

"I'm sorry, Max. But...no."

His skin paled. He stepped back, shoving his hands in the front pockets of his jeans. "I can't say I blame you," he said evenly.

She looked away, dashing her hand over her face.

"I don't want to make you cry, Sarah. I never wanted that."

"I know." She pressed her hands to her stomach. "I... just... I need you to—"

"Sshh." He reached out and thumbed away another tear from her cheek. "I know. I'll go."

And a moment later, he did.

She watched him close the kitchen door after himself. Heard his boots walk down the steps.

She moved to the door and slowly turned the lock.

And then she sat down, her back against the door, and wept.

Chapter 15

The badge sat on her table for hours.

She knew it was there when she finally dragged herself off the floor of her kitchen and went into the bathroom to soak her face.

She knew it was there when she changed out of her dress and pulled on the oldest, warmest, softest sweater and jeans that she possessed.

She particularly knew it was there when she sat down and clutched it in her hand until the engraving on it made a dent in her palm.

Sooner or later, Max would need it, if only to turn in to Sawyer when he changed his mind about staying in Weaver.

She tucked it in her pocket, found her wallet and let herself out of the house. The afternoon was brilliant and cold, the promise of snow tickling at her nose. She walked downtown and headed to the sheriff's office.

She'd leave the badge for Max with the dispatcher, pick up her car and go back home.

Simple steps seemed all she could manage.

There was only one cruiser parked beside the office when she got there. Her car was still sitting where she'd left it in the lot. If she'd had her wits about her, she would have just picked it up after she'd left the church earlier that day.

But wits seemed in short supply these days.

She pushed open the door. The blinds on the back of the window swayed as it swung closed behind her. "I need to drop this off…" Her voice trailed off. The badge she'd pulled from her pocket slipped loosely out of her hand.

Max and Pamela Rasmussen were standing against the wall facing Tommy Potter.

Tommy Potter who held a gun in his hand.

Sarah's shocked gaze met Max's.

"Get over there." Tommy gestured with his gun. "With them."

Sarah couldn't have uttered a word to save her soul. She slowly crossed the room, giving the deputy a wide berth. Pamela was crying softly. She grabbed Sarah's hand in a death grip.

"Locked doors," Max murmured.

"Shut up." Tommy reached behind him, though, and flipped the lock on the office door.

"What do you think you're gonna accomplish, Tommy? Let the women go." Max's voice was calm.

The deputy looked harried. "I need the product from the trailer. Tell me where it is, and I'll be outta here."

"Call it what it really is, man," Max said. "It's meth. It's what's going to work its way into the schools here. It's what's going to start killing kids and adults. Anyone who's not strong enough to say no when it's suddenly so easily available. Because of people like you."

"I'm not like that!" He lifted his gun and dashed his hand over his forehead, but sweat still gleamed there. "We're not getting rid of it here."

"Just dumping it on some other unsuspecting, vulnerable town."

"It's a lot of money. You think a guy can get ahead on a deputy salary?" His laugh was short and harsh and horribly, horribly sad. "There's no woman here who'd live on that."

Max slowly took a step forward. Tommy didn't seem to notice, but Sarah tightened her grip on Pamela's hand. The other woman squeezed back. Her shoulder was pressed against Sarah's and she could feel her shaking.

Or maybe it was Sarah who was shaking. Twice now in less than two days, she'd seen guns waving around.

Only then, it had been Max and Brody, both of whom she'd trusted not to lose their heads while she'd stood between them.

Tommy? She would never have believed it of him if she weren't witnessing it with her own eyes. He'd been in Weaver for *years*. Always quiet around women, she'd *thought* he was a decent guy. *Everyone* thought he was a decent guy. But there was no question. He wielded that gun as if he were fully prepared to use it.

"So this is *really* about a girl? Who? Dude, if she doesn't know what a catch you are on a deputy's salary, what would you want with her anyway? Plenty of fish in the sea."

Tommy snorted. "Yeah. You'd say that. You're screwing the Untouchable Teach." His gaze cut to Sarah for a moment.

She swallowed, pressing her lips together. From the

corner of her vision, she saw Max's hands fist and just as abruptly uncurl. "And I'm doing it on a deputy's salary," he said. "Hell, Tommy. You're ten years younger 'n me and in a helluva lot better shape. All you'd have to do is crook your finger and Dee Crowder would come running."

Tommy was evidently tired of the topic. He leveled the gun at Max. "You have another salary and everyone in this town knows it now, thanks to motormouth there." He jerked his chin toward Pamela.

"You're calling me a gossip? Oh, that's rich coming from *you*." Pamela bit her lip, and went silent when Max gave her a sideways look.

"Where's the package?" Tommy demanded. "I know Jefferson turned it in here. Sawyer told me."

Max slowly lifted his hands, and shook his head. "If I knew, don't you think I'd tell you just so you'd put that gun away? The sheriff handled it himself. Why don't we call him and ask."

"You're a regular laugh factory," Tommy said. He gestured with the gun. "Everybody go. Into Sawyer's office."

Pamela kept her death grip on Sarah's hand. Max turned, giving them an almost imperceptible nod. Sarah felt like her heart was going to explode out of her chest. She and Pamela turned and started walking toward the dispatcher's desk. They had to pass it before they could reach Sawyer's office beyond it.

As they neared the desk, Pamela stumbled, knocking into Sarah. Her hip hit the desk.

"What are you trying to pull?" Tommy's voice was loud. "Move it."

"I'm sorry!" Pamela had started crying again. Soft, frightened snuffles.

"Get some backbone," Tommy snapped.

Sarah turned her head and glared at the man. "I never realized you were a jerk," she snapped. "I'm glad now that I never went out with you when you asked."

Max's eyes looked like murky pools of green water. He shook his head sharply.

"Shut up," Tommy ordered.

Sarah turned. She and Pamela passed the desk, Max crowding closely behind them.

They entered Sawyer's office. Tommy stood in the doorway, blocking their exit. "Open every drawer," he said flatly. "Every cabinet."

"Most of them are locked," Max pointed out.

Tommy swore. "Open…every…one."

Max shrugged. He nodded toward the filing cabinet in the far corner of the room. "Sarah, you try there. Sawyer keeps his key to it in the top drawer of his desk. Pam, check the desk drawers."

"Glad you're being helpful," Tommy said snidely.

Sarah fumbled open the top drawer. There was a metal key ring inside holding a few small keys. She pulled it out and turned toward the filing cabinet. Pamela was yanking at the other drawers of the desk.

Max had flipped back the cupboard door on the wall that hid the locking safe. "Afraid I failed safecracking at the academy."

Tommy muttered an oath. He strode over to Sarah, snatching the keys out of her hand. He shoved them at Max. "Try these."

Max just looked at the keys. "Tommy, it's a combination lock. It doesn't take a key. Look for yourself."

The deputy shoved Pamela out of his way. The woman stumbled again, falling against the desk. Sarah caught her, trying to steady her. Tommy gestured at Max. "Move."

Max shifted. Tommy moved closer to see around the cupboard door. "That's not a comb—"

Max slammed the cupboard door in Tommy's face.

Pamela cried out.

Sarah froze.

Tommy fell back, grunting. But he swung around in a crouch and went at Max.

The two men crashed to the floor, knocking wildly into the two chairs in front of Sawyer's. Sarah shoved at Pam. "Go. Call help."

"But—"

"Go!" She grabbed the letter opener she'd managed to palm when they'd first knocked into Pamela's desk. But the two men were wrestling, arms locked in terrifying battle and Sarah didn't know *what* to do. She should have used the opener on Tommy when he'd grabbed the keys—

"Get out," Max said through gritted teeth. He sent his elbow into Tommy's jaw.

"I'm not leaving you!"

"*Now* you say that." His head snapped back as Tommy's fist caught him, and Sarah cried out as the men rolled again, this time with Tommy on top.

She grabbed the desk chair that was blocking her way to the door and smashed it over Tommy's back. The wood splintered. He swore violently and turned on her, snatching her ankle, yanking her off her feet.

Max latched his arms around Tommy's neck. "One... more...move," he said, breathing hard. "Come on, Tommy. Give me a reason."

Sarah scrambled back, pulling her legs out of Tommy's reach. But the deputy was scrabbling at the arm cutting off his oxygen.

She snatched up the gun that he'd finally dropped, and pushed to her feet, holding it between both hands. "Enough!"

Max didn't respond. Tommy's face was brilliant red. "Max, please. Stop."

Slowly, infinitesimally, she saw him begin to relax his hold.

Tommy sagged, sucking in gulping breaths.

Max shoved him onto the ground and came over to Sarah, lifting the gun carefully out of her tight grip. "It's okay. Everything's okay now." He worked the gun loose.

From outside in the lobby, they could hear commotion.

But Tommy was finally too spent to fight anymore.

Sawyer appeared in the office doorway, tight-lipped. His blue eyes traveled over Sarah. "You okay?"

She nodded, hugging her arms around herself.

His gaze slid to Max. There was a cut near his eye, and a trickle of blood was working its way down his chin. "Peaceful town you got here, Sheriff," he said, and handed over Tommy's weapon to the man.

Then he went over to Tommy and pulled the cuffs off the man's belt and clipped them around his wrists. "Get up, you miserable puke."

Dave Ruiz, the other deputy, had appeared, too. "If I weren't seeing this with my own eyes, I wouldn't have believed it when the sheriff filled me in." He took Tommy's arm from Max. "I'll put him in lockup." He led the disgraced deputy away.

Sawyer eyed the chaotic office. "I'm finally losing my taste for this. When a man you thought you knew could go so off track—" He shook his head. "Good thing you'll be taking over soon, Max."

Sarah's lips parted.

Sawyer eyed them both. "We can do the paperwork on this tomorrow."

Max nodded. "Fine with me." His voice was weary.

"One question, though." Sawyer eyed him. "What were you even doing here, today? Thought you were off."

"I was. But Tommy bugging us about changing shifts kept niggling at me. Dave told me he'd kept on him about it until he finally gave in and switched. I wanted to know why Tommy was so anxious to be on duty today."

Sawyer frowned. "He was after the stuff that *you* had me announce was here. Could have let me know which fish you were baiting, son."

"After the mess with Paine, I wasn't sure I trusted my own hunch. Didn't expect you to. I definitely didn't expect visitors." He slanted Sarah a look.

Sawyer sighed. "Maybe we've all been a little short-sighted. If I'd seen what Tommy was up to sooner…"

"Not every case is perfect," Max said.

Sarah knew he was thinking of E.J. "So if the package of drugs isn't *here*, where is it?"

"The field office has already taken it," Max said.

"Along with your resignation," Sawyer added. He shook his head. "Ironic timing." He stepped out of the office. "Pam won't be back, I'll bet. Gonna need *another* dispatcher." He tilted back his head. Smiled faintly. "That'll be *your* headache, Max. Now go on. Let Sarah mop you up."

Max's gaze slanted toward Sarah. "She's not in the

mopping business, I'm afraid." He went out into the lobby area, his movements stiff.

Sarah chewed the inside of her lip as she followed him. "Wait."

Max stopped. He sent her a look that had her heart aching. She was barely aware of Sawyer quietly disappearing back into his office where he closed the door.

"You don't have to, Sarah. I'm capable of cleaning up my own wounds."

She pressed her palms together and slowly walked toward him. "I'm afraid I do have to help." She knelt down and picked up his badge that she'd dropped when she'd come in. She opened her palm and held it up to him. "Because I don't think I can heal *my* wounds if I let you walk away."

She looked up at him. Frowned at the cuts on his face. "I thought it would hurt more if I let you back in here—" she touched her chest over her charging heartbeat "—and you left again. But—but seeing you with Tommy like that, I knew that I couldn't wait around for that day to happen—for that day when you walked away." Her eyes flooded with tears. "He could have shot you. Right then and there. I'd have lost you without ever having been *with* you. I don't want that to happen, Max. I love you. And if I haven't already ruined—"

He caught her face in his hands and covered her mouth with his.

She opened her mouth to him, and he swallowed her soft cry. "I love you," she said against him.

He circled his arms around her and pulled her closer. "Don't ever stop."

She shook her head. Slid her arms around his shoulders and held on.

For life.

Epilogue

"Merry Christmas, Mrs. Scalise."

Sarah looked up from the photo album on her lap as Max came into the room.

They'd gotten married only a week before. A small affair, held in the living room at the Double-C, with just their immediate family and a few friends.

Sarah had worn her mother's wedding gown and Max had been in his dress uniform. Eli had been best man, and though he'd dropped the ring, he'd quickly found it. Leandra had been matron of honor and had laughed that Sarah had taken her "simple" wedding advice seriously.

It had been quickly put together and beautiful and far more perfect than any elaborate wedding Sarah might have dreamed up as a girl.

Now, they were staying with Genna, at least until her cast came off in a few weeks. Beyond that, they hadn't yet determined where they would end up living.

Her house was comfortable enough for two, but with Eli, they would definitely be tight. Unfortunately, moving out to one of the newer houses on the far side of town held little appeal for any of them.

Now, she was just happy where they were. She smiled up at him. "Merry Christmas, Sheriff." The speed at which Sawyer had resigned had been daunting. Max had been appointed acting sheriff until the special election was held in January and he could officially be voted into office.

He moved next to her and she ran her hand up his leg. He laughed softly and bent down to sit beside her on the soft rug. He wore dark blue pajama bottoms in deference to the other people in the house, and a terrycloth robe that hung loose from his wide shoulders. "Couldn't sleep, or did you come down here to rattle a few packages?"

Behind them, the fire that she'd started when she'd come downstairs was beginning to catch. It crackled softly.

"I had a few things to deliver on Santa's behalf," she said.

He looked over at the fireplace. The stocking that Eli had hung was bulging with little gifts. "Santa's been busy," he murmured, smiling faintly, because the stocking looked even fuller than it had when *he'd* delivered a few things, too. "What're you looking at?"

She lifted the album that Genna had given her the evening before as a gift. "You were such a pretty boy, Max."

"Exactly what every *man* wants to hear," he drawled. He reached over and angled the book on her lap so he could see. "God. Those *are* old pictures. What did my mother do? Raid the storage boxes in the attic or something?"

"I love this album," Sarah said, smiling and holding it protectively to her bosom.

"Sentimental woman," he accused, but his lips were curving. He ran his palm up her spine. "You know, it'll probably be another hour, at least, before Eli shows his face. Even on a Christmas morning that kid hasn't made it up before dawn."

"Shocking." Sarah leaned back against him and sighed as his hand drifted over her shoulder, grazing her breast through her robe. "Derek and I were *always* up before the sun. Dad always complained that he wished we were so perky during the rest of the year when there were chores to be done."

"Yeah, well, be grateful for small mercies." Max's lips nibbled at the nape of her neck and shivers danced down her spine. "It's hard enough finding a few minutes alone to make love to my bride." He reached around her and pulled the album from her loose grasp, then slowly nudged her down onto the rug.

She smiled, looking up into his eyes. "I have a Christmas gift for you."

His lips curved. His eyes were heavy-lidded and full of intent. "My favorite kind of gift," he assured.

She laughed softly. "Well, there's that, too."

He propped his elbow beside her head and slowly drew his fingers through her hair, spreading it around her head. "Do I get to unwrap it?"

"Not for another eight months or so."

He froze. "What?"

She squelched the quick dart of nervousness accosting her. "I know we haven't talked about it yet or anything."

"You're pregnant?"

She slowly nodded. "I... I got up early this morning and did a home test thing."

"You know this early?"

"The lines turned bright pink. According to the directions, you get false negatives, but not false positives."

His gaze was turning decidedly worried. "What about what happened before?"

She slid her hands around his neck. "Now that I *know* about the problem, they can take measures to prevent a miscarriage. I talked with Rebecca about it last week when I started to suspect. I might have to be off my feet for a while somewhere along the way, but there's no reason I can't carry our baby to term."

"And you're happy about it?" His eyes searched her face.

She drew his head closer. "Most definitely." She lifted her head and brushed her lips over his. He deepened the kiss for a moment that was entirely too brief before he was lifting his head again.

She made a protesting sound.

"We're *really* going to need a bigger house," he said.

She laughed softly. "We'll figure it out. My uncle Daniel can *build* us a house. Another bedroom is no big deal." She leaned up to catch his lips once more. Her legs moved restlessly against his.

He closed his hands over her shoulders, gently pinning her to the rug. "Another two bedrooms," he said.

"Well, one for Eli. One for the baby. So two bedrooms. Besides ours, of course." She drew her foot along his calf.

"One for Eli. One for the baby." His hand swept gently down over her abdomen, his expression a combination of awe and possession that she would carry with her for the rest of her days. "And one for Megan."

She blinked. "What?" The words sank in a little more fully. She scrambled from beneath him, pushing him down onto the rug and peering into his face. "Megan?" She'd talked to Tristan a half-dozen times but her uncle had never once indicated he'd have any sway with her placement.

"Here." He fumbled in his robe and pulled an envelope out of his pocket. "It came yesterday. You and Ma were in the kitchen cooking."

She took the envelope and pulled out the single sheet inside. "It's a telegram from Coleman Black." She frowned, shooting Max a look. "And it's addressed to *you.* You're not keeping any secrets about Hollins-Winword from me, are you?"

He snorted softly. "Think there're enough folks in your family involved with them. I'll stick to sheriffing, thanks."

"Then how did you reach him? Tristan kept telling me there wasn't anything he could do."

"You just didn't go to enough uncles, darling. Between Daniel and Jefferson, they managed to pull some magic with the guy. Evidently, he had a lot to do with your cousin Angeline making it into the country when she was a child, and helping get through the red tape of Maggie and Daniel adopting her."

Sarah focused on the telegram again, but it was hard to read when her hand was shaking. "She's going to be here by New Year's Day." She cast a look at Max. "What if she doesn't *want* to live with us? What if Eli doesn't want her here?"

He pushed his fingers through her hair. "She will," he promised. "He will."

Sarah looked into his eyes and saw nothing but the future written there.

It wouldn't all be smooth sailing, she knew.

What was?

But she knew that whatever their lives brought, they'd meet it all, together. "I love you, Max."

He smiled slowly and drew her down with him. "I love you, too."

On the stairs above them, Genna Scalise smiled softly, looked to the heavens and gave a silent prayer. Then she quietly thumped her way back to bed.

She didn't *have* to get up and start breakfast just yet...

* * * * *